Mark Venekamp & Claire Chang© 著

餐飲英語 easy說

Conversational English For Restaurant Workers

作者 序

I hope that this book will help you achieve your goal of better conversational skills in English. Please use this book as a guide, but keep in mind that the best way to learn English is to speak it. Practice and use your English as often as you can.

I am thankful to all the people I've met in my 20 years in the restaurant business. Thanks to the staff at Death Valley and Yellowstone National Parks in the USA for teaching me the right way to do things. I hope you will also meet good teachers along the way.

請使用這本書做為敲門磚，希望這本書能協助你實現更好的英語會話技能。請記住，學習英語的最好方式是要開口說出來，並且經常盡你所能地練習和使用。

我很感謝在過去 20 年餐飲經驗裡所有遇到的人。尤其是在美國死亡谷和黃石國家公園工作期間，那些工作人員教導我做事的正確方式。最後，希望你能在餐飲職業的這條路上遇見好老師。

【經歷：畢業於太平洋路德大學 Pacific Lutheran University 英文系，曾在黃石國家公園湖區飯店餐廳服務多年，目前從事兒童美語教學和撰稿工作。】

Mark Venekamp　張馬克

特約作者 序

愛吃是我的一項優點。

高中起，我便熱愛呼朋引伴到處品嘗值得停車光顧的美食，舉凡路邊小吃到飯店、高級餐廳，或隱身山間的野店，坐落住宅區內的精緻餐館，都是我們尋覓品嘗的重點，因此造就了我不工作時便是四處遊玩、吃東西的習慣。

工作後，因為工作薪資不錯，身邊資金更加無虞，我開始放縱自己有時間就吃到海外去，從北半球吃到南半球，從東邊吃到西邊去，例如中美料理、歐式料理、東南亞料理、印度料理等，連西藏人的犛牛餐，我都不惜請假飛出去品嘗。又因自身工作為服務規劃，對於品嘗過的餐廳、下榻的飯店等服務，更有著自己的堅持與見解。

於本書我拿出自身的服務經驗、餐飲知識、職場技能，以 6 大主題提供你未來工作職場上的知能補給，讓你可以輕輕鬆鬆邁入餐飲的花花世界，順利稱霸職場。

Cheryl Lin　林瑜娟

【經歷：文化大學社工系，從事客戶服務領域已有 12 年，曾任服務資深講師、服務流程規劃師、服務品質管理師，專精規劃電話服務、餐廳現場服務、櫃檯服務（face to face service）等。】

特約編輯 序

在書店拿起這本書，心裡面應該對餐飲領域有著濃厚的興趣，不論是正從事這工作的專業人員，或是就學中的學生，還是正懷抱著夢想前往國外旅遊打工夢想的你，這本書能給你滿滿實在的交戰實錄，就帶著它回家與你一同成長吧！

國內的餐飲管理教育非常地完善，新聞報導總可以聽到屢獲大獎的佳績，專業項目都是數一數二的強手，但發現嗎？這些優秀的孩子在往國際舞台或是未來的職場上，還欠缺著把自己秀出來的語文能力，也許因為如此而無法把自己推上更高的層次，真的令人覺得惋惜，身邊也認識這樣的孩子嗎？或是你就是這樣的學生，那麼這本書可以提供的，正是一個嶄新的機會。

台灣的科技業持續發展，也帶進來自商務活動的商機，想要進大型商務觀光旅館或餐廳工作嗎？第一基本要求，你必須具有與客戶溝通的基礎能力！這本書幫你準備好了你的所需，給自己一次機會，打開它～跟著一起 easy 說。懷有旅遊打工計畫、也正想投入餐飲領域的你，更是別把這本書給錯過了，不論是要從事服務性質或是管理階層的工作，就在本書裡可以找到每個職階的特定需求，讓你在打工旅遊過程中，有如吃了一顆定心丸。

本書收錄了餐飲職場中各個環節的工作會話，除了以老外常說的英語對話呈現，更符合國際餐飲職場的實務需求；不僅是實戰對話一次收錄，更包含了職場上所需注意的細節部份，這些都是集結業界專業人士所提供的珍貴資訊。每個對話單元的人物安排與職場定位，更是以專業技能角度去安排，除針對自己本身所需加以學習之外，更可以 360 度視野去瞭解對應人員的立場與想法，如此工作上有了共同認知，你的努力也會更有收獲。

本書另一重要內容－職場補給站－更是不可錯過的部分。餐飲職場上有哪些不知道的 Know － How，由達人一一解析加以闡述，在補給站這裡你會有全新的發現，希望你能細細體驗本書附錄的新穎資訊，輕鬆提升餐飲職場專業知識。

張蘋　Claire Chang

推薦 序

很偶然的狀況下，在回台度假時認識了 Mark 以及他可愛的一家人。離開台灣工作十幾年，很少在國外遇到從事餐飲業或在飯店工作的台灣人。之前短暫回國工作的經驗中，在面試新員工時，由於工作團隊的關係，除了工作能力，英語程度也是錄取員工時考量的重要因素之一。有不少經驗及能力都不錯的應徵者，最後都因為英文程度不足以達到工作上的需求而無法錄取，令我不禁為他們惋惜。在英國及杜拜工作時，共事過的同事國籍近五十國，台灣人的工作能力和效率都數一數二，但由於語言的關係，知道的人少之又少。

Mark 本身有深厚的服務業經驗，這樣的一本書由他來撰寫，真的再適合也不過了。書中除了專有名詞及用法的解說，針對各種餐飲從業人員日常工作中會遇到的各式狀況，也很詳實而仔細地列舉。因此，這本書除了適合想加強英語能力的餐飲從業同仁，也很適合當作餐飲業新手入門的第一本書！

Patti　何孟澔

【經歷：寮國龍坡邦東方快車酒店集團 La Residence Phou Vao by Orient Express 餐飲部經理。】

編者 序

這本書真可說是「麻雀雖小，五臟俱全」，裡面所囊括的內容不只適合有志此行的專業人士，也適合消費者，更適合常去餐廳宴客的企業主管。尤其台灣近年來，許多家庭早已習慣不在家裡吃年夜飯，統統移師到大飯店去享受年節家族聚餐的歡樂氣氛及被服侍的便利感。

無可諱言，台灣越來越國際化，但國人的英語能力水準與其他鄰國間的落差卻越來越大，包括輸給公認不容易把英文學好的日本人。若要找可以捷進餐飲職場英語能力的書籍，本書當仁不讓。常言道「理論是死的，經驗是活的」，本書正是透過作者的經驗，以生動的會話方式，涵括餐飲業六大主題。

書中單元藉由資深餐飲老鳥引導新進人員或見習生巡行餐廳各部門，介紹、剖析、回答問題，帶領讀者彷如身歷其境般，親身了解餐廳各層面的情況。流暢的情境進行讓人很容易熟悉、背誦相關的生字。相信本書絕對是您書架上不可或缺的英文能力捷進利器。

倍斯特　編輯部

目 次 CONTENTS

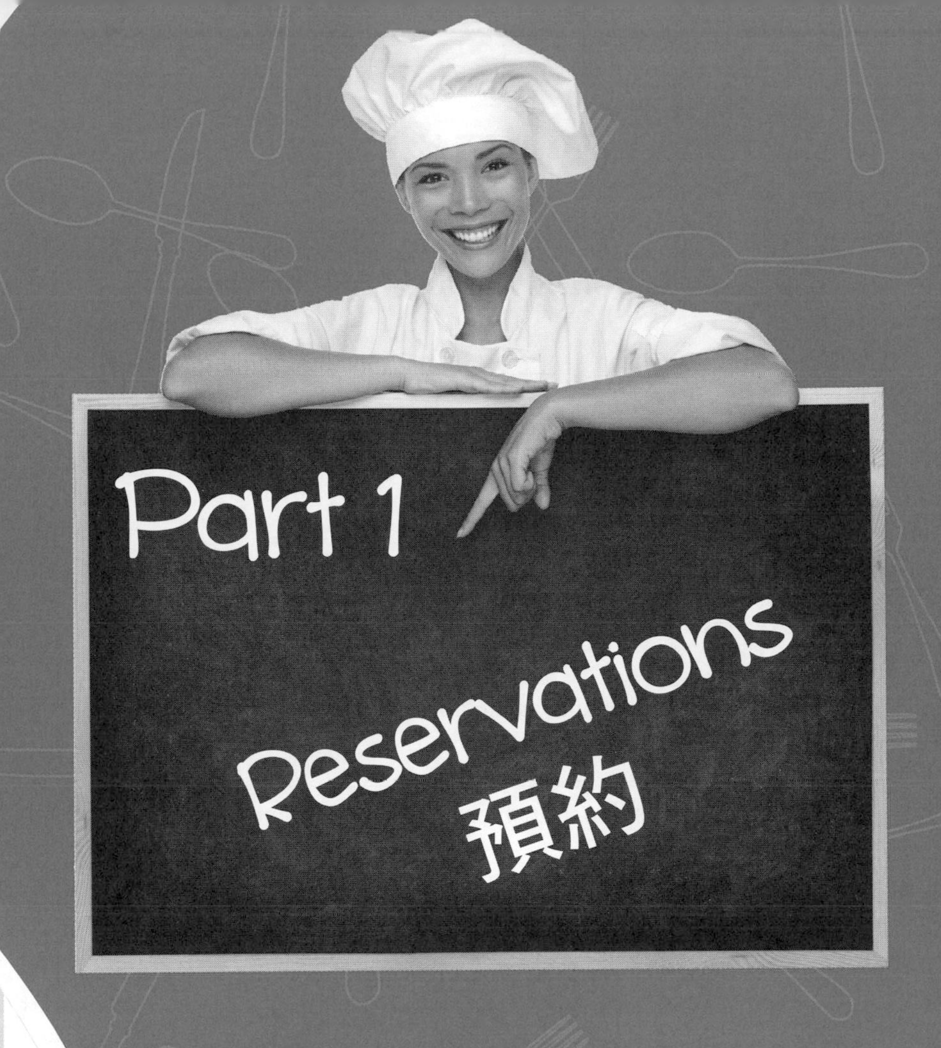
Part 1
Reservations
預約

Unit 01 預約訂位

1 *Making a Reservation* 預約訂位

Track 01

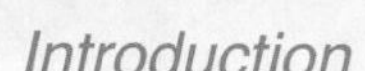

Introduction

A guest calls up to make a reservation for a busy night. 一位顧客來電想在一個繁忙的夜晚預約訂位。

Characters

George Mason - Guest	顧客
Simone - Host	領檯
Jennifer - Host	領檯

Conversation

George	Hi, I'd like to make a reservation for Friday night.	你好，我想預約星期五的位子。
Simone	That's fine, how many are in your **party**?	好的，請問會有幾位嘉賓來用餐呢？
George	There will be six of us.	總共會有六位。
Simone	What time were you thinking of coming in? We can't really take anything of that size from 7:00 through 7:45, but we can fit you in **earlier** or **later** than that.	請問您預計幾點鐘過來？您的用餐人數較多，我們沒有辦法幫您安排 7:00 到 7:45 之間的位子。但是我們可以安排早些或晚些。
George	Oh really, I was hoping we could come in at 7:30. Are you sure there's no way you can **accommodate** us at that time?	真的嗎？我本來是希望可以在 7:30 入座的。你確定你們沒有辦法在那時間接待我們嗎？
Simone	I'm sorry, sir, but that is our **busiest** time, and Friday is one of our busiest nights. 8:00 is only a half hour later. Wouldn't that be OK?	真的很抱歉，因為那是我們最繁忙的時段，而且星期五也是我們最忙碌的一晚。8:00 只比 7:30 晚了半小時，方便嗎？
George	I'll have to talk that over with my **associates** and see.	我必須先和我的同事商量看看。

Simone	We can take you at any time from 5:00 until 6:45, and then from 8:00 until we close at 10:00.	5:00 到 6:45，或是從 8:00 一直到我們 10:00 打烊，都歡迎您預約訂位。
George	All right, I'll see what we want to do and call back.	好的，我會看看我們要如何再回撥。
	(later)	（稍後）
Jennifer	Good afternoon, Best **Steakhouse**, how can I help you?	午安，Best Steakhouse，有什麼可以為您效勞嗎？
George	Hi, my name is George Mason, and I called earlier about getting a reservation for six people on Friday night.	嗨，我是 George Mason，稍早撥了電話過來，想要在星期五預約六個人的位子。
Jennifer	Yes, Mr. Mason, what time would you like?	好的，Mason 先生，您想預約什麼時間呢？
George	I really wanted 7:30, but I was told that wasn't possible. Can I check and see if you're still full at that time?	我真的很想約 7:30，但是我被告知那是不可能的。我可以再確認看看那時間是不是客滿的嗎？
Jennifer	Yes, all of our slots are full between 7:00 and 7:45. Is there another time you would consider?	是的，我們所有的位子在 7:00 至 7:45 之間都已經訂滿了。有其他您願意考慮的時間嗎？
George	I see; then 8:00 will be all right.	我知道了；那就八點吧。
Jennifer	Mr. Mason, I have you down for a party of six at 8:00. We'll see you on Friday night.	Mason 先生，那就幫您預約六位嘉賓於晚上八點用餐。恭候您星期五晚上光臨。

Word Bank

reservation *n.[C]* 預約　party *n.[C]* 派對　earlier *adj.* 稍早的
later *adj.* 稍晚的　accommodate *v.* 接待；容納　busiest *adj.* 最忙碌的
associate(s) *n.[C]* 同事；同僚　steakhouse *n.[C]* 牛排館

Unit 01 預約訂位

Booking Online 線上預約

Track 02

Introduction

A couple talks about going out to dinner, then makes reservations online. 一對情侶正討論要去哪吃飯，並利用網路做線上訂位。

Characters

Rosemary - Guest 顧客
Robert - Guest 顧客

Conversation

Robert	Where do you want to go Saturday night? I'd love to see that new **action movie**. What do you think?	你星期六晚上想去哪裡呢？我想要去看那部新上映的動作片。你覺得呢？
Rosemary	That sounds good to me, but I get to choose the movie next time.	聽起來還不錯，但下次輪到我選電影。
Robert	Since this isn't **your first choice** in movies, why don't I let you **choose** a restaurant?	既然這部電影不是你的首選，不然餐廳就給你挑吧？
Rosemary	Oh, are we eating dinner, too? That sounds good. Where do you want to go?	噢，我們還要吃晚餐啊？聽起來真不錯。那你想去哪吃？
Robert	I said it was **up to you**. You choose.	我就說餐廳給你挑呀。你選吧。
Rosemary	I'd like to go to Best Steakhouse. I really enjoyed it when we went there with the girls last month. The food was really good, and we had a great waiter.	那我想去 Best Steakhouse。上個月我們跟我的好姐妹去時，我就很喜歡那裡。食物真的很好吃，而且我們遇到很棒的服務生。
Robert	That sounds good. I think we can make reservations online. Why don't we do it right now? Here's their **site**. What time do we want to go out?	聽起來還不賴。我想我們應該可以上網訂位。不如現在就訂吧？這是他們的網站。我們打算幾點去呢？

Rosemary	I think if we eat about 6:00, we can spend a good amount of time there and enjoy our dinner, and then we can make it to the 8:00 **show**.	我想如果我們 6:00 左右到，就能有足夠的時間慢慢在那裡享用晚餐，接著可以去看 8:00 的那場電影。
Robert	Wow! This is really easy. All I have to do is enter what time we want and the size of our party, and we have a reservation. That's very **convenient**. It only takes a minute or so.	哇！這超簡單。我只要輸入我們想要的時間跟用餐人數就訂好位了。這超方便的。共花一兩分鐘即可搞定。
Rosemary	That's good. Now let's look up the movie times and see what's playing after dinner.	好極了。現在讓我們來查查場次，看看晚餐後放映的電影有哪些。

Word Bank

online *adv.* 線上；連接網際網路　action movie 動作片；武打片

your first choice 你的首選　choose *v.* 挑選；選擇

up to you 由你決定；（口）隨便你　site *n.[C]* 網站

show *n.[C]* 演出；節目　convenient *adj.* 方便的；便利的

Unit 01 預約訂位

3 *Canceling a Reservation* 取消訂位

Track 03

Introduction

A couple who had made a reservation find that they have to cancel it. 一對已經預約訂位的情侶發現不克前往，必須取消訂位。

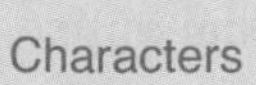

Characters

Rosemary - Guest	顧客
Robert - Guest	顧客
Jennifer - Host	領檯

Conversation

Rosemary	Hi, this is Rosemary. I don't think I'm going to be able to make it after all on Saturday. I have to get some work done, and I just don't have enough time for dinner and a movie.	嘿，我是 Rosemary。我想我星期六是去不成了。我必須處理完一些工作，我沒有時間去吃飯又看電影。
Robert	I'm sorry to hear that. We'll have to go some other time. How about next week?	真是遺憾。那我們再另外約時間去吧。下禮拜如何？
Rosemary	I really don't want to wait until next weekend. What if we go on Tuesday **instead**. I should be done with my **project** by then.	我實在不想等到下個週末。不如改到這星期二。那時我應該已經完成我的任務了。
Robert	That sounds good. The restaurant shouldn't be quite as busy then, either.	聽起來不錯。那天餐廳應該也不會有那麼多人。
	(later)	（稍晚）
Jennifer	Hello, Best Steakhouse, you'll love our service. How may I help you?	您好，Best Steakhouse，提供您賓至如歸的服務。有什麼可以為您效勞的嗎？

Robert	My name is Robert Rodman, and I have a reservation for 6:00 on Saturday. I need to cancel it, but I couldn't find a way to do that online.	我是 Robert Rodman，我預約了星期六晚上 6:00 的位子。現在我必須取消它，但是我在網站上找不到取消的方法。
Jennifer	We do have online reservations, but for right now we just **deal with cancellations** on the phone. Your reservation was for 6:00 Saturday, you said? Oh, here it is; I'll cancel your table. Thanks for letting us know, so we can give it to someone else.	我們是有線上預約的服務，但目前還是必須來電取消預約。您說您是預約星期六晚上 6:00 嗎？喔，有了；我會取消您的訂位。感謝您的告知，這樣我們就可以把位子讓給其他顧客。
Robert	Actually, I was hoping I could make **another** reservation right now.	其實，我希望現在可以再預約另一個時間。
Jennifer	That's not a problem. When would you like to come in?	沒有問題。您想要什麼時候前來呢？
Robert	Do you have any **openings** at about 6:00 Tuesday night?	你們星期二晚上 6:00 左右還有空位嗎？
Jennifer	Yes, we do. We don't have a lot of **bookings** for Tuesday yet. How many are in your party?	是的，有。我們星期二還沒有很多訂位。是幾位用餐呢？
Robert	It will be a party of two.	總共會有兩位。
Jennifer	All right, we'll see you at 6 pm on Tuesday.	好的，期待您於星期二晚上 6:00 光臨。

Word Bank

cancel *v.* 取消　instead *adv.* 取而代之；作為替代　project *n.[C]* 企劃；任務
deal with 處理；應付　cancellation(s) *n.[C]* 取消　another *adj.* 另一個
opening(s) *n.[C]* 空缺　booking(s) *n.[C]* 預約；預訂

預約訂位

Talking About Reservations 探討預約事宜

Introduction

*A new **host** is being taught how to take reservations.*
一位新手領檯正在學習如何接受預約。

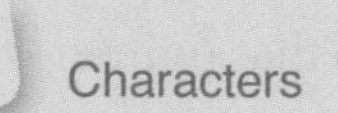

Georgia - Host 領檯
Simone - Host 領檯

Conversation

Georgia	It's nice of you to train me and show me how everything works here.	你真好，教我又示範給我看這裡的每件事怎麼運作。
Simone	I usually do the training because I've been here for a while. This isn't a really hard job, but you do have to have a nice smile and pay attention to **details**.	因為我在這有段時間了，所以通常都是由我負責訓練。這工作其實不難，但你必須保有親切的笑容，還要注意小細節。
Georgia	What kind of details are you talking about?	你指的是哪種小細節？
Simone	One important thing is taking reservations. You have to **pay attention**, or the **pace** of the whole night could be upset.	好比說接受客人預約就是件很重要的事。你必須特別小心，否則整個晚上的步調可能就會大亂。
Georgia	How do we take reservations?	那我們該如何接受預約呢？
Simone	We use this book. Every night is **listed** for several months ahead. The lines you see under the times are how many tables we can take at that time. When someone reserves a table, we fill in their name on the line.	我們用這本本子記錄。裡面列有未來好幾個月的每晚時間表。每個時段下方畫了幾條線就代表那個時段可接受的訂位桌數。每當有顧客預訂，我們就把他們的名字填上去。
Georgia	Why are there more lines at some times than others?	為什麼有些時段的訂位線比較多？

Simone	We take more people in early, so we get a lot of the tables full. But we can't fill all of them right away, or else people who come in later won't have anywhere to sit. That's why there are more lines under 5:00 than during the really busy time between seven and eight.	我們會在開始營業時盡量多接點顧客好填滿許多桌位。但是不能馬上就讓所有的桌數都滿席，否則之後現場光臨的顧客就沒位子坐了。所以 5:00 這個時段的訂位線才會比七八點還多。
Georgia	Do we ever take someone in who doesn't have a reservation?	那我們還是會接受未事先預約的顧客囉？
Simone	Yes, those are called **walk-ins**, and we usually take some of them. It takes a little **experience** to learn how many you can take.	當然，他們是所謂的機動客人，通常我們會接一些。這需要一點經驗來判斷可以接多少。
Georgia	What happens if someone shows up with a reservation but all the tables are full?	那如果已預約的顧客光臨，但那時桌數卻都滿了，會怎麼樣？
Simone	Then they have to wait, which we try to **avoid**. That's where knowing how many walk-ins you can take counts. Just smile and watch how we do things for a while; you'll catch on.	那他們就必須稍等了，這是我們要盡量避免的。所以知道可以接多少機動客人是關鍵點。保持笑容並從旁觀察我們一陣子；你會明白的。

Word Bank

host *n.[C]* 領檯　detail(s) *n.[C]* 細節　pay attention 注意；關注
pace *n.[C]* 步調　list(ed) *v.* 列舉；列表　fill *v.* 填滿
walk-in(s) *n.* 臨時客；未經預約便前來者　experience *n.[U]* 經驗；閱歷
avoid *v.* 避免

Unit 01 預約訂位

Tips for Workplace Happiness
職場補給站
加油大使 Cheryl 來充電！

請問幾位？位置將為您保留 10 分鐘

客人：「你好，我要訂位，時間是今天中午 12 點。」
服務生：「好的，請問幾位？」
客人：「6 位。」
服務生：「好的，為您預訂 6 位，位置為您保留 10 分鐘。」

以上的對話，相信大家一定不陌生，餐廳提供訂位服務對於餐廳與客戶來說是個雙贏策略，餐廳贏得事先了解當天來客狀況，方便評估人力與食材；客戶贏得想吃不用久等與可能撲空的風險。電話訂位是大家所熟知的，也是最方便的方式，但除此之外，還有那些方式呢？

電話訂位

這是一般客戶最常使用的方式，通常店家也十分樂意客戶以此方式進行訂位，電話中直接詢問客戶的資訊，並可第一時間回覆訂位狀況，免去繁瑣的後續連繫作業。

現場訂位

此訂位模式多用於預定大型宴會、喜宴，藉由現場洽詢可第一時間了解餐廳的空間、桌椅配置、佈置擺設、裝潢氣氛，亦可讓餐廳人員更清楚客戶需求，配合安排相關事宜。

網路訂位

網路化時代，知名連鎖餐廳、飯店紛紛推出了網路訂位服務，不管是自家的官網，或是透過訂位系統業者的網路平台，方便客戶隨時隨地皆可訂位，不用受限於餐廳的營業時間，同時餐廳也可搭配多樣化的優惠活動進行促銷。

信函／傳真訂位

信函／傳真訂位多用於較正式且簽約性質之訂位，客戶於紙本上載明需求，後續由餐廳以信函、E-mail 或是傳真方式回覆，此模式最大的缺點便是溝通與作業時間冗長。通常以此形式進行訂位的客戶，大多為宴席、團體訂餐等，通常需要簽署簡單契約，雙方各持一份訂位說明與約定條款，條款內容記載價格、桌數、菜色以及其他特殊需求等，付款的方式則會採訂金訂位或是分批付款。

了解了客戶可能會使用的訂位方式後，實際接待服務時，服務人員是否清楚什麼樣的服務流程可免去訂位資訊落差呢？而哪一種服務的流程可以讓客戶感覺到自己沒有訂錯餐廳，期待用餐時間的來臨呢？

訂位第一步　迎賓招呼與應對

來者是客，這泛用於任何一個接待的場景，面對客戶洽尋適當的自我介紹與稱呼對方是必要的，例如：「倍斯特西餐廳您好，敝姓林，有什麼地方可以為您服務的呢？」。

訂位第二步　瞭解顧客訂位需求

訂位確定一般會確認人數、時間、是否須先點菜和特殊需求外，亦會有餐廳主動說明優惠活動，提供客戶消費時選擇。

訂位第三步　查詢訂位當日桌次與訂席狀況

桌次安排是一門很大的學問，餐廳若有 10 張桌子，每桌 4 個位置，現在共 10 組客戶訂位，且每組皆為 2 名客戶，那你該如何安排？考量餐廳營收將一張桌子拆成兩個小桌，客戶擠一點，但還有 5 張桌子可以接待其他客戶。還是著重客戶用餐舒適，告訴第 11 名客戶訂位已滿，建議他挑選其他時間。這是需要經驗，一般餐廳多有其一套實行已久的模式。

訂位第四步　登錄訂位顧客資料

客戶資料基本上會登錄客戶姓氏、電話、訂餐時間、用餐人數（桌數）、餐點菜色以及其他特殊註記，例如：是否有素食限制、需要兒童椅等等。

訂位第五步　覆誦與再次確認訂位內容

覆誦確保記錄資料正確，並讓客戶了解其訂位的細節，例如：「陳先生，您明天中午的訂位共 6 位，1 位素食，已為您完成訂位」。

訂位第六步　收受訂金以及開立收據（宴席訂位使用）

一般餐廳訂位多為口頭確認即可，不需支付訂金或是書面約定，惟大型宴會訂席，因準備較為繁瑣，且支出成本較高，故大型訂位餐廳皆會制定訂金收取，亦會依照合約模式提供訂位細節與訂金收取狀況。

訂位第七步　感謝客戶安排後續事宜

確認訂位資訊後，依據客戶的需求開始準備，當然若訂位時間尚久，訂位日期前則會由專人開始準備。

訂位七步驟簡單、好記，當然您可依照餐廳性質或是規模而增減步驟，但要牢記服務態度需誠懇、正確、應對得宜。

Unit 02 在接待櫃檯

 Seat Arrangement 座位配置  Track 05

Introduction

The new host learns about how tables are seated.
新手領檯學習如何安排座位。

Characters

Simone - Host	領檯
Georgia - Host	領檯

Conversation

Simone	Hi, Georgia, how was class today?	嘿，Georgia，今天的課程如何？
Georgia	I learned a lot, but I'm not sure when I'll have time to do all the reading.	我學到很多新東西，但是我不確定我什麼時候有空讀完所有的教材。
Simone	I'm sure you'll find time. Anyway, don't worry about that now. Working will help you forget about how busy you are.	總會有時間的。好了，現在別擔心那些。工作會讓你忘記你有多忙碌。
Georgia	I have a question. You **explained** yesterday how to take reservations, but how do you know which table to **assign** them to? If you give them a table, how can you be sure that it will be ready in time?	我其實有個問題。你昨天解釋了要怎麼接受訂位，但是你怎麼知道要指定哪個桌號給訂位顧客？如果你答應給他某一桌，又怎麼保證桌子到時真的會空出來？
Simone	We don't actually assign a certain table to a reservation. We make an **educated guess** as to how many tables we'll need at any time, and then we give whichever one is open to people when they show up.	我們並不會真的在訂位的時候就給客人分配特定桌號。我們會依據經驗推測每一時段需要的桌量，當顧客抵達後，就給他們任何一張空出來的桌子。
Georgia	So, the guests can't ask for a certain table?	所以顧客們不可以指定桌號囉？

Simone	Not really, although if they want to, we tell them they'll have to wait if it's not **clear** when they **arrive**. People are usually happy if we can get them in to any table, as long as they don't have to wait. Now, do you remember your table numbers from yesterday?	不盡然；儘管如果他們想要指定的話，我們會告知他們抵達後必須等到該座位空出來了才行。其實只要不用等，大多數的顧客都會欣然接受我們給的位子。好了，你還記得昨天教你的桌號編制嗎？
Georgia	Yes, the 100s are against the left windows, so they go from table 101 at the front to 108 at the back. The 500s are against the other windows, then the rest are in the **middle**. I think I know them by now.	記得。100 開頭的是靠左邊窗戶那一排，從前頭的 101 依序到後頭的 108。500 開頭的是靠另一邊的窗戶，其它的在中間。我想我現在有概念了。
Simone	Very good; let's just walk through seating guests a few times. I have **a party of** six. Could you take them to 305?	很好，我們來演練幾次帶客入座。我有一組顧客共六位。你可以帶他們去 305 桌嗎？
Georgia	I would, except that 305 isn't big enough for a **6-top**.	我很樂意，只是 305 桌無法不能容納六個人。
Simone	That's good; you passed the test. You'll need to know that if you work as the **lead** host.	很好，你通過測試了。如果想要做好首席領檯工作，這個都是你該知道的。

Word Bank

seat(ed) *v.* 使就座　explain(ed) *v.* 解釋　assign *v.* 指定；指派
educated guess 有根據的揣測；以經驗或知識為依據的推測
clear *adj.* 清空的　arrive *v.* 抵達　middle *n.[C]* 中間
a party of 一團人；一組人；一行人　6-top (X-top) *n.[C]* 六人組；六人桌
lead *adj.* 領導的；先導的；首席的

Unit 02 在接待櫃檯

2 Planning Seating 座位的安排

Track 06

Introduction

The hosts plan special seating needed for the evening. 領檯們正在規畫今晚有特殊需求的座位。

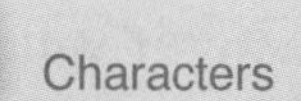

Characters

Simone - Host	領檯
Jennifer - Host	領檯
Georgia - Host	領檯

Conversation

Simone	Hi guys, are you all ready to go? Looks like we have a big night coming up, with a few large parties.	嗨，大家都準備好了嗎？看來今晚會特別忙碌，有幾桌都是團體桌。
Jennifer	Oh, my favorite! How many 24-tops all want to sit together?	噢，我的最愛！有多少想坐一起的 24 人桌呢？
Simone	None of those, **thankfully**, but we do have a lot of big families.	感謝老天，一個都沒有，但是有許多大家庭要來。
Georgia	What do we do when we get parties like that? I know our biggest tables only hold six people. What about larger parties?	當我們接到那麼大組的客人，該怎麼辦？我知道我們最大的桌子只能容納六個人。更多人的團體都怎麼安排？
Simone	What we usually do is put two tables together. Sometimes people want to put a whole party of 20 or 24, as Jennifer said, all at one table. Not only is that very hard to **serve**, it **blocks up** the kitchen for a long period of time.	我們通常會把兩張桌子併在一起。如同 Jennifer 剛剛說的，有的時候會有人想要 20 或 24 人一起坐一桌。那樣不但服務有難度，也會讓廚房塞車好一陣子。

Jennifer	That's right. That's why we make our biggest tables for twelve. That's three tables **slid** together. If there are more guests than that, we put them in groups of eight at different tables **side-by-side**.	沒錯。所以我們最大桌只能容納12人。那是並排三張桌子。如果超過12個人，我們就會拆成8個人一桌、鄰近著坐。
Simone	That way more than one waiter can serve them. It makes everything run more efficiently.	這樣就不只一個服務生可以照顧到他們。做起事來也更有效率。
Georgia	So, what do we have tonight?	所以，我們今晚的情況如何呢？
Simone	There's a group of ten coming in early. We're going to use 401, 2 and 3 for them, so Georgia, can you **set that up** when we get done? There will be an 8-top and a 10-top at 7:30, so we'll have to remember to save tables next to each other for them.	有一組10人的團體會來的蠻早的。我們會安排他們在401、402和403號桌，所以Georgia，可以請你在我們討論完後做好準備嗎？然後在7:30左右，會有一組8人和一組10人的顧客，得記得幫他們留相鄰的桌子。
Jennifer	Let's see what else is **on the books**. It looks like a family of nine at 8:30; that shouldn't be much trouble. Then there are quite a few sixes, but we can just use the **expandable** tables for that.	來看看我們還有什麼訂位紀錄。看來8:30會有一組9人的家族，應該不會太麻煩。然後有好幾組6人的訂位，用延展桌應該就行了。
Simone	Well, let's get into position and go. It should be an interesting night.	那我們準備就定位開工了。今晚應該會很有意思。

Word Bank

thankfully *adv.* 感激的；滿懷感謝的 serve *v.* 服務
block(s) up 堵塞；阻礙 slid *v.* 滑動；滑行 (slide-slid-slid)
side-by-side *adv.* 緊貼著的；並排著的 set that up 準備；預備；建立
on the books 在名冊上；在名單上 expandable *adj.* 可延伸的；可延展的

Unit 02 在接待櫃檯

3 *Answering the Phone* 電話應對 Track 07

Introduction

The hosts talk about answering the phone. 領檯們正在談論如何接聽電話。

Characters 

Simone - Host	領檯
Jennifer - Host	領檯
Georgia - Host	領檯
Jeanette - Guest	顧客
Jim - Guest	顧客

Conversation

Georgia	So, how do we **determine** which one of us answers the phone?	那我們要如何決定誰該去接聽電話呢？
Jennifer	Well, the phone rings here at the **host desk**, although if it's before any of us are on, the manager in the office answers it. If it's during **open hours**, though, whichever of us gets there first has the **duty** to answer it.	嗯，當領檯處的電話響起時，如果是在我們上班就定位之前，經理會在辦公室接聽電話。然而一旦開始營業後，就看誰離領檯處最近就負責接電話。
Georgia	What do we say? Is there a **script** we're supposed to follow?	那我們要說什麼？有什麼要依循的制式話術嗎？
Jennifer	Yes, there is. We're supposed to say, "Thanks for calling Best Steakhouse, you'll love our service." They change it **from time to time**. It used to be "Thank you for calling Best Steakhouse, the home of **prime rib**". It just depends on what they're **emphasizing** at that point in time.	是的，有。我們應該要說，「感謝您來電 Best Steakhouse，提供您賓至如歸的服務。」不過話術也會不時更換，比如以前我們是說，「感謝您來電 Best Steakhouse，牛肋排的首選之家。」所以會依據公司想要強調的重點訊息，來做開場白的更換。
Simone	And watch out; you might end up answering the phone at your house that way! It is an important part of the business, but just listen to us for a while; you'll catch on.	要小心喔，你可能之後在家接電話都會說成這樣！其實對公司來說，接電話是很重要的一環，但只要你觀察我們一陣子，就會抓到訣竅了。

	(the phone rings)	(電話響起)
Jennifer	Thanks for calling Best Steakhouse, you'll love our service.	感謝您來電 Best Steakhouse，提供您賓至如歸的服務。
Jeanette	Hi, I just want to know what time you close today?	你好，我想知道你們今天幾點打烊？
Jennifer	Our hours today are 11:00 am to 10:00 pm. On Friday and Saturday, we're open until 11:00.	我們今天的營業時間是從早上 11 點開始到晚上 10 點。星期五與星期六則延長至晚間 11 點鐘。
	(another phone call)	(另一通電話)
Simone	Thanks for calling Best Steakhouse, you'll love our service.	感謝您來電 Best Steakhouse，提供您賓至如歸的服務。
Jim	Hi, I was wondering whether you still had the **surf & turf** with shrimp on your menu?	嗨，我想知道你們菜單上是否還有海陸鮮蝦全餐？
Simone	Yes, we do. That's one of our most popular dishes. I love it, myself.	有的。那是我們最受歡迎的菜色之一，連我自己也很愛呢。
Jim	Thank you, and can I make a reservation?	謝謝，那我可以訂位嗎？
Simone	Yes, just hold on one second and we'll be right with you.	可以，請您稍後，這就來。
	(to Georgia)	(面對 Georgia)
Simone	Georgia, this is your chance. Could you make a reservation for the man on the phone?	Georgia，你的機會來了。你可以幫電話中這位先生安排訂位嗎？

Word Bank

answer(ing) *v.* 回答；應答　determine *v.* 確定；決定　host desk 接待櫃台
open hours 營業時間　duty *n.[C/U]* 責任；職責　script *n.[C]* 腳本；底稿
from time to time 三不五時；有時；偶爾　prime rib 牛肋條
emphasizing *v.* 強調（emphasize）　surf & turf 海陸全餐

Unit 02 在接待櫃檯

 *Guest Interaction* 與客人互動  Track 08

Introduction

The hosts are preparing to seat the first tables at lunch time. 領檯們正準備為今日午餐時段的第一桌客人帶位。

Characters 

Brianna - Manager	經理
Simone - Host	領檯
Jennifer - Host	領檯
Georgia - Host	領檯
Bill - Guest	顧客
Judy - Guest	顧客

Conversation

Brianna	Are you all ready? I should open the doors in about a minute.	你們都準備好了嗎？再一分鐘我就要把門打開了。
Simone	I'm **set**, but I think Georgia is in the bathroom **freshening up**. I'll go get her.	我好了，但是我想 Georgia 還在洗手間做梳洗。我去叫她。
Georgia	Here I am. Let's get these people in here and get going.	我好了。讓顧客進來吧，我們開始上工了。
Brianna	All right, I'm opening the doors. It's Friday, so we should have a busy lunch.	好，那我們開門營業囉。今天是星期五，午餐時段想必相當忙碌。
	(a party walks in)	（一組客人進入餐廳）
Simone	Good afternoon, welcome to Best Steakhouse. How many are in your party?	午安，歡迎光臨 Best Steakhouse。請問幾位呢？
Bill	There are just the two of us. Would it be possible to have a window seat?	只有我們兩位。有可能給我們靠窗的座位嗎？
Simone	Yes, that would be no problem. Jennifer, would you please take this **couple** to table 103? Jennifer will **see you** to your table.	好的，沒有問題。Jennifer，麻煩你帶這兩位去 103 桌好嗎？Jennifer 將會送您到您的餐桌。

Jennifer	This way, please. Your table is right over here. Let me pull out the chair for you, ma'am. Here is a menu for you, and one for you, sir. I'll put a copy of the **wine list** here in the middle of the table. Your waiter will be here in just a minute.	這邊請。您的餐桌在這。這位女士，讓我幫你拉椅子吧。這一份菜單給您，另外這份給先生。我把一張酒單放在桌面中間。您的服務生稍後就來為您服務。
Bill	Thank you. This table is perfect.	謝謝你。這位子好極了。
	(another party arrives)	（另一組顧客進入餐廳）
Simone	Good afternoon, how many are in your party?	午安。請問幾位呢？
Judy	There are six of us. Would it be possible to have a window table?	我們有 6 位。還有可能坐到靠窗的位子嗎？
Simone	I'm sorry, but all our window tables are currently full. The tables in the **second row** have a pretty good view, though. They're **offset**, so you don't have to look through someone's head to see outside. And you won't have to wait.	很抱歉，目前靠窗的座位都客滿了。第二排座位區視野也很不錯，座位跟第一排是交錯開來的，所以不會被擋住視線。而且，現在不必等就有空位。
Judy	I think that will be fine, thank you.	那就這樣也可以，謝謝你。
Simone	Georgia, could you please take these people to table 504? Enjoy your lunch.	Georgia，麻煩你帶這客人去 504 桌好嗎？祝您用餐愉快。

Word Bank

preparing *v.* 準備（prepare） seat *v.* 使就位 set *adj.* 準備好的
freshening up 梳洗；恢復精神 couple *n.[C]* 情侶；一對；兩位
see you 護送你；照看你 wine list 酒單 second row 第二排；第二行
offset *adj.* 錯開的；偏移的；不對齊的

Unit 02 在接待櫃檯

給好動的小朋友一個空間——餐廳區域規劃

調皮的小孩不只是惱怒爸媽的引爆彈，也是餐廳服務員最頭痛的天使。某次我前往一家全台知名連鎖的西餐廳用餐，當時我先抵達餐廳，同行親友尚未抵達。服務人員帶位前，禮貌詢問我今天幾位貴賓，不假思索的我直覺回應三個人，但我未提及其中一位是小朋友。

人員引領我到一個靠窗的四人坐位，遠遠眺望窗外淡水河景致氣氛非常好，但位置有點小，適合只有你跟我的情侶約會用餐。在我們三個人都入座後，點餐的服務人員發現我們之間有一個正值睪酮素旺盛期的小朋友，窗邊的小位置讓這個小朋友無法好好的活動，貼心的服務人員發現了這件事，快速的詢問我：「小姐，不好意思。因領位人員沒發現您有個小朋友，這四人位置可能無法讓你照顧好小朋友，需要幫您更換到空間較大的沙發區嗎？」

從上述餐廳帶位的小故事，我們可以想像一下餐廳的位置安排。靠窗的景致浪漫有情調適合情侶約會談心，設計上當然是越靠近越甜蜜。轉到空間較大的沙發區，位置上可以多樣利用，適合家庭、團體用餐。可見這家餐廳有用心在規劃他們的位置，那什麼是合宜的區域劃分呢？

餐廳前場營業區

前場可分為出入口區、接待區、座位區、通道、客用洗手間、服務工作站、結帳櫃檯、出菜口等，相關區域配置規則與座位規劃如下：

- 同質性的作業區應在同一樓層或區域，例如：出入口與接待區需同一區
- 依照功能規劃空間大小，例如：出菜區需能容納 2-3 人
- 廚房面積達到餐廳外場的 1/2
- 座位區與出菜口（廚房）的距離需適中，不可過遠
- 基於衛生，食物製備區及服務作業區應留有一定的區隔空間
- 周全設置安檢的空間及特殊設施，例如：逃生門與無障礙出口

⊙依據服務方式、風格屬性來決定桌椅間距，餐桌高度 70~75cm
⊙顧客活動空間最少 50cm，椅子間距最少 80cm，椅面高寬深皆需介於 40~45cm 間
⊙兩桌距離最少 50cm，如有推車經過則須加大

餐廳後場作業區

後場可分為配菜間、廚房、倉庫、員工休息區、後門出入口等，相關區域配置規則與座位規劃如下：

⊙客戶、服務人員、食品與設備器皿使用空間需區分清楚
⊙餐廳服務通道寬度以 75cm 為宜（宴會廳 60~75cm，高級西餐廳 90cm）
⊙食材物料出入口應獨立設置，不可與服務人員一起使用
⊙上菜與撤席通道要分開，確保服務人員安全
⊙考量安全與菜餚溫度，出菜口與座席或自助餐檯勿離太遠
⊙服務顧客的動線應求效率，不要太遠
⊙人員備餐間區域需避免顧客通行，以免危險
⊙員工休息區亦需完備，且須避免與食材物料設立一起

1987 年麥當勞經營者發想在餐廳內撥點空間，設立第一個兒童遊戲區。當時稱為「麥當勞樂園」，內設爬行管內有球和溜滑梯，這項決定無疑地大大減少餐廳座位區，客戶來店消費理所當然的也降低。但是，當時這個決定並未讓麥當勞來客數降低，這樣的空間犧牲反而帶來不一樣的銷售量與來客數。

來到麥當勞，爸媽只要將小朋友丟入遊戲區，他們就可以輕鬆地喘口氣，喝杯咖啡，享受兩人時光。若遇到孩子生日，也可在這裡辦生日派對。正因為麥當勞將孩子當成店裡主要貴賓，動點腦筋規劃了小小貴賓專屬區域，因此成功將麥當勞轉化成小孩用餐遊樂園的強烈形象。

現在你還會說犧牲部分座位區域，改為客戶專屬服務區，只有降低客戶席次的缺點嗎？

Unit 03 公司聚會

Banquet Reservation 宴會訂位

Track 09

Introduction

A guest is making a reservation for a large group.

一位顧客想要做團體訂位。

Characters

Joseph - Guest	顧客
June - Assistant Manager	副理

Conversation

Joseph I'm interested in having a party to honor some of our retiring employees. Do you have a separate room for things like that?

我想辦一場宴會來表揚一些即將退休的員工。你們有類似包廂的場地可供使用嗎？

June No, but for really large parties, we often rent out the entire restaurant. You can have the party here and have **a full bar** in addition to dinner. How many people will you have?

沒有喔，但如果人數眾多，我們通常會把整個餐廳做包場服務。您在這辦宴會，除了晚餐外，還可以享用吧檯所有的飲品。這場宴會大概會有多少人？

Joseph There will be about 65 people, and we'd like to come in about the 15th of next month.

大概會有 65 人，我們希望可以在下個月 15 號舉辦。

June Let me look on the calendar. Yes, that date is still open. What kind of **banquet** were you interested in having?

讓我看一下行事曆。沒有問題，那天還沒有被訂走。怎樣安排宴會形式您會比較喜歡？

Joseph We want to have a **cocktail hour** first, and then dinner afterwards. Then we'll have some **presentations** and speeches after that. It'll probably last three to four hours.

我們想要在吃飯前先有閒聊小酌的雞尾酒時間，再來是用餐。爾後會有些發表與致詞等等。整晚下來大概需要三至四個小時。

June	We can certainly accommodate you. We have a couple different styles to choose from. There is a buffet choice; that's the least expensive, and there are three, four, and five-**course** options as well. There is **a variety** of foods you can choose from within those **categories**, or you can work with our chef and design your own menu, if you like.	我們可以接待你們沒有問題。我們有幾種不同的宴會風格可以選擇。有自助的形式，會是最實惠的選擇，菜式組合也可以有三道、四道或五道菜的選擇。每組菜式提供多樣化的食物內容供您選擇，或者您想要的話，也可以與我們的行政主廚討論，設計自己的菜單。
Joseph	That sounds good. I'm going to need some time to decide, but I'm sure we want one of the **sit-down** options.	聽起來好極了。我需要一些時間做決定，但是肯定的是，我們會想要選擇一種由服務生上菜的用餐方式。
June	I can send all the information to you. We have a **packet** that will give you all the options and price **guidelines**. Then you can take your time and decide on what you would like.	我可以將所有的相關資料寄給您。我們的套裝方案裡會有所有的選項與參考價錢。您可以慢慢決定自己喜好的方式。
Joseph	I'll take a look at your information and discuss it with my staff. We'll get back to you.	我會參考你的資料，並與我的同仁們討論。之後會再聯絡你們。

Word Bank

assistant *adj.* 助理的；輔助的　a full bar 各式酒水齊備的酒吧
banquet *n.[C]* 宴會　cocktail hour 雞尾酒時間；正式用餐前的小酌時間
presentation(s) *n.[C/U]* 演出；發表　course *n.[C]* 一道菜
a variety 諸多種類；各式各樣　categories *n.[C]* 選項；類別（category）
sit-down *adj.* 非自助式的；坐定等待者上菜的　packet *n.[C]* 套裝方案；事先規劃好的計畫或行程　guidelines *n.[C]* 方針；原則

Unit 03 公司聚會

2 *Cocktail Hour Arrangements* 雞尾酒會安排  Track 10

Introduction

The guests who are having a retirement party are talking to the assistant manager about bar arrangements. 將舉辦退休送別宴會的顧客，正在與副理討論吧檯安排。

Characters

Joseph - Guest	顧客
June - Assistant Manager	副理

Conversation

June	I guess the first thing we need to discuss is the cocktail hour. Do you want to have a full bar, or are you just interested in beer and wine?	我想首先我們要討論的是雞尾酒會的安排。您想要整座吧檯的齊全供應，還是只需要啤酒與葡萄酒？
Joseph	I think some of my employees are **expecting** to have more than just wine, so we need to go with the full bar **option**.	我想我的員工們應該會期待不只有葡萄酒，所以我們需要走完整吧檯供應的方案。
June	Is the company going to pay for the drinks, or do you want the **individuals** to pay as they order?	那麼飲料是由公司買單，還是您希望員工們各自隨點隨付？
Joseph	I want the company to pay, as that will make it more relaxed for the employees. But I don't want everyone to get really **drunk** on free **alcohol**. What do you suggest?	我想就由公司買單，這樣員工們才會更為放鬆。只是我不想有人因為有免費的酒喝而喝到爛醉。你有什麼好建議嗎？
June	You could give each guest **vouchers** for two or three drinks each. That way you can control the cost and how much each person has. Or you could provide wine, soft drinks, and beer **free of charge**, and have the guests pay for any **mixed drinks**.	您可以給每位員工兩杯至三杯飲料的兌換卷，如此一來不但可以控管成本，也可以防止大家喝太多。或是你可以免費提供一般紅白酒、氣泡飲料和啤酒，但是調酒就必須要自費。

Joseph	I think we should go with the vouchers. If we also have wine on the tables, then I think everyone will be happy. I don't want the focus of the evening to be on drinking, anyway.	我想就用兌換券吧。如果餐桌上也提供紅白酒，就應該夠大家開心了。反正我不想把整晚的焦點變成光是喝酒而已。
June	I'll give you a copy of our wine list, so you don't have to decide what you'd like right now. If you buy at least eight bottles, we give a discount of 15%.	我會給您一份我們的酒單，所以您不用馬上決定。如果您購買超過八瓶酒，我們會提供 85 折的優惠。
Joseph	I think that will make for a good cocktail hour. Now, let's talk about the rest of the evening.	我想這樣應該會有個很棒的雞尾酒會。好了，現在就來討論其餘的晚宴細節吧。

Word Bank

arrangement(s) *n.[C]* 安排　expect(ing) *v.* 期待；期盼

option *n.[C]* 選項；選擇　individual(s) *n.[C]* 個人　drunk *adj.* 酒醉的

alcohol *n.[C]* 酒；酒精　voucher(s) *n.[C]* 禮券；優惠券

free of charge 免費　mixed drinks 調酒

Unit 03 公司聚會

3 *Menu Discussion* 討論菜色

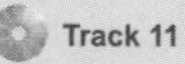
Track 11

Introduction

The chef is discussing menu options for the large party. 行政主廚正在討論團體宴會的菜色選擇。

Characters

Joseph - Guest	顧客
June - Assistant Manager	副理
Geno - Chef	行政主廚

Conversation

June	Geno, this is Joseph. He's the manager I told you about who is having a party for his retiring employees in a few weeks.	Geno，這位是 Joseph。他就是我提過的那位再過幾週要為退休員工舉辦宴會的經理。
Geno	Hello, Joseph. Have you thought about what kind of food you'd like for this party?	Joseph，您好。您想過要在宴會上提供哪些菜色了嗎？
Joseph	I looked **briefly** at the **materials** June gave me, and I think we want to go with one of the four-course meals.	我很快地看過 June 提供給我的資料了，我想我們會選一個有四道菜的菜式組合。
Geno	Would you like **appetizers**, then salad, entrée, and dessert, or soup, salad, entrée and dessert?	那您會想要開胃菜、沙拉、主餐、然後甜點的樣式，還是湯品、沙拉、主餐、跟甜點？
Joseph	I hadn't really thought about it. I think appetizers would **go over well**. What do you have that we might like?	我還沒認真地想過這個。我想開胃菜應該比較受大家歡迎。你們有什麼是廣受喜愛的呢？
Geno	A lot of people like to get a variety of appetizers. Each table gets three or four different ones and they share.	很多人喜歡開胃菜種類豐富些。每桌可以一起分享三或四種不同的菜色。
Joseph	That sounds like what we want. That way, everyone can try something a little different.	聽起來很合我意。這樣大家都可以嘗試一些不一樣的東西。

Geno	Here's a **list** of our most popular appetizer **selections**. What about entrées?	這邊有張我們最受歡迎的開胃菜選擇清單。那主菜呢？
Joseph	Since this is a steakhouse, I really wanted to get beef.	既然這是間牛排館，應該要選牛肉吧。
Geno	We do **specialize** in that. We have several different preparations that work well with larger parties. Since king crab is **in season** right now, our petit filet with crab **sauce** is popular. Or we could serve prime rib. That's always popular. Here's a list of suggestions. Why don't you take a look at it later? There's no hurry to decide.	牛肉的確是我們的專長。我們有好幾種適合大型宴會的不同烹調方式。由於目前是帝王蟹產季，我們的嫩煎小腓力佐蟹醬很受歡迎。或是牛肋排，一向是很熱門的菜色。這邊列出了我們的建議，您可以花些時間慢慢看，不必急著做決定。
Joseph	Thank you. I'll take a look at this and the appetizer list you gave me. Can I call you back in a day or two?	謝謝你。我會連你給的開胃菜清單一起好好研究。我可以過一到兩天再回電給你嗎？
Geno	That will be fine. And if you want to, we can create something especially for your group. Just get back with me and we'll discuss it.	沒有問題。如果您希望，我們也可以為您設計專屬菜色。儘管回覆我們，都可以再討論。

Word Bank

briefly *adv.* 簡短地；短暫地　material(s) *n.[C]* 材料；素材；資料
appetizer(s) *n.[C]* 開胃菜　go over well 被接受；受歡迎
list *n.[C]* 清單；列表　selection(s) *n.[C]* 被挑選出的人或物
specialize *v.* 專精；特長　in season 當季的；盛產期的　sauce *n.[U/C]* 醬汁

Unit 03 公司聚會

Final Seating and Menu Discussion 最終的座位安排與菜單討論

Track 12

Introduction

The final arrangements are being made for the retirement party. 退休宴會拍板定案。

Characters 

Joseph - Guest	顧客
June - Assistant Manager	副理
Geno - Chef	行政主廚

Conversation

Geno	Have you made any **decisions** since we talked on the phone the other day?	自從上次我們在電話中討論後，您做決定好什麼了嗎？
Joseph	Yes, I think we're all set. We've decided on a four-course meal, with three appetizers per table.	有的，我想大致上都確定了。我們決定選四道菜的菜式，每桌都有三種不同的前菜。
Geno	Very good, and which appetizers have you decided on?	好極了，您決定要哪幾種前菜呢？
Joseph	We'd like the mozzarella **cheese sticks**, **shrimp cocktail**, and the spicy mushroom **dip**.	我們想要莫札瑞拉起司條、雞尾酒蝦、還有香辣蘑菇沾醬。
Geno	That sounds like a good **combination**. What about entrées?	這組合聽起來不錯。那主餐呢？
Joseph	We're going to go with the steak and crab sauce you suggested, and also the teriyaki chicken with grilled shrimp. And I think we've decided on the raspberries in fresh **cream** for dessert.	我們要選你推薦的牛排佐蟹醬，還有照燒雞與碳烤明蝦。還有我想甜點就決定是覆盆子佐鮮奶油。

Geno	If there's nothing else you need to know about the food, then I'll let you and June finish the rest of your plans.	如果您對食物都定案了，那麼，我就讓您與 June 一起敲定其他事宜。
June	We just need to discuss the seating arrangements. How many people will be at the **head table**?	我們現在只需要討論座位安排。有多少人會坐在主桌呢？
Joseph	We'll have about ten. The company president and his wife, and then the retirees and their guests. It might be as many as twelve.	大約會有 10 人。公司總裁跟夫人，還有退休員工與他們的賓客。可能會有 12 人之多。
June	We can set it up for twelve and make changes **as needed**. As for the rest of the tables, we usually find that tables of eight and six work well in our dining room.	那我們會先預設 12 人的位子，然後視需要再做調整。至於用餐區的其他桌子，八或六人桌會是最適當的。
Joseph	Can you show me how the dining room will be **laid out**? I'm going to need to decide where everyone will sit.	你可以讓我看一下餐區會怎麼配置嗎？我需要決定與會人員的座位。
June	Here are some **charts** showing different ways we can set things up. You can take a look at them and get back to me.	這裡有一些圖表呈現不同的可行配置。您可以看過之後再回覆我。
Joseph	Thank you, I think that's all for now. I'll contact you if any more details need to be worked out.	謝謝你，我想大致上就先這樣了。如果還有什麼細節需要再討論的，我會再跟你聯繫。

Word Bank

decision(s) *n.[C]* 決定；決擇　cheese stick(s) 起司條
shrimp cocktail 雞尾酒蝦　dip *n.[C/U]* 沾醬；醬料
combination *n.[C]* 組合；搭配　cream *n.[U]* 鮮奶油　head table 主桌
as needed 依照需求　laid out 安排；設置

Unit 03 公司聚會

舉辦活動我最行——宴會活動策劃

如果你找過喜宴場地，你一定被推銷過婚禮秘書，這個新名詞近幾年快速竄紅崛起。婚禮秘書的工作主要是幫忙新人安排活動、迎賓禮物、餐廳布置與餐廳溝通等，往往因為你的宴客地點就是這家餐廳，包套服務價格優惠且方便。

婚禮秘書只做婚宴安排嗎？其實他可以做的事情很多，舉凡大型宴會、尾牙、公司活動等，這個秘書都可滿足客戶的需求，當然也有部分餐廳主攻婚宴，此點在訂席時都需要特別留意跟詢問。

除此之外，近幾年餐廳也開始提供結合餐點與活動的大型外燴服務，省下餐廳的空間，營造客製化的專屬服務，將主廚與服務團隊拉到外場，節省下客戶前往餐廳的時間與活動安排的方便性。

那麼，舉辦大型活動很困難嗎？我可以辦到嗎？當然可以，只要掌握好幾個原則，就可以把活動辦得精彩豐富。

活動策劃技巧

情報要正確

舉辦活動一定有目的、主題，參加的主要對象也都會有設定，舉行活動也會有費用上的限制，事前以上這幾個重點一定要抓牢，任何一個都不能遺漏。若想再提供更好的服務，賓客與主辦者的喜好有時也是需要納入活動舉辦的主軸。

分析要精準

分析需要依賴情報，若上述功課做的好，加上懂得觀察，分析將可得心應手。精準的分析將輔助活動發想的邏輯性與正確性，分析有時需要經驗，提供一個新手分析小技巧：面對客戶就是多問、多了解並記錄下來；背對客戶後，筆記認真看，抓出客戶喜好或活動重點。

發想有邏輯

發想是活動舉辦的靈魂，舉辦婚禮氣氛當然是溫馨、感人；舉辦尾牙場面應該是快樂、活潑；舉辦同學會，回憶與感恩將是不可少。這樣的發想邏輯很簡單，若要求客製化，當然就需要些不同的元素來激發，給新手一個小小建議，有時間可多參加各類活動，並將每次參加的活動心得改成企劃案，這有助於企劃發想！

企劃完整 執行確實

有了以上的情報、分析、發想後，要落實到企劃與執行上。企劃時，切記要制訂關鍵績效指標（KPI, Key Performance Indicators），將需要執行的重點與時間詳細地制定下來，並且合理地預估費用，完整地將流程一一擬訂。另外擅用餐廳資源進行企劃的包裝，亦將使得企劃完整。最後執行時，確實依照企劃書執行。若遇無法執行之處，亦須記錄下來，後續檢討修正。若遇到緊急狀況，首要是，要讓活動正常地進行下去。除非已攸關安全，不然切勿讓活動暫停或終止。

看到這裡，相信你會問我，餐廳真的有這樣的時間安排這麼多服務嗎？我想當然沒有。對餐廳來說，活動安排僅是訂席的一項額外加值服務。許多餐廳早已研擬好一套相同模式的活動服務方式，僅是現在餐廳宴會競爭激烈，部分的餐廳亦已將活動策劃獨立出來，甚至成立一家專屬的公司。從此亦可知，未來餐廳客製化的活動策劃將會越來越完整且盛行。

Unit 04 假日訂位

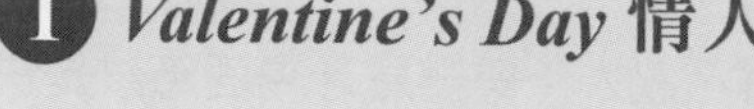

1 Valentine's Day 情人節

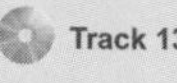
Track 13

Introduction

Employees discuss special preparations for Valentine's Day. 員工們討論情人節的特別準備。

Characters

Brianna - Manager	經理
Geno - Chef	行政主廚
Eldon - Waiter	服務生

Conversation

Brianna	The most **romantic** day of the year is coming up.	整年最浪漫的一天要來了耶！
Eldon	If it's so romantic, then why is it held in February?	如果真的那麼浪漫，為什麼偏要選在二月份慶祝？
Brianna	Because that's when someone decided to celebrate Saint Valentine. You've become a little **cynical**, haven't you? Or maybe it's just because you don't have a valentine.	因為那是有人為了聖人聖瓦倫丁阿而慶祝的時候。你變得有點憤世嫉俗，是不是？還是可能只是因為沒有情人可以一起過吧。
Eldon	Let's leave my love life out of this. And waiters are always cynical. What are we going to serve – **champagne**, I suppose? Can't we do something different this year?	我們別扯到我的感情生活吧！服務生當久了都會有點憤世嫉俗的。我猜我們今年還是要提供香檳吧？難道就不能來點別的嗎？
Brianna	I was thinking of having James come up with a special love cocktail, **in addition to** the champagne. He's usually good with new drinks.	除了香檳之外，我考慮請 James 想出一種特別的愛情雞尾酒。他對研發新飲品通常很有一套。
Eldon	Let's talk about food. We usually serve the regular menu and also a **set menu**. Can we maybe have a special with a **cut of meat** we don't usually serve?	來談談食物吧。我們通常提供經常性餐點，加上一種套餐。或許今年可以用我們平常沒有供應的牛肉部位做個特餐？

Geno	I was thinking about that, too. I'm considering a **roast**, topped with a special Valentine's sauce. Something red and white; probably raspberry-based.	我也在想這個。我想到一道菜是烤牛肉淋上特製情人節醬汁。某種紅紅白白的，也許是以覆盆子為基底的醬汁。
Brianna	That sounds good. And we should include dessert as well.	這聽起來不錯。還應該搭配甜點才行。
Geno	I think heart-shaped cakes topped with fresh strawberries and cream sounds good.	我想心形的蛋糕上頭鋪上新鮮草莓和鮮奶油應該不錯。
Eldon	What about reservations? Should we stay open a little later than usual?	那訂位呢？我們要稍微延長營業時間嗎？
Brianna	I'm not sure about that. Most people eat dinner and go somewhere else later. Why don't we just take our normal reservations and tell the hosts to let us know if there's any **demand** for **late-night** tables?	這我還不確定。許多人吃完晚餐還會去其它地方。先照一般時間接受訂位，再請領檯留意是否有深夜時段的訂位需求？
Eldon	Of course, most of the tables will be set as 2-tops. And we'll have the lights a little lower than usual. I'll make sure to get the extra candles out of the storeroom.	好的，當天會把大多數的餐桌設置成兩人座，也會把燈光調的比平日暗些。我還會去倉儲室多拿些蠟燭出來備用。
Brianna	Thanks guys, and let me know if you have any **brainstorms** in the next few days.	感謝大家的配合。未來幾天如果大家有任何新想法，務必讓我知道。

Word Bank

romantic *adj.* 浪漫的　cynical *adj.* 憤世嫉俗；不屑的
champagne *n.[C]* 香檳；本指法國香檳區產的氣泡酒
in addition to 除此之外；附加的　set menu 套餐
cut of meat 肉類主餐　roast *n.[C/U]* 烤肉　demand *n.[U]* 需求
late-night *adj.* 深夜的（11:00 過後）　brainstorm(s) *n.[C]* 妙計；新想法

Unit 04 假日訂位

2 Christmas Dinner 聖誕晚餐 Track 14

Introduction

The host talks about the upcoming Christmas holiday with guests. 領檯人員跟顧客們談論到即將來臨的聖誕假期。

Characters  

Jennifer - Host	領檯
Donald - Guest	顧客
Marian - Guest	顧客

Conversation

Jennifer	Thanks for coming in, **folks**. We hope to see you again soon.	大夥兒們，感謝您們的光臨。希望很快又可以再看到您們。
Donald	Oh, that reminds me. Are you going to be open on Christmas?	噢，這倒提醒了我。你們聖誕節會營業嗎？
Jennifer	Yes, we are. Would you like to make a reservation right now?	是的，我們會。您想要現在訂位嗎？
Donald	I might. Could you tell me what will be on the menu? Will you be doing anything special for the day?	或許會。你可以先告訴我菜單會有些什麼嗎？當天會有什麼特別的嗎？
Jennifer	Yes, we will. Here is a copy of the Christmas Day menu. It will include **squash** soup, salad, and then your choice of ham or turkey, with all the **trimmings**.	是的，會有喔。這是一份聖誕節菜單。裡面包含了南瓜濃湯、時蔬沙拉，您可以選擇火腿或是火雞當主菜，而且兩樣都有配菜。
Donald	Oh, look, you're even having **cranberry sauce**! That sounds just like the dinner we used to have at Mom's house growing up.	噢，你看看，居然有蔓越莓果醬！這聽起來就跟小時候媽媽做的聖誕節晚餐一模一樣。

Jennifer	Our managers wanted it to be like eating at home, for those people who live too far away to go home, or for people who just don't feel like cooking a big **feast**.	我們經理們就是想帶給那些無法返家，或是不想大費周章做菜的顧客們一份家的感覺。
Donald	And **pumpkin pie** for dessert. Sounds yummy. Can I make a reservation for seven people?	還有南瓜派當甜點，聽起來太可口了。我可以預訂七個人的位子嗎？
	(later, on the phone)	（稍後，電話中）
Jennifer	Thanks for calling Best Steakhouse, you'll love our service. What can I do for you this afternoon?	感謝您來電 Best Steakhouse，提供您賓至如歸的服務。有什麼可以為您效勞的嗎？
Marian	I'm interested in making a reservation for Christmas day. Do you have anything for kids on the menu?	我想要預約聖誕節的座位。你們有兒童餐點嗎？
Jennifer	Kids can choose from either the ham or turkey dinners on the set menu. They'll get a half **portion** at half price.	兒童可以選擇火腿或火雞套餐。份量與價錢都是普通菜單的一半。
Marian	That sounds like a winner. My two boys really like ham. I'd like to make a reservation, if I could.	聽起來正是我想要的。我的兩個兒子很喜歡火腿。可以的話，我想訂位。
Jennifer	Certainly, what time would you like to come in? And how many are in your party?	當然。您想要在哪個時段前來呢？有多少人會一起來用餐呢？

Word Bank

upcoming *adj.* 即將到來的　folks *n.* 大家；人們
squash *n.[C]* 南瓜　trimmings *n.* 盤飾；配菜
cranberry sauce 蔓越莓果醬　feast *n.[C]* 饗宴；大餐
pumpkin pie 南瓜派　portion *n.[C]* 份量；一份

Unit 04 假日訂位

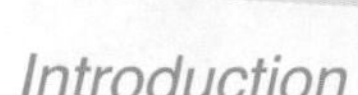

3 *New Year's Eve* 跨年夜

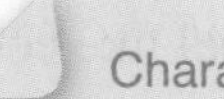

Introduction

The staff are gathered together to discuss plans for New Year's Eve. 員工們被召聚在一起計劃跨年夜。

Characters

Brianna - Manager	經理
Geno - Chef	行政主廚
Andy - Waiter	服務生
Eldon - Waiter	服務生

Conversation

Brianna	We called this meeting to let you know what we're planning for New Year's Eve this year. Last year we stayed open all the way through past **midnight**, but we didn't do a lot of business because people just stayed all night.	我們召開這會議是要讓大家知道今年跨年夜的計畫。去年我們延長了營業時間直到午夜過後，生意卻不盡理想，因為所有的賓客都整晚待著不走。
Andy	How are we going to avoid the same thing happening this year?	那我們要如何避免今年再重蹈覆轍呢？
Brianna	For this New Year's, we're going to serve our regular menu until 9:00. After that, we'll move all the chairs and tables and have a big cocktail party. That will start at 10:30.	今年的跨年夜，我們將會供應經常性餐點到 9:00。之後，我們將會移開所有的桌椅，在 10:30 開始舉行一場盛大的雞尾酒派對。
Eldon	So, how is this going to keep people from sitting all night?	那這樣要如何避免客人坐著不走呢？
Brianna	After we serve the last dinner, we'll close the doors and get the **remaining** people to leave. Then, we'll **reopen** the doors at 10:30.	當廚房完成最後一張晚餐點單的時候，我們就會先關門、讓剩下的客人離開。然後一直到 10：30 才會再開門營業。
Andy	Won't that **upset** some people?	這樣會不會造成某些賓客不愉快？

Brianna	I don't think so. We'll **make it clear** that they have to leave by 10:15. That will give them plenty of time to eat, and while they are eating we can get all the **noisemakers** and other party items together.	我想不會。我們會清楚告知他們必須在 10:15 前離開，這給了他們很充裕的時間享用餐點。同時，我們也可以備妥紙笛、派對吹捲與其它所需要的道具。
Geno	We're going to have a buffet set up on one side of the main dining room. There will be appetizers and **finger foods** there. The **waitstaff** that is left will be serving cocktails to order.	我們將在用餐區的一邊設置自助餐吧檯。那裡會供應一些開味菜與小餐點。留下的服務生們則會負責供應顧客們所點的雞尾酒。
Eldon	So, some of us will get to go home?	所以，我們有些人可以先回家嗎？
Brianna	Yes, we shouldn't need all of you here. But for those who do stay, there will be dancing, and then fireworks at midnight. Everyone will be in a **festive** mood, so it should be a lot of fun.	是的，我們並不需要所有的人手。但是對於留下來的人，這裡會有舞會，午夜也會有煙火秀。所有人都會沉浸在歡樂的氣氛中，所以應該會很有趣。

Word Bank

midnight *n.[C]* 午夜；凌晨 12:00　remaining *adj.* 剩下的；剩餘的
reopen *v.* 重新開始　upset *v.* 使不安；使心煩　make it clear 澄清；申明
noisemaker(s) *n.[C]* 指用來炒熱氣氛的發聲道具
finger food(s) 用手即可取食的食物；小餐點　waitstaff *n.[C]* 送餐服務生
festive *adj.* 喜慶的；歡樂的；節日的

Unit 04 假日訂位

4 *Mother's Day* 母親節 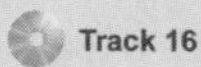 Track 16

Introduction

The staff make plans for one of the busiest days of the year. 員工們為一年之中最忙的某一天做準備。

Characters 

Georgia - Host	領檯
Andy - Waiter	服務生
June - Assistant Manager	副理

Conversation

Georgia	Hey, Andy, I was **wondering** about something.	嘿，Andy，我一直想知道一件事。
Andy	Yeah, Georgia, what is it? Did you forget your table numbers again?	嗯，Georgia，怎麼了？你又忘了桌號配置了嗎？
Georgia	You're so funny. I was looking at the books for Mother's Day, and I can't believe how many reservations we're taking. And they're all **huge**, like 10 or more guests. How are we going to **fit them all in**?	不好笑。我剛剛在看母親節的訂位，實在不敢相信我們接了那麼多的訂位，而且每桌人數都超多，10 個人以上都不只，甚至更多。我們要如何容納這麼多的客人？
Andy	What we do is take out all the regular tables and bring in some large ones. You should see how **crowded** it gets in here then. It's absolutely **nuts**!	我們會將一般餐桌挪走，換成大張的餐桌。屆時你就會看到這裡的擁擠盛況，簡直是像瘋了一樣！
Georgia	Is Mother's Day really **that big a deal**? I didn't **realize** we'd be quite so busy.	母親節真的有那麼嚴重嗎？我從沒想過我們在這天會這麼忙碌。
Andy	Think about it: Would you want your mom to cook on her special day? Didn't think so. And most other people think the same way. That makes us really busy, and means we have to be super-organized **beforehand**. You'll see at the meeting later this week.	你想想，你會想讓你媽媽在屬於她的特別日子下廚嗎？我可不這麼認為。多數人也跟我們有一樣的想法。所以我們才會這麼忙碌，也因此我們必須在事前做好超有條理的規劃，過幾天開會時你就會明白了。

(at the meeting)

（會議中）

June Hi, everybody. As you all know, Mother's Day is one of our busiest days. So, we have to be prepared. The first thing is to realize that we're going to do two and a half to three times as much business as on a normal Sunday.

大家好。我想大家都知道，母親節是我們一年中幾個最忙日子之一，所以我們要做好萬全的準備。首先，大家要瞭解的是那天我們將會有比一般星期日多出 2.5 至 3 倍的顧客量。

Georgia Won't that really back up the kitchen? I can't imagine doing that many more people.

這樣廚房不會忙不過來嗎？我實在無法想像要接待多那麼多的顧客。

June We'll be doing buffet-only service that day. It's the only way we can make enough food to serve everybody. And, just in case you were wondering, nobody gets the day off, so take your mom out on Monday.

那天我們只會有自助式的用餐方式，唯有如此才可以確保每個客人都有足夠的食物。還有，如大家猜測的，當天沒有人可以休假，所以請星期一再帶媽媽過母親節吧。

Word Bank

wonder(ing) *v.* 疑惑；納悶　huge *adj.* 巨大的　fit them all in 完全容納
crowded *adj.* 擁擠的　nuts *adj.* 發瘋的　that big a deal 那麼重大的事
realize *v.* 明瞭　beforehand *adv.* 事先；事前；早一步

Unit 04 假日訂位

特殊節慶的行銷——神奇求婚桌

「我要跟女朋友求婚，情人節哪天想訂神奇求婚桌用餐」。這是去年在一家餐廳用餐時遇到的故事，一個先生急忙進入餐廳告訴服務人員，無論如何情人節那天，那張求婚桌一定要讓給他，這關係他一生的幸福。從旁聽起來，當天若那張桌子沒給他，似乎他的人生就黑暗了，事情也就糟糕了。

你相信在那張神奇的桌子用餐求婚，就一定會成功嗎？換一張就不行嗎？相信懂得科學驗證的人都清楚，這只是個商業噱頭。

一個好的噱頭可創造好的業績。韓國從 2002 年開始錄製一系列的韓流偶像劇，結合戲劇、美食與旅遊，打造一系列偶像劇拍攝景點話題，以增加觀光營收。台灣旅行社嗅到這股風潮，特地規劃偶像劇拍攝景點之旅，使得業績大增，造就了韓國觀光風氣。

泰國潑水節可說是泰國境內一年一度的大事，許多觀光客會在此時前往泰國旅遊，但這些觀光客潑完水祈福後，便無其它吸引他再來泰國的理由。聰明的商人了解到這一點，於是他們將部分傳統食物挪到潑水節期間才提供，讓這個傳統食物變成季節限定版，加強觀光客特地於潑水節前往泰國的意願。

再回到神奇求婚桌，我們可以理解餐廳求婚桌、偶像劇景點、泰國潑水節傳統食物，其實都是包裝出來的商品。若沒包裝，它們充其量只是一個平凡的桌子、景點以及食物，然而我們要相信創造一個神奇求婚桌或特別景點其實不難，同樣一句老話，用對方法就可以。以下我歸納出一套簡單且容易執行的流程。

首要找出有趣的點子

一個有趣的點子可以引起人的好奇心，運用人的好奇心，將可以開發無窮的想像力，讓需要、喜愛想像的人，開始追著點子繞，並且認真的相信它是真實的。就像求婚桌，說明白它就是一張用餐用的餐桌，但套上一個點子，它瞬間變得神奇。

讓點子引起話題

套上點子後，你還需要讓它登上大螢幕，讓它成為大家會口耳相傳的話題。當然這個話題必須是正面的、吸引人的。當大家開始爭相想體驗這個點子時，表示這個點子出名了，例如：亞都麗緻巴黎廳那張 32 年歷史的求婚桌，用歷史創造話題（它就是那個先生一定要訂到的桌子）。

保持點子的特殊性

從小我們都聽過國旗歌，其歌詞中寫到創業維艱、守成不易，創造點子猶如歌詞中寫的創業維艱，保持點子的特殊性與新鮮感就如歌詞中寫的守成不易，創造好的點子確實非簡單的事。而保持其特殊性更是不容易，畢竟人心是喜新厭舊的。如何在不同時間抓住客戶的那顆心，這便是訣竅。

將點子升級

加強客戶印象，除了維持點子特殊性外，還有一個重點：時間到了就該讓它升級。有時將原來的點子加入已觀察出來的客戶需求，可以讓這個點子更加迎合客戶，也讓點子的影響效果更加倍。

上述幾種方式提供大家運用，它除了可用於節慶行銷活動外，對於餐廳品牌的設定與建立亦可同理使用之，各位千萬要好好的掌握上述的重點。

Unit 05 私人宴會

 Birthday Party 生日派對  Track 17

Introduction

A husband wants to give a big party for his wife's birthday. 一位先生想為太太的生日舉辦一場盛大派對。

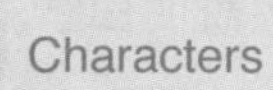 

Characters

Andrew - Guest	顧客
Simone - Host	領檯
June - Assistant Manager	副理

Conversation

Andrew	My wife is going to be **turning 50** next month, and I'd like to do something special for her. I was thinking of having a big party, and inviting all her **co-workers** and friends, and also a lot of **relatives**. Is that possible?	我太太下個月將滿 50 歲，我想做件特別的事來幫她慶生。我想辦一個盛大的派對，邀請她所有的好友、同事與親人來參加。這樣可行嗎？
Simone	We do that quite often. You can **rent** the entire restaurant for an evening, and our **management** will help you plan it. Let me get your phone number, and I'll have one of our managers call you.	這方面我們還蠻有經驗的。您可以包下餐廳一整個晚上，我們的管理階層會協助您做規劃。讓我留下您的聯絡電話，我會請我們一位經理與您聯繫。
	(on the phone)	（電話中）
June	Hello, this is June from Best Steakhouse. I understand you'd like to rent our dining room for a party?	您好，我是 Best Steakhouse 的 June。就我瞭解，您想要包下我們的餐區辦派對是嗎？
Andrew	Yes, I want to make my wife's 50th birthday special. I thought a big party would be nice.	是的，我想讓我太太的 50 歲生日很特別。我想舉辦一場盛大派對應該是個好主意。
June	I **assume** you'd like to do this in the evening. Are you interested in having a sit-down dinner or just a buffet?	我想您應該希望在傍晚舉行。您會比較喜歡由服務生上菜，還是自助式用餐呢？

Andrew	We'd like to **go all the way**: cocktails first, then dinner, dessert, and **socializing** time with drinks after dinner.	我們想要隆重點：先來些雞尾酒，然後用餐、甜點，最後還要有些飲料類讓大家閒聊一下。
June	I'll send you our menu that we use for special occasions. What would you like to do about party decorations?	我會寄給您特別包場所使用的菜單。那您對宴會佈置有什麼想法呢？
Andrew	I thought we could do balloons, candles, and have flowers on each table, with a couple big **bouquets** around the room. And I'd like to have a big display showing pictures of my wife through her life.	我想可以有些汽球、蠟燭，每張餐桌上都有些鮮花，房間四周也要有些大型花束。我還想要一個大展示區，好陳列我太太從小到大的照片。
June	That sounds wonderful. I'm sure she'll be happy that you did all that work for her. I can give you the name of a florist we use. It will save you some money, since we get a **volume discount**. Call me when you're ready to discuss your other options, and thank you.	聽起來真棒。我想她一定會很開心您為她做了這麼多。我可以提供您我們配合的花店，利用我們大量採購的折扣，應該可以讓您節省一些預算。如果您準備好討論其他項目，請再撥電話跟我聯繫，謝謝您。

Word Bank

turn(ing) 50 滿 50 歲　co-worker(s) *n.[C]* 同事　relative(s) *n.[C]* 親戚；家屬
rent *v.* 租借　management *n.[C]* 管理階層　assume *v.* 推測；假設
go all the way 完整的；全套式　socializing *v.* 交際；參與社交（socialize）
bouquet(s) *n.[C]* 花束　volume discount 大量購買折扣；量販折扣；批發折扣

Unit 05 私人宴會

2 Wedding Reception 婚宴 Track 18

Introduction

The father and mother of the bride are going over the details of a wedding reception. 新娘的父母親正在討論婚宴接待的細節。

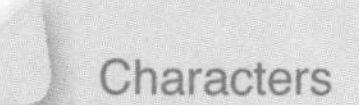

Characters

Sam - Guest	顧客
Diane - Guest	顧客
Brianna - Manager	經理

Conversation

Diane	Yes, we'd like to have a full sit-down dinner. Our guests will be hungry at that time of day.	是的，我們想要整套的上菜式晚宴。到那個時候，賓客們應該都飢腸轆轆了。
Brianna	Have you looked over the menu yet?	您們看過菜單了嗎？
Sam	Yes, I think we'd like prime rib, with a choice of the salmon pasta for those who don't want beef. And we'll have just one or two vegetarians.	看過了，我想我們要牛肋排，然後為不想吃牛肉的賓客準備些鮭魚義大利麵。應該也會有一兩位的素食賓客。
Brianna	What about after dinner? Will you want us to make the cake, or do you have that arranged already?	那麼晚餐過後呢？會需要我們幫忙準備蛋糕嗎？還是您已經安排好了呢？
Diane	We have a family friend who is going to do that. We're using the same small **bride** and **groom** on the top as my husband and I had on our cake.	我們有位朋友會處理這一部分。我們會用當年我跟我先生婚禮蛋糕上的新郎新娘小人偶來裝飾我女兒的蛋糕。
Brianna	That's sweet. What kind of **refreshments** would you like to have, in addition to the cake? Would you like to serve drinks?	好甜蜜呀！除了蛋糕以外，您們還想要什麼樣的小點心？需要一些飲品來做搭配嗎？

Sam	Since champagne is **traditional**, we thought we might as well go along with tradition. Most people like champagne, anyway.	既然香檳是傳統必備的，我想我們就跟著傳統走吧。反正大多數的人也都喜歡香檳。
Brianna	One thing we can do is a champagne **fountain**. Those are always popular.	我們可以弄個香檳噴泉塔，這一直是個很受歡迎的項目。
Diane	What's that? Is it like a regular water fountain, but with champagne? Wouldn't that make the champagne go **flat**?	那是什麼？你是說像一般噴泉一樣，只是噴出的不是水，而是香檳？這樣香檳不會沒氣嗎？
Brianna	It's actually more of a **pyramid**. We **stack** the glasses up high, with one at the top, just like a pyramid. Then, when we start pouring the wine into the top one, it **overflows** and fills the ones **underneath** it. Then the bride and groom can share the top glass, and everyone else gets a glass, too.	那其實比較像是金字塔。我們把酒杯疊起來，疊成最高處只有一個酒杯，像座金字塔。然後，當我們把香檳從最頂端倒進去，香檳會溢出來流入下一層，直到每個杯子都有香檳。新郎新娘可以分享最上面的那杯香檳，其他賓客也可以各自拿到一杯。
Diane	That sounds really neat. This is going to be such a good day!	這聽來真棒。我想那天會很圓滿！

Word Bank

wedding reception 婚宴；喜酒　bride *n.[C]* 新娘　groom *n.[C]* 新郎
refreshment(s) *n.[C]* 開味小點　traditional *adj.* 傳統的
fountain *n.[C]* 噴泉；噴水池　flat *adj.* 走味的；沒氣泡的
pyramid *n.[C]* 金字塔　stack *v.* 堆疊　overflow(s) *v.* 滿溢；洋溢
underneath *prep.* 在底下；在下面

Unit 05 私人宴會

3 *Personal Party* 個人派對 Track 19

Introduction

A group of friends want to rent the restaurant for a party. 一群好友想包下餐廳舉辦派對。

Characters 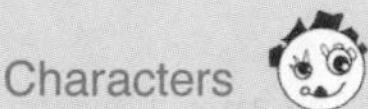

Martin - Guest	顧客
Dave - Guest	顧客
June - Assistant Manager	副理

Conversation

Martin	Hello? Oh, hi, Dave, how's it going? I haven't heard from you for a long time.	喂？噢，Dave，近來可好啊？好久沒有聽到你的消息了。
Dave	That's kind of what I called about. There are a lot of people I haven't heard from for a long time. I want to get us all together some night, so we can **catch up**.	所以我才打電話來呀。我跟好多人很久沒聯繫了。我想找個晚上大家聚一聚，好聊聊近況。
Martin	Where do you think we should go? A **club**?	你覺得我們應該去哪？夜店嗎？
Dave	I thought about that, but it would be too noisy to talk, and there would be too many people there we didn't know. I've been talking to Best Steakhouse. They will rent out the whole restaurant for us.	我想過，但是那裡太吵，根本沒有辦法好好說話，而且那邊會有太多我們根本不認識的人。我跟 Best Steakhouse 談過了，他們可以將整個餐廳包場給我們。
Martin	I think that's a great idea. Do you think we can get everyone to agree on it?	我覺得好極了！你覺得大家會贊同嗎？
Dave	I've already talked to a lot of people, and most of them want to come. Do you want to go with me when I go to Best and help me decide on **stuff**?	我已經跟很多人提過了，多數人都想參加。你想跟我一起去 Best 餐廳嗎？順便幫我做些決定。
	(at the restaurant)	（在餐廳內）

June	What I would **suggest** for food for your party is a buffet. Since you don't know when everyone is going to show up, they can eat whenever they get there.	因為你們不知道大家幾點鐘會到，所以我建議用自助餐的方式。這樣不論任何時間來，都可以立即用餐。
Dave	Of course, we want to have a bar, but can we do it **pay-as-you-go**?	當然好。我們還需要一個酒吧，但可以讓大家各付各的嗎？
June	Sure, that's called a **no-host bar**. That way, everyone pays for their own drinks, and they can drink as much or as little as they're **comfortable with**.	當然，這稱為自費酒吧。喝多少付多少，如此一來，每個人可以依照自己的狀況來決定要暢飲多少量。
Martin	How about dancing? I have a friend who's a **DJ**. Can we bring him in?	安排舞池如何？我有一個 DJ 朋友，可以讓他來嗎？
June	You're paying for the restaurant; you can do what you want. There's plenty of room for us to move tables out of the way for a **dance floor**.	你們付錢包下了整個餐廳，可以做任何你們想做的事。只要把桌子移開，就可以騰出個大空間來充當舞池。
Dave	That sounds great. It's going to be good to see our old friends again.	聽起來太棒了。跟老朋友重逢一定會很有趣。

Part I
Part II
Part III
Part IV
Part V
Part VI

Word Bank

catch up 趕上；追上　club *n.[C]* 夜店；俱樂部　stuff *n.[C]* 東西；物品
suggest *v.* 建議　pay-as-you-go 消費多少付多少
no-host bar 自費性的酒吧　comfortable with 可接受的；可容忍的
DJ *abbr.* DiscJockey；播放安排音樂的人　dance floor 舞池

Unit 05 私人宴會

Political Fundraiser 政治募款餐會

Track 20

Introduction

A political candidate wants to use the restaurant to raise money for her campaign. 一位政壇候選人想要在餐廳辦餐會，為選戰募款。

Characters

Susan - Campaign Manager 競選總幹事

June - Assistant Manager 副理

Conversation

June	I assume you're going to need a **podium** and a **stage**, for making speeches. How many people do you expect to show up?	為了發表演說，我想您應該會需要一個講台跟一個平台。您預期有多少人會來呢？
Susan	We're planning on 75, in addition to the campaign staff. We'll need about ten seats at the head table, and six chairs on the stage for the after-dinner speeches.	除了競選工作人員，我們以 75 人來規劃。主桌大概需要 10 個座位，然後餐後演說需要 6 張椅子在平台上。
June	Would you like the rest of the tables arranged in groups of four, six, or eight?	至於其它的桌子，您會希望安排成四人、六人還是八人一桌呢？
Susan	I think groups of eight would work. Will they fit in your dining room?	我想八人一桌應該是可行的。你們的用餐區容納得下嗎？
June	Yes, we can fit up to 12 at one table, but it's kind of hard to carry on a conversation with that many people. I'd recommend a **maximum** of eight.	可以的，我們一桌最多可以容納十二個人，但是那麼多人其實不易進行交談，所以我們建議最多八個人一桌。
Susan	That's what we'll do, then. We want to have drinks available before dinner, and then wine on all the tables. Red and white, so two wine glasses **per person**, please.	那我們就這樣做吧。我們希望在用餐前可以提供些飲品，而在餐桌上都需要有紅白酒。所以麻煩幫每個人準備兩只酒杯。

June	Do you have a **microphone** system that you can use, or would you like to use ours?	您們自己有的麥克風設備可用嗎？還是需要我們提供呢？
Susan	We do these things all the time, so we have our own sound system. We just need to make sure there are enough **electrical wires** up on the stage.	這方面我們已經很有經驗了，我們有自己的音效系統。我們只需要確定台上有足夠的電源線供我們使用即可。
June	We've already gone over the menu, so is there anything else you need to know?	我們已經討論過菜單了，其他還有什麼您想要知道的嗎？
Susan	I still need to decide on the wine, but other than that, I think we're ready to go. Thank you for your **cooperation**, and I hope we have a lot of people turn up, so we can get our **message** out.	我還需要再決定一下酒單，除此之外，我想應該定案了。謝謝你的配合，我希望當天會有很多人出席，這樣才能有效地宣達我們的政見。

Word Bank

political candidate 政壇選舉候選人　campaign *n.[C]* 競選；系列活動；戰役
podium *n.[C]* 演講台　stage *n.[C]* 舞台；講台　maximum *n.[C]* 最大限度
per person 每人　microphone *n.[C]* 麥克風　electrical wire(s) 電源線；電線
cooperation *n.[U]* 合作；協力　message *n.[C]* 訊息；消息；理念

私人宴會

難忘的慶生會——包場服務

小 Amber 即將滿 5 歲，Amber 爸媽想給她一場難忘的生日派對，苦思了幾天，他們決定包下一家餐廳邀請親朋好友一起來為小 Amber 慶生，上網查詢各家餐廳包場服務的價格，發現服務的模式真是多樣化，讓他們難以選擇。

包場是一個近幾年流行於餐廳的服務模式，包場的初期需求主要是因應宴會而生，目前市場的包場服務，除宴會需求外，另外還有慶生會、單身派對、同學會、研討會、行銷使用的商品說明會等，當然也有些比較特殊的包場原因，例如：親子研習營、婚紗拍照、電視錄影或是畢業典禮等。

包場的計費模式

一次性場地費用：

報價以單一場地費用提報，不限入場人數，且不需控管入場狀況，通常這類的計價模式多為開放性研討會或是商品說明會等為主，且通常不提供餐點服務，若有需要則需另外計價。

依參加人數收費：

此種計價模式為依人頭收費，針對每個人進場做一個單一定價，不限入場人數，但需控管入場狀況，通常此類的計價多為慶生會、同學會等，餐廳除提供場地外，亦會提供少量的餐點。

計算場地費與參加人數：

高級飯店多設定此報價模式，針對場地部份與參加人數分別計價，而餐點的準備則依據參加人數來提供，通常此類的計價多為封閉性研討會或是同學會等。

僅收餐點費用：

這類的計費模式可說是最優惠客戶，當然通常會有這樣的計費模式多為小餐廳或是規模不大的咖啡廳，依據客戶點的餐點價格來計費，在場地利用上較自由，也較多樣化。

包套：

這類計費模式通常是包含場地與佈置、餐點、商務需求（器材租借）等，當然也包含客戶的特別需求，價格組合上也較多樣化，且多為簽約模式。

後續小 Amber 的爸媽選擇了一間家庭式且非常溫馨的咖啡廳，當做這次慶生會的場地，計價模式老闆娘非常大方，說明僅以參加人數來計費即可，餐點部份則依照人數來提供，好不容易訂好了餐廳，小 Amber 的爸媽開始苦惱，那會場的佈置該怎麼進行？親友該怎麼通知？咖啡廳又可以提供什麼？是否需要另外計價呢？

一場正式的包場服務，基本包含餐點、會場佈置、器材提供（投影機、麥克風），當然也有單純提供場地的服務模式，而在餐廳的包場作業流程則有以下幾個步驟。

- 依照客戶需求確定當日訂位狀況
- 洽談需求細節，並簽訂合約（部分餐廳以口頭約定即可），溝通付款方式，付款方式依照餐廳規定，並無特別的標準
- 約訂日前 1 周（部分餐廳為前 3 日）確認菜單與參加人數
- 通知廚房備餐與外場準備當日服務人力
- 約訂日前一天確認當天會場佈置與器材租借狀況
- 約訂日當天，宴會完成後結帳作業

老闆娘了解了小 Amber 爸媽的苦惱，非常大方的協助佈置事宜，慶生會當天咖啡廳掛滿了小 Amber 喜愛的粉紅色氣球，在小 Amber 的坐位後方綁上一隻可愛的 Hello Kitty 大氣球。氣球上並寫著應景的 Amber 生日快樂。就這樣在咖啡廳歡愉、溫馨的氛圍下，大家大聲齊唱生日快樂，慶祝小 Amber 5 歲的生日，讓小 Amber 留下難忘的回憶。

Part 2
Upscale American Restaurant
高檔美式餐廳

Unit 06 服務生準備

1 *Table Setting* 餐桌桌面擺設

Track 21

Introduction

A new waiter is learning how to properly set a table. 一位新手服務生正在學習正確擺設餐桌。

Characters

Eddie - Waiter 服務生
Malcolm - Waiter Trainee 實習生

Conversation

Malcolm	Tell me again why we're **polishing** all these glasses? We didn't do this at my last job.	再跟我說一次為什麼我們要幫這些玻璃杯拋光？我上個工作是不這麼做的。
Eddie	The water here leaves lots of **spots** on the glasses, so we have to polish them so they look nice on the table.	這裡的水很容易在杯子上留下水漬，所以我們要替杯子拋光，杯在桌上才會好看。
Malcolm	And why are there two different wine glasses?	那為什麼又需要兩種不同的酒杯？
Eddie	One is for red wine, the other for white. We put both glasses on every table.	一個是紅酒杯，另一個是白酒杯。我們會在每桌都放上兩種酒杯。
Malcolm	So we're ready, no matter what the guests order. I understand.	這樣不管客人點什麼，我們都有萬全的準備。我明白了。
Eddie	Let's go put these on the table, and we'll see if you remember your table setup.	那把這些杯子都放到桌上吧，讓我看看你還記不記得怎麼擺設餐桌。
Malcolm	The **base plate** goes in the middle, about 1 cm from the edge. Then the forks go to the left, 2 cm off the edge of the table. The **dinner fork** is first, then the **salad fork** to the left, and the **cocktail fork** on the outside.	底盤放在中央，約離桌緣一公分的距離。然後叉子在左邊，離桌緣兩公分的距離。先是主餐叉，然後依序往左是沙拉叉，開胃品小叉則在最外側。

Eddie	And why are they in that order?	那為什麼是這樣的順序呢？
Malcolm	So the guests can pick up each fork as they need it, from left to right.	好讓客人可以依由左而右的順序，搭配用餐需求使用。
Eddie	Where do the glasses go?	那杯子又該怎麼擺放？
Malcolm	The water glass goes about 6 cm above the base plate, even with 2 o'clock. The wine glasses are to the right of the water glass and just a little lower.	水杯在底盤的兩點鐘方向，距底盤約 6 公分。酒杯則在水杯的右邊，略為下方。
Eddie	And the rest of the table?	餐桌的其他擺設呢？
Malcolm	The bread plate goes to the left of the forks, with the **bread knife** across it at eleven and one o'clock. The dessert fork and coffee spoon go above the plate, and the knife and **soup spoon** go to the right of the base plate.	麵包盤在叉子的左邊，奶油刀橫放在上跨居十一點與一點鐘位置。甜點叉和咖啡匙則在盤子上方。刀與湯匙則是在底盤的右手邊。
Eddie	You've got it. For the next lesson, we'll set up our station out here on the floor.	我想你懂了。下一堂課，我們要準備工作站。

Word Bank

set a table 餐桌的配置　polish(ing) *v.* 拋光　spot(s) *n.[C]* 汙點；斑點
base plate 底盤（每道菜上桌時會連盤擺放的位置）　dinner fork 主菜叉
salad fork 沙拉叉　cocktail fork 開胃菜叉
bread knife 麵包刀；本文指奶油刀　soup spoon 喝湯用湯匙

Unit 06 服務生準備

2 Station Setup 餐務櫃的準備 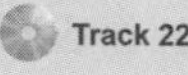

Track 22

Introduction

The new waiter learns how to set up the station out on the floor. 新手服務生學習怎麼準備現場的餐務櫃。

Characters

Eddie - Waiter	服務生
Malcolm - Waiter Trainee	實習生
Maddie - Busser	打雜工

Conversation

Eddie	This is where we come to get anything we need while we're out on the floor. It has to be **stocked** really well before the shift, and restocked as we go.	這裡就是我們拿取在現場會用到的所有東西的地方。必須要在交班前確實存放好，然後在我們離開前還要再補齊一次。
Malcolm	I'm sure it's better to have everything here than to have to run back to the kitchen for an extra fork or water glass.	我相信這比為了一支叉子或一個水杯就得跑回廚房來的好得多。
Eddie	That's right. Now, the glasses we just polished are right here on top. The **silverware** goes in those **bins** right next to the glasses. And the **napkins** are in that drawer down below.	沒錯。我們剛剛拋光過的杯子就在最上面，餐具組就放在杯子旁邊這些餐具收納盒裡。紙巾則是在下方的抽屜裡。
Malcolm	I notice those are already **folded**. I suppose it's asking too much to hope that someone else folds those for us?	我注意到那些餐巾已經摺好了。我猜想期待有人幫我們摺紙巾是不是要求太多啦？
Eddie	Our **bussers** will do some, but we have to help, and that's our responsibility that the drawer is full at the end of the shift. This is Maddie; she'll be our busser tonight. You'll find she's very helpful, especially if you do a good job yourself.	我們的打雜工會摺一些，但是我們也要幫忙，下班前確保抽屜備齊是我們的責任。這位是 Maddie，她是我們今晚的打雜工。你會發現她是個很好的幫手，尤其當你自己也表現稱職。

Maddie	Oh thanks, Eddie. I do my best.	噢，謝謝你，Eddie。我會盡全力的。
Eddie	And your best is always very good. Maddie is in charge of making sure we have water pitchers and ice out here. She'll usually fill the water glasses for the guests, too, but going around with a water pitcher in your hand is a good way for the waiter to check and see if any of his tables need anything.	你只要盡力，表現一向都很好。Maddie 會負責確認水瓶和冰塊都有準備好。一般而言她也會幫顧客們加水。但是身為服務生，當你要察看每張桌子是否有什麼需求的時候，手上拿著水瓶巡視是個好方法。
Malcolm	What else do we need out here?	我們在現場還需要什麼其它的嗎？
Eddie	There's some spray cleaner down below, and the **tablecloths** are under the ice bin. We don't keep a lot of things here; just what's needed for resetting tables. For our next task, see those empty silverware bins? Guess who gets to polish it.	清潔噴霧用品在下方，冰桶下面有桌巾。除了桌面擺設用的東西外，我們並不會放太多東西在這。好了，下一個任務，看到那些空的餐具收納盒嗎？猜猜是誰該把他們擦乾淨吧。

Word Bank

on the floor 地板上；本文指現場　stock(ed) *v.* 物品充足；補料
silverware *n.[U]* 餐具　bin(s) *n.[C]* 盒子；箱子；有蓋容器
napkin(s) *n.[C]* 餐巾　fold(ed) *v.* 摺　busser(s) *n.[C]* 助理服務生；打雜工
pitcher(s) *n.[C]* 水瓶　tablecloth(s) *n.[C]* 桌巾；桌布

Unit 06 服務生準備

3 *Kitchen Setup* 廚房準備  Track 23

Introduction

It's time to set up the kitchen for the next shift.
差不多該為下一個輪班時段先把廚房準備好囉。

Characters  

Eddie - Waiter 服務生
Malcolm - Waiter Trainee 實習生

Conversation

Eddie	This is a setup shift, so we have a little extra work to do. It doesn't take too long, as long as everyone shows up on time. Let's do the bread right now.	因為這是負責開店準備的早班，所以有些額外的工作要做。只要大家都準時出現，並不會花太多時間。現在，我們來處理麵包吧。
Malcolm	Where does the bread come from?	麵包是從哪裡來的呢？
Eddie	We get it from a **local bakery**. What we have to do is put it in these **heated** drawers to warm up. We put a wet towel in a coffee cup in there as well, to keep the bread from **drying out** too much. And we have to make sure the bread **baskets** all have napkins in them.	是從一間當地的烘焙坊。我們只要把它們放進加熱的抽屜保溫就好。然後再把一條濕毛巾放進咖啡杯中一起擺進去，可以避免麵包乾掉。再來就是確保每個麵包籃內都有紙巾。
Malcolm	What else do we have to do?	接下來還要做些什麼？
Eddie	Over here by the **soda machine**, we need to fill the ice bin. Then we need to make sure there's water in the **soup warmer**. The cooks will bring us the soup later on. Another **responsibility** in the soup area is making sure there are enough **crackers** in the cracker baskets.	冰桶在飲料機旁邊，我們要把冰塊加滿。廚師們等會兒會將湯端出來給我們，所以要確保湯鍋保溫器內有水。湯區的另外一項工作就是要確保餅籃裡的餅乾足夠。

Malcolm	Do we have to do anything to set up the bar area?	我們需要為吧檯區做些什麼準備嗎？
Eddie	No, we have our own **bartender** back here in the kitchen. She takes care of all the bar setup.	不大需要，廚房有我們店裡的酒保在，她負責吧檯所有的準備工作。
Malcolm	What else do the setup people have to worry about?	那還有什麼是早班人員需要操心的？
Eddie	The **salad dressings** are full; that's good. And let's see – the salad plates are stocked.	沙拉醬是滿的，不錯；我看看，而且沙拉盤也備齊了。
Malcolm	Who gets more of those if we run out?	那當它沒了的時候，誰要負責填滿？
Eddie	Whoever takes the last one is supposed to go back to the dishroom and get more. It's nice if you get some before the last one's gone, though.	只要是發現剩最後一個盤子的人，就必須去餐具室拿盤子出來補滿。不過最好是在用完最後一個前就補滿。
Malcolm	So, is that it?	所以，就這些嗎？
Eddie	I think so. The doors will be open in a few minutes, and we'll be getting our first table.	我想應該就這些了。再過幾分鐘就要開門了，準備迎接我們第一桌客人吧。

Part I
Part II
Part III
Part IV
Part V
Part VI

Word Bank

local *adj.* 當地的　bakery *n.[C]* 麵包店；烘焙坊　heated *adj.* 加熱的
dry(ing) out 脫水；乾掉　basket(s) *n.[C]* 籃子　soda machine 汽水機
soup warmer 湯鍋保溫器　responsibility *n.[C]* 職責；責任
cracker(s) *n.[C]* 薄脆餅乾；蘇打餅　bartender *n.[C]* 酒保
salad dressing(s) 沙拉醬

Unit 06 服務生準備

4 *Taking Payment* 結帳  Track 24

Introduction

Eddie talks to his trainee about taking payment from the guests. Eddie 教導實習生如何幫客人結帳。

Characters

Eddie - Waiter	服務生
Malcolm - Waiter Trainee	實習生

Conversation

Malcolm	Hey, Eddie, I didn't notice a **cashier**. Where do the guests pay for their meals?	Eddie，我沒看到有收銀員，客人要去哪裡結帳呢？
Eddie	That's one of the more **unpleasant** and **time-consuming** parts of this job. We run our own banks and have to **process** the payment for our guests.	這就是這份工作中令人比較不愉快又耗時的地方了。我們各自保管所收款項並自備零錢，且必須親自為顧客處理結帳事宜。
Malcolm	Why is that bad? Does it really add a lot of work for you?	那有這麼糟嗎？真的會增加很多工作量嗎？
Eddie	There are a couple things bad about it. In the old days, when I worked places that had cashiers, we had a lot more time to take care of our tables. Being a cashier and a waiter takes away from the time we can spend paying attention to the guests.	是有幾個缺點。以前我在有收銀員的地方工作時，服務生有較多的時間可以好好招呼顧客們。但在這裡又要結帳、又要服務，會耗去我們照顧到顧客需求的時間。
Malcolm	You said there were a couple things you didn't like.	你剛說有好幾個你不喜歡的點？
Eddie	The other one is having to run our own banks. If we make a mistake, we pay for it out of **our own pocket**.	另一點就是我們必須負責處理並保管款項。如果我們出了錯，必須要自掏腰包將錢補足。
Malcolm	Really? I had no idea about that.	真的嗎？我完全沒想過耶。

Eddie	I think most people don't know that about waiters. That's why we have to be really careful when we **make change**. That's kind of difficult when you're in a hurry and trying to do a thousand other things at the same time.	我想大多數的人都不知道服務生必須如此。這就是為什麼找錢的時候要非常小心。當你急著又要算錢、又要顧及一堆其它事的時候實在有點難。
Malcolm	What forms of payment do we take?	我們接受哪些付款方式呢？
Eddie	We take the usual **credit cards**: Visa, MasterCard, and American Express. And cash, of course, but most people use cards these days.	我們接受一般信用卡，如 Visa、萬事達、和美國運通卡，當然還有現金，只是現在大部份的人都喜歡刷卡付帳。
Malcolm	What about **checks**?	那支票呢？
Eddie	Is there anywhere that still takes checks? We sure don't. And no traveler's checks, either. I'll show you how to run the credit cards once our first table is ready to pay.	現在還有地方接受支票嗎？我們是確定不收的，旅行支票也不行。當第一桌客人準備結帳時，我會再教你怎麼刷卡結帳。

Word Bank

payment *n.[C]* 付款；款項　cashier *n.[C]* 收銀員；收銀台
unpleasant *adj.* 不愉悅的　time-consuming *adj.* 耗時的
process *v.* 處理　our own pocket 自掏腰包
make change 找零　credit card(s) 信用卡　check(s) *n.[C]* 支票

Unit 06 服務生準備

刀叉由外向內使用——西式擺設

你第一次拿刀叉吃西餐是什麼時候呢？看到滿桌的餐具時，心裡有沒有一堆疑問，該從那個餐具開始使用？湯匙這麼多支，喝湯要用那一支？明明只有一道主菜，為什麼刀子有兩支？這不是你會有的疑問，而是很多人也會有的疑問。

服務於餐廳的各位，相信會遇到的餐具絕對比一般客戶更多樣，每個餐具間的擺設更是困擾著剛踏入餐飲業的新鮮人，因此本章節，我們要來淺談西式餐具的擺設。

餐具擺設原則與重點

展示盤（Show Plate）或口巾需先定位

西式餐點通常會擺放底盤、展示盤或是服務盤（Service Plate），一般會以展示盤做為定位標準，所以展示盤要先擺定。

餐具擺放由內往外、由下而上

客人用餐使用餐具是由外往內取用，服務人員在擺設時，需依照此邏輯進行。

擺放位置有規則

以展示盤為中心，餐刀、湯匙擺放右側，叉類、麵包盤擺放左側，點心叉、匙放置上方，記得刀刃應朝左，匙面和叉齒應向上，點心叉在下、叉齒朝右，點心匙在上、匙面朝左。

餐具以擺放三套為原則

一般用餐空間大約為 55 到 65 公分的距離，通常擺設餐具時，需注意第一道菜和主菜餐具先擺放上桌，後續再追加需使用的餐具，避免因餐具過多影響其隔鄰客戶用餐。

相同餐具、杯子或特殊的餐具不同時擺放桌面

為免客戶混亂，類似的餐具不同時放置，可依餐點順序逐一追加放置。

餐具定位再擺放杯子、調味罐

為使餐具整齊，間距適當，餐具杯子擺設完成後，最後再擺放調味罐或花瓶等擺飾物。

水杯 / 酒杯擺放有規則

水杯需定位於餐刀正上方，其餘的杯子則依照客人飲用酒類順序擺放，以右下 45 度角的方向擺放，擺放杯子依舊以不超過三個為原則，若有需要可再追加。

「練習時間」講解完擺放的原則與重點後，讓我們實際來擺放一次吧！

西餐餐具擺設步驟

1. 檢視桌面鋪設檯布
2. 展示盤定位
3. 擺設刀、叉、匙，遵守由內往外、由下而上的原則進行
4. 刀、匙擺放在展示盤的右側，叉類擺放在展示盤的左側，刀刃向左，匙面和叉齒向上。
5. 擺設麵包盤與奶油刀
6. 擺設點心餐具（叉或匙）
7. 水杯定位餐刀正上方，注意杯腳與餐刀垂直對齊
8. 酒杯擺設以水杯為主，右下 45 度角依序擺放紅酒杯、白酒杯
9. 擺設口巾
10. 擺設調味品或花瓶
11. 擺設咖啡杯組
12. 其他相關物品放置

Unit 07 用餐服務

 Service Briefing and Specials 服務簡報與主廚精選  Track 25

Introduction

The staff goes to the pre-meal meeting. 員工們進行餐前會議。

Characters

Eddie - Waiter	服務生
Malcolm - Waiter Trainee	實習生
Larry - Waiter	服務生
Elizabeth - Assistant Dining Room Manager	餐區副理
Julia - Chef	行政主廚

Conversation

Eddie	We'll finish setting up in a few minutes. Right now, it's time for service briefing.	餐廳擺設再過幾分鐘就完成了，現在我們要做服務簡報。
Malcolm	What does that mean?	那是什麼意思？
Eddie	Service briefing is a **meeting** we have before every shift. They let us know the **specials**, and anything important that may be different from normal.	服務簡報是我們在每次交班前要開的一個會議。會議中會告訴我們今日的主廚精選特餐，還有要格外注意的特殊狀況。
	(at the meeting)	（會議中）
Elizabeth	Good afternoon, everyone. This will be nice and short. We're going to be pretty busy. The books are full until 9:00, and pretty full after that.	各位，午安。我會讓報告簡潔扼要些。今天我們會非常忙碌。直到 9:00 的訂位都已全滿，在那之後也是相當滿的。
Julia	Today we have **trout** almondine. That's covered with toasted **almonds**, then sautéed in butter and white wine.	今天我們有杏香鱒魚，撒上烤過的杏仁片，再用奶油和白酒來嫩煎。
Larry	Is that **farm-raised** trout?	鱒魚是養殖的嗎？

Julia	No, it comes from Alaska. It's wild trout, and it's **fresh**, of course.	不是，鱒魚來自阿拉斯加，是野生的，而且絕對新鮮。
Larry	What's on the side?	配菜有什麼？
Julia	The vegetable of the day is asparagus steamed in red wine, with a side of sage butter. The trout comes with baby red **potatoes**.	今日時蔬是紅酒蒸蘆筍佐上鼠尾草牛油醬。鱒魚會配上紅皮小洋芋。
Malcolm	Are there any more specials, or just the one?	還有其他主廚精選嗎？還是只有一道？
Julia	You're new, aren't you? My name's Julia, by the way.	你是新來的，對吧？對了，我叫Julia。
Malcolm	I'm Malcolm, and yes, I'm new. I'm trying to learn everything as fast as I can.	我是Malcolm。是的，我是新進人員。我想盡快把所有東西都學會。
Julia	That's OK, Malcolm. We'll help you out. We have two specials every day, and once in a while we have three. The second one today is fettuccine Bolognese, which has **veal** and **bacon** in a tomato sauce. It's topped with fresh parmesan cheese and a sprig of parsley. It's served with garlic bread from the bakery.	很好，Malcolm，我們會幫你的。我們每天都會推出兩道主廚精選，有時候會出三道。今天的第二道是波隆那肉醬寬扁麵，番茄紅醬裡有小牛肉和培根。上面會撒上新鮮的帕瑪森起司，再放上一小枝荷蘭芹。另外會附上一塊烘焙坊做的大蒜麵包。
Elizabeth	If that's all the specials, let's get going. Make sure your stand is well-stocked, and be ready for a couple of tables right when we open.	如果主廚精選都介紹過了，那就上工了。確定你們備餐檯的東西都備好了，而且一開始營業就要準備好迎接好幾桌客人。

Word Bank

meeting *n.[C]* 會議　special(s) *n.[C]* 主廚特餐；特色菜
trout *n.[C]* 鱒魚 almond(s) *n.[C]* 杏仁　farm-raised *adj.* 養殖的
fresh *adj.* 新鮮　potato(es) *n.[C]* 馬鈴薯；洋芋
veal *n.[U]* 小牛肉　bacon *n.[U]* 培根

Unit 07 用餐服務

2 *Appetizers and Entrées* 開胃菜和主菜

Track 26

Introduction

A waiter is telling a guest about options on the menu. 服務生向客人介紹菜單上的菜色選擇。

Characters

Larry - Waiter 服務生

Susan - Guest 顧客

Conversation

Susan	I'm interested in getting an appetizer, but I'm not sure which one. What would you recommend?	我想點一道開胃菜，但是不知道哪一道比較好。你推薦哪一道？
Larry	My favorite is the French onion soup. It's made from beef **stock**, with melted Swiss cheese over a large **crouton** on top. It's really tasty.	我最推薦我們的法式洋蔥湯，它是用牛高湯熬製，上頭放了裹著融化的瑞士起司的大塊麵包丁，真的很美味。
Susan	What else would you suggest? I don't really want soup.	你還推薦哪道？我不是很想喝湯。
Larry	Shrimp cocktail is always popular, or if you want your shrimp fried, there's the **beer batter** shrimp. I think both of those are really delicious.	雞尾酒蝦一直很受歡迎，或者如果你想要吃炸蝦，我們有酥炸啤酒蝦。我覺得這兩道都非常好吃。
Susan	I haven't had a shrimp cocktail for a long time. Let me have one of those. What entrée would you recommend?	我好久沒吃雞尾酒蝦了，就給我來一個雞尾酒蝦吧。主菜的話你推薦哪道？

Larry	It kind of depends on what you're looking for, but I like the **salmon** fettuccine. It's made with **marinated** and **smoked** salmon, in a dill cream sauce. You really taste the smoky flavor.	這就要看您想吃什麼了，我個人喜歡這道鮭魚寬麵，是用醃過的燻鮭魚佐上蒔蘿奶油醬汁製成，吃得到煙燻的風味。
Susan	No cream sauce for me. I'm trying to lose a little weight.	我不吃奶油醬，我正試著減肥呢。
Larry	Then you may like the **poached** salmon. It's poached in a white wine bath, and served with a side of low-fat lemon peppercorn sauce.	那您應該會喜歡煎煮鮭魚。鮭魚浸在白酒裡頭煎煮，佐上低脂的檸檬胡椒醬汁。
Susan	Maybe I'd like meat instead. What's your best steak?	也許我可以點個肉。你們最好吃的牛排是哪一道？
Larry	The filet, definitely. It's wrapped with bacon and then char-broiled, and topped with béarnaise sauce. It's a classic.	絕對是腓力。這道腓力外面包著培根碳烤後，上頭佐以法式貝亞恩醬。是一道經典名菜。
Susan	That sounds really good. I'll have that, please.	聽起來真不錯。我就點這道，謝謝。
Larry	And how would you like that done?	請問您的牛排要幾分熟？
Susan	**Medium rare**, thank you.	三分熟，謝謝。
Larry	All right then, I'll be back with your drinks to start with in just a couple minutes.	好的。我待會先幫您送飲料過來。

Part I Part II Part III Part IV Part V Part VI

Word Bank

entrées *n.[C]* 主菜　stock *n.[C]* 高湯　crouton *n.[C]* 烤或炸過的麵包丁　beer batter 啤酒麵糊　salmon *n.[C/U]* 鮭魚　marinated *adj.* 醃製的　smoked *adj.* 煙燻的　poached *adj.* 煎煮的　medium rare 三分熟

Unit 07 用餐服務

3 *Drinks* 飲料 Track 27

Introduction

Guests are ordering drinks before dinner. 顧客正在點餐前飲料。

Characters

Joseph - Guest	顧客
Eddie - Waiter	服務生
Judy - Guest	顧客

Conversation

Eddie	Good evening, can I get anything for you to drink while you're looking at the menu?	晚安。您在看菜單的同時，要不要來點什麼飲料呢？
Joseph	Yes, I think we'll have cocktails before dinner, and then I'd like some time to look over the wine list.	好，我們要餐前雞尾酒，然後我想花點時間看一下酒單。
Eddie	Certainly, what can I get for you to start?	沒問題，您想從什麼酒開始呢？
Joseph	I'll have Bushmills Irish **Whiskey on the rocks**, and my wife would like a Tom Collins. What do you have for the kids?	我要布什米爾斯愛爾蘭威士忌加冰塊，我太太要一杯杜松子果汁酒。你們有什麼可以給孩子喝的？
Eddie	You can get the usual Roy Rogers or Shirley Temple, but we have a couple other things that are interesting. One is an Arnold Palmer, which is half iced tea and half **lemonade**, and we also have a really good **raspberry** lemonade.	你們可以點羅伊羅傑斯（可樂加黑櫻桃汁和石榴汁等）或是莎利譚寶（薑汁汽水加黑櫻桃汁和石榴汁等）無酒精雞尾酒，不過，我們另外還有一些孩子會喜歡的飲品，一個叫阿諾德帕爾默，是一種半冰茶半檸檬汁的飲料，我們還有很好喝的覆盆子檸檬汁。
Joseph	I think we'll take one of each of the last two.	我想我們點後面那兩樣各一杯。
Eddie	Ok, thanks. I'll be back with those in a couple minutes and give you some time to look at the menu.	好的，謝謝。我待會兒會再回來上飲料，先讓你們看一下菜單。

	(at another table)	（在另一桌）
Eddie	Good evening, would you like something to drink while you're **deciding**?	晚安。在你們決定菜色時要喝點什麼嗎？
Judy	I think we just want a couple glasses of wine for right now. What would you recommend?	我想先給我們幾杯紅酒就好。你推薦什麼？
Eddie	We have a really good Chardonnay by the glass, but if you want something **drier**, our Sauvignon Blanc is quite tasty. Or were you thinking about reds?	我們單杯的夏多內葡萄酒很好喝，如果你們想喝比較不甜的，我們的白蘇維濃也很可口。或是說，你們想喝紅酒？
Judy	What reds do you have **by the glass**?	你們有哪些單杯的紅酒？
Eddie	We have cabernet, and also a **lighter** Pinot Noir. Or if you prefer French wine, we have a big, **bold** Bordeaux. But you might not want that before dinner. It goes better with **red meat**.	我們有卡本內紅酒，還有淡一點的黑比諾。如果您比較喜歡法國酒，我們有強勁濃烈的波爾多紅酒。但是可能不適合餐前喝，它搭紅肉一起用比較理想。
Judy	A glass of Sauvignon Blanc and one of Pinot Noir, please. We'll decide what we want with dinner a little later.	請給我們一杯白蘇維濃和一杯黑比諾，謝謝。我們等一下再決定要點什麼配晚餐。
Eddie	I'll just leave the wine list with you, then, and I'll be right back.	那麼，酒單先留給你們，我馬上回來。

Word Bank

whiskey *n.[U/C]* 威士忌　on the rocks 加冰塊的　lemonade *n.[U/C]* 檸檬水
raspberry *n.[C]* 覆盆莓　deciding *v.* 決定（decide）　drier *adj.* 比較不甜的
by the glass 單杯　lighter *adj.* 淡一點的　bold *adj.* 濃烈的
red meat 紅肉

Unit 07 用餐服務

 *Desserts and After-Dinner Drinks* 甜點及餐後飲料  Track 28

Introduction

The waiter is taking orders for dessert. 顧客向服務生點甜點。

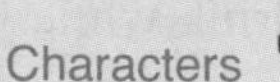

Joseph - Guest 顧客
Eddie - Waiter 服務生

Conversation

Joseph	We're interested in getting dessert. What do you have?	我們想吃甜點。你們有什麼樣的點心？
Eddie	Give me a minute or two to **get caught up** and I'll bring over the **dessert tray** and let you take a look.	請等我幾分鐘，讓我好好處理一下。我會拿甜品拼盤過來給你們參考。
	(Eddie returns)	（Eddie 回到餐桌邊）
Eddie	Hi, I'm back. This one here is my favorite: the brownie sundae. It's a homemade fudge brownie, topped with vanilla ice cream and **hot fudge**. It's so delicious.	您好，我拿甜品盤來了。這一樣是我最喜歡的：巧克力布朗尼聖代。這是手工熔岩布朗尼，上頭搭配香草冰淇淋和熱巧克力醬，非常好吃。
Joseph	I'm not really **in the mood** for chocolate. What's this over here?	我不是很想吃巧克力。那邊那個是什麼？
Eddie	That is our fresh raspberries and cream. It's simple but delicious.	那是覆盆莓佐鮮奶油。很簡單的甜點，不過很美味。
Joseph	What's the other thing with berries on it?	另一個上面有莓子的是什麼？
Eddie	That's another one of my favorites. It's strawberry shortcake. It has white angel food cake, with fresh strawberries and fresh **whipped cream**. It's almost as good as my mom used to make.	那也是我的最愛之一，那是草莓酥餅。它裡面有白天使蛋糕、新鮮草莓，以及鮮奶油。這簡直跟我母親以前做的一樣好吃。

Joseph	And that pie I see?	還有，那個是派嗎？
Eddie	Yes, today's pie is blackberry. The pie changes depending on what we have in season locally.	對，今天的派是黑莓口味。派的口味會依照本地季節性食材變化。
Joseph	I think I'll go for the raspberries and cream. And the other three are going to **split** a brownie sundae.	我想我點一個鮮奶油覆盆莓。然後其他三位分食一份巧克力布朗尼聖代。
Eddie	That's fine; it's pretty large. I'll bring three forks and some extra plates. Would you like anything to drink, either coffee or an after-dinner drink?	好的，布朗尼蠻大一份的。我會拿三支叉子和多點盤子過來。你們要喝什麼嗎？咖啡或是餐後飲料？
Joseph	I would like some **Cognac**, and my wife wants some of that **licorice**-flavored stuff. What's that called?	我要一些干邑白蘭地，我太太要那種帶有甘草味的酒。那叫什麼來著？
Eddie	I think you mean Sambuca, served with coffee beans?	我想你說的應該是杉布卡茴香酒，配上咖啡豆那種？
Joseph	Yes, that's it. Bring those in **snifters**, please. And a cappuccino for her and a latte for me.	對，就是那個。請用一口杯裝一點來，謝謝。然後再一杯卡布奇諾給她，一杯拿鐵給我。
Eddie	All right, I'll be back with your desserts in just a few minutes.	好的。我待會就幫你們送甜點來。

Word Bank

get caught up 投入；專注於　dessert tray 點心拼盤　hot fudge 熱巧克力醬
in the mood 想要；有心情　simple *adj.* 簡單　whipped cream 打發的鮮奶油
split *v.* 分享；分擔；切開　Cognac *n.[U/C]* 干邑白蘭地
licorice *n.[U/C]* 甘草　snifter(s) *n.[C]* 小口大肚酒杯；一口杯

Unit 07 用餐服務

迷人的高級美式餐點

大家對於美式餐點應該都是停留在漢堡、薯條、熱狗、貝果以及奶油玉米等，其時在曼哈頓的街上林立了各式價格不斐、佈置典雅高級的高級西餐廳，這類的餐廳提供的餐點，通常是擺盤細緻，且多為一個組合餐點，餐點組合通常會有前菜、主菜、甜點、飲料等，用餐中也會依據食用的主菜來搭配酒，服務生的素質亦是經過專業訓練，有別於一般賣漢堡的平價美式餐廳。

高級美國餐廳早期受到法國烹飪影響，多會於食材中加入香料提味，烹調肉或海鮮時，廚師認為香料可以消除腥味，保留魚肉原始風味，更可提升佐料的美味度。例如在美國餐廳鮭魚料理是非常受歡迎的一道菜，烹調時廚師除了加入鹽、白酒等基本佐料外，亦會加入芳香的迷迭香（Rosemary），此烹飪方式不像中國菜的烹調，喜歡放醬油、薑片或蒜頭等提味，而是以簡單的香料點綴而已。

廚師在料理肉品時，也喜歡將鼠尾草與洋蔥攪拌均勻後用來幫助肉品提味，例如在料理雞鴨時，將這些香料塞進其腹內，藉由香料強烈的味道刺激，讓食物口味變得強烈，引起顧客的品嘗慾望，打造迷人的食材香氣。然而除了上述幾種香料外，另外百里香（Thymus）、月桂（Bay）、薄荷（Mint）、羅勒（Ocimum Basilicum）、薰衣草（Lavandula）、蒔蘿（Anethum Graveolens）、啤酒花（Humulus Lupulus）、芫荽（Coriandrum Sativum）等，都是深受美國家庭主婦及高級餐廳廚師們所愛的香料，使用上也相當的廣泛。

在餐廳也會看到各式辣味調料（Spicy），例如我們熟知的黑胡椒、白胡椒、蒜頭粉、薑粉、辣椒粉、肉桂粉等，而這些香料的使用也延伸到美國的一般家庭裡，許多主婦也會利用辣味香料來料理食物，它可說是西式餐點的真髓。

你一定想問美式餐點一定用香料來提味嗎？那樣不是無法吃到食材的原味？其實並非如此，在美式的高級餐點裡，也講求原味品嚐，尤其是各式單純的牛肉，餐廳所提供的烤牛排，幾乎都是原味烹調，僅利用少部分的紅酒、白蘭地去腥提味，你品嚐到的僅會有牛肉本身的鮮味，也因此在烹調時，肉品的鮮度就是重要的控制指標。

美式高級餐點也延續美國人的飲食習慣，其搭配的配菜或是點心都非常簡單，你能想像一客要價 50 美金的餐點搭配的副食是烤馬鈴薯、奶油玉米、燙花椰菜嗎？其實搭配這樣簡易且味道單純的配菜，主要是為了保留主餐牛肉或海鮮的鮮味，並且美國人相信簡單的飲食有助於健康的維持、營養的均衡，而這樣的搭配方式亦顯示了美國人對馬鈴薯與玉米的熱愛！

Unit 08 服務生訓練

 *Talking to Tables* 點餐接待  Track 29

Introduction

The new waiter is learning what to do at a table.

新手服務生正在學習如何做點餐服務。

Characters 

Eddie - Waiter	服務生
Malcolm - Waiter Trainee	實習生

Conversation

Malcolm	I'd like to find out what you do when you talk to tables. I realize everybody is different, but what are some **general** guidelines I should know about?	我想知道你都怎麼和客人交談？我瞭解每個人都有自己的服務方式，但是哪些原則是我應該要知道的？
Eddie	The **initial greeting** is very important. Once the people are **settled down**, you should go up to them and say hello. That gives them a chance to order drinks if they want them, and it lets them know who their waiter is.	一開始的問候很重要。一旦客人就座之後，你要上前去打招呼。這時候若客人需要，就可以先點飲料，這樣客人也就知道他們的服務生就是你。
Malcolm	How do you **introduce** yourself?	你都怎麼介紹自己？
Eddie	I just walk up and say good morning, or whatever time it is. When I first started waiting, it was normal to tell the table your name, but I **don't bother** with that anymore. It's more important that they remember your face than your name. That's why it's important to greet them as soon as you can.	我會走上前說早安，或是看你那時的時間。當我剛開始當服務生時，先向客人報上自己的名字很正常，但是我現在不這麼做了。讓客人記住你的長相比記住你的名字更重要。所以越早跟他們問候越好。
Malcolm	What do you do after you bring them their drinks? Do you take the order then?	你送上飲料之後會做什麼？那時就讓客人點餐了嗎？

Eddie	It depends. I usually ask them, "Are you ready to order, or would you like a little more time to decide?" If it's **obvious** that they're not ready, I just say, "I'll be back in a few minutes, when you've had some more time to look over the menu." Lots of people want to take their time, especially at dinner, so don't **rush** them if they're not in a hurry.	看情況。我通常會問他們：「準備好要點餐了嗎？或者您還需要一些時間決定嗎？」如果很明顯他們還沒準備好點餐，我就會說：「給你們一點時間看菜單，我待會再回來。」很多客人想慢慢來，尤其是晚餐時間，所以他們若不趕時間就不催他們。
Malcolm	So, you take their order and bring out the courses. What do you do while they're eating the entrées?	所以他們點了餐，然後你上菜。客人在用主菜時你都做些什麼？
Eddie	Check back once, to make sure everything is cooked the way they want it, or they don't need anything else. After that, just be around, in case they need anything, but don't **interrupt** them until they're finished.	再回頭確認一次，看菜餚是不是都依照客人的意思做好，或是看看客人還需要什麼其他的。然後就在一旁待命以免客人有什麼需要，客人用完餐之前不要打擾他們。

Word Bank

general *adj.* 一般的　initial greeting 初次問候　settle(d) down 安頓下來
introduce *v.* 介紹　don't bother 不費心這麼做　obvious *adj.* 明顯的
rush *v.* 催促　interrupt *v.* 打擾

Unit 08 服務生訓練

2 Recommending Dishes 推薦菜色

Track 30

Introduction

A waiter is answering guest questions. 一位服務生正在回答顧客的詢問

Characters

Larry - Waiter	服務生
Kevin - Guest	顧客

Conversation

Larry	Hello again. Have you had enough time to decide on dinner?	您好，我回來了。已經決定好要點什麼了嗎？
Kevin	We have a few questions about the menu. I'm **interested** in having meat, but I don't really want a big steak. What do you think?	我有一些關於菜單的問題。我想吃肉，但是我不是很想點一大塊牛排，你有什麼建議？
Larry	Have you had **lamb** before?	您吃過小羊肉嗎？
Kevin	Yes, but it was a long time ago. What is lamb like?	吃過，但是那是好久以前的事了？你們的小羊肉是怎麼樣的？
Larry	These are lamb **chops**, so they look like steak, but they have their own special flavor, lighter than beef. If you're looking for red meat, but want something different, I think that would be the way to go.	我們的是小羊排，所以看起來像牛排，但它有自己的獨特風味，份量不像牛排那麼重。如果你想吃紅肉，又想嘗點不一樣的，小羊排應該錯不了。
Kevin	All right, I'll try that. I have a question about the salmon pasta, too. What does it mean when it says it's marinated?	好啊，那我試試小羊排。另外，我還想請問一下，你們的鮭魚義大利麵上寫的「醃製」是什麼意思？
Larry	That just means they put it in a mixture of olive oil and white wine and let it sit for a while. Do you like a **cream sauce** on your pasta?	那是指我們把鮭魚放在混了橄欖油和白酒的醃料中，浸泡一陣子。您喜歡義大利麵淋上奶油白醬嗎？

Kevin	No, I really don't want cream. Does that one have a cream sauce?	不了，我完全不想吃奶油。鮭魚義大利麵裡有奶油白醬嗎？
Larry	Yes, it does. If you still want salmon, I'd suggest the **grilled** salmon. It's much **lower in fat** than the pasta, and we can put the dill butter on the side.	對，裡頭有。如果您還是想吃鮭魚，我會建議您點烤鮭魚，它比鮭魚義大利麵低脂，我們可以在一旁佐上蒔蘿牛油醬。
Kevin	We'd also like to get a little wine, but I'm not sure what would go well with our dinner.	我們還要喝一點酒，但是我不確定什麼酒配今天的晚餐比較好。
Larry	Let's see, you're having the lamb, and she's having grilled salmon. I'd recommend either a lighter red or a white. I wouldn't go with a cabernet, or something heavy like that. You don't want the wine to **overpower** your food.	我看一下，您點的是小羊排，她點的是烤鮭魚。我會建議來點不那麼強烈的紅酒或白酒。我不建議卡本內紅酒，或是類似的重口味酒類。您不會想讓您的酒壓過食物的鋒頭。
Kevin	I agree. What do you think would be a good, light red wine?	我同意。那你覺得好喝又清淡的紅酒是哪一種？
Larry	We have a good Pinot Noir. You can get that in either a full or **half bottle**.	我們的黑比諾不錯，點整瓶或半瓶都可以。

Part I
Part II
Part III
Part IV
Part V
Part VI

Word Bank

interested *adj.* 感興趣的 lamb *n.[U/C]* 小羊肉 chop(s) *n.[C]* 肉排；排骨
cream sauce 奶油白醬 grilled *adj.* 燒烤的 lower in fat 低脂
overpower *v.* 壓過 half bottle 半瓶

Unit 08 服務生訓練

3 *Restaurant Promotions* 餐廳促銷

Track 31

Introduction

A waiter explains some of the restaurant's promotions. 服務生介紹餐廳的促銷方案。

Characters

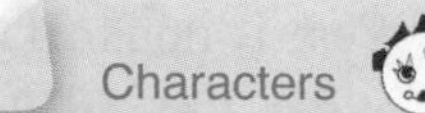

Eddie - Waiter	服務生
Malcolm - Waiter Trainee	實習生
Bob - Guest	顧客
Joan - Guest	顧客
Melinda - Guest	顧客

Conversation

	(in the kitchen)	（廚房內）
Malcolm	Table 52 just told me that they have a birthday. I know we give a free dinner on someone's birthday. How do we do that?	52 桌的客人剛剛告訴我，他們有人生日。我知道客人生日的時候，我們會招待免費的晚餐。通常是怎麼做的？
Eddie	I'll go talk to them. Listen and learn.	我去招呼他們。你邊聽邊學。
	(at the table)	（餐桌旁）
Eddie	Hi, I understand it's somebody's birthday tonight?	你們好，據我所知今晚有人是壽星？
Bob	Yes, my wife is a year older today.	沒錯，我老婆今天又老了一歲。
Eddie	Congratulations! I just need to see your ID, and then we take off the **least expensive** adult entrée. Happy birthday.	恭喜！我只需要看一下您的證件，然後您餐點裡價格最低的一道主菜是免費的。生日快樂！
Joan	Here's my **driver's license**. Just don't tell anyone how old I am.	這是我的駕照。別讓任何人知道我幾歲喔！
Eddie	Oh, your **secret** is safe with me.	噢！我不會洩漏您的秘密的。
	(back in the kitchen)	（回到廚房）

Eddie	OK, Malcolm, here's what we do with this. We **enter it into the computer** just like a regular order, then we get the manager to change the price to zero.	好了，Malcolm，我們的做法是，像一般點餐程序一樣輸入電腦系統，然後請經理把價格改成零。
Malcolm	Why did you say we take off the least expensive meal? Why not give the **discount** on what the birthday person orders?	為什麼你剛才說，餐點裡價格最低的一道主菜不算錢？為什麼不是算壽星那份餐點免費就好？
Eddie	That's to keep people from **taking advantage of** the offer. Some people might try ordering one expensive meal, and just a bunch of appetizers or salads for everyone else.	這是要避免顧客利用這種優惠佔我們便宜。有些人會點一道昂貴的主餐，然後讓其他人點一些開胃小菜或沙拉什麼的。
	(at another table)	（在另一桌）
Eddie	Hi, folks, how are you tonight?	嗨，你們好，今晚都好嗎？
Melinda	We're doing just fine, thanks. I want to know about this Restaurant Entertainment card we have. We're supposed to get a free meal with it. How does that work?	我們很好，謝謝。我們有你們餐廳的享樂卡，我想瞭解一下該怎麼用，應該可以抵掉一頓餐，對嗎？
Eddie	It's as simple as you said. We give you the least expensive meal for free. Now, can I get you something to drink while you're deciding on dinner?	就跟你說的一樣簡單實惠。您餐點裡價格最低的一道主菜不算錢。那在點菜的同時，你們要喝點什麼嗎？
	(at the sidestand)	（在備餐檯）
Malcolm	We sure **give away** a lot of free meals. How do we make money?	想當然我們送出很多免費的餐點。那我們賺什麼呢？
Eddie	These promotions bring people in. We hope that they will spend extra money on drinks, appetizers, and desserts, and we also hope that they like us enough to come back, and to recommend us to their friends.	這些促銷活動把客人帶上門。我們希望客人能多點一些飲料、開胃菜和點心，也希望他們很滿意而願意再回來用餐，並把我們的餐廳推薦給他們的朋友。

Word Bank

promotion(s) *n.[C]* 促銷　least expensive 最低價的　driver's license 駕照
secret *n.[C]* 秘密　enter it into the computer 輸入電腦
discount *n.[C/U]* 折扣　taking advantage of 佔便宜　give away 免費送出

Unit 08 服務生訓練

 Providing Professional Advice 提供專業建議  Track 32

Introduction

A waiter is helping a guest decide what to get.

服務生協助客人選擇餐點。

Characters

Larry - Waiter	服務生
Mia - Guest	顧客

Conversation

Larry	Good evening, let me give you some time to settle in and take a look at your menus.	晚安，您就座後可以花點時間慢慢看看我們的菜單。
Mia	I need a little **advice**. I've never been here before, and I'm not really sure where to start on the menu. What do you suggest?	我需要一點建議。我沒來過這裡，不知道要怎麼看菜單。你推薦什麼？
Larry	I think we have a lot of good **items** to choose from. Let's try to **narrow it down** a little. Are you interested in red meat, fish, pasta, or **white meat**?	我們有很多不錯的菜色可選。先把範圍縮小一點看看。你想吃紅肉、魚、義大利麵還是白肉？
Mia	I was thinking of something **light**, so probably white meat. I'm not in the mood for anything too heavy.	我想吃份量小一點的餐，也許白肉吧。我不是很想吃份量太多的菜。
Larry	I'd recommend our teriyaki chicken breast with lobster. It's marinated in a Japanese-style teriyaki sauce, then topped with fresh lobster and a tarragon **beurre blanc**.	那麼，我推薦這道照燒雞胸佐龍蝦。雞胸肉是用日式照燒醬汁醃過，上頭擺放新鮮的龍蝦，淋上龍蒿白酒奶油醬。
Mia	That sounds pretty good. What other white meat dishes do you think I should try?	聽起來真不錯。你還推薦什麼其他白肉的餐點？

Larry	I like our **pork** tenderloin. It's lean pork, thinly sliced, with a rosemary white wine sauce.	我很喜歡店裡的這道豬里肌，它是切成薄片的瘦肉，佐上迷迭香白酒醬。
Mia	Does that have cream in it?	那裡頭有奶油嗎？
Larry	There is some milk in the sauce, but no cream. It's a very light dish; tasty, but low in fat. I think you'd like it.	白醬裡頭有些牛奶，但不是奶油。是非常輕食的一道菜，美味又低脂。我想您一定會喜歡的。
Mia	I think so, too. I'll get that. I also want something to start with. Which of the shrimp appetizers do you recommend?	我也覺得。那麼，我點這道。我還想點些前菜。你推薦哪一道有蝦子的開胃菜？
Larry	I really like the beer batter shrimp, but it's not terribly light. For you, I think the shrimp cocktail would be good. It's a classic, but it's still really tasty.	我非常喜歡我們的酥炸啤酒蝦，但是這道菜熱量不是很低。您的話，我想應該吃雞尾酒蝦比較適合。這是傳統的經典開胃菜，但仍然非常好吃。
Mia	What kind of sauce comes with that?	雞尾酒蝦是搭配哪種醬料呢？
Larry	It's just a tomato sauce, with some spices and **horseradish** in it. It really brings out the flavor of the shrimp.	基本上是番茄醬和一些香料及辣根調製。這種醬料很能將蝦子的鮮味襯托出來。
Mia	Thank you for your help. Could you give us just a few more minutes, please?	謝謝你的幫忙。可以再給我幾分鐘的時間考慮嗎？

Word Bank

advice *n.[U]* 建議；忠告　item(s) *n.[C]* 項目；品項
narrow it down 縮小範圍　white meat 白肉　light *adj.* 輕盈的
beurre blanc 白酒奶油醬　pork *n.[U]* 豬肉　horseradish *n.[C/U]* 辣根

Unit 08 服務生訓練

他只相信你——推薦的藝術

當客戶第一次來到你的餐廳，通常第一句話你會詢問他：請問今天想點些什麼呢？而客戶總會回應：你有什麼推薦？

是的，服務人員的推薦往往是客戶點餐的一個重要指標，曾經我也遇到過服務不佳的餐廳，當我依照客戶的慣性詢問有什麼推薦的餐點，服務人員直接、快速告訴我：我覺得好吃的，不見得你也覺得好。雖然他説的是事實，但相信這樣的服務客戶絕對不會想感受第二次，當下我也為他解套找了理由，可能他擔心推薦錯誤的餐點給我，所以希望我自己決定。

推薦餐點其實是有些簡單的訣竅可以依循，我做了一個簡易歸納如下。

推薦的藝術

預算：

詢問客戶消費預算，在預算內提供一整套完整的餐點推薦，若有相關的優惠活動，亦需提供客戶了解。

喜好：

了解客戶喜好，從詢問預算中，可以進階詢問客戶是否有什麼比較無法接受的食材，再提供符合預算的餐點。

主廚推薦：

當客戶無任何想法時，往往可以推薦主廚主推的餐點，通常這樣的餐點都是有計算過成本與分析過客戶喜好而配置，客戶無法接受的機率會較低。

知名：

每家餐廳多少都有自己較知名或得獎的餐點，對於預算內且不排斥食材的客戶，亦可直接提供普羅大眾喜愛的菜色，避免推薦太過冷門的食材，而引起客戶的無法適應。

適量：

推薦餐點時，當然服務人員會提供多樣化的組合給於客戶參考，但當發現客戶點的份量過多時，亦需主動提醒，避免客戶事後有被強迫推銷的感受。

情境：

依照情境推薦有時需要點觀察力，當您發現用餐的客戶為看似親密的一男一女，理當該推薦情人套餐，但若觀察不夠敏銳，可能會造成客戶的尷尬，故若依照當時情境推薦，則須要先了解客戶的狀況。

完成點餐作業，當餐點一一上桌後，服務人員可以自行檢視，推薦的餐點是否有符合客戶的喜愛，觀察客戶是否將餐點通通食用完畢，若未食用完畢，也務必確認是否菜色不符合他的期望，或是菜量過多。

了解實際的狀況後，對於客戶的建議與回應，可整理為下次推薦時的注意要點，相信你的推薦會越來越精準且令客戶滿意。

Unit 09 廚房見習

1 *Understanding Special Ingredients* 瞭解特殊食材

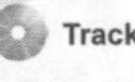 Track 33

Introduction

At the service briefing, the chef explains the evening's specials. 服務簡報時，行政主廚解說今晚的主廚精選。

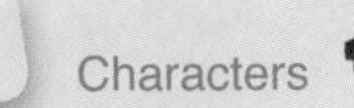

Characters

Elizabeth - Assistant Dining Room Manager 餐區副理
Julia - Chef 行政主廚
Malcolm - Waiter Trainee 實習生

Conversation

Elizabeth	Hi, everybody. It looks like we'll be **moderately** busy. The books aren't full, but hopefully we'll get some walk-ins to fill things up. Let me turn this over to Julia for the specials.	各位好，看來今天只是小忙。訂位還沒滿，希望會有機動客來撐場。現在把時間交給 Julia 介紹主廚精選。
Julia	The first special is veal scaloppini. It's thinly sliced veal, dredged in flour, then sautéed. It's topped with a tomato sauce and fresh, ground **parmesan cheese**.	第一道主廚精選是嫩煎牛小排。牛小排切成薄片，撒上一些麵粉然後嫩煎。上頭會淋上茄汁醬，再撒點新鮮的帕瑪森起司粉。
Malcolm	Is the cheese **melted** on top?	起司是融化在上頭嗎？
Julia	No, we'll have the cheese out on the **counter**. You'll have to put it on top right before you take it out. That way it will only be **slightly** melted when it gets to the table.	不是。我們會把起司拿出來放在工作檯上。你送菜出去之前，要把起司撒上去。這樣當菜送到客人桌上時，起司只稍稍融化而已。
Malcolm	How is it cooked? Is it cooked all the way through?	牛小排幾分熟？全熟嗎？

Julia	No, we usually serve veal medium rare to medium. It really loses a lot of **flavor** if it's too well done. But don't take a temperature on it. We can do it **well done**, but only if the guest asks for it that way.	不，我們的牛小排通常做三分到五分熟。若做到全熟，就會失去很多牛肉的風味。但幾分熟不是問題，如果客人要求全熟，我們也是照著做全熟給他。
Julia	The second special is Alaskan crab with a petit filet and a side of oregano-thyme beurre blanc.	第二道主廚精選是阿拉斯加蟹、配上小菲力，佐以奧勒岡百里香白酒醬。
Malcolm	I've never heard of beurre blanc. How would you describe it?	我沒聽過「beurre blanc」。可以請你解釋一下嗎？
Julia	Beurre blanc is French for "white butter". It's a simple, classic sauce made from butter and white wine. We add the oregano and thyme to it, as the sauce itself doesn't have a real flavor of its own. It can take on many different flavors, depending on what you put in it.	「Beurre blanc」是法文「白奶油」的意思。它是一種簡單又經典的醬汁，用牛油和白酒做的。因為白酒醬本身沒有什麼味道，我們加入奧勒岡和百里香來提味。這種白酒醬可以依照個人喜好，加入不同香料做出不同口味。
Elizabeth	The vegetable of the day is zucchini, and the soups are clam chowder and vegetarian vegetable. If there aren't any more questions, let's get going. Have a good night, everybody.	今日鮮蔬是櫛瓜，湯品有蛤蜊巧達濃湯，以及素食可用的蔬菜湯。如果沒有其他問題，我們開工吧。今晚加油！各位。

Word Bank

ingredient(s) *n.[C]* 成分；原料　evening *n.[C/U]* 傍晚
moderately *adv.* 適度地　parmesan cheese 帕瑪森起司
melted *adj.* 融化的　counter *n.[C]* 櫃檯　slightly *adv.* 些微地
flavor *n.[C/U]* 味道；風味；口味　well done 全熟的

Unit 09 廚房見習

2 *Cooking Methods* 烹調方式 Track 34

Introduction

Julia takes some of the newer waitstaff through the kitchen to explain how things are cooked.

Julia 帶著幾名新進的服務生到廚房裡，向他們解釋食物烹調過程。

Characters  

Julia - Chef	行政主廚
Malcolm - Waiter Trainee	實習生
Alex - Waiter	服務生

Conversation

Julia	Let's head to the first station. This is the **fryer**, which we tend to use **sparingly**. We use vegetable oil in the fryer, at about 180 degrees.	我們到第一個工作點去。這是油炸鍋，要很謹慎地使用。油炸鍋裡面用的是植物油，溫度約 180 度。
Malcolm	What do you use the fryer for, besides French fries?	油炸鍋除了炸薯條，還炸什麼？
Julia	The beer batter shrimp appetizer is also fried, and we sometimes use it for a special, such as fish and chips.	乾燒啤酒蝦這道開胃菜也是用油鍋炸的，有時候也會拿來做主廚精選的菜，像是炸魚或是炸薯片。
Alex	What's next? I used to work at McDonald's; I know all about fryers.	下一個是什麼？我以前在麥當勞工作過，很瞭解油炸鍋。
Julia	While we're here on the line, let's look at the **sauté** area. Sautéing is when thin or small pieces of food are cooked in oil very quickly in one of these **shallow** pans.	既然我們在這條工作區塊上，可以過來看看煎炒區。嫩煎，指的是將薄透細碎的這類食材、放在淺鍋子裡用油快速烹調。
Malcolm	This is one of the busiest area in the kitchen, isn't it?	這是廚房裡最忙碌區域之一，對吧？

Julia	Yes, it is. It's where we cook a lot of fish, and also some of the thinner meats. We sometimes do the vegetables this way, too.	沒錯。我們在這裡烹調許多魚類、還有細薄肉類。有時候蔬菜也是這樣料理。
Alex	The broiler is here on the line, too, isn't it?	碳烤爐也在這個區域，是嗎？
Julia	Yes, this is the char **broiler**. It's where we cook steaks and other kinds of meat. You can see the **gas** underneath, and the metal ribs that put the black lines on the steaks.	對，這就是碳烤爐。我們在這裡烹調牛排和其他肉類。你可以看到瓦斯在下方，然後這些鐵條會在牛排上留下黑色烙痕。
Alex	But you don't cook all meats like that, right?	但是，不是所有的肉都是這樣處理的對吧？
Julia	Correct; back here in the **prep area** you'll see how we do a lot of meats. These ovens are where we do the **roasting**.	沒錯，回到準備區你就可以看到我們怎麼處理大量肉品。我們用這些烤箱來烤東西。
Malcolm	So, roasting is a lot like **baking**.	所以，烘烤的過程很類似烘焙囉。
Julia	Yes, but baking usually refers to bread and cakes. Roasting cooks meats slowly. It's what we use for prime rib and things like the pork tenderloin.	對，但是烘焙通常是指烘焙麵包和蛋糕。肉要慢慢地去烤，肋排或是像豬里肌之類的肉品都是這樣烹調。
Alex	Thanks for the tour. I know this will help us do our jobs better.	謝謝你的導覽。這些解說對我們的工作有很大的幫助。

Word Bank

fryer *n.[C]* 油炸鍋；煎鍋　sparingly *adv.* 謹慎地；愛惜地　sauté *v.* 炒；嫩煎
shallow *adj.* 淺的　broiler *n.[C]* 烤箱；烤爐　gas *n.[U]* 瓦斯
prep area 準備區　roasting *n.[U]* 烘烤　baking *n.[U]* 烘焙

Unit 09 廚房見習

3 *Timing and Placing Orders* 上菜時機與廚房下單

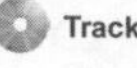 Track 35

Introduction

Eddie is explaining the ordering system to his trainee. Eddie 正在向實習生解釋點餐流程如何運作。

Characters

Eddie - Waiter	服務生
Malcolm - Waiter Trainee	實習生
Justin - Guest	顧客

Conversation

Eddie	OK, so that's two shrimp cocktails to start, and then a lamb chops and prime rib. The appetizers should be ready in **just a bit**.	好的，所以你們要兩個雞尾酒蝦做前菜，然後是小羊排和肋排。開胃菜一會兒就會先上。
Justin	We'd like some time to **sip** our cocktails first, so could you hold off on the shrimp for ten minutes or so?	我們想先慢慢品嘗一下雞尾酒，能不能請你們過十分鐘左右再上蝦子？
Eddie	That'll be no problem.	沒問題。
	(at the sidestand)	（在備餐檯）
Eddie	So Malcolm, what can we learn from the way this table ordered?	那 Malcolm 你從這桌的點餐過程中觀察到什麼？
Malcolm	They don't seem like they're **in a hurry**. They wanted to wait for the appetizers.	他們似乎不趕時間，還想讓開胃菜晚點上。
Eddie	That's right. You need to learn to read tables and figure out which ones are in a hurry and which aren't. If they order appetizers and wine, they're not.	對了。你要學著去觀察餐桌的客人，判斷他們哪幾桌在趕時間，哪幾桌不趕。通常點了開胃菜和餐前酒的客人都不趕時間。
Malcolm	So, how do you **figure out** when to bring out everything?	那麼，你怎麼判斷何時出餐？

Eddie	Well, they ordered a bottle of wine, so we'll bring that out when they've **nearly** finished their cocktails. And we'll place the order for the appetizers right now. We don't know how long those will take.	嗯，那一桌的客人點了一瓶酒，所以我會在他們快喝完雞尾酒的時候先送上酒。然後跟廚房下開胃菜的出菜單吧。因為不知道要等多久。
Malcolm	What about the rest of the food? It's going to be a while before they get to the entrée course.	那其他的菜呢？到上主菜之前，還有一段時間。
Eddie	We'll ring the whole order into the computer right now. That way the cooks know what they have coming up.	趁這個時候，我們會把整個點單鍵入電腦裡。這樣廚師就知道要準備什麼。
Malcolm	But won't the food get **overdone** if we order it right now?	但是如果這時候就跟廚房下單，菜不會煮過頭嗎？
Eddie	They won't start cooking most of it for a while. We'll **fire the order** when the guests are about half done with their salads. Then, it'll be ready just a little after they finish them.	大部份的菜，廚房還不會這麼早開始烹煮。客人的沙拉用到大約一半的時候，我們就會跟催廚房開始出單。所以，在客人用完沙拉不用多久，主菜也就準備好了。
Malcolm	Does it always take the same amount of time to get things after you fire them?	跟催廚房開始出單以後，出菜時間都能抓得差不多嗎？
Eddie	No, on busy nights we have to fire things really early. You'll get used to it.	不會，在很忙碌的晚餐時間，我們得很早就跟催廚房出單。久了你就習慣了。

Word Bank

order(ing) *v.* 點餐　just a bit 一點兒；一會兒　sip *v.* 啜飲　in a hurry 趕時間
figure out 判斷　nearly *adv.* 近乎；將近　overdone *adj.* 煮過頭的；過度的
fire the order 跟催廚房出單

Unit 09 廚房見習

4 Interaction Between Cooks and Waiters
廚師與服務生的互動

Track 36

Introduction

Eddie explains how to communicate with the cooks. Eddie 說明如何與廚師溝通。

Characters

Eddie - Waiter	服務生
Malcolm - Waiter Trainee	實習生
Caleb - Expeditor	傳菜領班

Conversation

Eddie	Malcolm, this is Caleb. He's the expeditor tonight.	Malcolm，這位是 Caleb，他是今晚的傳菜領班。
Malcolm	Hi, Caleb, this is my first night. What is it you do, exactly?	你好，Caleb。今晚是我第一次上班，你的工作職掌是什麼？
Caleb	I'm the **middle man** between the waits and the cooks. I **organize** the orders as they come up, and make sure the waits know when their food is ready.	我是介在服務生和廚師間的協調人員。我負責整理傳進來的點單，並確保服務生知道他們的餐點已經備妥。
Malcolm	That sounds like a pretty **complicated** job. How long have you been here?	聽起來是非常複雜的工作。你在這裡多久了？
Caleb	I started out as a dishwasher about two years ago. I work as a busser on the nights I'm not expediting. This does get a little complicated, especially if the cooks get behind.	我二年前剛來的時候是個洗碗工。不做傳菜領班的晚餐時段，我是打雜工。這個工作的確有點複雜，尤其是廚師做菜進度落後的時候。
Malcolm	What do you do when that happens?	那時候你怎麼辦？

Caleb	Tell everyone to wait. The guys on the cooks' line do a good job; it's just that sometimes they get too much to do in a really short time.	告訴大家等一等。工作線上的廚師都很盡心盡力，只是有時候經常在很短的時間內，要處理太多東西。
Eddie	One thing about working here is that everything you need from the cooks goes through the expeditor. So, if you need a **side** of sauce, you ask Caleb, and he gets it for you. It's better than having ten people all trying to talk to the cooks at once.	在這裡工作要注意的一件事是，所有你跟廚師要的東西，都要經由傳菜領班交付給你。所以，你如果要一碟沾醬，得跟 Caleb 要，他會要廚師做給你。這比讓十個人同時跟廚師溝通來的好。
Malcolm	What does Caleb do once your order is ready?	那麼，當我們點的餐好了以後，Caleb 會怎麼做？
Eddie	In the old days, he would shout your name. That led to some **confusion**, because when it's really noisy "Eddie" sounds just like "Jenny" or "Larry". Now we have these nifty little **pagers** that **buzz** when our order is ready.	以往他會叫我們的名字。但是如果現場太吵，會造成很多混淆，有時候「Eddie」聽起來像「Jenny」或「Larry」。現在我們有這種新潮的小呼叫器，當我們的菜好的時候，它會響起通知我們。
Malcolm	What happens when there isn't an expeditor?	如果當天沒有傳菜領班會怎樣？
Eddie	That's usually when it's not too busy. You talk to the wheel man then. He's the one in the middle of the line organizing everything. Just be patient, and they'll take care of you.	那通常是不太忙的時候。到時你要跟領頭的廚師溝通。他是工作區中統籌大小事的那一位。耐心點，他們會關照你的。

Word Bank

interaction *n.[C/U]* 互動　communicate *v.* 溝通　expeditor *n.[C]* 傳菜領班
middle man 中間人　organize *v.* 整理；組織　complicated *adj.* 複雜的
side *n.[C]* 指一碟　confusion *n.[U]* 混淆　pager(s) *n.[C]* 呼叫器　buzz *v.* 響

Unit 09 廚房見習

Tips for Workplace Happiness
職場補給站
加油大使 Cheryl 來充電！

平民美式料理特色

快速、簡單一直是美式餐點的主要特色。1920 年代美國的「白色城堡」(White Castle），為全球第一家美式餐廳，當時講求的就是便宜快速又簡單的販售方式，一個漢堡訂價約 5 分錢美金，為加快料理時間，業者更將肉餅上打 5 個洞，好讓肉熟得更快，來加速販售服務。

不過真正引發全世界美式速食風潮的應該要算是麥當勞。麥當勞於 1948 年以一個聖地牙哥熱狗攤名字的形式出現，創始人克雷克（Mr. Ray A. Kroc）在 1954 年正式將熱狗攤設立為麥當勞餐廳，從此麥當勞便變成美式速食的代名詞。

大家所了解的美式餐點大部分是漢堡、薯條、起司等食物組合而成，而它們共同的特色就是烹煮簡單、適合久放、冷了也可以食用，以上描述雖很簡單，卻大約已經點出美國人一般的飲食習慣。

美式餐點的特點

生冷：

美式餐點很多部份都是冷的，蔬菜以水洗淨，加些沙拉醬或是油醋，點綴些堅果，就是一道菜。此跟美國人的飲食習慣有關，美式的菜餚大多不需要太過烹煮，很多部分是原汁原味地上桌，也造就了生冷飲食的模式。

重鹽：

美式餐點另一個重點是鹽的使用會比一般餐點多，且僅是很單純的使用鹽，這一點你可以從薯條看出端倪，台灣人吃薯條並沒有那麼喜愛用鹽調味，但純美式餐廳，薯條旁一定會附上鹽等佐料。

嗜甜：

要說美國人是螞蟻演化而成的，我絕對舉雙手贊成，美式的甜點、糕點清一色就是甜死人不償命，美式甜點用糖的比例可以說是台灣的好幾倍，造就美式餐點餐後甜點多為冰淇淋、甜派等，因為這樣的甜點才可以容下比例極高的砂糖。

愛油膩：

美式餐點的油膩其實是因為製作方式而起的，因餐點的製作多為快速且簡單的方式進行，油煎、生烤都容易使得食物依附大量的油，加上美式餐點多使用牛油烹調，也就使得餐點的油膩感會比一般料理多一些。

絕無內臟：

要在美式餐點看到內臟那是不可能的，美國人對於吃內臟可是深感不可思議，他們就是覺得動物的內臟很噁心，只能丟棄，不能吃，另外他們雖吃動物的肉，但動物的頭則一定要去掉，絕不可上桌。

使用的食材

馬鈴薯、玉米

馬鈴薯與玉米可以說是美式餐點的靈魂，使用的範圍幾乎佔了美式餐點的 70%，尤其是馬鈴薯，不管是什麼場合、時間都會用到它，當然也因為馬鈴薯變化性大，使用範圍自然較廣。

紅蘿蔔、洋蔥、花椰菜、西洋芹菜、蘑菇、甜椒、甜豆

生菜飲食的關係，美式餐點大量使用可生食的蔬果，這一點你只要走一趟美式超商就可以看出端倪。

碎牛肉、雞肉、培根、火腿

肉品的使用，美式餐點依舊偏愛牛肉與醃製類肉品，主要可能與美式餐點重鹽有些關連，肉品的烹煮也偏向簡單煎、烤。

雞蛋、麵包

雞蛋的使用，美式餐點用的就是煎蛋和炒蛋這兩種，但看似簡單，其實它們的應用和變化很廣泛。

奶油、糖、起司、牛奶、醃酸黃瓜、花生醬

醬料的運用在美式餐點裡使用上多是單純的，不像法式料理，醬料的處理遠遠複雜過主餐，在美式餐點你很少看到多樣的醬料組合，最多就是酸黃瓜加番茄醬這類的組合模式。

看到以上的介紹，對於美式的餐點是否有些了解了？嚴格說來很多人說美國人是個不懂吃的民族，吃對他們來說只是為了吃飽、維持生命，但也因為這樣的文化特質，發展出一套快速、便利的飲食模式，讓現今忙碌工作的上班族有另一種快速飲食的選擇。

Unit 10 食材管理與餐廳清潔

Ordering Food 採購食材

Track 37

Introduction

Malcolm learns how food is ordered at the restaurant. Malcolm 學習如何採購餐廳食材。

Characters

Boris - Storekeeper 店長
Malcolm - Waiter Trainee 實習生

Conversation

Boris	I guess I'm supposed to show you how we get everything here in the restaurant.	我想我應該要向你示範我們餐廳是如何準備所有食材的。
Malcolm	Yeah, there sure are a lot of different things you need to keep **in stock**. How do you keep track of it all?	是啊，餐廳裡一定有各種各樣的東西需要隨時備妥。你都怎麼管理材料的？
Boris	For the things on the regular menu, we have what is known as a **par** system. I have a big list of everything we usually need. It shows how much we should have in stock; that's the par. If we don't have as many as the par, then I have to order more.	我們用這套 PAR 系統，來準備平日菜單上的食材。我建置了一大張清單，記錄我們常用到的東西。PAR 系統會告訴我們什麼東西該備多少料。如果某樣東西少於 PAR 該有的數量，我就得採購補足。
Malcolm	Who determines what the par is?	那麼，誰決定哪些東西要用 PAR 系統管理？
Boris	Every time they **make changes to** the menu, I sit down with the chef and one of the managers and we figure it out. The idea of the par system is that we should never **run out of** anything we sell every day.	每當他們變更菜單時，我就會和行政主廚以及其中一位經理共同討論出結果。PAR 系統的用意就是絕不能發生缺料的情形。
Malcolm	What about specials? You **obviously** can't do a par on those.	那麼主廚精選呢？你顯然不能用 PAR系統去管理主廚精選的食材。

Boris	That's one time when I don't always do the ordering. Julia can call up the supplier herself and make orders for special things she needs.	這就是我不必負責採購的時候了。Julia 會自行連絡供應商，下單採購她需要的特殊食材。
Malcolm	Who **puts things away** when the order arrives?	貨到了以後，由誰收貨呢？
Boris	I do, usually. I'm used to the system, and since I'm the one who placed the order, it's easiest for me to be the one who checks it. I have to check everything that comes in and make sure we got what we ordered. That's just as important as **placing** the order.	通常是我。我對系統很熟悉，而且既然是我做的採購，由我來點貨也最省事。我要清點所有送來的東西，確保東西都送齊了。這個動作跟下採購單一樣重要。
Malcolm	Thanks for showing me around. I'll keep you in mind if we ever need anything.	謝謝你帶我參觀。當我們有什麼需要補貨時，我會記得找你。

Word Bank

storekeeper *n.[C]* 店長；店主　in stock 備有庫存；現貨供應
par *n.* par 庫存系統　make changes to 變更……　run out of 用盡……
obviously *adv.* 明顯地　put(s) things away 收起；儲存　placing *v.* 下單（place）

Unit 10 食材管理與餐廳清潔

2 Clean As You Go 隨手清潔 Track 38

Introduction

Larry explains to his trainee how to keep the restaurant clean during open hours. Larry 向實習生解釋，如何在營業時間維持餐廳清潔。

Characters

Larry - Waiter 服務生
Hunter - Waiter Trainee 實習生

Conversation

Hunter	This place is really clean. How do you all **manage to** keep it looking so good when you're so busy all the time?	我們這裡真的很乾淨。你們平時都這麼忙碌，到底是怎麼將這個地方維持得這麼好？
Larry	That's one thing that management always **stresses**. We not only have to worry about health **inspections**, but just out of **concern for** the guests, we need to keep this place as clean as we can.	那一向是我們的管理重點之一。我們不僅要應付衛生稽查，為了顧客著想，我們還得盡可能維持餐廳的乾淨整潔。
Hunter	Everybody seems to be doing a good job of it.	每個人似乎都很賣力工作。
Larry	Part of it is the sidework that we do at the end of every shift, but a lot of cleaning is done on a "**clean as you go**" basis.	有一部分要歸功於每班結束之前要做的雜務工作，但是大部分的清掃都是在「隨手清潔」原則下完成的。
Hunter	That sounds like a good idea. How do you make it work?	聽起來是很好的辦法。通常怎麼進行？
Larry	It's simple: If you make a **mess**, you clean it up right away. Not everyone does that all the time, but there are enough good employees that it usually works.	很簡單，如果你製造了髒亂，你就馬上將它清理乾淨。並不是每個人每次都做得到，但還是有夠多的好員工能做到，所以還是蠻有效果。

Hunter	What do you do if you find something that someone didn't bother to clean up?	如果你發現有人懶得清理自己製造的髒亂呢？
Larry	If someone **makes a habit of** not cleaning up after themselves, we usually **confront** them with it. If it gets really bad, we can let management deal with it. But most of the time, I just go ahead and clean it up.	如果有人養成了不清理自己製造的髒亂的這種習慣，我們通常會當面提點他們。如果情況真的很糟，將會交由管理部處理。但多數時候，我都自己前去清理乾淨。
Hunter	What do you use to clean with?	你都用什麼來打掃？
Larry	There are towels in **sanitizing** water located throughout the kitchen. For instance, right now we should clean up a little around the salad dressings. Why don't you grab a towel from that bucket and just wipe up a little.	廚房各處都放有浸在消毒水裡的抹布。比如說，我們現在應該稍微清理一下沙拉醬汁周邊。你要不要去那個桶子裡拿條抹布來，將它稍微擦掉一下？
Hunter	That's no problem. It's nice working somewhere where people take their jobs seriously.	沒問題。能夠在大家都認真工作的地方工作真的很棒。

Word Bank

manage to 辦到　stress(es) *v.* 重視；強調　inspection(s) *n.[C]* 稽查；審視
concern for ……的擔憂　clean as you go 隨手清潔　mess *n.[C]* 髒亂
make(s) a habit of 養成……的習慣　confront *v.* 當面告知
sanitizing *adj.* 消毒的

Unit 10 食材管理與餐廳清潔

3 Sidework 雜務工作 Track 39

Introduction

Larry and a trainee go over sidework after the shift. Larry 和一位實習生下班後在處理雜務工作。

Characters  

Larry - Waiter	服務生
Hunter - Waiter Trainee	實習生

Conversation

Larry	Sidework is part of the job that everybody **grumbles** about, but it has to be done. So, don't let me hear you complaining about it, OK?	雜務工作是所有人都抱怨連連的工作項目，但是總要有人完成這些事。所以，別讓我聽到你發出埋怨，好嗎？
Hunter	Whatever you say. I'll try not to.	你說的是。我盡量不抱怨。
Larry	Actually, I don't care how much you complain, as long as you get your work done. A lot of people are just **eager** to get off work, so they **resent** the time it takes to do the sidework.	其實我不在意你怎麼埋怨這些雜事，只要你能將工作完成就好。很多員工都急著想盡早下班，所以對這些雜務工作所耗費掉的時間相當不滿。
Hunter	I'll try not to get too **anxious** about leaving, then.	好吧，那我盡量不要急著走。
Larry	Our sidework tonight is to put away all the salad dressings and clean the area around where they're kept. It's not too hard to do, so I'll show you the sidework **sheet**. That shows what needs to be done each night. Each waiter is assigned a different sidework, depending on which **section** they have that night.	今晚我們的雜務工作，是要將所有的沙拉醬收拾好，再將擺放沙拉醬的地方清理乾淨。不是太難的工作，那麼來看一下雜務工作表。上面列出了每晚要進行的工作項目，每個服務生會根據當晚負責的區域，被安排一項雜務工作。

Hunter	What's the worst one?	最麻煩的雜務工作是哪一項？
Larry	That's a matter of **opinion**. I hate **sweeping**, so doing the kitchen floor is the one I don't like. But everyone has their own least favorite. Here's the list. See, someone has to clean up around the soup wells and restock the bowls and things. Another one is to clean the soda machine and restock there. It's all pretty easy to figure out. It's just that if you don't do it, it makes it harder for someone else.	那得看個人喜好。我恨死掃地，所以我不喜歡清掃廚房地板。但每個人都有自己最不愛的項目。這張是工作表。瞧，有人要清理湯爐並補齊碗盤；有人得清理飲料機並補料。這些都不是太困難的事，只是你如果不完成自己的工作，就會造成其他人的困擾。
Hunter	What happens if it doesn't get done?	如果雜務工作沒完成會如何？
Larry	A manager has to check it before you can leave, so they make sure it's done.	將有個經理負責在你離開前檢查你的雜務工作，他們會確定你完成你的工作了。
Hunter	I'll try to do the best I can.	我會盡我所能去完成。
Larry	If you just do everything it says to do on the sidework sheet, you'll have no problems.	若你老實按著雜務工作表安排的工作執行，應該不會有問題的。

Word Bank

sidework *n.[U]* 雜務工作　grumble(s) *v.* 抱怨　eager *adj.* 急切的；熱切的
resent *v.* 不情願；厭惡　anxious *adj.* 焦急的　sheet *n.[C]* 表單
section *n.[C]* 區域　opinion *n.[C/U]* 看法；意見　sweeping *n.[C/U]* 掃地

Unit 10 食材管理與餐廳清潔

Deep Cleaning and Insect Control 大掃除與害蟲防治

Track 40

Introduction

Larry explains what to do when the restaurant needs to be deep-cleaned. Larry 說明餐廳如何進行大掃除。

Characters

Larry - Waiter 服務生
Hunter - Waiter Trainee 實習生

Conversation

Larry	This is what we **affectionately** call "bug night".	今天就是我們暱稱的「除蟲之夜」。
Hunter	Bug night? That doesn't sound very **pleasant**.	除蟲之夜？聽起來不是很愉快的事。
Larry	It's **inevitable**, really. In any restaurant, you have a lot of food. Food attracts **insects**, and any decent restaurant needs to get rid of them. So, once a month someone comes in to spray **bug killer** around.	沒辦法避免，真的。不管哪一家餐廳，都放了一堆食物。有食物就引來蟲子，有水準的餐廳都會想辦法驅除牠們。所以每個月都會有人進來噴一次殺蟲劑。
Hunter	Is that safe?	這樣安全嗎？
Larry	Well, it's pretty mild stuff, but we can't leave any of the settings on the table. We have to put everything away just in case.	其實，這東西還算溫和，但是我們還是要注意不能把這些物品留在桌上。所有東西都要收好，以防萬一。
Hunter	Where would you like me to start?	那你要我從哪裡開始呢？
Larry	Take the silverware from our station and put it in the walk-in. And take all the glasses and put them in the dishroom. The dishwashers will wash them all after the bug guys are done.	將餐具組從工作站拿進壁櫥，再將所有的玻璃器皿拿進洗碗室。除蟲人員噴完殺蟲劑以後，洗碗工會全部洗過一次。

Hunter	What about the tables?	桌子怎麼處理？
Larry	We just leave them **bare**. The **centerpieces** get put away and covered in the back, then we wipe off the tables and reset them before the first shift tomorrow.	桌子就淨空放在原處，餐桌中央的擺飾收起來，放在後頭用東西覆蓋。明天開張前我們要擦拭一下桌面，再將擺飾品放回去。
Hunter	This happens once a month?	這一個月做一次？
Larry	Yes, and there is one other time we don't reset the tables after the shift. That's when they do the floor. They have someone come in and polish the **wood floor**, so we have to move all the tables to one side.	是的。另外，有人要來維護地板的時候，我們下了班也不必整理桌子。到時會有人進來給木地板打蠟，所以我們必須將所有的桌子移到一側。
Hunter	And those days are just like tomorrow; we have to reset everything in the morning.	那些日子就會像明天，我們必須要在早上將所有東西重新排回去。
Larry	Yes, it's a little more work, but it makes the restaurant cleaner and makes it look better, so it's better for everybody.	對，這是額外要做的一些工作，但餐廳會因此變得較乾淨，也更美觀，這對大家都好。

Word Bank

deep-clean(ed) *v.* 大掃除　affectionately *adv.* 親暱地；有感情地
pleasant *adj.* 令人愉快的　inevitable *adj.* 無可避免的
insect(s) *n.[C]* 昆蟲　bug killer 殺蟲劑　bare *adj.* 裸露的；空無一物的
centerpiece(s) *n.[C]* 餐桌中央的擺飾　wood floor 木地板

Unit 10 食材管理與餐廳清潔

我是大廚師——衛生是我的任務

電影「料理鼠王」的法國餐廳主廚能隨手煮出讓客戶滿意且一再光顧的美食，理所當然，影片裡料理評鑑家亦是給予最高級的肯定，這樣一個好手藝的廚師，當然是各餐廳爭相洽談，但沒人了解這主廚——牠是隻愛美食的老鼠。這一切都是電影裡的情節，試想一家裝潢華麗、食材高級的餐廳廚房有老鼠橫行，天啊！這是多麼恐怖的事。

廚房有鼠輩這到底是誰的責任呢？就職務區分衛生是主廚需要負責的，那大飯店或是高級餐廳主廚的職責有那些呢？以下讓我們來逐一說明。

配合老闆策略與營運要求

餐廳的營運是老闆的職責，然後菜色、食材成本都需要由主廚提供專業的建議，而主廚所提出的建議更需搭配老闆經營的策略與考量，若未思考到餐廳實際的營運，而只顧主廚的喜好，將導致餐廳的虧損。

相關法令、安全、衛生的處理

餐飲業對於衛生與安全是格外用心謹慎，尤其細菌滋生、食物中毒等問題，不能掉以輕心，對於各種病菌的特性、發作和潛伏期，更要瞭如指掌嚴格防範，而這些都需要主廚多加了解與注意，並將這些細節教育下去。

了解顧客喜好

所謂要抓住老公的心，就是要先抓住他的胃。這適用於新婚夫妻，也適用於餐廳主廚，要抓住客戶的心，首重要抓住客戶的胃。每個人都有其喜愛的味道、食材、料理的方式，怎麼樣可以吸引客戶，留住客戶，這都需要主廚動動腦筋，方式很簡單，經常走出廚房進入餐廳內，看看客戶用餐的表情，端出去的餐點是否通通食用完畢，哪一道菜經常性地有剩餘，這些細節都是主廚需要了解的，惟有了解歸納修正後，才可以真正地抓住客戶的心。

硬體設施的安排

主廚對於生財器具，如鍋碗、加熱設備、爐灶、冰箱的添購更新，廚房動線的規劃，器材擺設的管理，都必須站在較高的角度全盤思索，使得廚房作業順暢與安全，而這些都是主廚的責任。

組織的完整

廚房需多少大廚、助理廚師、廚工、清潔員，搭配多少的作業平台，這都是主廚需處理的，怎麼樣讓餐廳順利運作，組織完整，這都是重要的課題。

講述了主廚職責後，是否了解到當個主廚並非容易的事，所需要了解與處理的事務並非僅有做好菜、煮好湯，還要兼負廚房的所有內外事務。面對這麼多事務，那廚房的衛生主廚又該如何輕鬆地掌控呢？以下有一套簡易的掌握規則。

- 食材洗滌順序：乾貨→加工食品類→蔬菜→牛肉→豬肉→雞肉→蛋類→海鮮。以此順序洗滌將可降低細菌互相感染的風險，並可讓食材保存時間長久。
- 器具洗滌順序：餐具→鍋具→刀具→砧板→抹布。器具的洗滌首重客戶用的先處理，清潔用的擺最後，切勿通通丟一起洗滌。
- 洗滌流程（三槽式）：預洗（第一槽）→洗滌（第二槽）→沖洗（第三槽）→消毒→風乾。
- 塑膠砧板多用於熟食，尤其白色。其餘則把握生、熟食避免交互污染即可，原則上以顏色區分，紅色用於肉類，藍色用於海鮮類，綠色用於蔬菜類。
- 乾貨倉庫一定要杜絕蟲鼠來源，有防蟲鼠入侵設施，維持乾燥，各式儲物架最好是不鏽鋼製品，標準庫存量為 4 到 7 天或 1 到 2 週（暫時性倉庫則為 3 天內）。
- 冷凍冷藏倉庫需具現代化溫度管理之管控器械及儀表標示（冷藏：7℃至凍結點，冷凍：-18℃以下），食材分區、分類標示要清楚，並且嚴格管控有效期限，冷凍冷藏櫃裝載容量以 50 至 60% 為限。

有了以上的控管流程，相信您的餐廳衛生絕對是一等一。

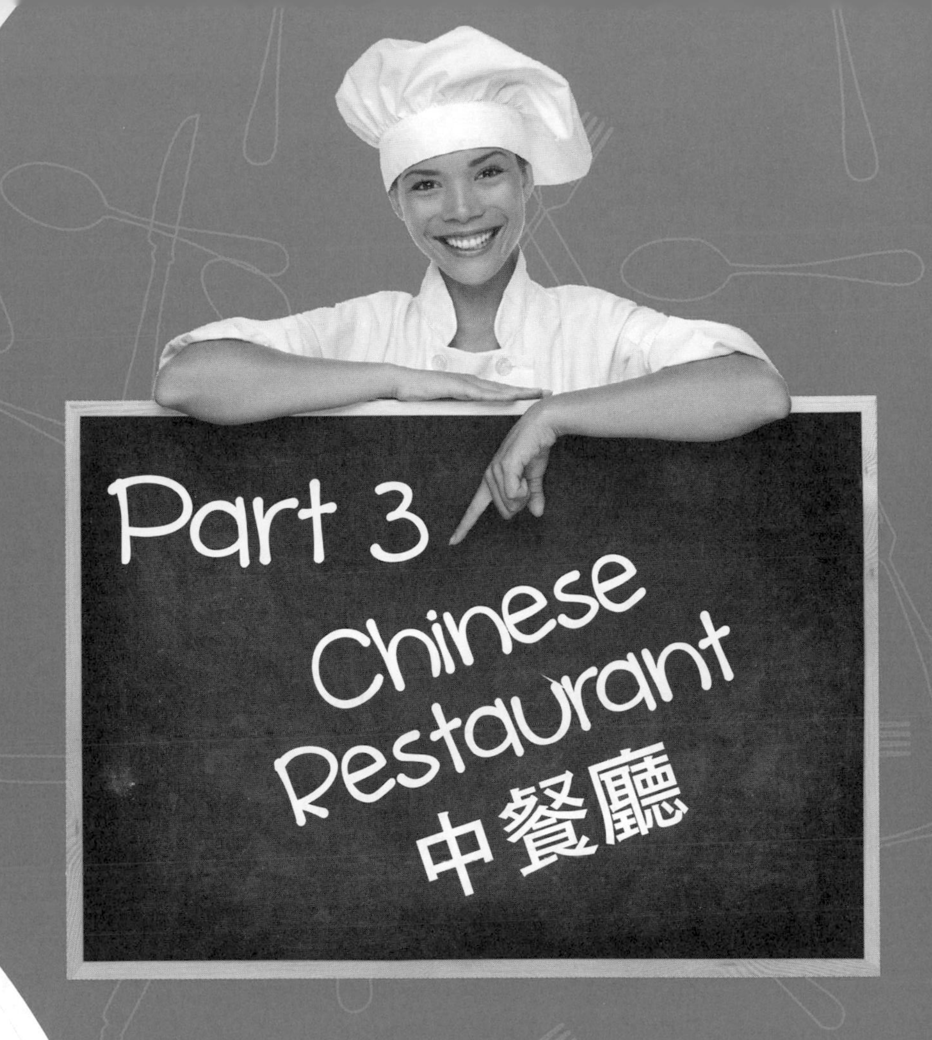
Part 3
Chinese
Restaurant
中餐廳

Unit 11 餐廳陳設

1 *Setting the Table* 餐桌桌面擺設 Track 41

Introduction

A server is showing a new server how to put everything in place on a table. 服務生給新進服務生示範、如何擺放餐桌上的物品。

Characters  

Chris - Server Trainee 實習生
Lily - Server 服務生

Conversation

Chris	We sure do a lot of large parties here. It's a little different than my last restaurant.	我們經常有大型宴會在這裡舉辦。這跟我上個工作的餐廳不大一樣。
Lily	That's right. One thing you'll find is that we serve most tables **family-style**. Everything goes on the **turntable** in the middle, and guests **help themselves** to what they want.	沒錯。你會發現，我們大都採家庭式的餐桌服務。所有的餐點都放在中間的轉盤上，讓客人隨自己的意思用餐。
Chris	So, the table setup is going to be a little different, too, right?	所以，桌面擺設也不太一樣，是嗎？
Lily	Some things, yes. We probably have more items on the table than what you're used to. But setting the table isn't all that hard.	對，某些東西不太一樣。跟你所習慣的比起來，我們應該是有較多物品要放在餐桌上。但桌面擺設並不總是那麼難。
Chris	What goes on first?	哪樣要先放呢？
Lily	The first thing we put on is the plate. That goes up two fingers from the **edge** of the table. The napkin goes on top of that. Then you put the **soup cup** above the plate, to the left. The **sauce dish** goes to the right of that.	第一樣要放的是這個盤子。要將盤子放在離餐桌邊緣二指寬的位置，再將餐巾置於其上。接著，湯杯放在盤子的左上角，沾醬碟則放在它右側。
Chris	It sort of looks like Mickey Mouse!	這樣擺看起來有點像米奇老鼠！

Lily	Yes it does, now that you pointed that out. Anyway, put the soup spoon inside the soup cup, with the handle point to 9:00.	真的耶，被你認出來了。如論如何，把湯匙放入湯碗內，湯杯把手指向九點鐘方向。
Chris	Then all that's left is the chopsticks.	然後就只剩筷子了。
Lily	Those go on the right, with the chopstick holder to the right of the sauce dish. Of course, we use nice, reusable chopsticks, not the throw-away bamboo kind like they do in cheap places.	筷子放在右側，筷架放在沾醬碟的右邊。當然，我們用的筷子品質好，且可重複使用，而不是那種在便宜餐館用一次就扔掉的免洗竹筷。
Chris	What about **glassware**?	玻璃器皿該怎麼處理？
Lily	We put the water glasses to the right of the chopsticks, above the top of the plate. Wine glasses go on the turntable, along with the spice and sauce **rack**.	我們將水杯放在筷子右邊，盤子的上緣附近。酒杯則放在轉盤上，跟佐料和醬汁碟架排在一起。
Chris	That covers it, then. Where to now?	這部分講的差不多了。再來呢？

Word Bank

in place 在合適的位置　family-style *adv.* 家庭式地　turntable *n.[C]* 餐桌轉盤
help themselves 自助　edge *n.[C/U]* 邊緣　soup cup 湯碗；湯杯
sauce dish 沾醬碟　glassware *n.[U]* 玻璃器皿　rack *n.[C]* 架子

Unit 11 餐廳陳設

2 *Stocking Front of House* 外場備品 Track 42

Introduction

Lily teaches Chris what needs to be stocked before a shift. Lily 教導 Chris 上工前需補足什麼。

Characters

Chris - Server Trainee	實習生
Lily - Server	服務生

Conversation

Chris	There's one thing I've been wondering about: How do we change the tablecloths on these tables?	有件事我一直不太明白：我們要如何更換這些餐桌的桌布？
Lily	I didn't know that myself when I first started working here. What we do is **remove** the turntable, then we can take the old tablecloth off **easily** and change to a new one.	我一開始在這裡工作時也不清楚。我們是將轉盤先移走，然後就能輕鬆地把舊桌布拆下，換上新的。
Chris	You'll have to show me once we get busy and there's a **dirty table** we need to do.	當我們一忙起來、有髒桌布需要更換時，請務必示範給我看。
Lily	Why don't we do one right now? That way we won't have to worry about it while we're busy during the shift. The tablecloths are in that cabinet right there. Grab one white and one red.	我們何不現在就來換一桌？這樣我們就不用擔心上工時太忙。桌布在那邊的櫥櫃裡。請你去拿一條白的和一條紅的來。
Chris	Here they are.	拿來了。
Lily	We just lift up the turntable like this, then set it over here. Then, the round white one goes on the bottom, and the red one goes **diagonally**, like a **diamond**. It looks good, and it's simple to do.	像這樣把轉盤抬起來，放到這邊。將白色圓布放在底下，然後將這條紅色的桌布放對角，成為菱形。看起來美觀，做起來也不難。

Chris	So, we need to get more tablecloths before we open. What else do we need to stock out here?	所以，開始營業前我們要多準備一些桌布。還有什麼東西我們需要先備妥？
Lily	We keep extra soup spoons and chopsticks in that drawer, and there are some steak knives and forks, too, if people **ask for** them. Then we also need some small **beer glasses**. Since it's Saturday, we need to make sure we have a lot of those.	我們會多放一些湯匙和筷子在那個抽屜裡，若客人需要，這裡也有些牛排刀和叉子。另外，我們還需要準備一些小啤酒杯。尤其今天是星期六，我們需要確定啤酒杯準備得夠多。
Chris	What about water pitchers?	那麼水壺呢？
Lily	Yes, come with me in the back and we'll get some of those. We also need to **refill** the ice bin while we're doing that.	對，跟我到後頭來，我們拿一些出來。在這同時，我們還要把冰桶填滿。
Chris	Are we ready?	我們都準備好了嗎？
Lily	I think so. Let's be prepared for our first table.	應該都好了。我們來準備迎接第一桌客人吧。

Word Bank

remove *v.* 移開　easily *adv.* 容易地；不費力地　dirty table 髒桌子
diagonally *adv.* 對邊地；對角地　diamond *n.[C]* 菱形；鑽石；方塊
ask for 要求　beer glass(es) 啤酒杯　refill *v.* 補充；再填滿

Unit 11 餐廳陳設

3 *Additional Waiter Setup* 額外的服務生準備工作

Track 43

Introduction

Servers are doing stocking after their shift, to get ready for the next one. 服務生下工後進行備料作業，為下一班做準備。

Characters

Chris - Server Trainee 實習生
Lily - Server 服務生

Conversation

Lily	At the end of every shift, we have to refill the **condiments** and make sure we have **enough** bottles of each one. I'll start with the soy sauce; why don't you do the **ketchup** bottles. Just pour them all together, then get a new one for each **empty** bottle you have.	每一班結束後，我們必須補充調味料，確定每種調味料的瓶數都足夠。我先從醬油開始，你何不處理一下蕃茄醬瓶。就把它們倒在一起，然後拿一瓶新的來置換空瓶。
Chris	I understand why we have soy sauce, but why ketchup? We don't serve hamburgers or French fries.	我能理解為何需要醬油，但是，為什麼會有蕃茄醬？我們並不賣漢堡和薯條。
Lily	We have to have it anyway, because some foreigners put ketchup on everything. They especially like it on anything with eggs, or any beef items.	我們還是必須準備蕃茄醬，因為有些外國顧客吃什麼東西都會加蕃茄醬，尤其是加在蛋類和牛肉料理上。
Chris	I see; it's as important to them as soy sauce is to us.	我明白了。蕃茄醬對他們而言，就像醬油對我們一樣重要。
Lily	That's right; go ahead and fill up those bottles. I'll show you where we get the new ones from in the back when we get all **finished**.	沒錯。去將那些瓶子都裝滿。我要帶你去後頭，讓你看看我們從哪裡拿新的醬料，來補充用完的。

	(later)	（稍後）
Chris	Now that the condiments are done, what else do we need to do?	既然所有的醬料都處理完了，我們還要做什麼？
Lily	We need to help the assistants get all the plates and silverware out here for tomorrow. It's actually their responsibility, but we don't go home until they do, so everyone **helps out**. Why don't you go find some chopsticks, chopstick holders, and soup spoons? Do you remember where those are?	我們要幫助理們將所有的餐盤和銀器拿出來，好供明天用。這其實是他們的責任，但是他們沒完成之前，我們也不能回家，所以大家都會幫忙。你何不去拿筷子、筷架以及湯匙？你記得在哪兒嗎？
Chris	Yes, I think so. I'll be back in just a couple minutes.	好，應該記得。我一會兒就回來。
	(later)	（稍後）
Lily	All right, Chris, we have the station stocked really well. Oh wait, I forgot about napkins. Let's grab a **bundle** and start folding. The assistants will help us with that, and then we'll **head home**.	很好，Chris，我們工作站的備料都弄好了。噢，等會兒，我忘了還有餐巾了。去拿一包來摺吧。助理會幫我們一起摺，然後我們才能下班回家。

Word Bank

condiment(s) *n.[C]* 調味料；佐料　enough *adj.* 足夠的
ketchup *n.[U]* 蕃茄醬　empty *adj.* 空的　finished *adj.* 用完的
help(s) out 幫忙；幫助　bundle *n.[C]* 包；捆；束　head home 回家

Unit 11 餐廳陳設

 Job Titles and Descriptions 職稱與工作說明  Track 44

Introduction

Lily shows a new server some of the front-of-house jobs. Lily 給新進服務生示範外場工作。

Chris - Server Trainee 實習生
Lily - Server 服務生
Brian - Assistant Service Manager 客服副理
Laura - Server Assistant 助理服務生

Conversation

Brian	Hi, I don't think I've met you yet. I'm Brian, one of the assistant service managers.	你好，我們應該還沒見過。我是 Brian，其中一位客服副理。
Chris	Hi, I'm Chris. This is my first day.	你好，我叫 Chris。今天是我第一天上班。
Brian	Well Chris, I think Lily should take you around and tell you what some of the different jobs are. That way, you'll **get a feeling for** the **teamwork** that's necessary for us to all do our jobs here.	很好，Chris。請 Lily 帶你到各處參觀一下，告訴你不同的工作內容。如此你就能對這份工作所需要的團隊精神有個概念。
Lily	Good idea, Brian. First of all, up in the front of the room are the hosts. They're the ones the guests see first when they enter the restaurant. They always make sure the guest is greeted in a friendly way.	好主意，Brian。首先，餐廳最外頭的是接待人員。客人一進門最先看到的就是他們。接待員要始終確定客人受到友善的歡迎。
Chris	They show guests to their tables, right? What else do they do?	他們為客人帶位，對嗎？他們還負責什麼？

Lily	They have to **keep track of** all the reservations and make sure we have enough tables for the number of people we have coming in.	他們還必須控管所有的訂位狀況，確保我們有足夠的桌次接應上門的顧客。
Chris	Who's next?	我還要跟哪位見面？
Lily	You've already met Brian. There's one service manager **on duty** all the time.	你已經見過 Brian 了。我們這裡隨時都有一位值班的服務經理。
Chris	What do they do?	他們的工作職掌是？
Lily	They **keep an eye on** things and help us front-of-house people out. This is Laura, our server assistant today. She'll help us keep water glasses full and turn tables when guests leave. Laura, say hi to Chris.	他們負責監督所有作業，並協助外場人員的工作。這位是 Laura，今天的助理服務生。她將幫我們為客人巡桌倒茶水，並在客人離開以後協助翻桌作業。Laura，跟 Chris 打個招呼。
Laura	Hi Chris, just let me know if you need anything during the shift.	Chris，你好。工作期間有什麼需要，都可以讓我知道。
Chris	Thanks, Laura. For right now, I'm just trying to learn where everything is, so I'll ask if I need help.	謝謝妳 Laura。目前我正想辦法瞭解這地方的概況，若我有困難，一定會找妳。
Lily	There is another important job here, and that's the cashiers. They take the money from the guests when they're ready to pay the **check**. I'll introduce you to more people as we go along.	這兒還有一項重要的工作，那就是收銀員。當客人要結帳時，收銀員就負責收取費用。我會順道給你介紹更多其他人。

Word Bank

front-of-house *adj.* 外場的　server assistant 助理服務生
get a feeling for 對……有概念　teamwork *n.[U]* 團隊合作
keep track of 掌控　on duty 值勤　keep an eye on 注意　check *n.[C]* 帳單

Unit 11 餐廳陳設

泡茶　喝茶——中式飲食習慣

自秦漢時代開始，中國人便懂得飲茶，不過茶在當時是皇宮貴族才能品嘗的飲料，民間飲茶的風氣還不盛行。西晉以後，飲茶才漸漸由奢侈品變為一般百姓所能享用的飲料，此時一般百姓對於飲茶的接受度漸漸轉高，當時有詩描述：「芳茶冠六清，溢味播九區」，可見茶葉當時在民間受歡迎的程度。

到了三國時代，飲茶更為風行，甚至出現「以茶代酒」的飲食習俗。飲茶風氣到了唐代可說是鼎盛時期，飲茶方式大為進步，陸羽更著有茶經一書，書中載明當時百姓對於泡茶時水質的選擇、烹煮方式、飲茶環境和茶葉品質等，都有深入的論述。

中國人用餐飲茶已有幾千年歷史，各地中式料理都有其用餐適合搭配的茶，以下為大家略做介紹。

川菜搭配茉莉花茶：
川菜中在烹煮時常常會加入糖，搭配茉莉花茶，能讓美味在口中留存更久。

山東菜（魯菜）搭配熟普洱茶：
因為山東菜製作較為油膩、重鹽，用熟普洱茶配山東菜，有去油膩、促消化和清火排毒的功效。

上海菜（本幫菜）搭配龍井茶：
搭配龍井茶主要為了增加客戶品嘗後原來食材的餘味。

廣東菜（粵菜）搭配烏龍茶：
烏龍茶的烘培留有果香餘味，此大大補足廣東菜中欠缺的果香氣味，因此廣東菜喜愛搭配烏龍茶。

一般台灣餐廳當然無法如上述模式區分得如此仔細，但飲茶卻時有些訣竅可依循，以下歸納了餐點飲茶的重點規則：

- 茶香可消除用餐後的油膩感，最佳飲用時間為用餐中後段
- 清蒸類及淡味海鮮等口味較淡的菜餚，可配搭青茶、文山包種茶
- 紅燒、油膩重味的菜餚，可搭配滋味較強勁的鐵觀音、普洱茶
- 提供熱茶需沖泡約二至三分鐘，待入味後再端上
- 上茶時，可先盛上杯子的 6 至 7 分滿，引起茶香
- 了解沖茶溫度，掌握茶的品質
  - ⊙低溫（70℃ -80℃）
    沖泡龍井、碧螺春等帶嫩芽的綠茶類與黃茶類
  - ⊙中溫（80℃ -90℃）
    沖泡白毫烏龍等嫩採的烏龍茶，瓜片等採開面葉的綠茶，以及雖帶嫩芽，但重萎凋的白茶與紅茶
- 高溫（90℃ -100℃）
  沖泡採開面葉為主的烏龍茶，如包種、凍頂、鐵觀音、水仙、武夷岩茶等，以及後發酵的普洱茶。

學會了以上簡單的沖茶與上茶技巧，相信你的服務絕對會達到客戶滿意。

Unit 12 用餐服務

 *Appetizers* 開胃菜 

Introduction

A waiter explains some of the appetizer alternatives to a guest. 服務生向顧客介紹開胃菜選擇。

Characters

Tony - Server	服務生
Janice - Guest	顧客

Conversation

Tony	Good afternoon, it's nice to see you all today. I'll come back when you've had some time to look at the menu.	午安，歡迎各位今日的光臨。你們有一些時間看看餐單，我待會兒會再回來。
Janice	I think we'd like to order something to eat while we're deciding.	趁著我們正在做決定的時間，我想點些東西吃。
Tony	Let me show you our appetizer section of the menu, then. We have some delicious ones to choose from.	好的，請先看看菜單的開胃菜區。我們有一些好吃的小菜可以點。
Janice	I think we'd like to get several and then just share them. What do you think of the wined shrimp?	我想我們要點幾樣小菜，待會和他們分享。紅酒蝦怎麼樣？
Tony	That's a really good choice. They're medium-sized shrimp, lightly sautéed in red wine. It's a simple dish, but really good.	那真是不錯的選擇。我們選用中型的蝦子，加入紅酒爆香。做法雖然簡單，但非常美味。
Janice	And can you describe the caramelized matsuzaka pork? What kind of pork is that?	能請你介紹一下這道焦糖松阪豬嗎？這是什麼樣的豬肉？

Tony	It's some of the best pork you can get. It's known for the light fat which is present all through it. It's a rare meat, as there is only a little bit of it on each animal. It's roasted in the oven, then served with a **brown sugar** and **cinnamon** apple sauce.	松阪豬是很高檔的豬肉。它出名之處在於低油脂，且油花散佈各處，是很稀有的肉品，每頭豬只有一小部分能成為松阪肉。進烤箱烤過後，搭配黑糖肉桂蘋果醬汁一起上菜。
Janice	That sounds really good. We'll take one of those. And how about the **shredded** jellyfish salad?	聽起來真棒。我們要點一份松阪豬。涼拌海蜇絲沙拉如何呢？
Tony	The jellyfish is **dried**, then **tossed** with sea salt and light **soy sauce**. It's served with radish slices over a bed of fresh, local greens. It's a really good, traditional dish.	我們將海蜇絲瀝乾，再用海鹽及薄鹽醬油攪拌入味。海蜇絲搭配蘿蔔片，底下鋪滿新鮮的本地蔬菜。這是道非常好吃的傳統小菜。
Janice	I don't think we really want salad after all. Maybe the seafood **assortment**, but I don't understand it.	我們可不是那麼想吃沙拉，也許來個海鮮拼盤，但我不是很懂菜單上的說明。
Tony	We get that question a lot. Sea ear is another word for abalone, and mullet roe is the eggs of the mullet fish, lightly salted and sun-dried. It's served **chilled**, with a light **sake vinegar** on the side.	我們時常被問到這個問題。海耳是鮑魚的另一個稱呼；烏魚子是烏魚的卵，是稍微鹽漬且曬乾的成品。海鮮拼盤是冷盤，一旁附上清酒醋做沾醬。
Janice	Thanks for your help. We'll have one of those, with the shrimp and the pork.	謝謝你的協助。我們就來一份海鮮拼盤，還要蝦子跟豬排。

Word Bank

alternative(s) *n.[C]* 可供選擇之事物　several *adj.* 幾個　brown sugar 黑糖
cinnamon *n.[C/U]* 肉桂　shredded *adj.* 切成絲的　dried *adj.* 乾燥的
toss(ed) *v.* 拌　soy sauce 醬油　assortment *n.[C]* 總匯；什錦；雜燴
chilled *adj.* 冷的；涼的　sake vinegar 清酒醋

Unit 12 用餐服務

2 Entrées 主菜 Track 46

Introduction

A server is explaining some of the entrée choices to a guest. 服務生向顧客介紹主菜菜色

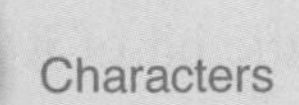

Characters

Lily - Server	服務生
Adam - Guest	顧客

Conversation

Adam	I really can't decide what I want. Can you give me some help?	我沒辦法決定要點什麼。你能給我一些建議嗎？
Lily	Sure, what would you like to know?	好的，您想瞭解什麼？
Adam	I'm interested in the crab with **ginger** and green onion. Do I have to take that out of the **shell** myself?	我想點這道薑蔥炒蟹。我需要自己剝蟹殼嗎？
Lily	No sir, that's already out of the shell.	不用的，先生。螃蟹已經去殼了。
Adam	And what about the **prawn** balls. I've never heard of those.	那麼，這個明蝦球是什麼？我沒聽過這道菜。
Lily	Those are shrimp that are ground up, like hamburger, then mixed with spices, a little red wine, onions, and **celery**. Then they're fried and served with the choices of sides you see on the menu. I like the black bean or pineapple sauce.	那是用蝦磨成泥做的，像漢堡肉一樣，再混入香料、些許紅酒、洋蔥和芹菜，然後油炸。蝦球可以搭配不同的配菜，如您在菜單上看到的。我喜歡配上豆豉或鳳梨醬吃。
Adam	Moving away from fish, which red meat would you recommend?	撇開魚不談，你會推薦哪一道紅肉？

Lily	The beef **slices** with **oyster sauce** is something you don't see every day. It's a good combination of meat with seafood.	不常看到的有蠔油牛肉這一道。它是一道肉食搭配海鮮的美好料理。
Adam	That sounds good. What other meats do you like?	聽起來很棒。你還想推薦什麼肉食？
Lily	The champagne pork **ribs** are really tasty. They get a little **messy** when you're eating them, but we give you a wet napkin to clean up with. Or, if you like chicken, the chicken with black bean sauce is nice.	我們的香檳肋排非常美味。食用時有點會弄髒自己，但我們提供濕紙巾給您清理。或是您若想吃雞肉，我們的豆豉醬雞很不錯。
Adam	You must like black beans.	你一定很喜歡豆豉吧。
Lily	I do, and our cooks do a really good job with them. This dish is sautéed in the sauce, then served on a bed of rice, with fresh vegetables, which today are asparagus.	的確，我們的廚師很會做豆豉料理。這道料理用豆豉醬爆香後，淋在飯上，再搭配新鮮蔬菜。今天的蔬菜是蘆筍。
Adam	That sounds really good, but I think I'll go with your recommendation and take the beef with oyster sauce.	聽起來真好吃，但是我想點你推薦的蠔油牛肉。
Lily	All right, I'll get that started for you, and I'll be back with your first course in a few minutes.	好的，就先由這一道開始。過一會兒，我會送上您的第一道菜。

Word Bank

choice(s) *n.[C]* 選擇　ginger *n.[U]* 薑　shell *n.[C/U]* 殼　prawn *n.[C]* 明蝦
celery *n.[U]* 芹菜　slice(s) *n.[C]* 薄片　oyster sauce 蠔油
rib(s) *n.[C]* 排骨；肋條　messy *adj.* 髒亂的

Unit 12 用餐服務

3 *Drinks* 飲料 Track 47

Introduction

A party of foreigners wants to try some different drinks. 一群外國顧客想嘗試不同的飲品。

Characters

Hermann - Guest	顧客
Tony - Server	服務生

Conversation

Hermann	Hi, we haven't been in Taipei very long. We'd like to try some drinks that are different from what we get **back home**.	嗨，我們剛來台北不久，想要試一試我們在家鄉喝不到的飲料。
Tony	Where are you from?	你們從哪兒來呢？
Hermann	We're from **Germany**.	我們來自德國。
Tony	Oh, then you must want beer.	噢，你們一定想喝啤酒吧。
Hermann	Oh, we've tried **Taiwan Beer**. We weren't too **thrilled** with it.	我們喝過台灣啤酒了，喝起來沒有太令人興奮。
Tony	You know, that's not the best beer, but then you figured that out already. For a long time, it was the only beer you could get in Taiwan. A lot of the locals still drink it, but it's not the only choice you have anymore.	你知道，那不是最好的啤酒，但你們已經領悟了。曾經有段很長的時間，在台灣只有台灣啤酒可以喝。很多在地人仍喝台灣啤酒，不過它已不再是你唯一的選擇了。
Hermann	We don't really want beer, anyway. We'd like tea to start.	反正，我們不是很想喝啤酒。我們想先點茶。
Tony	In Taiwan, that usually means **green tea**. I know a lot of restaurants in other countries serve **black tea**.	茶在台灣通常指的是綠茶。據我所知，其他國家的餐廳提供的是紅茶。

Hermann	No, green is just fine. It's supposed to be **healthy** for you, and most of us like it.	綠茶很好。對身體健康很有幫助，我們大部分人都很喜歡綠茶。
Tony	One other thing while you're thinking about tea: when you're out on the streets of Taiwan, there are lots of little drinks shops that serve **bubble tea**, which is sometimes called boba.	說到茶，還有另外一件事。你若走在台灣街上，會看到很多小茶飲店在賣珍珠奶茶，有時又稱波霸奶茶。
Hermann	You don't serve that? And what is it?	你們沒有珍珠奶茶嗎？那是什麼？
Tony	No, we don't have it, but it's a very Taiwanese drink. They serve it with these fat **straws** because it has little pieces of pudding inside. You eat them as you drink the tea. You should try it sometime.	沒有，我們沒賣珍珠奶茶。這是很有台灣特色的飲料。我們用粗吸管喝它，因為茶裡頭有小顆粒的粉圓。一邊喝茶，一邊吃粉圓。有機會應該要試試。
Hermann	I think we will. We want to try as many local things as we can while we're here.	我們會的。在這裡的這段期間，我們會盡可能多多嘗試地方小吃。
Tony	For now, I could recommend our mango juice blend. It's fresh mango juice and coconut milk, topped with chopped mango. That's probably something you won't find in Germany!	目前，我會推薦我們的芒果爽。這是用新鮮芒果跟椰奶攪打而成，上頭再鋪上芒果丁。你在德國可能喝不到！
Hermann	We'll try three of those, and green tea for everyone.	請給我們三杯芒果爽，再一人一杯綠茶。

Word Bank

foreigner(s) *n.[C]* 外國人　back home 回到家鄉　Germany *n.* 德國
Taiwan Beer 台灣啤酒　thrilled *adj.* 感到驚奇的　green tea 綠茶
black tea 紅茶　healthy *adj.* 健康的　bubble tea 珍珠奶茶
straw(s) *n.[C]* 吸管

Unit 12 用餐服務

4 *Desserts* 甜點 Track 48

Introduction

The foreigners want to try some desserts. 外國顧客想品嘗甜點。

Characters 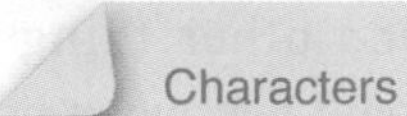 

Klaus - Guest 顧客
Tony - Server 服務生

Conversation

Tony	Here's the dessert menu. I'll be back when you've had some time to speak German to each other.	這是我們的甜點菜單。你們有點時間用德語討論一下，我待會兒回來。
	(Tony comes back)	（Tony 回到桌邊）
Tony	Hi, do you have any questions about the desserts?	你們好，關於甜點，有沒有什麼疑問？
Klaus	We'd like to know about the pumpkin **pastry**. It sounds a lot like the pumpkin pie we have at home.	我們想瞭解一下這個南瓜酥，聽起來很像我們那邊的南瓜派。
Tony	It's not really pie; it's a square, light flour pastry filled with an egg **custard** made from pumpkin. It has a cinnamon **glaze** on top, and is served with a small bit of whipped cream.	那不太像是派，它是方形的油酥餅，裡頭填滿用南瓜做的奶黃。南瓜酥上塗了一層薄肉桂，配上一點生奶油一起用。
Klaus	We like pumpkin, so we might think about that one. What else do you like?	我們喜歡南瓜，應該會想點南瓜酥。還有什麼你推薦的？
Tony	If you like something that is very Taiwanese, you should try the mango **sago** cream with **pomelo**.	如果你想來點台灣道地的點心，你應該嘗嘗這個柚香芒果西米露。

Klaus	Wow! That has a lot of different ingredients.	哇！這裡頭有很多種不同的食材。
Tony	Yes, it does. The mango makes it sweet, and it has some sago, made from **palm trees**, which holds it together. The pomelo is a tree we grow locally. The fruit looks and tastes like grapefruit, but it can be as big as a volleyball. Things grow really well in the Taiwan **climate**.	是的。芒果增添甜味，裡頭的西米是棕櫚樹提煉成，才能凝固成西米。柚子來自本土種植的柚樹，它果實的外觀和口味都很像葡萄柚，但柚子能長得跟一顆排球一樣大。在台灣的氣候下，作物長得很好。
Klaus	Yes, we have noticed that it's very green. Does it rain a lot?	沒錯，我們注意到台灣十分綠意盎然。這裡常下雨嗎？
Tony	Yes, you have to be able to appreciate rain if you live here, especially in the north. What other desserts were you thinking of?	對，您若住在這兒，會見識到這裡的雨量，尤其在北部。您還想到哪些甜點？
Klaus	Can you explain the **lotus seed** with **red bean** pasta? We've never had pasta for dessert before.	可以請你介紹這道蓮子紅豆沙包嗎？我們沒吃過豆沙包之類的點心。
Tony	Lotus seeds are a traditional, healthy snack. They even use some types in **Chinese medicine**. Red beans are sweet beans and are very popular in Taiwan. So it's a sweet pasta, not like spaghetti.	蓮子是一道傳統又健康的點心，也被當成中藥使用。紅豆是有甜味的豆子，在台灣非常普遍。這道是甜味酥包，不是像義大利麵條那種。
Klaus	We'll talk this over a bit. Meanwhile, could you bring us all some coffee?	我們會再討論一下。同時可以請你先給我們大家咖啡嗎？

Word Bank

pastry *n.[C/U]* 油酥餅　custard *n.[U]* 奶黃醬；卡士達醬
glaze *n.[C/U]* 使食物有光澤的糖液外層　sago *n.[U]* 西米
pomelo *n.[C/U]* 柚子　palm tree(s) 棕櫚樹　climate *n.[C/U]* 氣候
lotus seed 蓮子　red bean 紅豆　Chinese medicine 中藥

Unit 12 用餐服務

Tips for Workplace Happiness
職場補給站
加油大使 Cheryl 來充電！

好吃派頭大的中式料理

中國菜區分有四大菜系（魯菜、川菜、粵菜、蘇菜）或是八大菜系（魯菜、川菜、粵菜、蘇菜、閩菜、浙菜、湘菜、徽菜），中國菜的特點被總結為色、香、味、意、形，被稱為國菜五品。按烹飪特點分又可分為選料、刀工、火候和調味四個方面。

中國菜的特色除了味道多樣化外，選材絕對是非常豐富，有一句俗語稱「山中走獸雲中燕，陸地牛羊海底鮮」，從中可知中國料理幾乎所有能吃的東西，都可以做為食材，但食材的選擇又關係到菜色的質量。

四大菜系特色

魯菜（山東菜）：

魯菜可說是北食的代表菜系，因所處區域靠山近海，菜色山海皆有，菜色體系包括沿海以海鮮為主的膠東菜和內陸的濟南菜以及孔府菜等三大流派。魯菜講究調味純正，口味偏鹹鮮，具有鮮、嫩、香、脆的特色，特點為清香、鮮嫩、味醇，十分講究清湯和奶湯的調製，清湯色清而鮮，奶湯色白而醇，且擅長以蔥香來調味，烹煮海鮮甚有特色。其代表菜有：糖醋黃河鯉魚 、濟南烤鴨、八寶鴨子、蔥燒海參。

川菜（四川菜）：

四川離海較遠，因此以河鮮、菌類、乾貨、山珍為特色，口味以麻、辣、鮮、香為特色，以一菜一味，百菜百味著名，其烹調有四個特點，一是選料認真、二是刀工精細、三是合理搭配、四是精心烹調。據傳川菜烹煮共有 38 種方式，特別在炒的方面有其獨到之處，川菜很多菜式都採用小炒方法，特點是時間短、火候急、汁水少、口味鮮嫩。其代表菜有：宮保雞丁、干燒魚、回鍋肉、麻婆豆腐、魚香肉絲。

粵菜（廣東菜）：

廣東菜最大的特點為花款多、味道鮮。廣東地處亞熱帶，瀕臨南海，雨量充沛，除海鮮外，亦會食用特殊野生動物如蛇等，又因天氣炎熱，食材不宜久存，以生猛、鮮為主，廣東菜烹煮特色為使用少量的香料，故對原料的新鮮程度要求嚴格。其代表菜有：鮑參翅肚、燕窩、烤乳豬、燒鴨、燒鵝、燒乳鴿、廣式點心、梅菜扣肉。

蘇菜（淮揚菜）：

淮揚菜的特色尤為注意鮮活、鮮嫩，口味清淡但強調本味，重視調湯風味清鮮，菜色著重製作精細注意刀工，且色彩搭配鮮艷清爽悅目，烹飪善用火候，擅長燉、燜、煨、蒸、燒、炒等。其代表菜有：叫化子雞、糖醋鱖魚、清燉蟹粉獅子頭，滿漢全席即為蘇菜的名宴之一。

Unit 13 服務生訓練

1 *Talking to Tables* 點餐接待

Track 49

Introduction

Lily talks to her trainee about interacting with guests. 莉莉教導她的實習生如何與客人互動。

Characters

Chris - Server Trainee	實習生
Lily - Server	服務生

Conversation

Lily	Now that we're open, I can start teaching you about serving the tables.	既然餐廳開門了，我來教你如何進行餐桌的服務。
Chris	That would be good. The idea of talking to them makes me a little **nervous**.	那很好。想到要跟客人說話讓我有點緊張。
Lily	That's pretty **normal**, but most people are nice. Pretend you're talking to your friends, and you'll be all right.	這很正常，但大多數的顧客都很和善。你只要當成是跟你的朋友說話，一切都會很順利。
Chris	Thanks, I'll try to remember that.	謝謝，我會記住這一點。
Lily	We just got our first table. Listen and watch for a while, and later I'll let you do some of it **on your own**.	我們的第一桌客人來了。先跟在我身旁邊聽邊看一會兒，然後再讓你親自做其中的一些服務。
Chris	Thanks, I'm very anxious to learn.	謝謝，我會非常渴望學習。
Lily	It'll take them a while to decide what they want to eat, and we want to give the assistants time to pour water for them, too. After they've been here a couple minutes, **wander** by and just let them know who is responsible for taking care of them.	客人需要一段時間去決定想要點些什麼，我們也希望給助理時間替他們倒水。他們待幾分鐘之後，你可以在附近走動一下，好讓他們知道誰負責服務他們。
Chris	What do people usually order first?	客人通常都先點什麼？

Lily	Some foreigners want to get something to drink **right away**, so if you have them, ask. Most other people will just order everything at once.	有些外國人習慣先點喝的，所以如果遇到這情形，先詢問看看。其他大部分人則會馬上點每一樣東西。
Chris	How do you tell when they're ready to order?	你怎麼知道他們什麼時候準備點餐？
Lily	Sometimes, you'll be able to see that everyone is done looking at the menu. Other times, the person who is going to order for everyone will **look around** for you. You'll figure it out soon enough.	有時，你會看見每個人都看完菜單。有時，幫大家點餐的那個人會東張西望地找你。你很快就會辨識出來。
Chris	Do we have to talk to each person, or do we just talk to the leader?	我們要問每一位客人要點什麼，還是只問那個帶頭幫大家點餐的人呢？
Lily	Since we serve family-style, one person will often order for the **whole** table. Just talk to that person, but look at the others, too. After that, you just need to be there through the meal, **in case** anyone needs anything else.	因為我們的服務性質偏向家庭式，所以通常都會有一個客人幫大家點整桌的菜。只要跟這個人討論就好，但也要注意其他客人。之後整餐飯間，你只需要隨侍在側，以防萬一有人需要加點別的。
Chris	That doesn't sound so bad. I think I can do it after all.	聽起來沒有那麼糟。我覺得我理當可以勝任。

Word Bank

interact(ing) with 與……誰互動　nervous *adj.* 緊張的　normal *adj.* 正常的
on your own 靠自己的　wander *v.* 走動；徘徊　right away 馬上
look around 尋找　whole *adj.* 全部的　in case 萬一；以免

Unit 13 服務生訓練

2 Recommending Dishes 推薦菜色 Track 50

Introduction

A server is recommending appetizers for a table.

服務生給客人的開胃菜建議。

Lily - Server	服務生
Iris - Guest	顧客
Josie - Guest	顧客
Rodney - Guest	顧客

Conversation

Iris	Your menu is huge!	你們的菜色真多啊！
Lily	Yes, we do have a lot of things to choose from. Do you have questions about anything?	沒錯，我們確實有很多東西可供選擇。您有任何疑問嗎？
Iris	I do; I have lots of questions. I want to get a **first course**. What would you suggest?	確實；我有很多問題。我想點第一道菜。你會建議什麼？
Lily	Most of our appetizers are **designed** to be shared, so you should just order several for your table. Then everyone can have a little of something different.	我們的開胃菜大多是設計成可以分食的份量，因此你可以替這一桌多點幾道菜。這樣每個人都可以吃到一些不同的小菜。
Iris	I still don't know where to start on the menu, though.	但我仍然不知道要從菜單的哪裡開始點起。
Lily	Well, let's narrow it down a little. Do you think you'd like salad, **poultry**, red meat, or fish?	好吧，我們把範圍縮小一些。您喜歡沙拉、禽肉、紅肉、或者魚呢？
Iris	I do think I want something with fish in it, but my **daughter** and her friend would **prefer** some red meat.	我很想吃有魚的餐點，但我女兒和她朋友比較喜歡有紅肉的餐點。

Lily	That's no problem. If, by fish, you also include shrimp, then the shrimp cocktail is something I always recommend. If you want a combination, the sliced abalone & goose palm gives you a little meat along with some seafood.	沒有問題。有魚的餐點，如果也包括蝦子，我大都建議客人點雞尾酒蝦。如果你想要一個綜合口味，餐裡還可放鮑魚片、鵝掌，組成一個海陸拼盤。
Iris	I know about abalone; what is goose palm?	鮑魚我知道，但鵝掌是什麼？
Lily	Those are the feet of the goose that are slowly cooked in orange peels and spices.	是用橙皮和香料慢火烹煮的鵝腳掌。
Iris	No thanks, that doesn't really sound like what I want.	不用了，謝謝，聽起來不像是我想吃的菜。
Lily	You said you were intercsted in red meat. How about pork? I really like the pork with shiitake mushrooms. What does your daughter think of that?	您説您有興趣嘗嘗紅肉。豬肉怎麼樣？我很喜歡豬肉配上香菇。不知您女兒意下如何？
Josie	I think pork and mushrooms sounds really good. Get that for Adrian and me, Mom.	豬肉配上蘑菇聽起來很美味。媽媽，請幫我跟 Adrian 都點這道菜吧。
Iris	OK, one of those, and one shrimp. Then we need one other, I think.	好的，除了這個。再一個蝦。我想，我們還需要加點另外一道。
Rodney	I'll take the goose palm. I've never had that before. I'm feeling adventurous.	我要鵝掌，我從來沒有吃過，想大膽嘗試一點新奇的東西。
Lily	Thank you, I'll get the cooks to start those for you.	謝謝，我請廚師開始製作您點的菜。

Word Bank

first course 第一道菜 design(ed) *v.* 設計 poultry *n.[U]* 家禽；家禽肉
daughter *n.[C]* 女兒 prefer *v.* 偏好 include *v.* 包括 abalone *n.[C]* 鮑魚
goose palm 鵝掌 peel(s) *n.[C]* 表皮 adventurous *adj.* 愛冒險的

Unit 13 服務生訓練

Special Promotions 特別促銷

Track 51

Introduction

A magazine promotion is discussed at a staff meeting. 員工會議上討論雜誌宣傳方法。

Characters

Arthur - General Manager 總經理
Lily - Server 服務生
Tony - Server 服務生
Laura - Server Assistant 助理服務生

Conversation

Arthur Thanks for coming to this meeting, everyone. We're going to be **placing an ad** in *Taipei Walker* **magazine** this month. We hope that it works and makes us a little busier, so I wanted you to know beforehand.
感謝大家出席本次會議。我們要在這個月的 Taipei Walker 雜誌刊登一則廣告。希望廣告能有效果，讓大家更忙一些，所以我想讓大家事先知道這件事。

Lily Is there any promotion with the ad, or is it just a general advertisement?
它是加了入促銷活動在內的廣告，還是一般廣告呢？

Arthur There is a promotion. We're giving **10% off** to anyone who says they saw it in *Taipei Walker*.
這個廣告有一項促銷活動。任何人只要說他們在 Taipei Walker 看到廣告，我們就提供九折優惠。

Tony There's no **coupon** or anything we have to worry about?
有沒有優惠券或任何我們要掛慮的地方？

Arthur No, they just have to say they saw the ad, and they get 10% off their **entire** check. This lets us know how many people actually saw the ad, and it will hopefully get people to **come back**, when they find out how good the food and service are.
沒有，只要他們說看過這則廣告，結帳時就可享有九折優惠。這可以讓我們知道，有多少人確實看到這則廣告，希望他們因為發現我們的食物與服務有多好，而再度光顧。

Lily	So, we have to make the food and service really good.	所以我們必須確實提供真正好的食物與服務。
Arthur	I'm not worried about that; just do your **usual** good job, and this promotion should bring us some more business now and in the future.	這我並不擔心，只要善盡你們平時的本份就好，這個廣告促銷應該會在此時與未來持續帶給我們更多生意。
Tony	How do we ring this up on the computer?	怎麼用電腦處理折扣優惠？
Arthur	Ring it in like any normal order. After everything is ordered, find a manager, and they'll take off the 10%. Make sure to remind the guests that they got the discount. That way, they'll remember they got a **good deal** here.	處理方式跟平常一樣。完成點餐後，請經理來將 10% 的折扣從帳單裡扣除。一定要將九折優惠告知顧客。這樣，他們便會記得在這裡得了一筆好交易。
Laura	How much extra business do you think this will bring in?	你認為這樣做會增加多少業績呢？
Arthur	It's a pretty popular magazine, so we expect some increase in business. We won't be putting any extra **staff** on yet, but we'll watch the books and see how it looks. Some of you may be able to get some more hours.	這是一本很受歡迎的雜誌，所以我們預期業績會有些增長。我們尚不增加員工，但會看看訂位反應如何。你們有些人可能工作時數會增加。

Word Bank

discuss(ed) *v.* 討論　placing an ad 放置廣告（place）　magazine *n.[U]* 雜誌
10% off 打九折　coupon *n.[C/U]* 優惠券　entire *adj.* 整個　come back 回來
usual *adj.* 通常的　a good deal 一個很划算的交易　staff *n.[C]* 工作人員

Unit 13 服務生訓練

 Providing Professional Advice 提供專業意見  Track 52

Introduction

A server is learning how to recommend a dish a guest will enjoy. 服務生學習如何向顧客推薦一道滿意餐點。

Characters

Chris - Server Trainee 實習生
Lily - Server 服務生

Conversation

Chris	What do you do when a guest asks for advice on what to order? What's the best thing on the menu?	當客人問你關於點菜的意見時，你要如何回答？什麼菜是菜單中最好的？
Lily	One thing you should realize is that there is no one "best" thing. You have to **read your guest** and ask them questions. Then you can figure out what will be the best thing for them.	你必須明白的是，菜單裡並沒有「最好」的菜。你必須讀出客人的心思，並問他們一些問題。那樣你才能揣摩得出對他們來說，什麼樣的菜色最好。
Chris	What **sorts** of things do you need to do when you read a guest?	要了解客人，你需要做哪類事情呢？
Lily	First of all, you need to get them to tell you what kind of food they're interested in. If you really like beef, but they want something low in calories, it won't matter what you like. You need to **steer** them to something they want.	首先，你要讓他們告訴你，那一類菜他們有興趣。如果你實在喜歡牛肉，但他們希望低卡食物，這與你的喜好無關。你需要朝他們想吃的去推薦。
Chris	What would you recommend if they want a **low-calorie** meal?	如果他們想要低卡路里餐，你有什麼建議嗎？

Lily	A lot of the seafood dishes are very healthy, and people who want healthy things will often like fish, anyway. I'd recommend something like the three sauce stewed **fish balls**, or one of the steamed fish entrées.	海鮮類的菜色都很健康，健康取向的人反正會喜歡魚料理。我會建議三杯魚丸或清蒸魚的主菜。
Chris	How about someone who wants something special, and they don't really care how many calories it has?	若是客人想要嘗鮮，但不在乎卡路里，你會怎麼建議？
Lily	Find out if they want red meat, chicken, or if they're **open to suggestions**. **For example**, the sweet & sour pork ribs are an **excellent** choice, as is the roasted chicken. But if they want a great suggestion, you should tell them about the seafood **curry**. That's my choice for best thing on the menu.	問他們想點紅肉、雞肉或者可聽聞建議。例如：糖醋排骨以及烤雞都是絕佳選擇。但如果他們要更好的意見，可以建議他們咖哩海鮮，這是我在菜單上最好的選擇。
Chris	That's of great help. I'll have to try that soon.	非常謝謝你的説明，我會試試看。
Lily	We'll get you back in the kitchen one day soon and let you try all the sauces and some of the dishes. That will make it a lot easier for you to make recommendations.	總有一天我們會儘快讓你回到廚房這一塊，讓你嘗過所有醬料及一些菜色。那將使你更容易對顧客做出建議。

Word Bank

enjoy *v.* 享受　read your guest 解讀你的客戶　sort(s) *n.[C]* 種類
steer *v.* 引導　low-calorie *adj.* 低熱量的　fish ball(s) 魚丸
open to suggestions 樂於接受建議　for example 例如
excellent *adj.* 出色的；優秀的　curry *n.[U]* 咖哩；咖哩粉

Unit 13 服務生訓練

服務是貼近需要，不是有就好——服務技巧

服務不是有就好，而是要貼近客戶的需要。提供飲水對於餐廳是一般迎賓的基礎流程，而以下我要分享的餐廳，對於這個基礎服務，卻堅持適時變更，配合貼近客戶需求。

日前我與友人敘舊，相約一家歷史悠久的連鎖餐廳，其實我是這家餐廳的常客，喜歡前往的原因沒有別的，就是人員的服務讓我感覺很接近我的需求。

餐廳區分為室內區與室外區，當天我們於室外區用餐。室外區難免會因天氣變化而感覺寒冷或是炎熱，那天我們於中午前往，天氣略為炎熱，服務人員於我們就座後，主動遞上冰涼的茶水，讓我們感覺舒適些，一瞬間不自覺得來到近傍晚，而傍晚的天氣稍冷，服務人員後續主動更換提供熱騰騰的茶，其實這是個小細節，我想對於很多人可能不會發現，但對於我來說這樣的服務卻非常貼近我的需求。

那怎樣的餐廳服務才可稱得上貼近客戶需要呢？讓我來細細說明給大家了解。

服務的基本——穩定

穩定的服務流程是服務的基本，一套好的服務需要明訂服務的方式，且穩定服務品質，每位服務人員的服務需無差異性，且達到公司確定之標準。

適當的問候用語

禮貌六句要常掛嘴邊：歡迎光臨、好的、請您稍後、讓您久等、對不起、謝謝，搭配微笑表達增加客戶喜愛。

服務要愉快

出自內心的喜愛服務，客戶是感受得到的，不急不徐的服務步驟，可以讓客戶跟著服務人員的節奏享受愉快的服務。

觀察、配合客戶

服務客戶時要顧及其他服務人員的方便性及客人的舒適性，其服務規則因空間、環境、客戶習慣而異，但其基本原則節錄如下

- 餐點需從客人的左邊、服務人員的左手端上
- 飲品需從客人的右邊、服務人員右手端上，湯則左右皆可
- 空盤子從客人的右邊、服務人員右手撤走
- 服務人員需從客人面前服務，千萬不可從背後出現

適時、適度關心

客戶用餐時，服務人員可適時地關心或詢問客戶的需求，例如餐具掉了，迅速更換新的餐具，客戶用餐中翻閱菜單，適時上前詢問是否有需要加點其他餐點。

以上的服務技巧看似簡單，其實不甚容易，畢竟餐廳用餐時間服務人員都是非常忙碌，是否有時間觀察到如此細微，有時需要些經驗及配合餐廳人力安排。

Unit 14 廚房概況

 Understanding Special Ingredients 瞭解特殊食材  Track 53

Introduction

The chef explains some menu items to some new servers. 行政主廚向新手服務生介紹菜單項目。

Characters

Greg - Chef	行政主廚
Chris - Server Trainee	實習生
Eric - Server Trainee	實習生

Conversation

Greg	We had you come in early today so I could explain some of the ingredients in our sauces and **recipes**. Does anyone have any questions before we start?	我們要你今天早點來，好讓我可以跟你解說一些醬汁和食譜的成分。在我們開始之前，有人有任何問題嗎？
Chris	I was wondering about **lemongrass**. I mean, lemons grow on trees, so what is lemongrass?	我有一點關於檸檬草（檸檬香茅）的疑問。我的意思是，既然檸檬是生長在樹上的，那怎麼會有檸檬「草」呢？
Greg	That's a good question, Chris. It's an **herb** we use in the poached salmon, which is one of the better-selling healthy dishes on our menu.	這是一個好問題，Chris。我們用檸檬草這種草本植物來給水煮鮭魚調味，這道菜是我們菜單上銷售很好的健康菜餚之一。
Eric	That is a good question; I'd never heard of lemongrass either, before I read our menu.	這是一個好問題；在閱讀我們的菜單之前，我從來沒聽說過檸檬香茅。
Greg	Lemongrass is actually a grass. It only has the "lemon" name because it has a flavor similar to lemons. It's used in lots of Asian dishes.	檸檬草確實是一種草。它之所以用「檸檬」來命名，只因它有類似檸檬的味道。許多亞洲美食都使用香茅調味。
Chris	Now I understand.	我現在明白了。

Greg	Let's talk about a couple other things. You'll notice we use a lot of ginger in our cooking. Ginger is a **root** that has a very **distinct**, almost **spicy** flavor. It's used worldwide but originally comes from Asia. This is what it looks like.	我們再來談談其他的一些事。你會注意到我們在餐點中使用了很多薑。薑是植物的根，它有非常獨特，幾近辛辣的味道。它在全世界廣泛受到使用，但最初源自於亞洲。這就是它的長相。
Eric	That looks like an ugly potato.	它看起來就像一個難看的洋芋。
Greg	They are both roots, so that's why you think they look similar. Over here, this is curry **powder**. I'm sure you've had curry before, but maybe you haven't seen how it's cooked. This is a green curry powder, but there are lots of different colors and combinations of spices available.	它們都是植物的根部，所以你會覺得它們看起來很相似。這兒，這是咖哩。我敢說，你們雖然曾經看過咖哩粉，但也許你們並不知道如何煮它。這是綠色的咖哩粉，但它還有許多不同的顏色，另有一些調味料組合可用。
Chris	So, it's not just one spice that's called curry?	所以說，咖哩並不是單指一種香料？
Greg	No, if you go to India, you'll find many different curry powder **blends**.	是的，如果在印度，你會看到許多不同的咖哩粉混合成的不同香料。
Eric	What else goes in a curry?	有什麼咖哩做成的料理嗎？
Greg	Our curry **laksa** soup has noodles and **coconut milk**. It's not for people who are afraid of a few **spices**, that's for sure. Now, over here...	我們的咖哩叻沙湯含麵條，是混合椰奶做的。不用說，怕辣的人不適合。現在，過來這裡……

Part I Part II Part III Part IV Part V Part VI

Word Bank

recipe(s) *n.[C]* 食譜　lemongrass *n.[U]* 香茅　herb *n.[U]* 草本植物
root *n.[C]* 根　distinct *adj.* 不同的　spicy *adj.* 辛辣的　powder *n.[U]* 粉
blend(s) *n.[C]* 混合品　laksa *n.[U]* 叻沙　coconut milk 椰奶
spice(s) *n.[C]* 辛香料

Unit 14 廚房概況

2 *Cooking Methods* 烹調方式 Track 54

Introduction

The kitchen tour continues, as Greg shows new servers how things are done. 繼續參觀廚房，Greg向新服務生示範烹調方式。

Characters

Greg - Chef	行政主廚
Chris - Server Trainee	實習生
Eric - Server Trainee	實習生

Conversation

Eric	Are we going to talk about cooking **methods** today, too? I'm a little weak in that area.	我們今天也會談論烹調方法嗎？我在這方面不太行。
Greg	I think that's a really good idea.	我認為這真是個好主題。
Eric	Then I have a question. What's a **casserole**? I saw our scallop chicken casserole on the menu. How is that **fixed**?	那麼我有個問題。焗烤是什麼？我看到我們的菜單上有焗烤干貝雞，那是怎麼混合的？
Greg	A casserole means that the dish is baked in the oven. Casseroles usually have a **crunchy** crust on top, and quite often have melted cheese on top as well.	焗烤是指這道餐點放在烤爐裡用高溫烘焙。焗烤上面通常會覆蓋一層碎麵包皮，且常會有融化的起司在上頭。
Chris	So, our scallop chicken is a baked item. How does that **differ from** roasting?	那麼，我們的焗烤干貝雞屬於烘焙類。與燒烤有何不同？
Greg	Roasting usually refers to meat. It's a way of cooking meat slowly in the oven. Casseroles go in the oven, too, but the meats inside are **already** cooked. The oven is just for heating all the ingredients and melting the cheese on the top.	燒烤通常用來指對生肉的烹調方法，就是將肉類放進烤箱慢慢烹調至熟。焗烤也在烤箱內烹調，但裡面的肉原本就已經煮熟。烤箱是要加熱所有食材，並且使頂部的起司融化。

Eric	What other cooking methods should we learn?	我們還要學習什麼其他的烹飪方法？
Greg	Let's talk about **steaming**. We do this with a lot of our fish, especially when they're served whole.	讓我們談談清蒸。我們菜單上的魚有很多都用這種方法料理，尤其是全魚料理。
Chris	Is steaming different from **boiling**?	清蒸與水煮有不一樣嗎？
Greg	Yes, in boiling you put the food right down into the water. Steaming just uses the heat from the boiling water to cook. It's a very healthy way to cook, and it keeps more of the **vitamins** in the food than boiling.	是不一樣，水煮是指把食物放進沸水中煮熟，而清蒸是用水滾開後的蒸氣蒸煮。清蒸是一種非常健康的烹調法，它比水煮保留了更多食物中的維生素。
Eric	I suppose **shabu shabu** is also a way of cooking. But we don't have to actually cook that, do we?	我想涮涮鍋是另一種烹調的方式。但是，我們並沒有實際參與烹調過程，對嗎？
Greg	The guests cook their own **hot pot**, but it involves a lot of prep work for us. It takes a long time to slice and cut all those ingredients, and to prepare the spiced **broth**.	雖然客人烹煮自己的火鍋食材，但我們仍須做很多的準備工作。所有食材都要先切成小塊和切片。準備高湯要花很多時間。
Eric	Thanks for the tour, Greg. It was very informative.	感謝您的導覽，Greg。我們獲益良多。

Word Bank

method(s) *n.[C]* 方法　casserole *n.[C/U]* 焗烤　fix(ed) *v.* 製作；準備
crunchy *adj.* 酥脆的　differ from 不同於　already *adv.* 已經
steam(ing) *v.* 蒸煮　boiling *adj.* 烹煮；沸騰　vitamin(s) *n.[C]* 維生素
shabu shabu 涮涮鍋　hot pot 火鍋　broth *n.[U]* 高湯；清湯

Unit 14 廚房概況

3 *Placing Orders* 下單 Track 55

Introduction

A server and a trainee are talking about how to order food from the kitchen. 一位服務生和一位實習生在談論如何下單給廚房。

Characters

Tony - Server 服務生
Eric - Server Trainee 實習生
Mardy - Guest 顧客

Conversation

Tony	Good evening, folks. Thanks for **coming in**. Would you like a little more time to take a look at the menu?	各位晚安，感謝光臨 。是否要更多一點時間看菜單？
Mardy	Yes, I think we need just a few minutes to **talk things over**.	是的，我們還需要再商量幾分鐘。
Tony	All right, I'll return **shortly**.	好的，我過一會再回來。
	(at the sidestand)	（在備餐檯旁邊）
Eric	I have a question: After you **take the order**, how do you know when to ring it in so you get the right courses in the **right order**?	我有個問題：客人點菜後，我們要如何依序向廚房下單，才能讓餐點依照正確順序出菜呢？
Tony	I'll show you as soon as we get the order from this table. I think they're ready.	等這桌客人點完菜後，我會示範給你看。他們的菜應該已經點好了。
	(back at the table)	（回到餐桌旁）
Tony	You'd like the seafood assortment and a jellyfish salad to start, then the **crispy** rice scallops, a garlic jumbo prawns, and one steamed grouper. After the meal, the crab pumpkin soup. And one big bottle of Taiwan Beer. Thank you, I'll be right back with your beer.	您點的前菜是海鮮拼盤和海蜇沙拉，然後是鍋巴扇貝、一個蒜香大蝦和一個清蒸石斑魚。吃完主餐，上蟹肉南瓜湯。再來一個大瓶台灣啤酒。謝謝你，我等會兒就先幫您將啤酒送過來。

	(by the computer)	（在電腦旁）
Eric	They ordered a lot of food. How do you time it?	他們點了好多食物。如何抓好時間呢？
Tony	They ordered beer and appetizers first, so that's what we'll ring in now. We need to put some beer glasses on the table.	他們先點了啤酒和開胃菜，所以我們請廚房先做開胃菜。我們先把一些啤酒杯擺好放桌上。
Eric	Then when do you order the rest of the food?	接下來，你要如何向廚房點其餘的菜色呢？
Tony	You have to learn which things take a long time and which ones are **pretty quick**. Since the steamed grouper is a whole fish, that will take a while. So, we'll order it right when the appetizers **come up**.	你必須了解哪些菜需要很長的烹調時間，而哪些菜很快可以完成。由於清蒸石斑魚是烹煮一整條魚，需要一段長時間。因此，上完開胃菜，就要立刻請廚房開始做魚。
Eric	Does everything else they ordered cook **slowly**, too?	他們點的菜還有什麼是需要較長時間烹煮的呢？
Tony	No, the prawns are really fast, but the baked scallops **take a while**. The soup is already made, so we just pick that up when they're ready for it. You just need to learn the menu, then it'll be easy. Let's go get their beer.	沒有了，蝦子可以很快完成，但烘烤扇貝需要一段時間。而湯品已經煮好備用，當客人需要時，我們就可以呈上。你只要確實了解菜單上的菜色，之後就很容易判定了。我們拿啤酒去給他們吧。

Word Bank

coming in 光臨（come） talk things over 商量事情 shortly *adv.* 不久；馬上
take the orders 拿到客人的點菜單 right order 正確的順序 crispy *adj.* 脆的
pretty quick 相當快 come up 來；出現 slowly *adv.* 慢慢地
take a while 花費一段時間

Unit 14 廚房概況

4 *Staff Interaction* 員工互動  Track 56

Introduction

The staff are talking to each other during the shift.

工作人員在送餐過程中互相交談。

Characters  

Eric - Server Trainee	實習生
Lily - Server	服務生
Laura - Server Assistant	助理服務生
Greg - Chef	行政主廚
Tony - Server	服務生
Jeff - Cook	廚師

Conversation

Eric	Hey Greg, I have a question about the special tonight, the spicy vinegar **pig's knuckle**. What exactly is a pig's knuckle?	嘿，Greg，我有一個關於今晚特餐酸辣豬蹄的問題。豬蹄到底是什麼？
Greg	A pig's knuckle is the **joint** that connects the foot to the leg. These are quite often made into **ham**, but we roast it slowly in a pan with the spicy vinegar.	豬蹄是指連接腳與腿的關節部位。這些部位經常被製成火腿，但我們這道菜是將這個部位用辣醋醬以慢火在平底鍋煎烤。
Eric	OK Greg, thanks. I'll get back out on the floor now.	瞭解了，Greg，謝謝。我先回到工作崗位上了。
	(at a table)	（在餐桌邊）
Laura	Hey Eric, could you help me change the tablecloth on this table? The one that's on there has a **tear** in it.	嗨，Eric，你能不能幫我替這張桌子換桌布？原本的那塊桌布有個破洞。
Eric	Sure, let me pick up the turntable first. Now we can get the round cloth on there.	當然可以，讓我先把桌上的旋轉盤拿起來。現在，我們可以把圓桌布鋪上去。

Laura	And now the diagonal one. Thanks for the help. Do you need anything?	再來是這塊鋪對角的桌布，感謝你的幫忙。有沒有需要我幫你忙的地方呢？
Eric	Not right now, but I'm sure I will later.	現在不用，但之後一定有。
Tony	Laura, can you help me? I need some water in those water pitchers, but I have to finish setting this table first.	Laura，可以請你幫個忙嗎？我得在這些水壺裡裝一些水，但是我必須先布置好這張桌子。
Laura	Which do you want me to do?	你要我做什麼？
Tony	Let me go get the water. Could you **place** all the settings on the table?	我要去裝水。你可以把所有的餐具擺在這張桌子上嗎？
Laura	Sure, I'd **be happy to**.	當然，我很樂意。
	(in the kitchen)	（在廚房裡）
Jeff	Lily, you have an **order up**.	Lily，你有一張單的餐點做好了。
Lily	OK, I'll be right there. Eric, could you check and make sure it's **complete**? And then you can carry it out, but wait for me first.	好的，我馬上就來。Eric，你能去檢查一下，確定菜已經備妥了嗎？然後你就可以上菜了，但要先等我一下。
Eric	Hey **wheel man**, I don't know your name, but we're missing a pig's knuckle on this order.	嘿，掌廚，我不知道你的名字，但這張單的豬蹄並沒有做。
Jeff	Oh yeah, it's sitting right here. I just forgot to **plate it up**. And my name's Jeff.	噢，是的，它已經準備在那兒了。我只是忘了裝盤。還有，我的名字叫 Jeff。
Eric	Thanks Jeff, that makes the order complete. Lily, are you ready to go?	謝謝你 Jeff，有了豬蹄，整張單的餐點就都到齊了。Lily，你準備好一起上菜了嗎？

Word Bank

pig's knuckle 豬蹄　joint *n.[C]* 關節　ham *n.[U/C]* 火腿　tear *n.[C]* 撕裂處
place *v.* 陳設；放置　be happy to 樂意　order up 指點單內容完成
complete *adj.* 完整的　wheel man 指主導一切的人　plate it up 裝盤

Unit 14 廚房概況

中式料理食材常客

延續 Unit12 好吃的中式餐點，我們介紹了中國菜的派系與特色，也了解中國菜如何複雜多樣，而在這一章節裡，我們要來實際討論中式料理的做法與食材。

中國菜無論那一個派系菜色的選材都是有其講究之處，從食材鮮度與部位選擇到食材搭配烹調方式與酌料，每項都有其邏輯與規則。

食材選取原則

符合當季時令：

食材依據動植物成熟時間不同，品質也不同，在烹飪與選擇上須留意處理，例如蘇菜便有刀魚不過清明，鰣魚不過端午的說法，可知中國菜講究食材須符合時令的堅持。

講究產地適宜：

不同區域生長的食材品質亦不同，例如台灣人愛吃的蟹，便以陽澄湖和盤錦產為佳。

依品種製作：

不同品種的食材則需有不同的做法，例如北京烤鴨，需用北京特有的填鴨做成，非一般台灣產的菜鴨，白斬雞則用三黃雞做成。

部位影響製作：

同樣食材，但不同的部位其製作的菜色就會不同，例如家常菜肉段應用里脊製作，北京烤鴨雖整隻烘烤，但實際品嘗也僅有背脊肉，其於部分可能做其他菜餚的處理。

講究鮮嫩：

中國菜要求食材鮮活，不鮮不用，例如醋溜黃魚，便是在拍昏黃魚下鍋油炸後，直接淋上酌料。

烹調方法與火候

中國菜烹調方法非常多，且各體系菜餚使用的方式皆不同，但亦有相同之處，例如涼拌、炒、爆、溜、煸、蒸、熬、煮、燉、煨、燴、汆、涮、燒、鹵、醬、煎、炸、燜、烤、焗、熏等幾十種，然而每種又分為好幾種小類。在中國菜製作過程中，尚十分講究火候，火候的控制深深影響菜色的味道，以最簡單的蒸排骨為例，蒸的時間長了，肉就老了，時間短了，則還沒熟透。

調味的藝術

中國菜的調料種類繁多，調味品會依據地區不同而有不同的使用方式，亦深深影響地方風味菜餚的原因之一。常用調料品有以下幾類：

- 調色使用：老抽醬油、紅曲米
- 調香使用：麻油、麻醬、黃醬、蔥、蒜、八角、茴香、桂皮、丁香、肉豆蔻、白豆蔻、草果、香菜、香菇、桂花、薄荷、三奈、香葉、砂仁、甘草、木香、
- 調味使用：食鹽、生抽醬油、醋、白糖、紅糖、蜂蜜、蚝油、豆豉、蝦皮、辣椒、生薑、胡椒、花椒
- 調型使用：生粉、菱粉、冰糖
- 滋補使用：枸杞、桂圓、党參、西洋參、黃芪、當歸、天麻、冬蟲夏草、川芎、茯苓、薏米、三七、蓮子、川芎
- 其他添加劑：高湯、味精。

看完了琳瑯滿目的中國菜介紹，是否了解到中國人重視飲食的層次呢？也許那天您服務到美食家，您也可以跟他淺談一下中國菜餚的特色。

Unit 15 清潔和食材管理

1 *Ordering Everyday Menu Items* 訂購每日菜單食材

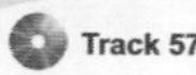

Introduction

The storekeeper talks about ordering food. 店長談到訂購食材。

Characters

Devan - New Sous Chef 新任大廚
Edward - Storekeeper 店長

Conversation

Edward	I usually go through the whole **inventory** once a day, or my **replacement** does it on my day off. But if there's anything we're really low on, let me know and I'll make sure to order it.	我每天通常會去清點食材庫存一次，若是我輪休，我的代理人也會執行我的工作事項。但是，如果真的有什麼是庫存不足的，一定要讓我知道，我會確認然後去訂購補足。
Devan	Thanks, it's good to know who to go to. But where does the order go when you send it in? Who do you send it to?	謝謝，很高興知道這是誰負責的。但是，當你送進訂單時，訂單是發到哪兒去？是發給誰呢？
Edward	If you mean, "Where does our food come from?" there is a huge amount of **restaurant supply companies** we use. But first, it has to go through the office.	如果你的意思是指「我們的食材從何而來？」的話，那麼有一大堆的餐廳食材供應商可以向他們訂購。但首先，所有的訂購需求都要統一由辦公室經辦。
Devan	You mean you can't order anything directly?	你的意思是不能直接向供應商下訂單嗎？
Edward	Not really, the **purchasing department** has to OK everything we order. If it's something on the regular menu, they usually just **rubber stamp** it, but the **paperwork** has to go through them, anyway.	不盡然，採購部門的職責是必須審核我們的訂購正確無誤。如果是經常性菜單食材，他們通常只是例行性地蓋上核可章，但文件流程仍然必須通過採購部門。
Devan	We don't have the **authority** to order anything on our own?	我們沒有權限自行下任何訂單嗎？

Edward	Everything we get has to meet the **budget**, so Purchasing has to look at all our orders before we can send them out. If everything is all right, then they issue a **purchase order**. That's when the order goes to the **supplier**.	餐廳裡要購買任何東西，都必須符合預算，所以在我們可以採買之前，採購部門必須檢閱過我們所有的訂購項目。如果一切都符合預算合需求，那麼他們就會送出採購訂單。這時候供應商也才會拿到訂單。
Devan	It sounds kind of complicated.	這聽起來有點複雜。
Edward	I suppose it is, but that's the way it goes when you work for a big company like this. We can't exactly buy eggs from the guy in the **blue truck** out on the street.	我想是的，在這樣的大公司工作就必須如此。我們畢竟無法隨意地在街上、向開藍色貨車的傢伙買雞蛋吧。
Devan	I suppose Purchasing decides on all the suppliers, so you can't get something special if you want to.	我想應該由採購部門決定所有供應商來源，所以你無法隨意訂購一些特別的東西。
Edward	They do have **contracts** with companies for the majority of the things we use. But sometimes Greg will order something himself for the specials, and they let him. You'll have to ask him about that, though.	我們與大量採買的供應商都簽有合約。但有時 Greg 會自己訂購一些東西，做特餐的食材，公司允准他這麼做。關於這部分，你必須問他本人才知道。

Word Bank

inventory *n.[C/U]* 庫存　replacement *n.[C]* 代替者
restaurant supply companies 餐廳食材供應公司（company）
purchasing department 採購部門　rubber stamp 橡皮圖章
paperwork *n.[U]* 文書工作　authority *n.[U]* 權威　budget *n.[C]* 預算
purchase order 採購訂單　supplier *n.[C]* 提供者；供應商
blue truck 藍色貨車　contract(s) *n.[C]* 合約

Unit 15 清潔和食材管理

2 *Ordering Specials* 主廚精選的食材採購 

Track 58

Introduction

The chef, sous chef, and general manager talk about ordering food for specials. 行政主廚，大廚及總經理談論主廚精選的食材採購事宜。

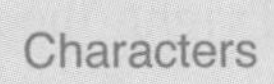

Characters

Greg - Chef 行政主廚
Devan - New Sous Chef 新任大廚
Arthur - General Manager 總經理

Conversation

Devan The storekeeper explained the food ordering **system** for me. It **sounds like** it's kind of difficult to get anything special.

店長對我解釋了食材採購制度。聽起來很難用這種方式買到什麼特別的東西。

Greg It's not always so bad. We can always get things that are on the regular menu. That way we never run out of anything.

清況不總是那麼糟糕。有了這種機制，例行菜單上的東西，我們隨時都會有備料，就絕不會有食材短缺的問題。

Devan But he said you could sometimes order materials for the specials yourself. How does that work?

但他說你有時可以自行訂購特餐的食材。你都怎麼做的呢？

Greg For the specials, we usually plan them two days ahead of time. I then talk to the **GM**, and he can OK the order. It still goes through the purchasing department, but we don't have to wait for them to **approve** it. That is a real **advantage** if we want to serve something that's only in season for a short time.

對於特餐所需的食材，我們通常會提前兩天計劃。然後，我會將訂購明細先告訴總經理，請他批准。訂單還是要呈交採購部門，但倒不必等待採購部核可。如果我們想提供以產季極短的當令食材製作的料理，這樣的程序便利多了。

Devan Those are the kinds of things people like to see in specials, aren't they?

這些食材都是客人想在特餐中吃到的，是嗎？

Greg	Yes, they are. Let's take a look at the specials for Thursday, and I'll show you how it works.	是的。讓我們來看看週四供應的特餐，我會告訴你它是如何運作的。
Devan	You're going to be serving Singapore-style seafood curry.	你要上的菜是新加坡風味的海鮮咖哩。
Greg	Yes, and I want to get a special curry powder for that one, because everyone's had **regular** Taiwanese curry. There's only one place I can get it. Arthur, can I talk to you just a minute?	是的，我希望為此餐點買到一種特殊的咖哩粉，因為之前每個人吃到的都是台灣一般常見的咖哩。只有一個地方能買到它。Arthur，跟你談一下？
Arthur	Yes, what do you need, Greg?	是的，有什麼可以幫忙的，Greg ？
Greg	I want to get a special curry powder, and I need **authorization** for it. Can I go ahead and order it?	我想要一種特殊的咖哩粉，需要核准。我可以直接去訂購嗎？
Arthur	Sure, just let me know the amount and price before you do. As long as the price isn't too **outrageous**, we shouldn't have to go through the office.	當然可以，在你買之前，要讓我知道你訂購的數量和價格。只要價格不是太離譜，我們應該不必經過辦公室核可。
Greg	Thanks Arthur, I'll **get back to** you.	謝謝你，Authur，我等會兒再回覆給你。

Word Bank

system *n.[C]* 系統　sound(s) like 聽起來像　GM=general manager 總經理
approve *v.* 批准　advantage *n.[C]* 優點　regular *adj.* 尋常的；標準的
authorization *n.[U]* 授權　outrageous *adj.* 過分的　get back to 回到；再通話

Unit 15 清潔和食材管理

3 *Washing the Dishes* 清洗碗碟

Track 59

Introduction

A new dishwasher is learning about his job. 一個新的洗碗工正學習他的工作內容。

Characters

Adam - Dishwasher 洗碗工

Brent - Dishwasher Trainee 實習洗碗工

Conversation

Brent	Hi, my name is Brent. I'm new, and Greg said you'd show me what to do here.	嗨，我的名字是 Brent。我是新來的，Greg 說，你會告訴我在這裡該做什麼。
Adam	Hi, my name is Adam. Grab a **rubber apron**, and we'll get started.	嗨，我叫 Adam。拿一件橡膠圍裙，我們開始吧。
Brent	How long have you been here?	你在這裡做多久了？
Adam	I've been working here for about a year.	我已經在這裡工作了大約一年。
Brent	So, you must like it.	所以，你一定很喜歡這份工作。
Adam	Well, it's not something you'd want to make a **career** out of, but it's not a bad **job**. I managed to save enough to get my motorcycle... But let's get to work. This window is where the servers and assistants drop off the dirty dishes. And over there is where they come out of the **dish machine** clean. **In between** is what we do.	嗯，這雖然不是你想發展生涯的工作，但它不算是一個壞工作。我計畫存夠錢買摩托車……但是，我們開始工作吧。服務生和助理會把收來的髒碗碟放置在這個窗口。那邊是這些碗盤從洗碗機出來的地方。我們的工作是完成在這過程之間的所有事情。
Brent	What's our first step? I know there'll be a lot of dishes coming in through that window. This is a really big restaurant.	第一個步驟是什麼？我知道會有一大堆的碗盤由那個窗口送進來洗。這是一個非常大的餐廳。

Adam	The servers do their best to **scrape** the food off the plates, but they're usually really busy, and they can only do so much. That's what this sprayer is for. We **spray** off as much food as we can. It's not good to have food run through the machine.	服務生會盡力把碗碟中的殘留物撥乾淨，但他們實在太忙了，只能做到這樣。這就是為何要有噴除器。我們儘可能把食物殘渣撥除掉。食物的殘渣最好不要進到洗碗機裡。
Brent	That's why we wear these aprons, right? There's a lot of water **splashing**.	這就是我們穿這種圍裙的原因，對不對？因為會被很多水花濺到。
Adam	That's right. After we spray them off, the dishes go through the machine. The water in there has to be hot enough to **sanitize** everything; that's a **minimum** of 72 degrees.	是的。我們用水噴灑清潔後，碗盤才會通過機器。機器裡的水溫至少要 72 度，才能熱到足以進行全面消毒。
Brent	I'll be careful; that's pretty hot.	那真是相當的熱，我會小心的。
Adam	And be especially careful of the final **rinse** before they come out. That can get up to 90.	碗盤送出來之前，最後的洗滌溫度高達 90 度。要特別小心。
Brent	So, that's the reason some of the people are wearing gloves. I'm ready to work. Let's go.	所以，這就是有些人戴著手套的原因。我已經準備好要工作了。開始吧。

Word Bank

rubber apron 橡膠圍裙　career *n.[C]* 事業　job *n.[C]* 工作
dish machine 洗碗機　in between 指中間步驟　scrape *v.* 刮；擦
spray *v.* 噴　splash(ing) *v.* 飛濺　sanitize *v.* 消毒
minimum *n.[C]* 最低限度　rinse *n.[C]* 沖洗

Unit 15 清潔和食材管理

 Cleaning the Restaurant 餐廳的清潔 

Introduction

A new waiter learns how the restaurant is cleaned every day. 新進服務生學習如何每天打掃餐廳。

Characters	
Eric - Server Trainee	實習生
Lily - Server	服務生
Jeff - Cook	廚師
Adam - Dishwasher	洗碗工

Conversation

Lily	Since we're still waiting for our last table to leave, let me take you around and show you how the restaurant gets cleaned.	既然我們仍在等最後一桌客人離桌，我先告訴你如何清理餐廳。
Eric	Isn't there a **cleaning crew**?	不是有清潔人員嗎？
Lily	For the most part, those of us who are working are **in charge of** cleaning our own areas.	大多數情況下，負責清潔自己負責的區域是我們每個人的工作。
Eric	I didn't expect that, but I guess that makes us do a better job of cleaning as we go.	我沒想到是這樣，但我想如此可以讓我們把清潔工作做的更好。
Lily	Let's start with our job. We have to use one of these **manual** carpet cleaners to do the floor. And we also have to clean our part of the back as part of our sidework.	我們開始動手吧。我們必須使用這些手動式地毯清潔劑來清潔地板。清理後場也是我們雜務工作的一部分。
	(in the kitchen)	（在廚房裡）
Lily	Hey Jeff, why don't you show Eric here what you're working on?	嘿，Jeff，示範給 Eric 看一下你的工作內容可以嗎？
Jeff	Now that we have all the meals out, we have to clean the **cooks' line**.	現在餐點全都出完了，我們來清潔廚師工作專區吧。

Eric	After a night like tonight, I guess it's a bit of a mess.	經過像今晚這樣忙碌的夜晚，這裡真的有點亂。
Jeff	We're about to turn on the **pressure washer**, so you should probably get out of the way. Unless you like being **covered** in **soapsuds**.	我們要打開高壓清洗機，所以你最好先離遠一點兒。除非你想要被肥皂泡沫噴得滿身都是。
Lily	We'll go see what Adam is doing in the **dishroom**. Hi Adam, why don't you tell Eric what you have to do to **close**.	我們去看看 Adam 在洗碗間做甚麼。Adam，你何不告訴 Eric 打烊前要做哪些事。
Adam	We keep things pretty clean most of the night. That's kind of our job here. All we have to do now is wipe down our counters, clean the floor, and **drain** and clean the dish machine.	整個晚上，我們都維持各種事物的清潔。這是我們在這裡的職責。現在我們要做的是擦拭櫃檯、拖地、排除洗碗機的髒水並清理。
Lily	You can see that each job has its own **cleanup** to do. Let's go see if that last table is gone. Then we can finish cleaning up ourselves.	你可以看到，每項工作都有相關的東西必須清理。我們去看看最後那桌客人走了沒。接著，我們就可以完成自己的清潔工作。

Part I
Part II
Part III
Part IV
Part V
Part VI

Word Bank

cleaning crew 清潔人員　in charge of 負責　manual *adj.* 手動的
cooks' line 廚師作業動線　pressure washer *n.* 高壓清洗機
covered *adj.* 覆蓋　soapsuds 肥皂泡沫　dishroom *n.[C]* 洗碗間
close *v.* 打烊　drain *v.* 排水　cleanup *n.[C]* 掃除；清潔工作

Unit 15 清潔和食材管理

我是大廚師——廚房動線與規劃

作業動線的順暢有助於品質管理與降低成本，餐廳裡的廚房在用餐時間可是非常忙碌，每個人的作業都需事前妥善的分工，這樣忙碌時，才不會手忙腳亂。

我們在 Unit10 介紹了主廚的職責，廚房的硬體規劃當然也是其職責之一，而硬體的規劃基礎，當然是建立在軟體作業動線上，而廚房硬體又是如何搭配動線來設計呢？

廚房格局規劃

- 廚房除了要預留適當的作業面積外，天花板、地板、配電、通風、照明、排水系統的設計都需要考量。
  - ✓廚房總面積 / 機械器具面積＝ 1.5-5.0
  - ✓扣除機械排列面積外，第一位廚房人員所需工作面積為 3.3 平方公尺，每增加一人則增加 1.7 平方公尺之面積。
  - ✓一般理想廚房面積與餐廳之比例為 1:3 左右。
- 廚房基本會規劃食材倉庫、食材處理區、烹調區、調理備餐區、廚餘垃圾暫存區、辦公室等，每個區域都需要做明確的區域界定，並考慮每個區域、餐飲衛生安全需求之區隔。
- 各區建置重點
  - ✓特別要重視食材處理區之衛生（避免食物汙染）。
  - ✓備餐區設菜梯，出入需分開，並設置冷藏或保溫設備。
  - ✓餐具洗滌需為三槽式。
  - ✓垃圾廚餘暫存區，需設置冷藏設施及垃圾分類。
  - ✓主廚辦公室以透明玻璃窗，以監控全場為主。
  - ✓烹調設備考量清潔問題。
  - ✓注意工作動線流暢，餐點運送及餐具回收順序。

- 設備規格要考量人體工學，避免長期工作引起傷害。
  - ✓工作台高 80-85cm 深度 75cm。
  - ✓壁架一般高度在 140-150cm。
  - ✓壁櫃一般高度在 150-210cm。
  - ✓吧台工作台深度一般在 75cm。
  - ✓保溫餐車高度在 140-150cm。
- 廚房冷／暖氣出口 16~18℃，但廚房及供膳場所需維持溫度 20~25℃，相對濕度控制在 50~60%。
- 廚房氣壓需小於外場氣壓，瓦斯警報器、一氧化碳偵測器、煙霧偵測器、油脂截流器、油煙處理器，皆應妥善規劃設置。

看到以上的廚房規劃規則，有沒有感覺到腦袋一陣昏眩，怎麼會規定這麼多呢？其實這樣的規定包含了安全與衛生的考量，畢竟餐飲第一考量是衛生，而廚房又屬危險的工作環境（用火、瓦斯、刀具等），若沒有完善的全盤規劃，後續造成憾事，我想將不是大家所樂見的，故在進行規劃時，務必要仔細謹慎。

Part 4
International
Restaurant
國際餐廳

Unit 16 陳設與準備

1 *Décor and Music* 布置和音樂 Track 61

Introduction

A new server learns about the restaurant's atmosphere. 一個新手服務生學習如何營造餐廳氣氛。

Characters

Colleen - Server Trainee 實習生
Cody - Server 服務生
Ben - Dining Room Manager 餐區經理

Conversation

Ben	Colleen, how do you like working here so far?	Colleen，到現在為止還喜歡這個工作嗎？
Colleen	I'm really happy. Everyone has been very friendly. I think I'll like being your **employee**.	我真的很喜歡，每個人都非常友善，我很樂意成為你的員工。
Ben	If there's anything I can do for you, just let me know.	如果有什麼事我可以幫忙你，儘管讓我知道。
Colleen	Come to think of it, there is one thing I have a question about. Who came up with the **décor** around here? It's kind of all mixed up.	我想想看，有件事我有些疑問。這裡的裝潢擺設是誰想出來的？有點像是融合各種風格。
Ben	You've seen our menu, haven't you? It's a **mixture** of food from all over, so that's what we wanted the **interior** to look like, too.	你已經看過我們的菜單，不是嗎？我們的餐點內容來自各地，因此餐廳內部風格也是如此呈現。
Colleen	Now I understand why there are **signs** in German, **posters** from the United States, and Italian **street scenes** on the walls. I like it. Is that the way the music is designed, too?	現在我明白為什麼牆上會出現德國標誌、美國海報、和意大利街頭場景。我喜歡，就連音樂也是同樣的設計嗎？

Ben	We have a **consultant** who advises us on the music. You might hear a Taiwanese or Korean pop song, followed by a traditional European song, then something from 1960s America. We use music that **attempts** to put people in an **international** mood.	我們有顧問會提供音樂建議。譬如會聽到一首台灣或韓國的流行歌，接著是歐洲傳統歌曲，然後是 60 年代美國音樂。我們用的音樂，是想讓客人感染一種國際氛圍。
Colleen	I'd say it's successful. It's easy to forget that you're in Taiwan when you're inside here.	我必須説這樣很成功。置身在這裡，很容易忘了身在台灣。
Cody	Colleen, let's go take a tour. I don't think you've seen the whole restaurant yet. Back here is one of my favorites.	Colleen，我帶你去看看，你可能還沒逛夠餐廳每個角落。這兒就是我的最愛之一。
Colleen	That's a gorgeous picture. Is it a movie poster?	這照片真讓人驚豔，是一部電影的海報吧。
Cody	Yes, it's from one of my favorite movies, The Sound Of Music.	是的，這是我最喜歡的一部電影：「真善美」。
Colleen	Where was the picture taken.	照片是在哪裡拍攝的呢。
Cody	That was taken in the Alps mountains in Europe. Doesn't it just make you want to run outside and sing?	在歐洲的阿爾卑斯山。看到這張照片，難道不會讓你有想跑到戶外歌唱的衝動嗎？
Colleen	It sure does. Do we have any Taiwan things in here?	確實。我們是否有任何關於台灣的東西在這裡？
Cody	Sure, we do. Right over here are some **vintage** local products.	當然，我們有。這裡可有一些經典本地產品。

Word Bank

atmosphere *n.[C/U]* 氣氛　employee *n.[C]* 僱員
décor *n.* 房內裝飾；室內裝潢　mixture *n.[C]* 混合物
interior *n.[C]* 內部　sign(s) *n.[C]* 標誌　poster(s) *n.[C]* 海報
street scene(s) 街景　consultant *n.[C]* 顧問　attempt(s) *v.* 試圖；企圖
international *adj.* 國際的　vintage *adj.* 經典的；古色古香的

Unit 16 陳設與準備

2 *Table Setup* 餐桌擺設 Track 62

Introduction

A new server is being quizzed on setting a table.

新進服務生正被問及如何進行餐桌擺設。

Characters  

Colleen - Server Trainee 實習生
Cody - Server 服務生

Conversation

Cody	Do you remember your table setup, Colleen?	你還記得如何擺餐嗎，Colleen？
Colleen	It's kind of hard to forget; it's pretty **basic**. Knife, fork, spoon, a **bread plate**, and a water glass.	這有點難忘記，因為這很基本。刀、叉、湯匙、麵包餐盤和裝水的玻璃杯。
Cody	And why do we only put those things on the table?	為什麼桌子上只放這些東西？
Colleen	Because we don't know what the guest is going to order. We don't put wine glasses on because we sell a lot of **beer**. It would **waste** too much time taking them off every table.	因為我們還不知道客人要點甚麼。我們不擺紅酒杯，因為啤酒是主力賣點。要每桌收走酒杯挺費時的。
Cody	Can you remember where we keep everything we need for the table?	你還記得，擺桌需要的項目都放哪兒嗎？
Colleen	We keep lots of extra bread plates on the **sidestand**.	我們將許多額外的麵包餐盤放在備餐檯。
Cody	What do we use those for?	那些做什麼用？
Colleen	In case the guest is getting an appetizer to share; also for desserts or **pizza**.	萬一客人要共享開胃菜；甜點或比薩也適用。
Cody	Very good. You're **getting an A** so far. What else is on the sidestand?	非常好。你目前的表現很好。還有什麼東西放在備餐檯？

Colleen	Wine glasses, in case they do have wine.	紅酒杯，萬一客人有點酒的話要用。
Cody	And when do we put the wine glasses on the table?	什麼時候該把酒杯拿出來擺桌？
Colleen	We put them on right when they order wine, and then we go get the bottle and open it **tableside**. The sidestand also has **pasta spoons** and **steak knives**, and we put them on before the guest's meal arrives.	當客人點了紅酒，就把酒杯拿出來放在他們右手邊，然後拿酒並在桌邊開酒。備餐檯也有麵匙和牛排刀，要在客人主餐端上來之前就擺好。
Cody	You are really good. What are the bottles in the center of the table for?	你回答得真不錯。餐桌中間的瓶罐是做什麼用的？
Colleen	The lighter one is **olive oil**, and the darker one is **balsamic vinegar**. You mix them together, Italian style, when you eat your bread.	顏色較淡的是橄欖油，顏色較深的是香醋。吃麵包時把它們混在一起，呈現義大利風味。
Cody	Very nice, Colleen. What else do we serve with bread?	很好，Colleen。我們還提供什麼來搭配麵包？
Colleen	Butter, but we teach the guests how to use the oil and vinegar, so they can learn a new way of eating.	奶油，不過我們還是教客人使用油和醋，學習新吃法。
Cody	Excellent! I think you're going to be ready to be on your own soon.	好極了！我想你很快就可獨當一面了。

Word Bank

quiz(zed) *v.* 提問；測驗　basic *adj.* 基本的　bread plate 麵包餐盤
beer *n.[U]* 啤酒　waste *v.* 浪費　sidestand *n.[C]* 指備餐檯
pizza *n.[U]* 比薩　getting an A 表現得很好　tableside *adv.* 在桌邊
pasta spoon(s) 麵食用湯匙　steak knives 牛排刀（knife）　olive oil 橄欖油
balsamic vinegar 甜醋

Unit 16 陳設與準備

3 *Utensils and Extras* 餐具與額外用具 Track 63

Introduction

A new server is learning what utensils and extras are needed for table service. 新進服務生學習餐桌服務所需要的餐具和額外物品。

Characters

Colleen - Server Trainee	實習生
Cody - Server	服務生

Conversation

Cody	Let's go over the order we got from that table. They're having a smoked salmon pizza to start. What **extra** things do we need to bring out for that?	我們來看看那桌點的菜單。他們前菜點了醺鮭魚比薩。要拿什麼額外餐具搭配出菜？
Colleen	We'll need an extra fork for everyone, along with a plate. Then, we'll need to bring out the **red peppers** and ask if they want some **grated** parmesan cheese on their pizza.	需要為每個人多放一支叉子和一個盤子。然後要提供些紅辣椒，詢問是否想在比薩餅上灑一些磨碎的巴馬乾酪。
Cody	And where do we get the parmesan from?	在哪可以拿到我們需要的巴馬乾酪？
Colleen	It's here on the sidestand. But I have a question: Won't it **go bad** if it stays out here all the time?	放在備餐檯上。但我想問：起司一直擺這難道不會壞？
Cody	No, parmesan is a hard cheese, and it can stay out here where it's easy for us to **grab**. Then, they're having a Caesar salad to split.	不會，巴馬乾酪是一種硬質乳酪，它可以一直擺這，方便取用。還有，他們點了一份凱撒沙拉要分食。

Colleen	For that, we need a **pepper mill**. We always offer fresh **ground pepper** with all salads. And we should ask if they'd like more parmesan, even though it already **comes with** it.	沙拉的話，我們需要一個胡椒碾磨罐。所有的沙拉餐點，都有新鮮胡椒粒可供使用。我們該問他們是否要多加一些乾酪，即使已經有了。
Cody	Let's see what they're having for dinner. A prime rib pasta and a tenderloin steak. What will we need for that?	看看他們晚餐點了哪些。一個肋排義大利麵和腓力牛排，我們要怎麼準備？
Colleen	We'll have to place a pasta spoon in front of one guest, and a steak knife for each of them.	必須在每一個客人前面擺上義大利麵湯匙，並給一人一支牛排刀。
Cody	That's right, and what else?	完全正確，還有什麼要注意的？
Colleen	We'll need the parmesan again for the pasta. And we can ask the guest if she wants steak sauce.	需要為義大利麵再準備些巴馬乾酪，同時詢問是否要加牛排醬。
Cody	One other thing: A lot of people like ground pepper on their **beef**, so you might want to ask them about that. But I think you've got it.	還有一件事：很多人喜歡在牛排上灑胡椒粒，所以你可能要問問看。不過我想你早就知道。

Word Bank

utensil(s) *n.[C]* 器皿；用具　extra *adj.* 額外的　red pepper(s) 紅辣椒
grate(d) *v.* 磨碎　go bad 變質；腐壞　grab *v.* 拿；取
pepper mill 胡椒碾磨器　ground pepper 磨碎的胡椒粒
come(s) with 帶有；搭配　beef *n.[U]* 牛肉

Unit 16 陳設與準備

4 *Serving the Table* 服務餐桌 Track 64

Introduction

The server serves the table and shows his trainee the placement of utensils. 服務生服侍客人用餐，並為實習生示範如何擺放餐具

Characters

Colleen - Server Trainee	實習生
Cody - Server	服務生
John - Guest	顧客
Melody - Guest	顧客

Conversation

Cody	Colleen, we're still in **watch and learn** mode, so I'm going to serve this table. You just **note** where everything goes, and watch the **timing** of the food and placement of all the utensils.	Collen，現在仍然是見習階段，所以由我來服務這桌客人。你只要注意每件事如何進行，並且注意上菜的時間和所有餐具的擺放。
Colleen	The first thing is to bring out everything for the pizza, right?	第一件事情，就是要供應吃比薩所需的每項東西，對嗎？
Cody	Yes, I'll go ahead and do that now.	是的，我會馬上進行。
	(at the table)	（在餐桌邊）
Cody	Here are some plates, so you can share your pizza. These are red peppers, and some extra forks so you can both try it. The pizza should be ready shortly.	這邊有幾個盤子，好讓你們可以共享比薩。還有紅辣椒和一些多出來的叉子，讓你們都能試一試。比薩應該很快就要上桌了。
	(a couple minutes later)	（過了一會兒）
Melody	There's our pizza. It looks delicious.	這就是我們的比薩，看起來真好吃。
Cody	Would you care for some fresh grated parmesan cheese?	您要不要來一些新鮮的現磨巴馬乾酪？
Melody	Just put a little bit on **half**, please.	只要在半邊放一點點就好了。
	(at the computer)	（在電腦旁邊）

Cody	Now, Colleen, we can order the Caesar salad. It should take **very little** time. When they finish with the pizza, could you **take away** the plates and forks, then give them each a salad fork?	Colleen，現在我們可以請廚房做凱撒沙拉。它應該只需要一點點時間。當他們吃完比薩，可以請你收走盤子和刀叉，然後給他們每人一份沙拉叉嗎？
	(at the table)	（在餐桌邊）
Cody	Here is your Caesar salad. Would you like some fresh ground pepper for that?	這是您的凱撒沙拉。您想加一點新鮮的現磨胡椒粒嗎？
John	Yes please, for **both** of us. And could we get a little extra parmesan cheese, too?	好的，我們兩個人都要。可否也再多給一點巴馬乾酪嗎？
Cody	Certainly; I'll give you some time now to enjoy your salads.	當然，請慢慢享用你的沙拉。
	(back at the computer)	（回到電腦旁邊）
Colleen	Now that they're done with the salads, we need to clear the plates and bring out the pasta spoon and steak knives. I'll go do that.	既然現在他們吃完沙拉了，我們需要清空沙拉盤，並換上麵食湯匙和牛排刀。讓我來吧。
	(returns to the table)	（回到餐桌邊）
Cody	Here is your pasta. Would you like some grated parmesan on that?	這是你的麵點。你要加一些磨碎的巴馬乾酪嗎？
John	Yes, that sounds really nice.	好的，聽起來真不錯。
Cody	And pepper on your steak?	你的牛排要加胡椒嗎？
Melody	No, thank you, but do you have any steak sauce?	不用了，謝謝你，但可否給我牛排醬？
Cody	Yes, it's right here. If there's nothing else you **require**, please enjoy your meal.	好的，在這裡。如果沒有要再點菜，敬請慢慢享用餐點。

Word Bank

placement *v.* 擺放；配置　watch and learn 見習；觀摩　note *v.* 注意
timing *n.* 時機　half *n.[C/U]* 一半　very little 微乎其微；非常少
take away 帶走；拿走　both *pron.* 兩者（都）　require *v.* 需要；要求

Unit 16 陳設與準備

喝酒的文化——酒與食材搭配

紅酒配紅肉、白酒配白肉是一般顧客認知的酒與食材的搭配方式，但這也是最有待討論的餐酒搭配原則。

廚師烹煮食物，對於食材的選擇有一定的堅持度，其會運用佐料或是保留食物原本的味道來讓客戶感受到他的用心。用餐飲酒文化發展的很早，早期在義大利很少人吃飯不搭配喝酒，會有此習慣主因為當地的葡萄所釀製出來的酒微酸，很適合作為餐酒，義大利人單喝酒時，常給人澀、酸、單薄無味的印象，但是搭配上口味濃郁的義大利菜，這些酒就徹底表現出它優秀的特質。

在歐洲用餐幾乎都一定會搭配酒食用，又因為歐洲多處地區為葡萄酒的重要產區，因此佐餐用酒就多以葡萄酒來搭配。葡萄酒基本有三種味道，分別為苦、甜、酸，這三種味道則是由酒內單寧、殘糖、酒石酸等三種主要成分而形成，當然近期專業的品酒亦將第四種主要成分酒精納入參考，尤其是品酒時酒精於喉嚨後方產生的熱量，則是影響酒濃淡的主因，故在搭配食物時，亦需考慮酒精餘熱對食物的影響。

葡萄酒這麼多該怎麼選擇呢？確實每種酒都有其各自的特性，而每種特性都有其適合搭配的食材，若要正確推薦客戶搭配，我們可以依照下表進行。

食物與酒品的搭配

食物類型	適合搭配的酒品
酸的食物	較酸的酒
鹹的食物	較甜或酸的酒
甜的食物	較甜或氣泡酒
辣的食物	氣泡酒
苦的食物	較苦的酒
油炸類食物	較酸的酒
有嚼勁的食物	較澀的酒

除以上依照食物味道搭配酒品外，另外也有一派以產區酒搭配產地特色餐點的搭配方式，此搭配的邏輯非常簡單，當產區釀什麼酒，就拿它來搭配當區特色餐點。早期歐洲部分地區以羊肉為主要肉食，這些地方產的葡萄酒被視為最適合搭配羊肉的酒，其中包括波爾多葡萄酒、希臘葡萄酒、西班牙的里奧哈酒、法國羅納葡萄酒以及普羅斯旺葡萄酒等。

葡萄酒小常識——葡萄酒分級

法國

✓普通日用餐酒（Vins de Table）
✓鄉村酒或地區餐酒（Vins de Pays）
✓優良品質餐酒（VDQS）
✓原產地法定區域管制餐酒（AOC）

德國

✓日常飲用餐酒
✓優質酒，簡稱 QbA
✓高級優質酒，簡稱 QmP

美國

✓附屬類
✓專屬品牌酒（Proprietary Wine）
✓葡萄品名餐酒（Varietal Wine）

義大利

✓一般日常酒（Vino da Tavola）
✓原產地區域管制酒（DOC）
✓原產地區域保證酒（DOCG）

Unit 17 用餐服務

1 *Appetizers and Pizza* 開胃菜和比薩

Track 65

Introduction

A server is making first-course recommendations.

服務生推薦前菜

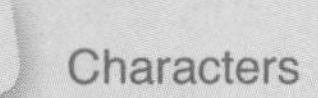

Characters

Jamie - Guest	顧客
Naomi - Server	服務生
Nancy - Guest	顧客

Conversation

Naomi	Good evening, and welcome. Can I get anything for you to drink while you're looking over the menu?	晚安，歡迎光臨。請問您看菜單的同時，需要先送上飲料嗎？
Jamie	We're actually interested in getting something to start, but we can't decide between appetizers or a pizza. How long does a pizza take?	是的，我們正想要點些什麼當前菜，但我們在猶豫要點開胃菜或比薩。點比薩要等多久？
Naomi	Our pizzas are **wood-fired** and have a **thin crust**, so they don't take much time at all. Appetizers are usually a little faster, but unless you're in a real **time crunch**, pizzas make a great first course.	我們的比薩是用木柴窯烤的，餅皮很薄，所以一點也不花時間。開胃菜通常會快一點，除非您非常趕時間，不然第一道菜點比薩是挺讚的。
Jamie	All right, you **convinced** me. What pizza would you recommend?	好吧，你說動我了。你會推薦什麼口味的比薩？
Naomi	I like spicy food, so I think our firehouse special is great. It has spicy sausage and a hot tomato sauce.	我喜歡吃辣，所以我覺得我們的辣味火烤比薩棒極了。它用了辣香腸和辣味番茄醬汁。
Jamie	Do you have recommendations for anything **milder**?	你有什麼口味較溫和的建議嗎？
Naomi	Sure, you can't go wrong with the basic **pepperoni**. When I was **growing up**, that was my friends' favorite.	當然，您一定不能錯過較不辣的義大利臘味香腸比薩。從小到大，它一直是我一群朋友的最愛。

Jamie	I like pepperoni, too, but I really want something different.	我也喜歡義大利臘味香腸比薩，但我想嚐點不一樣的。
Naomi	If different is what you want, you should try the seafood pizza. It comes with fresh shrimp, **scallops**, and **squid**, with garlic and basil in a tomato sauce. You can get it in a **clam sauce**, too.	如果您想嘗點不同的口味，您應該試試海鮮比薩。它的配料有新鮮的蝦、扇貝和魷魚，加大蒜和羅勒番茄醬汁。您也可以配蛤蜊醬吃。
Jamie	That sounds really good. One of those, please.	聽起來很不錯。請幫我點一份。
Nancy	Dad, can Mary and I share a pizza? I think we want that firehouse one.	爸爸，Mary 和我可以共享一個比薩餅嗎？我們要一個辣味火烤比薩。
Jamie	Sure, you can get whatever you want. OK, one of those for the girls, and one of the seafood pizzas.	當然，你可以點任何想吃的。好吧，給我女兒們來個辣味火烤，再加一分海鮮比薩。
Naomi	Tomato or clam sauce on that?	要番茄醬汁，還是蛤蜊醬？
Jamie	We'd like the tomato sauce. And just **out of curiosity**, which appetizer would you have recommended?	我們想要番茄醬汁。只是好奇想知道，你可以推薦哪道開胃菜？
Naomi	I really like the king crab **quiche** with lobster sauce, but I think you'll like your pizza. Maybe you can try that the next time.	我很推薦蟹肉鹹派佐龍蝦醬，但我想您一定會喜歡剛點的比薩。也許下次可以再點那道菜試試。

Word Bank

wood-fired *adj.* 柴燒的　thin crust 薄脆餅皮　time crunch 時間緊絀
convince(d) *v.* 說服　grow(ing) up 長大　milder *adj.* 較溫和的
pepperoni *n.[C/U]* 義大利辣味香腸　scallop(s) *n.[C]* 扇貝
squid *n.[C/U]* 烏賊　clam sauce 蛤蜊醬　out of curiosity 出於好奇
quiche *n.[C/U]* 鹹派

Unit 17 用餐服務

2 *Entrées* 主菜 Track 66

Introduction

A server gives advice to two different tables. 一個服務生分別建議兩桌客人。

Characters

Naomi - Server	服務生
Werner - Guest	顧客
Vivian - Guest	顧客

Conversation

Werner	We're **going out** to dinner later, and we just want to get something light for right now. What would you suggest?	我們等會兒要到別處吃晚飯，現在只想點些輕食。你有什麼建議嗎？
Naomi	You might want one of our **sandwiches**. Even though most people think of them as just being for lunch, we have some good ones to choose from. I especially like the club sandwich. It has smoked **chicken breast** and bacon, with cheddar cheese and tomato. That's served with fries or **potato salad**.	嘗嘗我們的三明治吧。儘管大多數人認為三明治只適合當午餐，我們仍有些很好的可供選擇。我特別推薦總匯三明治，配料有煙燻雞胸肉和培根，以及巧達起司和番茄。附餐是薯條或馬鈴薯沙拉。
Werner	That sounds really good. What other smaller things do you think are good?	聽起來很不錯。還有什麼其他少份量的東西你覺得不錯？
Naomi	You really can't go wrong with the pizza, and I really like our **dumplings**. The spicy shrimp are really good. They won't leave you too full, but you'll be **satisfied**.	你真的不能錯過比薩，還有我實在喜歡我們的餃子。香辣蝦餃真的好。這些都不會讓你吃得太撐，卻會感到滿足。
Werner	OK, we'll have one order of the dumplings and one club sandwich. And two **mineral waters** to drink.	好的，我們就點一份餃子和總匯三明治，再加兩瓶礦泉水。

Naomi	Thank you, and I'll be right back with your water.	謝謝你，我馬上就幫你拿水過來。
	(at a second table)	（在另一桌）
Naomi	Good afternoon, are you ready to order, or do you need a little more time?	午安，您現在可以點菜了嗎？還是需要多一點的時間考慮？
Vivian	We really want steak. Which one would you recommend?	我們很想要點牛排。你推薦哪一種？
Naomi	We have a couple of different ways you can get steak. One is the prime rib linguine. It's a beef pasta with **a choice of** four different sauces. We also have a beef steak noodle soup that's really good. For a traditional steak, I'd recommend the tenderloin. It's not big, but it's really good and will leave room for appetizers or dessert.	我們有幾種不同的牛排吃法。一種是肋排義大利麵，這是一種可以選擇四種醬汁的牛肉類麵食。我們也有風味絕倫的牛排湯麵。至於傳統的牛排餐，我推薦菲力牛排。它份量不大。但味道真的很好，讓你不會太飽，好騰出肚子來吃開胃菜或甜點。
Vivian	Which pasta sauce do you like?	你推薦哪一種義大利麵醬？
Naomi	I like the olive oil and **chilis**. It's simple, spicy, and really good with the beef.	我喜歡橄欖油和辣椒。味道單純、帶辣，與牛肉一起享用真是絕配。
Vivian	Thanks for your advice. We'll talk it over for a few minutes.	謝謝你的建議。我們先商量幾分鐘。

Part I Part II Part III Part IV Part V Part VI

Word Bank

go(ing) out 出去；外出　sandwich(es) *n.[C]* 三明治　chicken breast 雞胸肉
potato salad 馬鈴薯沙拉　dumpling(s) *n.[C]* 餃子　satisfied *adj.* 滿意的
mineral water 礦泉水　a choice of 精選的；優質的　chili(s) *n.[C]* 辣椒

Unit 17 用餐服務

3 Drinks 飲料 Track 67

Introduction

A table wants to know about beers served at the restaurant. 有一桌客人想瞭解餐廳供應的啤酒。

Characters

Cody - Server 服務生
James - Guest 顧客

Conversation

James	Hi, we'd like some advice. You have a lot of beers **on tap**, but I'm not really **familiar** with some of them. What would you recommend?	你好，我們想要一些建議。你們有很多種桶裝啤酒，但有些我不太熟悉。你有什麼建議嗎？
Cody	I think you should try them all. Well, not all of them, but we have a **sampler**. That gives you a small glass of each of our best-selling tap beers.	我想您應該全部都試試。噢，不是指全部都點，而是我們有小量試喝。每一種最暢銷的啤酒都給您一小杯嚐嚐味道。
James	I think that's a good idea. We'll take one of those to start. Then maybe we can decide on one we'd like a bigger glass of.	好主意，我們就先試喝其中一種組合再開始。也許這樣就可以決定要點一大杯某種口味的。
Cody	All right, I'll be back with your sampler in a few minutes.	好的，我待會兒就把試喝酒拿過來。
	(Cody returns)	（Cody 回到餐桌）
James	Ahh, look at all that delicious beer.	啊，看看這些啤酒多美味。
Cody	I'll give you a short **rundown** on what you have here. This first one is a **lager**. It's what people normally think of when they think of beer. The next is a Hefeweizen.	我來為您做個簡短的介紹。第一種是淡啤酒。通常大家想到啤酒時，就會想到這一種。接下來是酵母小麥啤酒。

James	A what?	什麼啤酒？
Cody	It's pronounced hef-uh-vite-zun. It's a wheat beer; they replace some of the **barley** with wheat. It's **unfiltered**, so it looks a little cloudy, and it has a mild, smooth taste.	它的發音是：hef-uh-vite-zun。是一種用小麥發酵的啤酒，但混有一些大麥一起發酵。因為未經過濾，所以看起來有點混濁。它的口感很溫和、順口。
James	What's this really dark one?	這種顏色較深的呢？
Cody	That's Guinness, a really strong-flavored beer from Ireland. It has a bit of a coffee taste.	這是健力士黑啤酒，是一種從愛爾蘭進口、風味濃烈的啤酒。帶點咖啡味道。
James	And the golden-colored one next to it?	在它旁邊金黃色的呢？
Cody	That's a pilsner. It's my favorite. It has a really **sharp** taste and was originally from the Czech Republic.	這是 Pilsner 啤酒。它是我最喜歡的。其口味非常強烈，它源自捷克。
James	That brown one next to it looks really good. Well, they all look really good, but I may have to **take it easy** with the Guinness.	在它旁邊褐色的啤酒看起來真的很不錯。好吧，他們看起來都挺好喝，但我較青睞健士力黑啤酒。
Cody	This one is a bitter. As the name **implies**, it's a little more **bitter** than a lager. It has a little sharper flavor. I like it.	這是苦啤酒。它的味道正如其名，比淡啤酒苦一點。但味道更強烈一點。我喜歡。
James	Thanks for all your help. We'll try these and see which ones we like.	謝謝你的幫助。我們會嚐嚐這些啤酒，看看喜歡哪幾種。

Word Bank

on tap 即時可取用的　familiar *adj.* 熟悉的　sampler *n.[C]* 樣品
rundown *n.[C]* 概要　lager *n.[C/U]* 淡啤酒　barley *n.[U]* 大麥
unfiltered *adj.* 未過濾的　sharp *adj.* 濃烈的；辛口的　take it easy 放輕鬆
implies *adj.* 意味著（imply）　bitter *adj.* 苦的

Unit 17 用餐服務

4 Desserts 甜點 Track 68

Introduction

A server explains some of the dessert choices.

服務生解釋一些甜點的選擇。

Characters 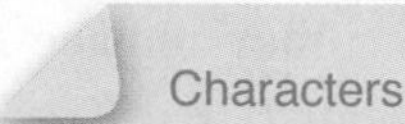 

Naomi - Server	服務生
Babette - Guest	顧客

Conversation

Naomi	Hi, are you ready for dessert?	嗨，準備點甜點了嗎？
Babette	We are, but everything on the menu looks so good. What would you have?	是的，但菜單上每個甜點看起來都很棒。你有什麼建議嗎？
Naomi	Tiramisu. It's the most popular dessert we have, **far and away**.	提拉米蘇，它是我們最暢銷的甜點，遠近馳名。
Babette	Isn't that Italian?	不是出自義大利嗎？
Naomi	Yes, it's a classic Italian dessert made from cream, eggs, and cheese. It has a touch of **espresso** in it, too, so it has **a hint of** coffee flavor.	是的，這是一種經典的義大利甜點，用奶油、雞蛋、乳酪做成，它也含有少許義式濃縮咖啡，所以有一股淡淡的咖啡風味。
Babette	That sounds really **heavy**. I'm already pretty full.	聽起來份量很大。我已經相當飽了。
Naomi	No, it's really not. It's whipped up all light and **airy**; it really **hits the spot**.	沒有，真的不會。它混合了輕柔滑潤的口感，一定合您的胃口。
Babette	What do you think of the raspberry **cheesecake**? Is it as good as it sounds?	若是點覆盆子乳酪蛋糕呢？它好得正如其名嗎？

Naomi	It sure is. It's a traditional cheesecake, made with fresh raspberries. It has a raspberry cream sauce on top. I'd **definitely** recommend it.	一點兒也沒錯，它是一種傳統的起司蛋糕，用新鮮的覆盆子做的。它還塗了一層覆盆子奶油醬在頂層，這個我絕對推薦。
Babette	We'll think about it. What's a tart?	我們會考慮一下。什麼是餡餅？
Naomi	A tart is a small pie. Instead of making a big pie, they make one big enough for one person. Our berry tart comes with a mixture of fresh berries, topped with a light powdered sugar glaze.	餡餅是一種小派餅。相對於大的派餅，它的大小剛好足夠一人食用。我們的漿果餡餅是用混合的新鮮漿果製成，並且在最上層撒上糖霜。
Babette	I think I'll pass on that. I know my mom used to make bread **pudding**; that sounds like something that would make me feel good. What's in it besides bread?	我想我先跳過這道。我母親以前做過麵包布丁，讓我十分回味。除了麵皮外，裡面有什麼餡料呢？
Naomi	The main flavor comes from cinnamon and **vanilla**, and it has raisins and spices, too. It's delicious, but it might not be as good as your mom's.	它的風味主要來自於肉桂跟香草，同時也添加了葡萄乾和香料。很美味，但可能比不上你母親親手做的。
Babette	I'll have that, and my husband would like a raspberry cheesecake.	我就點這個，我先生想來一個覆盆子乳酪蛋糕。
Naomi	Thank you, and would either of you like coffee right now?	謝謝你，你們兩位現在想來點咖啡嗎？

Word Bank

far and away 無疑地　espresso *n.[U/C]* 義式濃縮咖啡
a hint of 少許；些微　heavy *adj.* 難消化的；份量大的　airy *adj.* 輕盈的
hit(s) the spot 正合我意；完全正確　cheesecake *n.[C/U]* 乳酪蛋糕
definitely *adv.* 無疑地；肯定地　pudding *n.[C/U]* 布丁　vanilla *n.[C/U]* 香草

Unit 17 用餐服務

耗時複雜的歐式料理——法國人的用餐文化

歐式料理我最推崇的是法式料理。法國人用餐的過程非常多樣，用餐時間也很長，主要是因為法式料理的上菜程序很多，且法國人用餐時話非常多，不管男女都可以天南地北地聊。

法國人用餐的程序依序

品酒：

法國人喝酒通常會依據當天的狀況搭配，但使用的狀況卻很講究，例如開胃菜有開胃菜的酒，主餐有主餐的酒，品嘗起司有品嘗起司的酒，連甜品也可以搭配酒。

開胃菜：

通常法國人於正式用餐前會於客廳或是餐桌上喝點酒，吃點小點心當開胃菜，而這些小點心多為精巧且用手即可方便取用，而搭配的酒會有香檳、伏特加、威士忌等各類的酒給客戶選擇，而這樣的過程通常需要 30 分鐘或長達一小時。

前菜：

前菜多為冷盤或是去油膩的料理，以區分開胃菜與主餐，而且有趣的是，法國人非常在意來賓品嘗後的滿足表情，所以對於料理的安排可是非常細緻，例如當開胃菜為海鮮類時，主餐則不會再搭配海鮮，則可能以肉類為主，而常用的前菜大致上有鵝肝醬、生蠔、蝦肉等。

主餐：

吃完一堆開胃菜、前菜，到了主餐，我想應該也飽了，其實不用擔心，通常吃到這裡，用餐時間大約也過了 2 小時，肚子應該也餓了。法國菜的主餐通常是非常的迷你，不似美國人豪氣，牛排通常是又厚又大，會有此差異主要是因為法國人喜愛精緻的餐點，若主餐為牛肉，廚師會用技巧的將牛肉切成一口即可品嘗的大小，精緻裝盤搭配大量的佐醬，讓你可以優雅品嘗肉汁的美味。

起司：

在進入甜點前，通常法國人會吃點起司來緩衝一下味道，並且讓自己再品嘗些不同的紅酒或是香檳等，讓氣氛更加地歡愉。

甜點：

一般來說，法國人吃了甜點後，表示他已經真的吃飽了，且將不會再品嘗任何鹹的食物，而在他們的甜點中，也喜愛搭配佐醬，增加甜味的層次感。

飲品：

終於來到了最後，來到這裡用餐時間大約已過 4 小時，餐後飲料多為簡單的茶或咖啡，進行至此也表示是時間該離開了。

法國人用餐其實有很多禮節，而這些禮節多源自於 16 世紀貴族制訂下來的用餐禮儀五十法則，聽起來似乎非常地多樣複雜，當然年代久遠，部分法則已不適用，現在我簡單摘要時下仍通行的禮儀規範。

- 一旦入座便不隨意離開。法國人覺得隨意離開座位是非常不禮貌，如真有非離座不可的理由（例如上廁所），也要不動聲色地離去，回來後再輕緩地入坐，切記大聲嚷嚷，這樣對於同桌的賓客是非常不禮貌的。
- 在飯桌時雙手應該放在桌上，讓同桌賓客看得見，放置桌下，同桌客戶會以為你對於談話的話題不喜歡。
- 法國人使用刀叉的技藝已爐火純青，舉凡炸雞、烤牛小排、蘆筍、水果都可以用刀叉取用，千萬不可使用手來拿取。
- 生菜用刀叉輕柔地折好，然後用叉子送食，切忌使用刀子切割，其實不使用刀切主要是生菜有醋，醋的酸性會讓刀鋒生鏽，故法國人養成了這樣的食用禮儀。
- 法國麵包一定要用手撕開食用，亦不可以用刀切，主要是為了避免碎屑彈進別人眼睛或衣服上。
- 喝湯時從湯匙末端喝或兩側面喝，這與我們平日所接受的用餐禮儀有點不一樣。
- 甜點與咖啡是兩道不同的餐飲，所以法國人不會讓這兩個餐點同時端上桌，此於我們一般的飲食方式有些不同。

看完了這一長串的法國人用餐介紹，當未來您服務於法國餐廳時，自然可以了解為何法國餐廳如此在意服務細緻度，對於法國人來說，用餐是件非常神聖且重要的事情，不可以輕率視之。

Unit 18 服務生

1 *Difference between Lunch and Dinner* 午餐和晚餐之間的差異

Track 69

Introduction

The new server wants to know the difference between working at lunch and dinner. 新進服務生想知道午餐和晚餐的工作差異。

Characters

Colleen - Server Trainee 實習生
Cody - Server 服務生

Conversation

Cody	Hi Colleen, how was your night last night?	嗨 Colleen，你昨晚工作如何？
Colleen	I think it went pretty well. I even took a couple tables.	我感覺相當不錯。我甚至服務了好些客人。
Cody	That's good; you should be ready to be on your own really soon.	相當不錯；你應該相當快就可以獨當一面了。
Colleen	Today is my first lunch shift. How does lunch **compare to** working at dinnertime?	今天是我第一次上午班。晚班與午班的工作有何差別呢？
Cody	It's a lot more **fast-paced**. Most people have an hour **or so** for lunch, so they don't have a lot of time to waste. You have to get to them quickly and take their order as soon as they're ready.	午餐的工作步調相對要快很多。多數人只有一個小時左右吃午飯，所以沒有多餘的時間等候。你必須儘快服務他們，一旦他們看好菜單後就儘快點餐。
Colleen	I see the menu isn't quite as big at lunch.	我看午餐菜單選擇性不若晚餐多。
Cody	No, it's **geared** more toward what we can put out fast. We don't have things that take a lot of time, liked the baked salmon.	是的，這樣設計是為了配合快速出餐。我們不會有要做很久的菜色，像是烤鮭魚。

Colleen	So, I bet we don't get a lot of appetizer or salad orders, either.	所以我敢說，也沒有太多人會點開胃菜或沙拉。
Cody	That's right. Most people just want to order their entrée, and that's all. Sometimes people will be having a long **business lunch** and get different courses, but that's **the exception to the rule**.	沒錯，大多數人只會點主餐，不會多點。有時，客人會花長時間邊吃午餐邊談公事，而且點好幾道菜，但這是極少的例外。
Colleen	What else should I know before I work my first lunch shift?	還有什麼是午餐工作需要知道的？
Cody	**Be prepared for** lots of **separate checks**. Many people are on **expense accounts**, and they need to put it on their own credit card. That makes some extra work for us.	要預備好會有很多分開結帳的情形。很多人都可報銷帳單，會先用自己的信用卡刷卡。這樣我們的工作就會額外增加。
Colleen	Thanks for the tips. I'll follow you around, and let me know anything else I need to learn.	感謝您的提示。我會跟在你左右，若有我需要學習的地方，請讓我知道。
Cody	**Will do**, and you can take some of the tables as soon as you get comfortable.	我會的，只要你覺得可以勝任，就可以自己服務客人了。

Word Bank

compare to 相較於　fast-paced *adj.* 步調快的　or so 大約
gear(ed) *v.* 配合；適應；調整；做好準備　business lunch 商務午餐
the exception to the rule 例外　be prepared for 為……做好準備
separate checks 分開結帳　expense account(s) 報銷帳單；支出帳目
will do 我會這樣做的；會的

Unit 18 服務生

2 *Asking Guest Preferences* 詢問客人的喜好

Track 70

Introduction

A server is making suggestions for a guest. 服務生提供建議給客人。

Characters

Seth - Server	服務生
Melody - Guest	顧客

Conversation

Melody	I have a couple questions about the menu.	我有幾個關於菜單的問題。
Seth	I hope I have some answers. What would you like to know?	希望我的答案能供你參考。您想知道些什麼呢？
Melody	I'll get the entrées in a couple minutes, but I want to get something different to start. I'm **tired of** salad and soup.	我過一會就會點主菜，但我希望嘗試些不同的前菜。老是點沙拉和湯挺煩的。
Seth	I know just the thing: **escargot**.	我就只推這一道：田螺。
Melody	Isn't that **snails**?	這不就是蝸牛嗎？
Seth	Yes, and I know people think it sounds **unappetizing**, but they're really good. They're served **on the shell**, with a garlic butter sauce. It's not something you can get every day, and I really like them. Besides, you can go home and tell your friends you ate snails for dinner.	是的，我知道有些人認為這聽起來難以開胃，但這道菜真的很不錯。蝸牛肉已幫客人從殼內挑到外殼上，佐以大蒜奶油醬。這不是平常想吃就點得到的菜色，我真的很喜歡這道。此外，您回去後，可以告訴朋友你晚餐吃了蝸牛。
Melody	Umm... I'll think about it. What other **starters** would you recommend?	嗯…我會考慮的。你還推薦其他什麼樣的開頭菜？
Seth	Do you like seafood?	您喜歡吃海鮮嗎？

Melody	Yes, I do. What do you think of the crab pudding?	是的，我喜歡。你覺得螃蟹布丁如何？
Seth	That's delicious. You don't usually think of seafood and pudding together, but this really works. It's made with fresh Alaskan king crab. The pudding is made from eggs, white wine, and cream.	這道很美味。一般人不會把海鮮跟布丁放在一起，但這二種食材一起卻很對味，而且很美味。海鮮的部分是用新鮮的阿拉斯加帝王蟹做的，而布丁則是用雞蛋、白酒和奶油做成。
Melody	I think that sounds better than snails. Now, about the entrées.	我覺得聽起來比蝸牛餐好。現在，談談主菜。
Seth	What were you thinking of?	你想吃甚麼呢？
Melody	Not red meat, but I don't want anything **vegetarian**, either.	我不想點紅肉，也不大想點素食類的。
Seth	I'm going to go for seafood again and recommend the **lobster** pasta. It's made with fresh Maine lobster, mushrooms, onions, and **caviar**. It's one of the things we're **known for**; you won't find anything like it **elsewhere**.	那我會再次推薦海鮮類，並建議你點龍蝦義大利麵。它是由新鮮的緬因州龍蝦，蘑菇，洋蔥，和魚子醬做成。這道是我們招牌名菜，其他地方吃不到的。
Melody	Caviar? Really?	魚子醬？真的嗎？
Seth	Yes, it makes the whole dish come alive.	是的，它為整道菜加分不少。
Melody	Give us some more time to think this over.	多給我們一些時間考慮一下。
Seth	All right, I'll check back in a couple minutes.	好的，我會在幾分鐘內回來幫您點菜。

Word Bank

tired of 厭倦　escargot *n.[C]* 田螺；食用蝸牛　snail(s) *n.[C]* 蝸牛
unappetizing *adj.* 倒胃口的　on the shell 帶殼地　starter(s) *n.[C]* 開胃菜
vegetarian *adj.* 素食的　lobster *n.[C]* 龍蝦　caviar *n.[U]* 魚子醬
known for 以……聞名　elsewhere *adv.* 在別處

Unit 18 服務生

Server Assistant's Job 助理服務生的工作 Track 71

Introduction

A new server assistant starts training. 一個新的助理服務生開始培訓。

Susan - Server Assistant 助理服務生

Marge - Server Assistant Trainee 實習助理服務生

Conversation

Susan	So, this is your first day, huh?	那麼，這是你來的第一天，對嗎？
Marge	Yes, and the manager said you would be training me.	是的，經理說你會負責訓練我。
Susan	What made you want to come work here?	什麼原因讓你想來這裡工作？
Marge	I wanted a job I could do after school and on weekends. Restaurants are good for that.	我想找一份可以在放學後和週末做的工作。餐廳很適合。
Susan	Yes, I'm in school, too. I'll start by showing you where everything is.	沒錯，我也仍在就學。首先，我會將所有配置告訴你。
Marge	I have one question before we start. What **exactly** does a server assistant do? I **applied** without really knowing what job I wanted. I **figured** I'd be a dishwasher. Then they told me I could be a server assistant if I wanted. It **sounded better than** washing dishes, so I took it.	在我們開始之前，我有一個問題要問。助理服務生到底要做什麼？我申請了工作，卻不大清楚內容，以為會是洗碗工。後來他們告訴我，如果我想要，可以當助理服務生。聽起來比洗碗工還好些，所以我答應了。
Susan	There's nothing wrong with washing dishes. I kind of liked it. You don't have to deal with anyone except yourself and a couple other people, but it gets kind of messy.	當洗碗工沒什麼不好的，我還算喜歡。除了自己和其他幾個人之外，你不用與任何人接觸，只是工作有點髒亂就是了。

Marge	So anyway, what's our job?	無論如何，談談我們的工作吧？
Susan	It's just like what it sounds. We assist the servers and do anything they don't have time for. In other places they call us bussers. Our **main** job is to **turn the tables**.	這工作就像它的名字一樣。我們協助服務生，忙不過來時幫忙分擔一些。在其他地方，他們稱我們為打雜工。我們的主要工作是清桌。
Marge	What does that mean?	這是什麼意思呢？
Susan	We're mostly responsible for making a dirty table into a clean table. We clear off anything that's still on the table when the guests leave, then **reset** it for the next party.	我們主要負責把髒桌子清理乾淨。當客人離開後，我們清除桌面殘留物，再重新擺設好讓下一批客人使用。
Marge	That sounds easy enough.	這聽起來很容易。
Susan	It's not too bad, but sometimes it gets a little **hectic**. We have a lot to do when it's busy and lots of people are leaving at once.	還好，但有時會很忙亂。若客人很多、迴轉率高，就有很多事情要做。
Marge	What else do we do?	我們還有哪些事要做？
Susan	When we're not turning tables, we restock the dishes. We also help the servers take away dirty dishes, keep the water glasses full, and do whatever else they ask us to do.	當我們不清理桌面時，必須將碗盤歸位。我們還可以幫忙服務生回收髒盤子、補滿水杯，做任何他們要求幫忙做的事。

Part I
Part II
Part III
Part IV
Part V
Part VI

Word Bank

train(ing) *v.* 訓練　exactly *adv.* 確切地　applied 申請；此指應徵（apply）
figured 以為；認為　sound(ed) better than 聽起來比……好
main *adj.* 主要的　turn the tables 換桌；翻桌；扭轉形勢
reset *v.* 重置；重設　hectic *adj.* 忙亂的；繁忙的

Unit 18 服務生

4 *Presenting the Check and Collecting Payment*
出示帳單和收取費用  Track 72

Introduction

A waiter is explaining to a trainee how the guests pay for their meals. 一位服務生向實習生解釋客人如何結帳。

Characters  

Seth - Server	服務生
Colleen - Server Trainee	實習生

Conversation

Seth	You've seen everything we have to do to serve a table. Now it's time to bring them the **bill** and process the payment.	你已經了解服務客人用餐的大小事。現在輪到出示帳單和處理付款的程序。
Colleen	Why do the servers have to do that?	為什麼服務生要做這些事呢？
Seth	It's become **standard operating procedure** a lot of places. I think it saves the boss money. That way, they don't have to hire any cashiers. And it makes it look like you're giving the guests extra **service**.	這已經成為許多餐廳的標準作業程序了。我想這樣做會省下老闆的成本，這樣一來，也不用聘請任何收銀員。而且這看起來像是在幫客人提供額外服務。
Colleen	What ways can people pay for their meals?	客人結帳方式有哪些？
Seth	We take all the usual credit cards, and **cash**, of course. We used to see a lot of cash, but more and more people put everything on their cards.	我們收所有常見的信用卡，當然也收現金。我們以往大都收現，但越來越多的人凡事刷卡。
Colleen	But some people do still use cash?	但有些人還是用現金？
Seth	Yes, and that's a little harder for us than credit cards. We have to bring a **bank** with us to make change for them.	是的，這樣是比用信用卡麻煩。我們必須自己準備現款來找零。

Colleen	What if you don't bring enough change?	如果零錢不夠怎麼辦？
Seth	You can get change from the manager. But it's not always easy to find one, so it's better if you bring your own bank.	你可以跟經理拿。但並不是甚麼時候都拿得到，所以最好自己準備現款。
Colleen	What happens if you make a **mistake** with the cash?	如果收付現金出錯會怎麼樣？
Seth	That's one reason why cash is more **difficult**. At the end of the day, you have to pay for all the checks from the tables you served. So, if you're **short**, you have to pay for it out of your own pocket.	這就是收現金比較麻煩的原因。每一天結束的時候，你必須繳出所有服務桌數的帳單金額。所以，如果錢有短少，你就要從自己口袋裡掏錢出來補。
Colleen	I'll be very careful when I count out my money. When do you give the check to the table?	我會小心核對我負責的款項。何時要出示帳單給客人呢？
Seth	You should wait until everyone is done eating, but quite often someone will ask for it ahead of time. In that case, you give it to them then. I'll show you how to process credit cards in just a minute.	你應該等到客人用完餐再送帳單，但通常有人會提前跟你要。這時，你就直接把帳單交給他們。我將告訴你如何在一分鐘內處理刷卡消費。

Word Bank

present(ing) *v.* 呈現；提出　bill *n.[C]* 帳單
standard operating procedure 標準作業程序
service *n.[U/C]* 服務　cash *n.[U]* 現金　bank *n.[C]* 此指現款與零錢
mistake *n.[C]* 錯誤　difficult *adj.* 困難的　short *adj.* 短缺的；不足的

Unit 18 服務生

小牙籤計價——西班牙小酒館

上一個章節我們品嘗了費時的法國料理，這個章節我們來點簡單的餐點。說到簡單又時尚的餐點，非西班牙的 Las Tapas 莫屬。所謂的 Tapas 就是在西班牙飲食中各式各樣小份量的前菜或點心的統稱，又稱 Pincho（西班牙語）。很多西班牙人會在晚上下班後先跟同事或是朋友去 Tapas Bar 吃 Tapas 然後再回家吃晚餐，它特殊的地方在於每個 Pincho 上面都會插著計價用的牙籤（Palillo）。

通常小酒館會有一個吧檯擺放著各式的 Pincho，客人可以依照自己的喜愛挑選想品嘗的，而這時小牙籤也發揮了些作用——方便客戶取用。通常牙籤有長有短，甚至於有些會用顏色標註，每種顏色或長短都有不同的價格，當用餐結束後，服務人員則會依照客戶盤子上的牙籤計算今天的消費，當然也有部分店家不將食物插滿牙籤，相信客戶會誠實的告訴他，他一共取用了幾個點心，依照客戶說的數字來收費。

在西班牙吃 Tapas 的時，你可以搭配上一杯冰涼的啤酒或是 Sangria 來品嘗，當然也有人搭配紅酒白酒等等各種飲料，這部分並無特殊的規定，端看客戶的喜好。現在讓我們來介紹一下常見和受歡迎的 Tapas 吧！

Patata Bravas 炸馬鈴薯塊佐美乃滋辣醬

這是一道西班牙是最經典的 Tapas，無論在哪一家店都一定可以吃的到。西班牙人也跟美國人一樣非常喜歡吃馬鈴薯，所以許多菜色中都一定會加上馬鈴薯，而這一道炸馬鈴薯更是人人都愛吃的一道菜。

Jam 和 Chorizo 生火腿 / 生香腸

西班牙生火腿是先將火腿醃過後拿去風乾，通常是切成薄片上桌，可單吃，也可配上一片法國麵包一起吃（義大利人通常使用此吃法）。Chorizo 則是西班牙香腸，一般也是生吃，常見的吃法是夾在法國長棍麵包 Baguette 中品嘗。

Croquetas 和 Bunyol 炸馬鈴薯肉泥 / 炸魚

馬鈴薯泥加上火腿或雞肉或牛肉或是鮪魚再裹粉炸，口感外酥脆內軟綿。Bunyol 就是炸鱈魚球，味道很簡單，品嘗起來跟日式的炸魚很類似。

Pulpo a la Gallega 章魚切片佐辣椒粉

是西班牙西北部 Galicia 地區道地的料理，講究的是新鮮，調味上也偏向重口味。

Pescadito Frito 炸小魚

這跟剛剛介紹的 Bunyol 不太一樣，Pescadito Frito 比較像是台灣的一般炸溪魚，小魚整條地品嘗，在西班牙也是常見的 Tapas 料理。

Champinon 炒菇類

做法很簡單就是利用橄欖油、青醬，加上季節蘑菇，佐些香料快火熱炒，簡單又好吃。

Esparragos Placho 煎綠蘆筍

季節綠蘆筍小火煎，起鍋後灑點鹽與起司，非常地清爽。

Montaditos 法式麵包佐上海鮮或肉或蔬菜

以一塊法式麵包，在麵包上面放上份量約一小口的食物，有時可以搭配海鮮，例如蝦子、章魚或是沙拉、肉泥等。

Tortilla Espanola 西班牙蛋餅

蛋加上馬鈴薯，通常還會加上洋蔥一起煎成蛋餅，這也是道地的西班牙料理，常常可以見到西班牙人拿 Tortilla 加在法國長棍麵包 Baguette 裡面一起品嘗，是道必點佳餚。

介紹了這麼多的 Tapas，你一定會問這真的是餐前的小點心嗎？是的，不要懷疑 Tapas 真的是西班牙人晚餐前約會或是交際必品嘗的食物，重點是品嘗完點心後，他們還是會準時回家與家人用餐。

Unit 19 服務生在廚房

 Special Ingredients 了解特殊食材 

Introduction

A new server asks about some menu items. 新手服務生詢問菜單菜色。

Characters  

Debra - Server Trainee 實習生
Ben - Dining Room Manager 餐區經理
Dean - Sous Chef 大廚

Conversation

Ben	It's our **policy** to have our new servers spend some time in every part of the kitchen.	餐廳規定，新來的服務生要花點時間到廚房各處見習。
Debra	That sounds like a good idea. That way I can learn how the cooks do their jobs, right?	聽起來不錯！這樣就可以了解廚師們怎麼做事的，對吧？
Ben	Yes, that's the idea. You've had some time to study the menu, so ask any questions you need to.	對，就是這樣！妳已經花了時間研究過菜單了，有問題都可以發問！
Debra	All right, you lead and I'll **follow**.	好，你帶頭，我跟後！
Ben	The first area we'll visit is the prep area. This is where all the food, sauces, and soups are prepared.	第一個要去的是準備區。這是所有的食物、醬料及各式湯品準備的地方。
Debra	Speaking of sauces, I'd like to know what's in the **tartar sauce** that comes with the **fish & chips**.	說到醬料，我想知道炸魚及炸薯條附的塔塔醬是甚麼成份？
Ben	You know, I'm not really sure about that. Why don't we see if Dean has enough time to explain it. Hi Dean, do you have a minute?	這個嘛，我不大清楚！為何不看看 Dean 是否有空解釋給我們聽？嗨，Dean，你有空嗎？

Dean	Sure, it's still a couple hours until we open. What would you like to know?	沒問題！開店還要好幾個小時。妳想知道甚麼呢？
Debra	What's in the tartar sauce?	塔塔醬裡有甚麼？
Dean	Usually, it's made from **mayonnaise** and chopped **pickles**. Here, we make it **from scratch**. We use eggs, a little oil, some white wine vinegar, and our special touch, which is just a hint of **jalapeno juice** and **Dijon mustard**.	通常有美乃滋及碎黃瓜。我們這裡則是全程自行製作。用蛋、一點油、一些白酒醋及一點特殊添加物，也就是加微量的墨西哥辣椒醬及法國狄戎芥末醬。
Debra	Thanks, and I have one more question. Where does our caviar come from?	謝啦！我還有一個問題。我們的魚子醬從哪來的？
Dean	Most of the caviar sold these days comes from Iran or Russia. Ours is **organic**, and comes from a farm in Spain.	現今大部分市售的魚子醬來自伊朗或俄羅斯。我們的魚子醬是有機的，來自西班牙某個養殖場。
Debra	That's a long way to come for some little fish eggs.	哇！這些小小的魚卵真是費了好大一番功夫才到這。
Dean	Yes, but it's really a tasty treat.	是啊！但這真是一道可口美食！

Word Bank

policy *n.[C/U]* 策略；方針　follow *v.* 跟隨　tartar sauce 塔塔醬
fish & chips 炸魚與炸薯條　mayonnaise *n.[U]* 美乃滋
pickle(s) *n.[C/U]* 酸黃瓜；漬物　from scratch 從頭做起；從零開始
jalapeno juice 墨西哥辣椒醬　Dijon mustard 法國狄戎芥末醬
organic *n.* 有機的

Unit 19 服務生在廚房

2 *Cooking Methods* 烹調方式

Track 74

Introduction

A server trainee is introduced to some cooking methods used at the restaurant. 向實習服務生介紹餐廳烹調方法。

Characters

Debra - Server Trainee 實習生
Ben - Dining Room Manager 餐區經理

Conversation

Ben	Let's continue our kitchen tour. I'll show you the **smoker**. It's back **in the back**.	繼續我們的廚房巡禮。我會讓妳看看煙燻爐，在廚房後面的後方處。
Debra	What do we use that for?	那是用來做什麼的？
Ben	Some of the meats and fish taste really good when they're cooked in smoke.	一些煙燻過後的肉及魚類，嘗起來真的很好吃！
Debra	How is it different from roasting?	那跟烘烤有甚麼差別？
Ben	It's basically the same, except that in roasting you can use anything to provide the heat. In smoking, we use wood. That **imparts** a great flavor to whatever is being smoked.	基本上是一樣的。差別在於烘烤時，用任何方式提供熱源都可以。然而煙燻時，我們用木材。那樣可以增添煙燻食物一種很棒的風味！
Debra	I see. I have another question. I haven't seen a **toaster** anywhere on this tour. I thought all restaurants had one.	明白了！ 我還有一個問題。到目前為止，沒看到廚房裡有烤麵包機。我以為每個餐廳至少都有一台。
Ben	We don't serve breakfast, so we don't need to toast bread very much. For the sandwiches that come with toasted bread, we just put the bread on the **grill** and toast it along with whatever is on the sandwich.	我們不供應早餐，所以不太需要烤麵包。至於那些要用到烤土司的三明治，只需把土司放到烤架上，跟吐司上的東西一起烘烤即可。

Debra	Why do we do it that way?	這樣做是為什麼？
Ben	That way, the bread gets some of the flavor of the rest of the sandwich. It makes it taste better. Did you have any more questions?	這樣，可以讓吐司增添其他食材的香味，使三明治更好吃。還有其他問題嗎？
Debra	Yeah, I know we have **barbecued** ribs on the menu, but I haven't seen a barbecue back here, either.	有的，我在菜單上看到有烤豬肋這道菜，但是在這我也看不到烤架。
Ben	Those are **American-style** barbecued ribs. They're roasted in the oven, then finished off on the char broiler. The "barbecue" really comes from the sauce that goes on top. It's a **mildly** spicy tomato sauce. In the US, it's called barbecue sauce.	因為那是美式的烤豬肋，是放在烤箱裡烘烤的，最後再放在木炭式燒烤爐上烤過。「Barbecue」這個字其實是指淋在上面的醬料，是一種微辣的番茄醬汁。在美國，叫做BBQ醬。
Debra	All right, I guess we still have some parts of the kitchen to look at. Thanks for the **tour**; I'm learning a lot.	好的，我想廚房的其他部分還有得看看。謝謝你的廚房巡禮，我學到很多！

Word Bank

smoker *n.[C]* 煙燻爐　in the back 在後方　impart(s) *v.* 給予
toaster *n.[C]* 烤麵包機　grill *n.[C]* 烤架
barbecued *adj.* 在篝火或地灶上烤炙的　American-style *adj.* 美式的
mildly *adv.* 略微地　tour *n.[C]* 參觀

Unit 19 服務生在廚房

3 *Timing Orders at Lunch* 午餐下單時機

 Track 75

Introduction

A server is explaining when to place guest orders in the kitchen. 一位服務生解釋何時該送單到廚房。

Characters 

Colleen - Server Trainee 實習生
Cody - Server 服務生

Conversation

Cody	I think your training is just about finished, Colleen. But we do still have to cover one important **aspect** of waiting tables.	Colleen，我想妳的訓練差不多完成了。但是我們還必須涵蓋一項重要的餐桌服務概念。
Colleen	What is that?	是什麼呢？
Cody	How to make sure the table gets their food at the **proper** time.	就是如何確定送餐時間點正確。
Colleen	Is that hard?	很難嗎？
Cody	It's one of the more difficult aspects of this job. You have to read each table and see if they're in a hurry or not. Then you have to **time** their meal **accordingly**.	這可是這份工作中比較難的部分之一。妳必須觀察每桌客人，看看他們是否急著要點東西。之後，妳還必須照點單按時上菜。
Colleen	Since it's lunchtime right now, do we assume that everyone is in a hurry?	既然現在是午餐時間，要假設每位客人都很趕嗎？
Cody	That's usually right. Most people have an hour, or maybe a little more, to get here, eat, and get back to work. But **every once in a while** you'll get a table that wants to take their time.	通常沒錯！大部分人有一小時時間，也許多一點點，趕來這吃飯，再回去上班。但偶爾你也會遇到想慢慢用餐的客人！
Colleen	How do you know if they do?	如何知道他們是這一類的？

Cody	You can often tell by what they order. If they get an appetizer or a bottle of wine, that **signals** to you that they're in no hurry and want to enjoy their meal.	藉由點單往往判斷得出來。如果點了一份開胃菜或是一瓶酒，就意味著他們不趕，想要享受美食。
Colleen	And if they just order entrées, you can usually assume they want to get out fast?	如果他們只點主菜，可否假設他們想快點吃完？
Cody	That's right. Look at this check. This table came in and ordered right away. They didn't get any soup or other starters.	沒錯！瞧瞧這份帳單。這桌客人一進來就立刻點菜，沒有點湯或其他前菜。
Colleen	So, with a check like that, you turn it into the kitchen **immediately**, right?	所以，像這樣的點單，就要立刻送單到廚房，對嗎？
Cody	Yes, but look at table 32 over there. They look like a couple who want to have a **leisurely** lunch. They ordered drinks first, and then waited to order until after they'd sipped them a while. So, I won't hurry their order through at all.	是的！但妳看看32桌的客人，看起來像是想悠閒享受午餐的一對。他們先點了飲料，等到輕啜幾口飲料後才會點其他的。所以，我完全不會催促廚房趕做他們的單。
Colleen	I hope it won't take me too long to get used to reading the tables.	希望我不會太久才逐漸習慣斷定何時點單出單。

Word Bank

aspect *n.[C]* 方面；觀點　proper *adj.* 適當的　time *v.* 安排時間；衡量時機
accordingly *adv.* 相應地；照著　every once in a while 偶爾
signal(s) *v.* 發出信號　immediately *adv.* 立刻地　leisurely *adj.* 從容不迫的

Unit 19 服務生在廚房

 Interaction between Cooks and Servers
廚師與服務生的互動  Track 76

Introduction

Several servers have to talk to the cooks about their orders. 幾位服務生必須跟廚師說明客人的點單。

Characters

Cody - Server	服務生
Jim - Cook	廚師
Naomi - Server	服務生
David - Expeditor	傳菜領班
Seth - Server	服務生

Conversation

Jim	Could you get Cody to come back here? I need to talk to him about an order.	可以把 Cody 叫過來嗎？我要問他點單的事情！
David	I just buzzed him. It should be just a minute.	我已經呼叫他了。應該快來了！
	(30 seconds later)	30 秒後
Cody	What did I get buzzed for? I shouldn't have any food up yet.	呼叫我有什麼事？應該還沒有要上的菜吧。
Jim	Cody, it's a little hard to cook a steak when you don't tell me what **temp** you want it.	Cody，你沒告訴我牛排要幾分熟，可是有點難煎的！
Cody	What table is that?	幾號桌呢？
Jim	It's the filet on table 27.	27 號桌菲力牛排。
Cody	Oh, sorry about that. It should be medium rare.	啊！真抱歉！應該是三分熟！
Jim	All right, thanks.	好，謝謝啦！
	(later)	稍後
Naomi	Jim, did you see on table 14 where I said "see me"?	Jim，你有沒有看到我在 14 桌的單上寫上「找我」的字樣呢？
Jim	Yeah, what do you need?	有啊！妳要什麼呢？

Naomi	The lady wants the caviar for the lobster pasta on the side. That won't **be any problem**, will it? I **hope**?	這位女士想要在龍蝦義大利麵旁邊放上魚子醬。沒問題的，對不對？可以吧？
Jim	Of course it won't. It's just **sprinkled** on top as a **garnish**.	當然沒問題！只要撒在上面當作配料即可。
Naomi	I didn't think you'd have any trouble. I just used "see me" because it was too hard to **type** it into the computer.	我想對你來說不成問題。我用「找我」字樣，因為太難直接輸入電腦了。
Jim	That's all right. Anything else?	沒關係！有其他要求嗎？
Naomi	No, not for them. But I'm sure I'll have some more requests before too long. It seems to be **substitution** night tonight.	沒有，這道菜都沒問題了。但是我肯定沒多久客人要求又會接踵而至。今晚似乎會有很多替換食材的要求。
	(later)	稍後
Seth	Hey guys, I have a special **request**.	嗨，夥伴們，我這兒有個特別要求！
David	Imagine that!	說來聽聽！
Seth	Is it **possible** to get the bread pudding served cold?	有沒有可能出冷盤的麵包布丁？
Jim	Sorry, but we keep that in the warmer. There's no way we can cool off a piece, unless it's going to be a while before they want it.	抱歉，我們把這道甜點放在保溫箱，不可能將它單塊冷卻，除非他們願意等一會兒。
Seth	No, they just ordered dessert. I'll just tell them there's not enough time for you to put it in the **freezer**.	不行這樣，因為他們只點了甜點而已。我會告訴他們時間不夠把這道甜點冰起來。

Word Bank

temp *n.[U]* 熟度　be any problem 有任何問題　hope *v.* 希望
sprinkle(d) *v.* 灑　garnish *n.[C]* 配菜　type *v.* 輸入　substitution *n.[U]* 替換
request *n.[C]* 要求　possible *adj.* 可能的　freezer *n.[C]* 冷藏箱

Unit 19 服務生在廚房

歐式料理食材常客

歐洲飲食可說是非常多元化，這都有賴於中世紀那些大大小小的戰爭，將歐亞大陸的飲食做了一個有趣的交流。

在歐洲的飲食文化裡，包含了法、英、德、義、波蘭、西班牙、拜占庭等各式的料理，使用的食材也是略有差異。

歐式料理食材主角

穀類

歐洲人最重要的主食就是麵包與麵條，而麵包與麵條便是由穀類製作而成。歐洲人一天會吃 1 至 1.5 公斤的麵包，其中裸麥、大麥、蕎麥、粟麥、燕麥最為盛行。當然除了麵包與麵條外，穀類有時也會煮成稀粥、乳粥，例如西班牙燉飯。

橄欖油

橄欖原產於地中海沿岸，是小亞細亞木犀科常綠喬木，目前有 500 個品種，地中海、愛琴海沿岸為主要產地，佔世界總量的 95%，且歐洲飲食絕對少不了它。橄欖油大致可分為精製橄欖油（extra virgin oil）、原味橄欖油（virgin oil）和純橄欖油（pure oil）等三大類。通常精製橄欖油用於生食，例如佐蔬菜，純橄欖油則用於火炒、煎炸使用。

鯡魚、鱈魚

於大西洋和波羅的海鯡魚是當地盛產的魚獲，曾對北歐經濟扮演舉足輕重的角色。這些魚獲歐洲人除了新鮮烹調外，也會將它們鹽醃、風乾，有時也會使用煙醺方式料理，醃鯡魚便是一項熱門的商品，曾由北海運到遙遠的君士坦丁堡出售。其他常見魚類有梭子魚、鯉魚、鱸魚、七鰓鰻、鮭魚、生蠔、青口、帶子是沿河或沿海居民經常的普遍食糧。

☑ 豬肉、羊肉

豬肉、羊肉在歐洲是非常常見的肉類，料理的方式也多是使用香料或是醬料進行醃製後火烤食用，比較少有炸肉的飲食方式，並且對於肉類的處理，不像美式料理喜愛單純地原味品嘗，這可能跟當地文化與農特產相關。

☑ 捲心菜、甜菜、洋蔥、蒜、胡蘿蔔、番茄、馬鈴薯

歐洲人經常食用的蔬菜基本上也是以搭配主餐（肉、魚）食用，不然便是食用沙拉的食材，當然也有些地區有其特殊的食用蔬菜，例如德國酸菜。

☑ 香料

歐洲是個種植許多香料的地區，其原生的香料，包括鼠尾草、芥末、香芹、香菜、薄荷、蒔蘿和茴香等。然而歐洲人愛香料的瘋狂心態到了大航海時代發揮到極致。在那時代，海運、陸運皆盛行，歐洲人開始懂得進口非當地生產的香料，例如黑椒、藏紅花、肉桂、桂皮、孜然、肉豆蔻、薑和丁香等，也因此讓歐式料理充滿了各式各樣的芳香，也造就了歐洲人料理時多愛用香料的基礎。

Unit 20 食材管理及餐廳清潔

1 *Restaurant Supply Companies* 餐廳食材供應商

 Track 77

Introduction

The managers talk about which restaurant supply companies they want to deal with and which ones need to change. 經理們談論哪家食材供應商要交涉，哪家需要替換掉。

Characters  

Betty - General Manager 總經理
Nora - Chef 行政主廚

Conversation

Betty	Hey, Nora, could you come in about an hour **early** tomorrow?	哈囉，Nora，你明天可以提早一小時來嗎？
Nora	Sure, what for?	可以啊！為了什麼事？
Betty	We need to talk about **updating** some of our suppliers.	我們要討論更替供應商的事情。
Nora	Not a problem. I've been thinking we might need to make a few **changes** myself.	沒問題！我自己也一直在想，應該要做一些改變了！
	(the next day)	（隔天早上）
Betty	Thanks for coming in. Let's start off with our **dry goods** supplier. Have you been happy with them?	謝謝你提早過來。我們先從乾貨供應商開始。你對他們滿意嗎？
Nora	Not really. I don't think their prices are all that good, and their service doesn't **warrant** their higher prices.	並不盡然。我不認為他們的價錢全都那麼合理，而且他們的高價位並不保證服務好。
Betty	That's sort of what I've been thinking.	這也是我一直在思考的事情。

Nora	They seem to get orders wrong more often than other people. This week I ordered five bags of **whole wheat** flour, and they sent me white instead. It took until the next day to fix, too.	他們似乎比其他供應商更常在訂單上出錯。這個星期我訂了五袋全麥麵粉，他們卻送來白麵粉！也要等到隔天才換到貨。
Betty	All right, well I think we should put the contract out for **bids**. We'll see if we can get a lower price, and ask around to see who is known for their service, too.	好吧！我想就開放這份合約來競標，看看是否能拿到較低價錢，也打聽一下哪家供應商以服務聞名。
Betty	The next thing is our cheese guys. They have a really good **product**, but it's just too expensive.	接下來是我們的起司供應夥伴。他們的東西品質好，但是價錢實在貴。
Nora	I'll talk to them and see if they can discount it a little more. How much do we need to save on that?	我會問問他們是否可給些折扣！我們該降低多少起司成本呢？
Betty	We need to get it down by at least 8% in order to make our **food cost** correct. Just see what they can do. I hope they can come down on price; I'd hate to have to go somewhere else.	必須減少至少 8% 的成本支出，才能使我們的食材成本合理。看看他們能怎麼做，希望他們可以砍些價格。我不想換廠商。
Nora	I have a couple more to talk about. Let's keep going.	我還有些問題要跟你討論，我們繼續吧！

Word Bank

early *adv.* 提早　updating *v.* 更新（update）　change(s) *n.[C]* 改變
dry goods 乾貨　warrant *v.* 保證　whole wheat 全麥的
bid(s) *n.* 減價；投標　product *n.[C]* 產品　food cost 食材成本

Unit 20 食材管理及餐廳清潔

2 Cleaning Up Spills 清理汙漬 Track 78

Introduction

Employees clean up a couple spills during the shift. 員工當班時清理一些灑出來的汙漬。

Characters

Cody - Server	服務生
Susan - Server Assistant	助理服務生
Ben - Dining Room Manager	餐區經理
Debra - Server Trainee	實習生
Justine - Guest	顧客
Naomi - Server	服務生
Seth - Server	服務生

Conversation

Debra	Hey Cody, your table 21 just spilled a glass of water. Do you want me to help you clean it up?	嗨，Cody，你 21 號桌的顧客剛弄翻一杯水。你要我幫你清理嗎？
Cody	Yeah, that'd be great. I'll go out there and get all the stuff off the table. Could you bring out another tablecloth?	好啊！如果可以就太棒了！我會過去把所有桌上的東西拿開。可以請妳拿另一條桌布過來嗎？
Susan	Do you need me to help you, too?	你也需要我幫忙嗎？
Cody	Yeah, could you bring out a big **tray** and put it on a **tray jack**?	好啊，可否請妳帶一個大的托盤、並把它放置在托盤架上？
	(at the table)	（在餐桌旁）
Cody	Hi folks, let me help you with this. It happens **all the time**. The easiest way to take care of this problem is to just **replace** the tablecloth. I'm going to put the centerpiece on the tray over here, along with your glasses and silverware.	各位，讓我帶你們做這個。這種事常發生，最簡單的處理方法就是替換桌布。我會把餐桌擺設物放到這邊的托盤上，還有其他的杯子和餐具組也要放過來。

Justine	Thanks very much. My son wasn't paying attention, and his **elbow** hit the glass.	非常謝謝你！我兒子不小心，手肘撞到了玻璃杯。
Cody	Now, if you can just pick up your dinner plates, we'll change tablecloths and you can keep on eating.	現在，請拿起你們的餐盤，我們換了桌布後，你們就可以繼續用餐了！
Susan	I'll get the water that's on the floor.	我會清理灑在地上的水。
Cody	And I'll be back with new bread plates and silverware in just a second.	那麼，我馬上回來放置新的麵包盤及餐具。
Justine	Thanks, we're sorry.	謝謝啦！真是不好意思！
Cody	No problem; we're **used to** doing this.	沒關係的！我們已經習慣處理這種事。
	(in a different part of the restaurant)	在餐廳的另一邊
Ben	Seth, could you help Naomi? She just dropped a salad off her tray.	Seth，可以幫一下 Naomi 嗎？ 她剛從托盤上掉了一盤沙拉下來。
Seth	Sure, I wouldn't want someone else to **slip** on it and fall. Here Naomi, I'll get the salad off the floor. You get back in the back and get the new salad you need.	好的，我也不想看見有人踩到而滑倒！ Naomi，我會去清理掉地上的沙拉，妳回去後面那拿盤新沙拉。
Naomi	Are you sure you're not too **busy**?	你確定忙得過來？
Seth	No, I'll just get a couple **towels** and a **broom** and this'll be no problem. You just serve your table.	沒問題的！我只要去拿幾條毛巾及掃把來清理，就沒問題了。妳去服務顧客吧。

Word Bank

spill(s) *n.[C]* 噴濺物　tray *n.[C]* 托盤　tray jack 托盤架
all the time 總是；一向　replace *v.* 替換　elbow *n.[C]* 手肘
used to 以往習慣於……　slip *v.* 滑倒　busy *adj.* 忙碌的
towel(s) *n.[C]* 毛巾　broom *n.[C]* 掃帚

Unit 20 食材管理及餐廳清潔

3 Sidework 雜務工作

 Track 79

Introduction

A waiter is explaining the day's sidework to a trainee. 一位服務生在為實習生解釋每日雜務工作。

Characters 

Debra - Server Trainee 實習生
Seth - Server 服務生

Conversation

Seth	Since our last table is still eating, why don't we get started on our sidework, so we can get out of here.	既然最後一桌客人還在用餐，我們何不開始做雜務呢？趕快弄就可早點走！
Debra	What is our sidework tonight?	今晚的雜務是什麼？
Seth	We have **restock**. Everywhere in the kitchen that there are dishes, we need to make sure there are **plenty** for tomorrow.	今天要做的是備盤。補齊廚房裡所有用到盤子的地方，必須確定明天有足量可以使用。
Debra	Where should I start?	該從哪裡開始？
Seth	We can start on the soup area. You need to **separate** these **doilies** and put one on each plate for the soup cup **underliners**. It takes a while to get them separated, so go ahead and start on that while I check and see how our tables are doing.	我們可以先從濃湯區開始。妳必須分開這些小飾巾，並在每個湯杯專用的小盤子上放一張飾巾。要花點時間才能把飾巾都分開，在我巡桌時，妳就可以開始去進行了！
	(a couple minutes later)	幾分鐘過後
Seth	I'm back. Everyone is doing fine. Table 44 is about ready to clear. How are the doilies doing?	我回來了，大家都做得很好，44桌已經差不多可以清理了。飾巾分得怎樣？
Debra	This is **kind of** slow.	有點慢！

Seth	Yeah, just **keep at it**, and get two big **stacks** of plates with doilies on them. I'll start on the silverware.	是啊，繼續做吧！去搬兩大疊上面有飾巾的盤子過來。我要開始擺放餐具組了！
Debra	What do we need for that?	還需要甚麼？
Seth	Right here by the soups we need spoons. And over on the line we need big pasta spoons and steak knives.	湯的旁邊需要一些湯匙。在另一邊需要大的通心麵湯匙及牛排刀。
Debra	Where are those **kept**?	那些餐具都放在哪？
Seth	Come with me into the dishroom and I'll show you right now. See, all the silverware is over there. Grab as many steak knives as you can, and I'll get the soup spoons.	跟我一起去餐盤室，我馬上可以告訴你放哪。看，所有的餐具組都在那邊。盡可能多拿一些牛排刀，我來拿湯匙。
Debra	I finished the underliners. What's next?	湯盤上的飾巾都擺放完成了。接下來做甚麼？
Seth	You'll never believe this, but we need more doilied plates. Count out about 25 of them and put them by the tea **station**. We serve the hot tea on those, too.	你永遠不會相信，但是我還需要更多放了飾巾的湯盤。算一下約拿二十五個湯盤，然後放在熱茶區。我們送熱茶時也要用到這些盤子。
Debra	Anything else?	還有其他的事嗎？
Seth	No, I think we have it all done. Now we just need to find a manager to **check** the sidework, and then we can go home.	沒了，我想我們都把事情完成了。現在只要把經理找來，檢查做好的雜務工作，就可以回家了。

Word Bank

restock *v.* 補貨　plenty *n.[U]* 大量；充足　separate *v.* 分開
doilies *n.[C]* 墊杯盤的小飾巾（doily）　underliner(s) *n.[C]* 底盤
kind of 有點兒；稍微　keep at it 堅持做；持續進行　stack(s) *n.[C]* 疊；堆
kept *v.* 存放；保管（keep）　station *n.[C]* 區；站　check *v.* 檢查

Unit 20 食材管理及餐廳清潔

 *Waitstaff and Cleaning* 全體服務生與清潔工作

Introduction

The waitstaff has special cleaning duties tonight.
全體服務生今晚有特別的清潔勤務。

Characters 

Debra - Server Trainee 實習生
Naomi - Server 服務生
Ben - Dining Room Manager 餐區經理

Conversation

Naomi	Tonight is deep cleaning night, so we'll be here about half an hour longer than normal.	今晚是例行性的大掃除，所以我們將比平常多待上半個小時。
Debra	I didn't know about that. **How often** does this happen?	我不是很懂。這件事多久進行一次？
Naomi	We do it once a month. It's always on a different night, so the same people don't **get stuck** doing it every time.	每個月進行一次，都不會在同一個晚間時段，這樣就不會每次都是同樣一群人擠著做。
Debra	That sounds fair. And it's only half an hour, right?	聽起來蠻公平的。每次都只要半個小時而已，對嗎？
Naomi	Well, sometimes it **runs on** a bit. But it does help make the restaurant look better.	這個嘛，有時候時間會超過一點。但這樣的確能使餐廳看起來乾淨許多。
	(at the end of the shift)	（晚班結束時）
Ben	OK everyone, **gather round** and I'll give you your duties. Naomi and Colleen, you're one team. You get the **undersides** of the tables.	好，大家這邊集合，我會分配該做的勤務。Naomi 與 Colleen，你們兩人一組。清理桌子下面。
Debra	What does this mean for us?	我們到底該怎麼做？

Naomi	We just have to clean the bottom of the tables.	我們只要清理桌子底部即可。
Debra	I guess those don't get done on a normal shift very often.	我想，這通常不會在正常上班時間拿來做。
Naomi	No, that's why we're doing it now.	沒錯，這就是為何我們現在得做。
Ben	Here you go, guys. Take your **scrapers**, and go get some rags from the back.	來吧，各位，拿著你們的刮刀，再到後面拿幾條抹布。
Debra	What are the scrapers for?	刮刀用來做甚麼呢？
Naomi	We have to remove any gum we find stuck to the bottom of the tables.	我們必須清掉所有黏在桌子底部的口香糖。
Debra	Ooh yuck, do people actually do that?	好噁心呦！客人真的會這樣？
Naomi	We don't see it too often, but it does happen. Some people can be kind of **gross**. We also have to make sure the bottoms of the tables don't have any dirt or food on them.	不常看到，但的確發生過。有些人會做些噁心的事。我們還必須確保桌子底部不會有任何污垢，或是殘留的食物在上面。
Debra	And then we do the table legs?	接下來就是清理桌腳嗎？
Naomi	Yes, and the **bases**. Those get a lot of dirt and dust from people's shoes on them. This isn't the best duty, but it's not the worst. And it won't take too long.	是啊，還有底座。 因為客人的鞋子踩在上面，常有許多灰塵與汙垢。這不是最好的差事，但也不是最糟的。而且不用花太久就可以完成。
Debra	All right, let's get **scrubbing**.	好了，咱們開始刷吧！

Word Bank

how often 多久一次；多頻繁　get stuck 困住；卡住　run(s) on 超時；持續
gather round 集合；聚攏　underside(s) *n.[C]* 底面　scraper(s) *n.[C]* 刮刀
gross *adj.* 噁心的　base(s) *n.[C]* 底座；基部　scrub(bing) *v.* 用力刷洗

Unit 20 食材管理及餐廳清潔

決定耶誕菜色——廚房分工

每年聖誕節各飯店、餐廳都會推出聖誕大餐，餐點的組合多為該餐廳最具特色或節慶限定的菜色，然而這個菜色是誰決定的呢？

歐洲的飯店大部份都具備有完整的廚師層級，每個人的職務都有其重要性，可說是分工細微、清楚。

廚師等級

- 行政主廚（Executive Chef）：是廚房最高階主管，Unit10 說明過其負責整個廚房的管理，所有的菜單與食譜都必須經過他的審核，才能推出讓顧客品嚐，當然其也決定食材與調味品的採購。另外他負責訓練廚師學徒，監督廚房的衛生等。
- 大廚（Deputy Kitchen Chef）：大廚是行政主廚的副手，受命於行政主廚管理廚房事物，通常範圍較小的餐廳僅有大廚，未有行政主廚。
- 二廚（Senior Chef）：通常專職負責主廚交辦特定作業站的烹調工作。在每一個作業站中，會安排一、二名廚師協助二廚執行。
- 三廚（Cook）：負責烹調某特定菜餚的廚師，通常會是牛排、海鮮、義大利麵等。
- 四廚（Junior Cook）：協助二廚的助理，專職負責準備烹調材料器材等。
- 學徒（Apprentice）：通常是餐飲學校的實習生，負責一般打雜與清掃工作。
- 調味師（Sauce Maker）：調製各式醬料、前菜，通常這個職務皆是由資深廚師擔任，其掌控了全餐廳調味的重責大任。
- 烤炸師（Roast Cook）：專職負責烤、炸食物的廚師，並受命於主廚或是二廚。
- 煎烙師（Grill Cook）：專職負責烤架上碳火煎烙食物的廚師，並受命於主廚或是二廚。
- 海鮮師（Fish Cook）：專職負責處理海鮮料裡的廚師，並受命於主廚或是二廚。
- 煮湯師（Soup Cook）：專職負責準備各式湯品的廚師，並受命於主廚或是二廚。
- 素菜師（Vegetable Cook）：專職負責生菜或各式蔬菜類食物的廚師，並受命於主廚或是二廚。
- 冷盤師（Pantry Supervisor）：專職負責準備與調理冷盤類食物的廚師，並受命於主廚或是二廚。

- 點心師（Pastry Cook）：專職負責製作蛋糕、甜點的廚師，並受命於主廚或是二廚。
- 伙食師：專職負責做餐點給飯店內部職員的廚師。
- 幫手（Spare Hand）：廚房協助廚師並執行各項雜務的廚工。
- 跑單員（Announcer）：將前檯服務人員所點之菜單交給廚房各作業站料理的廚師。
- 碗盤洗滌員（Dishwasher）：負責清洗所有餐具、廚具、杯皿等。
- 鍋鑊洗滌員（Pot and Pan Washer）：在超大型廚房中更細的工作分類，負責清洗廚師用的鍋、鑊、盆、烤箱等。

看完了上述的廚師等級，我們可以知道當一個飯店要規劃即將來到的聖誕節大餐時，首先須由行政主廚或主廚選定菜單，挑選菜色，搭配相關的餐酒、前菜、主餐、點心、餐後茶或咖啡，再由二廚、三廚、四廚依據當天的客戶訂單進行烹調，出餐的控制則由跑單員掌控，當客戶完成用餐開心離開後，再由碗盤洗滌員協助清理餐具，完成一年一度忙碌的聖誕節大餐活動。

Part 5
Personnel
Management
人事管理

Unit 21 徵聘廚師

 Manager to Chef 經理與行政主廚對話  Track 81

Introduction

A restaurant needs to find a new **second in command** *for its kitchen.* 餐廳要為廚房找一位新副手

Characters

Ned - Chef	行政主廚
Barry - Manager	經理

Conversation

Barry	Eric just gave me his **two weeks' notice**. Guess we have to find a new **sous chef**.	Eric 剛剛告知我再二個禮拜就要離職，我想我們要開始找一個新的二廚。
Ned	Oh really, why is he quitting?	啊，真的嗎？他為何要離職？
Barry	He found a chef job somewhere else. That's good for him, I suppose.	他在別的地方找到了行政主廚的工作，我想他覺得不錯吧。
Ned	Yes, I think he'll do well. But now we have to **hire** someone else. Where do we start?	是啊，我想他會做得很好。但是我們現在得聘雇其他人了。要從哪開始找起？
Barry	We have to decide what kind of person we want for the job. Do we have anyone you would consider moving up?	我們必須先決定要找甚麼樣的人來做這份工作！有沒有任何員工是你考慮升為大廚的？
Ned	We have some good cooks, but there's no one with the kind of training I think we need.	我們有幾位不錯的廚師，但是沒有一個受過我們需要的訓練。
Barry	So, you want to get someone who's been to cooking school.	所以，你想要找一個上過烹飪學校的廚師。
Ned	Yes, and one of the better ones. What should be our first move?	是的，而且要找比較優秀的。我們首先該怎麼做？

Barry	We can put out job **vacancy** notices on the internet job sites. I'm not sure if that will **accomplish** what we want, though. We might not be able to find the right person that way.	我們可以把工作空缺的消息放到求職網站。雖然我不確定那樣做可以達成目的，也有可能那樣做仍然無法找到想要的人！
Ned	When I was in chef's school, there was a **referral** program. People who had just graduated could see a list of **employers** who were looking for people with their training. They probably still do something similar to that.	當我就讀廚藝學校時，有一個建教合作計畫。應屆畢業生可以看到一張表，列著在尋找受過訓練之廚師的雇主名單。這所學校可能仍在進行類似的計畫。
Barry	Go ahead and contact your school. I'll **get ahold of** the other major schools and see if they have something similar. They may even have a referral service for their older graduates who are looking for something better.	快去連絡你的學校吧！我會去找其他主要的廚藝學校，看看他們有沒有提供類似計畫。他們或許還會提供轉介服務給正在尋找更好工作的老校友。
Ned	That's a good idea. We don't need someone with a lot of experience. I can train a newer graduate. But if they have the right **background**, that would be all right, too.	好主意！我們不一定得聘用有豐富經驗的人，我可以訓練剛畢業的廚師。但是他們如果有恰當的訓練背景，那也很好。

Word Bank

second in command 副手　chef *n.[C]* 主廚　two weeks' notice 二個禮拜前提出的離職告知訊息　sous chef 二廚　hire *v.* 聘僱
vacancy *n.[C]* 職務空缺　accomplish *v.* 完成（任務）
referral *n.[C]* 推薦；介紹　employer(s) *n.[C]* 雇主
get ahold of 掌握；聯繫　background *n.[C/U]* 養成背景

Unit 21 徵聘廚師

 Interview 面試  Track 82

Introduction

A potential sous chef comes in for an interview.

一位符合資格的二廚應徵者前來面試。

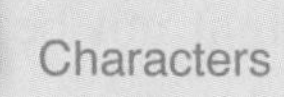

Characters

Ned - Chef	行政主廚
Missy - Hostess	女領檯
Bernie - Applicant	應徵者

Conversation

Missy	Good afternoon, table for one, or are you waiting for someone else?	午安，請問一位嗎？還是在等人呢？
Bernie	No, I'm here for a job interview with Ned Bergstrom. My name is Bernie Middleton.	喔，不是，我是來這與 Ned Bergstrom 面試的。我的名字是 Bernie Middleton.
Missy	Oh, you need to see the chef. Have a seat, and I'll let him know you're here.	啊，你待會要跟行政主廚面談。請坐，我會告知他你到了。
	(a couple minutes later)	（幾分鐘過後）
Ned	Hi, my name is Ned.	嗨，我是 Ned.。
Bernie	Mine is Bernie. I'm here about the sous chef job.	我是 Bernie. 我來面談大廚這份工作。
Ned	Go ahead and sit down. I already looked at your **resume**, of course, and you look like the kind of person we're looking for. What made you decide to **go into** cooking?	請坐。當然，我已經看過你的履歷表，你的確看來像是我們在找的人。說說看你為何走這一行？
Bernie	When I was in high school, I worked **part-time** in a restaurant. I started as a dishwasher, then learned how to do prep work and eventually ended up on the line.	我讀高中時，曾在一家餐廳兼職打工。一開始從洗碗工開始做起，之後學著如何準備食材，最後就上線去做菜。

Ned	How many years have you been cooking?	你從事烹飪工作幾年了？
Bernie	It was about a year and a half in high school, then I worked **full-time** for almost two years. That was when I decided to go to cooking school and make cooking my career.	在高中時就已經做了大約一年半左右，接著就做了二年全職的廚師工作。也就在那時，我決定去念廚藝學校，並把烹飪作為職志。
Ned	What did you like most about school?	你最喜歡學校什麼課程？
Bernie	I like that we learned about most kinds of **cuisine**. We not only studied different Taiwanese **regional** foods, but we also spent a lot of time on Western and other Asian cuisines.	我喜歡學習各種做菜技巧。我們不單只是學做台灣小吃，也花許多時間在學習西餐及其他亞洲菜。
Ned	What is your favorite type of food to cook?	你最喜愛料理哪種菜？
Bernie	I really like French cooking, but I liked **pretty much** everything we learned there.	我鍾愛法國菜，但是學校裡學的一切我都很喜歡。
Ned	That's good. We do a little bit of everything here.	很好！我們這家餐廳什麼菜都有一些。
Bernie	That would be nice. I'd look forward to cooking a variety of meals.	那很棒！我很期待能做不同類型的餐點。
Ned	Thanks for coming in. Someone will call you for a second interview in a day or two.	感謝你前來面試。這一兩天內會有人致電給你二次面試。
Bernie	Thank you for taking the time to talk to me.	謝謝你撥空與我面談。

Word Bank

potential *adj.* 可能的；潛在的　interview *n.[C]* 面試
applicant *n.[C]* 申請者　resume *n.[C]* 履歷表　go into 從事（某一行業）
part-time *adv.* 兼職地　full-time *adv.* 全職地　cuisine *n.[U]* 烹調法；菜餚
regional *n.* 地區性的　pretty much 非常；相當

Unit 21 徵聘廚師

 Final Decision 最終決定 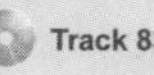 Track 83

Introduction

The chef and the manager talk about who they want to hire for the sous chef position. 行政主廚與餐廳經理討論該聘僱誰做二廚這個職務。

Characters

Ned - Chef	行政主廚
Barry - Manager	經理

Conversation

Barry	We have to decide today who we want to hire for sous chef. What do you think?	今天就要決定聘僱的二廚人選。你認為呢？
Ned	We interviewed some good people, and I think there are a couple who would work. Let's **eliminate** a couple first, and then we can talk about our **final** choices.	已經面試了一些不錯的人，其中有幾位應該可以勝任。我們先刪除掉一些，接著就可以進入決選。
Barry	One person who I didn't think would **be right** is Shirley. She didn't seem very friendly, and I don't think she'd fit in in our kitchen really well.	有一位我覺得不適合的是 Shirley。她似乎不是很友善，而且我覺得她要與廚房磨合有困難。
Ned	I felt that, too. We want someone who is **serious** about her job, but she needs to be friendly, too. Who else did you eliminate?	我也覺得如此。我們要的是一位認真看待工作的人，但她也必須要很隨和才行。還有誰要刪掉？
Barry	I don't know about George. He didn't have much experience, and he didn't come from a very good school. I know you said you could train the right person. What do you think?	我不知道該不該刪掉 Geroge。他不是很有經驗，且也非出身名校。我知道你說過你可以訓練合適的人。你有甚麼看法？

Ned	I don't really like his **qualifications**, either. He doesn't have as much background in different cuisines as I'd like. Let's take him off the list.	我其實也不是很欣賞他的資歷。他並沒有我想要的，做過各種菜式的背景。把他刪掉吧。
Barry	Who did you like?	那你覺得哪位適合呢？
Ned	I thought Bernie sounded really good. He has some kitchen experience, and his **schooling** was **well-rounded**. I liked Carol, too. How about you?	我覺得 Bernie 似乎蠻適合的！他有些廚房經驗，而且學校表現也是面面俱到。我覺得 Carol 也不錯，你覺得呢？
Barry	I'm **leaning toward** Bernie, too. He seemed to have the right **attitude**, and I think he would fit in really well. Carol would work, but I think Bernie is the better choice.	我也比較傾向選擇 Bernie。他似乎態度良好，而且應該能跟大家相處融洽。Carol 也行，但 Bernie 應該更適合！
Ned	I agree. I really liked how he interviewed. What do you say we go ahead and hire him?	我同意！我真的欣賞他面試時的表現。你說，我們要不要就決定聘用他？
Barry	That sounds good to me.	我也這麼想！
Ned	You can send out a letter and contract to him. Ask him if he can start soon. Eric is going to **be gone** in a week or so.	你可以寄一封通知信及合約給他，問問他可否儘快上班。Eric 再過一周左右就要離職了

Word Bank

eliminate *v.* 刪除掉　final *adj.* 最終的　be right 適當
serious *adj.* 認真對待事物的　qualification(s) *n.[C]* 資歷
schooling *n.[U]* 學業表現　well-rounded *a.* 面面俱到的；多才多藝的
lean(ing) toward 傾向於　attitude *n.[C]* 態度　be gone 離開

Unit 21 徵聘廚師

4 Beginning Training 開始訓練

Track 84

Introduction

The new sous chef starts work. 新的二廚開始工作。

Characters

Missy - Hostess	女領檯
Bernie - Sous Chef	二廚
Ned - Chef	行政主廚
Benji - Cook	廚師

Conversation

Missy	Welcome, how are you? Oh, I know you. You were here last week looking for a job.	歡迎，你好嗎？ 啊，我認得你，你上星期來這應徵工作。
Bernie	Yes, and Ned and Barry hired me. This is my first day.	是的，Ned 與 Barry 雇用了我。今天是我第一天上班。
Missy	I'm glad you got the job. Go on back; I'm sure they're waiting for you.	很高興你獲得這份工作。快過去吧！我確信他們正在等你！
	(in the kitchen)	（在廚房）
Ned	Hi Bernie, how are you doing?	嗨 Bernie，一切順利嗎？
Bernie	I'm a little nervous. I always get a little anxious the first day of anything new.	我有點緊張。第一天上班總是對任何新事物感到焦慮。
Ned	Well, you did **just fine** in your interview, and your **grades** from school are good. I don't think you have anything to worry about. Let me show you around.	嗯，你在面試中表現很好，而且你在學校的成績也不錯。我想你不需要擔心。我帶你到處看看。
Bernie	That'd be great.	那太好了！

Ned	We'll have you spend some time in the prep area today, so you can get used to **what goes on** there. As chef and sous chef, we still spend some time doing prep. We don't stay in the office all day, like some other places. We try to be **hands-on**, so we know what's really happening in our kitchen.	今天會讓你花些時間待在準備區，你就可逐漸習慣那一區的工作。身為行政主廚及大廚，我們依然要花時間做準備工作，而不是像其他地方一樣，整天待在辦公室。我們要試著親自動手備料，才能清楚在廚房內真正發生的各種狀況。
	(in the prep area)	（在準備區）
Benji	Hi, I'm Benji. You must be the new sous chef.	嗨，我是 Benji。你一定是新來的大廚。
Bernie	I am; my name is Bernie.	我就是，我叫做 Bernie。
Benji	Glad to meet you. This is a good place to work. I'm sure you'll like it here.	很高興認識你。這裡的工作環境很好。我保證你會喜歡這裡的。
Bernie	What are you **working on** right now?	你現在正在做甚麼呢？
Benji	Just basic **chopping**. We're doing lemons, onions, and salad ingredients right now. I see you have your own knives. Do you want to **jump in** and **give us a hand**?	只是一些基本的切菜工作。現在正在準備檸檬、洋蔥及沙拉物料的準備。我看到你已經有自己的刀具。要不要加入，幫幫我們呢
Bernie	Sure, there's **no time like now** to start.	好啊，現在正是開始工作的好時間。
Ned	Benji, after you guys get done, bring Bernie back to me. I'll give him something else to do.	Benji，你們完成工作後，把 Bernie 帶過來。我會給他其他的事情做。

Part I Part II Part III Part IV Part V Part VI

Word Bank

just fine 很好　grade(s) *n.[C]* 成績　what goes on 在運作的事情
hands-on *adj.* 親手去做的；躬親的　work(ing) on 工作；做事
chop(ping) *v.* 切（菜）　jump in 加入　give a hand 幫忙
no time like now 沒有比現在更好的時機

Unit 21 徵聘廚師

我有證照——新人選拔

電視廣告有這樣一段對話：沒人罩也要有證照。是的，證照對於社會新鮮人來說在面試時，是個非常好的競爭武器。餐飲的證照在台灣有非常多的類別，從一般的中西式烹調證照到調酒證照皆十足完備。

一般台灣的證照區分有丙級與乙級，丙級為一般初階必備，考試內容較為簡易跟多樣，取得丙級證照後，面試時已經足夠，若需要進階，可再依照各項證照所需條件進階再取得乙級證照，通常乙級證照會有較多的限制，且必須取得初階的丙級方可報名這是基本門檻。

台灣餐飲類證照介紹（丙級類）

證照名稱	證照考試內容	可應徵職務
丙級餐旅服務技術士	學、術科測驗內容包括基礎餐飲及旅館知識與技能，主要內容明細如下。 1. 餐具認識與餐桌擺設 2. 餐飲服勤方式 3. 飲料服務 4. 餐飲安全與衛生 5. 客房作業 6. 相關法規與職業道德	餐飲服務生、飯店工作人員
丙級西餐烹調技術士	學科為選擇題 80 題，每題 1.25 分，答錯不倒扣。 術科為實作共 90 道菜，每個主題需完成 6 道。 301 菜式（A、B、C、D、E 組）共 30 道菜 302 菜式（A、B、C、D、E 組）共 30 道菜 303 菜式（A、B、C、D、E 組）共 30 道菜 筆試考試內容範圍包含： 1. 職業道德 2. 食物的性質及選購 3. 食物貯存與製備 4. 器皿與盤飾 5. 設備與器具	中餐廚師、西餐廚師、其他類廚師

	6. 營養知識 7. 成本控制 8. 安全措施 9. 衛生知識與衛生法規	
丙級中餐烹調技術士	同丙級西餐烹調技術士	中餐廚師、其他類廚師
丙級烘焙食品技術士	術科測驗依產品類別分為：麵包、西點蛋糕、餅乾等三項。應檢者可自行從三項中，任選一項參加術科測驗，檢定合格後，技術士證上註明所選項別之名稱，各單項產品，丙級製作 2 種或 2 種以上為原則。	麵包師、食品衛生管理師
丙級飲料調製技術士	丙級技能檢定著重於有關飲料知識及實務操作。證照考試內容包含材料知識、製作原理、實際飲品製作等。	餐飲服務生、西餐廚師、調酒師／吧台人員、餐廚助手
丙級調酒技術士	考試範圍： 1. 吧台清潔 2. 作業準備 3. 飲料調製 調製有酒精飲料 調製無酒精飲料 5. 職業道德 6. 安全知識與衛生法規	調酒師／吧台人員

上述丙級證照為目前餐飲類的證照總類，大部分皆相同設立有乙級證照可進階得，僅是調酒技術士較為特殊，其未有設立乙級。

Unit 22 排班

 Writing the Waiter Schedule 安排外場服務生班表  Track 85

Introduction

The managers are writing the work schedule for the waitstaff. 經理幫服務生排班。

Characters

Josie - Dining Room Manager 餐區經理

Melvin - Assistant Dining Room Manager 餐區副理

Conversation

Josie	Hey Mel, guess what you get to help me do tomorrow?	嗨 Mel，猜猜看你明天得幫我做些什麼？
Melvin	What's that? I see you scheduled me to come in an hour early.	是什麼呢？我看到你安排我提早一小時來上班。
Josie	We get to write the schedule for the waits. It's so **exciting**.	我們必須幫外場服務生排班。真是令人興奮！
Melvin	You are **kidding**, aren't you?	你在開玩笑，是嗎？
Josie	Yes, I am. It's one of the most **challenging** parts of this job. See you in the morning.	沒錯，我是在開玩笑。這份工作最具挑戰性的地方就是排班。明早見！
	(the next day)	（隔天）
Melvin	Hi Josie, ready to go on the schedule?	嗨 Josie，準備來排班了嗎？
Josie	Yes, I am. Here is the first thing we need to look at: the **forecast** for the coming week.	嗯，準備好了！以下是第一件我們要注意的事情：預測下星期餐廳業務狀況。
Melvin	What does it tell us?	這麼做會知道什麼？

Josie	It usually just tells us about how much staff we will need for each day. As you can see, Monday isn't going to be busy, so we can **get by with** seven waits. But there's a concert on Wednesday, which is usually not busy. We expect to get some business from that.	通常能讓我們知道每天需要多少人力。如你可以看到的，星期一不會很忙，所以只要七位服務生就可以應付。星期三有一個音樂會，但那天通常不忙。我們預估從那天之後才會有一些生意。
Melvin	How many servers do you usually have on on Wednesday?	通常星期三都安排幾位服務生工作？
Josie	It's usually eight, but with the concert we're going to **run with** eleven.	通常八位，但因為音樂會的關係，我們會安排十一位外場服務生。
Melvin	Does that mean that some people won't get their usual day off?	這是不是意味著一些員工無法像平時一樣，在那天休假？
Josie	Yes, but we have people like Maggie who like to **pick up** extra shifts. We can use them on days like this.	沒錯。但是有些員工像 Maggie，喜歡多排些班。因此可以幫他們在這種日子排班。
Melvin	How do you **decide** which days off each person gets?	你如何決定每個人的休假日？
Josie	We try to give them the same two days off every week, but that doesn't always work out. See these **slips of paper**? These are time off requests. The hardest thing to do is to try to give everyone the time off they want and still keep people's days off the same.	我們試著每週給他們固定日休二天，但並非都能如願。看到這些小紙條了嗎？這些是排休請假單。最難的就是給每個人他們想要的排休日，同時還能維持每個人有相同日數的排休。
Melvin	Let's keep going and see how our **juggling** works.	我們繼續看看我們的安排有什麼效果。

Word Bank

schedule *n.[C]* 班表；時間表　exciting *adj.* 令人興奮的　kid(ding) *v.* 開玩笑
challenging *adj.* 富有挑戰性的　forecast *n.[C]* 預測　get by with 應付得了
run with 以……進行　pick up 獲得；指排班　decide *v.* 決定
slip(s) of paper 紙條　juggling *n.[U]* 此指安排調度

Unit 22 排班

2 *Back of House Scheduling* 內場員工排班 

Introduction

The chef is writing the schedule for the back of house employees. 行政主廚正在為內場員工排班。

Characters 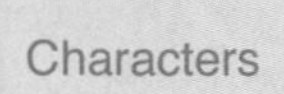 

Ned - Chef 行政主廚
Bernie - Sous Chef 二廚

Conversation

Ned	Hey, Bernie, why don't you sit down and help me **make out** our schedule.	嗨 Bernie，何不坐一下幫我擬出排班表呢？
Bernie	You mean for you and me?	你是指為我和你排班？
Ned	No, not just for us. We'll be working 10 or 12 hours a day, six **days a week**, until you get **trained**. After that, you'll work on my **days off**, and I'll work on yours, and we'll both work over the weekends.	不，不是只為我們兩個。我們必須一天工作十到十二小時，一星期上班六天，直到你完成訓練。之後，你就要在我休假時上班，而我會在你休假時上班。週末時我們都要上班。
Bernie	So, we're going to do the cooks' schedule?	所以現在是為內場廚師排班？
Ned	Not just them. We have the dishwashers', too. That one's actually harder because they **come and go** so much. But we'll look at the cooks' first.	不光是他們，我們也要為洗碗工排班。但是他們的班比較難排，因為他們流動率很高。但首先，我們還是來看看廚師們的班表。
Bernie	How hard is it to write a schedule for them?	為他們排班有多困難呢？
Ned	It's not too bad. **Unlike** the front of the house, I don't let people ask for time off **whenever** they want it. We have a set schedule, and if they want a different day off, they have to find someone to **trade** with.	實際上不是那麼難。不同於外場，我不會讓大家想休就休。我們有固定班表。如果他們想要換一天排休，就必須找到人調班。

Bernie	I suppose that makes it easier for our people to **plan** their lives ahead of time.	我認為這會讓我們內場的人更容易事先安排生活。
Ned	Yes, that's the **general idea**. Sometimes, if it's not going to be too busy, I can let someone have an extra day off, but usually our guys like knowing when their days off are going to be.	沒錯！大致上就是這個理念。有時候，如果不太忙，我可以讓某人再多休一天，但是我們的人通常想要知道他們會在哪幾天休假。
Bernie	What about the dishwashers? You said they come and go a lot.	那洗碗工怎麼辦？你說過，他們流動率很高。
Ned	It's not the greatest job in the world, so we end up with a lot of new faces back there. But many of them want to work a lot, so if we have a vacancy, we can usually fill it **at short notice**.	那的確不是世界上最好的工作，所以總是不斷見到新面孔來做這份工作。但是他們大多想要多做些工作，所以一有空缺，班表很快就能補上。
Bernie	That's good.	很好。

Word Bank

back of house 內場　make out 填寫　days a week 一週若干天
train(ed) *v.* 訓練　day(s) off 休假　come and go 來來去去的
unlike *prep.* 不同於　whenever *conj.* 每當　trade *v.* 交換　at short notice 一通知就馬上行動　plan *v.* 事先計劃　general idea 大概的理念

Unit 22 排班

3 *Scheduling Vacations* 排休  Track 87

Introduction

The managers are discussing employee vacations.
經理正在討論員工休假事宜。

Characters

Barry - Manager 經理
Jolene - Assistant Manager 副理

Conversation

Barry	It's a good thing everyone didn't decide to take their vacation in July this year.	今年都沒有人決定要在七月休假，真是件好事。
Jolene	It's too bad no one wants to take one in January, when it's slow. I guess we do have to expect quite a few July vacations, since we don't let anyone **go away** for two weeks in June.	沒有人想在一月生意的淡季休假，這很糟糕。我猜想必定會有人想在七月休假，因為六月不讓任何人排休二個星期。
Barry	Nope, too many weddings. Anyway, let's see what we have requested for July and August. That's when the people with kids usually want to take time off.	不能排啊，因為很多人這個月結婚。不管怎樣，看看七、八月大家怎麼要求排假。有小孩的人通常會在這兩個月排休。
Jolene	Jody wants the last week in July and the first one in August.	Jody 想要在七月最後一週及八月第一週排假。
Barry	That'll be no problem. She's a **model employee**, and she got her notice in early. Steve, **on the other hand**, didn't ask until last week, and he wants about the same time.	應該沒問題！她是模範員工，而且也會提早申請。至於 Steve 呢，相反的，直到上星期才申請要在同個時段排假。
Jolene	What should we do about that?	那該怎麼辦？

Barry	Try to get him to **switch** his days. Either that or he doesn't get a vacation. We can't let them both go at the same time. That's a pretty busy time as it is.	試著讓他換到別的時間休假。要嘛這樣，不然他就不准休。不能讓他們兩個同時不在。那段時間會很忙的！
Jolene	What are the chefs doing about their vacations?	那廚師們排假的狀況如何呢？
Barry	Ned only ever takes a week at a time, and he always picks **slow periods** to do it. He really likes to keep an eye on his kitchen. Since Bernie just started, we're not going to worry about him going on vacation for a while.	Ned 一次就只休一星期，而且他總是挑淡季的月份排假。他真地非常關心自己的廚房。Bernie 既然才剛來上班，暫時不用擔心他會排假。
Jolene	And what about the managers? I'm **flexible**. My boyfriend doesn't really mind when we go. We just need a little **advance notice**. Actually, we were talking about going to Japan in September to see the **fall colors**.	那經理們呢？我的排休蠻彈性的。我男朋友不會介意玩的時間點，只要能略微提早告知我們即可。事實上，我們正討論九月要去日本欣賞秋景。
Barry	Why don't you do that. Since my son is in school, we'll go sometime in July.	為何不就這麼定了？因為我的兒子仍在學校讀書，我想在七月排假。

Word Bank

vacation(s) *n.[C]* 假期　model employee 模範員工
on the other hand 相反地　switch *v.* 調換
slow period(s) 不忙的月份；淡季　flexible *adj.* 有彈性的
advance notice 提前告知　fall colors 指秋季美景　go away 離開；指休假

Unit 22 排班

 Day Off Requests 排休請假單 

Introduction

The front of house managers are looking at which days off people want for next week. 外場經理正在研究、員工們下星期可在哪幾天排休。

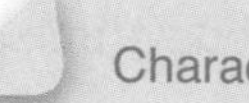 

Josie - Dining Room Manager 餐區經理
Melvin - Assistant Dining Room Manager 餐區副理

Conversation

Josie	Now we have to look at the day off request slips and see if we can **make that work** with the number of people we need each day. Who's first?	現在得審察這些排休請假單，看看能否在每日必要的員工需求量下，順利進行排休。從誰的先呢？
Melvin	Amy, June, and Bob all want Tuesday night off. There's some **special** concert in town.	Amy、Jnue 及 Bob 都想在星期二晚上排休，因為城區有場特別的演唱會。
Josie	It's a good thing it's on a Tuesday and not Friday or Saturday. It shouldn't be too busy that day. It's **normally** Robbie's day off. We'll ask him if he **wouldn't mind** coming in that day.	還好是在星期二，而不是在星期五或星期六。那天應該不會太忙。通常 Robbie 會那天排休。我們會問他是否不介意那天來上班。
Melvin	Here's one that Kathy gave me yesterday. It looks like she wants Tuesday off, too.	這是昨天 Kathy 給我的排休單，看來她也想在星期二排休。
Josie	Sorry, but she won't get it. Everyone knows that our policy is that you have to have requests **turned in** by Saturday for the next week. Too many other people want that night off.	很抱歉，她不能這樣排休。每個人都要了解公司的政策，員工得在星期六前呈交下星期的排休單，這次有太多人想在那一晚排休了！

Melvin	If it wasn't this week, that might be OK, right?	如果不是在這個星期，那應該沒問題，是嗎？
Josie	No, I try to **keep a firm hand**. If they want a **particular** day off, they need to ask for it **in time**. Now, the best she can do is trade with someone else.	不，我試著強硬。如果他們想在某一特定日子排休，就需要及時提出申請。現在她最好跟其他人調班。
Melvin	Hopefully someone will be **willing**.	希望有人會願意。
Josie	Who has the next request?	接下來是誰的假條？
Melvin	Dora wants to go to Tainan with her family over the whole weekend. That's not really possible, is it?	Dora 整個週末想要跟她的家人一起去台南。那應該不太可能，是吧？
Josie	Maybe for her. We'll have to **put together** the **rough draft**. Then we'll know if we can give that to her or not. Anybody else?	或許對她來說有可能。先把大致的排休表排出來，就知道能否讓她在週末排休。還有誰要請假？
Melvin	There are a few more we have to talk about.	還有一些我們得再討論的。

Word Bank

make that work 使……順利進行　special *adj.* 特別的
normally *adv.* 一般而言地　wouldn't mind 不會介意　turn(ed) in 呈交上來
keep a firm hand 強硬一些　particular *adj.* 特定的　in time 及時
willing *adj.* 樂意的　put together 統整　rough draft 初稿

Unit 22 排班

體力透支的新年——外場排班

念書時為了賺取學費，有好幾年奔波於各大飯店餐廳打工，每每到了年節佳日，領班總會急忙來電詢問是否有時間過去幫忙，甚至於加費用希望你過去幫忙，依上述描述其實已簡單說明餐廳的排班模式。

在餐廳排班會區分為忙碌期與非忙碌期，而通常中餐廳與西餐廳的人力安排又有不同，以下是幾個簡單的人力安排的邏輯。

非忙碌期靠正職、忙碌期靠兼職

在餐廳其實僅安排少量正職人員進行管理，主要是正職人員需要支付的成本與福利較高，故在餐廳的人力安排上，多以兼職人力支撐，比例大約為佔 50%-60%，尤其是特殊節慶時，餐廳都會需要找尋兼職人員協助，而兼職人員的來源多為學生或是實習生，在外國也是如此的安排模式，也就造就非忙碌期多靠正職，忙碌期多靠兼職的狀況。

非忙碌期多休假、忙碌期先加班

只要是排班的工作都會有這樣的一個現象，非忙碌期時請人員多消化休假，忙碌期時，則多安排加班，當然此現象不分行業，僅要需要人力調整的工作都會依照此法則進行人力的運用與調節。

提早訂位有助人力安排

節慶運用提早訂位來達到有效掌控人力的目的。許多知名或是大型的餐廳多使用此方式來掌控當天食材進貨與服務人力的安排，而這樣的訂位模式也避免客戶久等的窘境，當已知當天的客戶數量後，自然可以有效地安排。

培養兼職口袋名單

排班要順利主要的是能在第一時間找到服務人力，這部份很多餐廳的排班人員都了解，往往在他們的口袋裡都藏有一份屬於自己的兼職名單，在緊急或是必要的時刻使用上他。

服務人員與客戶比例為 1:15

一名服務人員至多可以服務幾位客戶呢？其實這是要看餐廳的服務模式與品質要求，基本上一般的服務比例以一名服務人員同時服務 12-15 位客戶（約 3-4 桌左右）為標準，當然部分高級餐廳會要求一名服務人員同時間僅服務一桌客戶，或是中餐廳一個服務人員僅服務一桌（約 10 位客戶），此端看餐廳規定而定。

如果你問餐廳的工作人員，最怕遇到什麼，相信你會得到的答案肯定是節慶值班，不管是過年、情人節、母親節、父親節或聖誕節，每次只要遇到節慶就是從早忙到晚，甚至於很多時候客戶吃得很滿意，而隨侍在側的服務人員可能已經餓了一整天。

未來若您也步上餓肚子的行業，請記得打開這本書，看看這個章節所提醒的人力安排的邏輯你是否有善加運用。

Unit 23 管理者的職責

 *Disciplinary Actions* 紀律維繫  Track 89

Introduction

The manager has to deal with some employee problems. 經理必須處理一些員工問題。

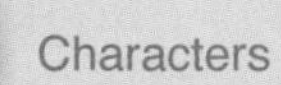 

Characters

Jolene - Assistant Manager	副理
Dora - Server	服務生
Bob - Server	服務生
June - Server Assistant	助理服務生

Conversation

Jolene	Dora, you're late again. That's the second time this week.	Dora，妳又遲到了。這是這星期第二次了。
Dora	I'm sorry, I just couldn't get going this morning.	很抱歉！今天早上就是沒辦法順行。
Jolene	I'm sorry, too. I'm going to have to **write you up**. When you're late, it puts extra **pressure** on the other people you work with. That's not fair to them.	我也感到抱歉，我必須把妳這狀況記個點。妳每次遲到，等於是為其他同事增添額外壓力，對他們並不公平。
Dora	I'll try to get started earlier in the morning.	我會盡量早上早點成行。
Jolene	What can we do to help you?	我們該怎麼幫助妳呢？
Dora	Not having any morning shifts would be nice.	如果不用排早班就太好了！
Jolene	But you know that's not possible. The only way we could do that is if we **demoted** you to server assistant.	但是妳知道這是不可能的，唯一可以不用排早班的辦法，就是把妳降職為助理服務生。
Dora	I'll really try to be on time from now on.	從現在開始我會努力準時來上班的。
Jolene	That's good. Just **keep in mind** that if you make a habit out of being late, further discipline will need to be taken.	很好。記得，如果妳養成了遲到習慣，我們就要進一步執行紀律。

	(later)	稍後
Jolene	Bob, what is it between you and June?	Bob，你和 June 之間到底有甚麼問題？
Bob	**I have no idea**. She just doesn't like me.	我也不知道，她就是不喜歡我！
Jolene	All right, I'll talk to her, but we can't have employees fighting **on the job**. It's bad for **morale**.	好吧，我會跟她談談看。但是我們不能容許員工在工作時起爭執，這對於整體工作士氣有負面影響
Bob	I'll try, but she has to, too.	我會努力改善的，但她也得努力。
	(later, to June)	稍後，與 June 會談
Jolene	June, can you come into the office for a minute?	June，可以到辦公室來一下嗎？
June	What is this about?	有甚麼事呢？
Jolene	How come you and Bob can't get along out there?	妳和 Bob 怎麼會無法好好相處呢？
June	He's just not a very nice person. He always demands more than anyone else, and he never asks anyone to do anything **politely**.	他不是一個隨和的人，老是比其他人要求的多，而且請別人做事時總是不禮貌。
Jolene	I'll **have a word with** him, but you have to do what you can to get along with him.	我會跟他談談，但是妳也必須盡可能與他好好相處。
June	It would help if I wasn't in his section.	如果我能調離他的部門，會比較理想。
Jolene	We'll look at the **assignments** and see if we can **arrange** that. Do your best, though, for now.	我們會仔細檢視工作分派，再看看是否可以安排。但是，現在你要盡力而為！

Word Bank

disciplinary *adj.* 紀律的　write you up 詳細記錄下你的工作狀況　pressure *n.[U]* 壓力　demot(ed) *v.* 降職　keep in mind 牢記在心　on the job 工作時　morale *n.[U]* 士氣　politely *adv.* 禮貌地　have a word with 與……談話　assignment(s) *n.[C]* 工作內容　arrange *v.* 安排　I have no idea 我不知道

Unit 23 管理者的職責

2 *Disciplinary Actions 2* 紀律維繫 2 Track 90

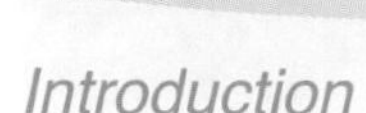

Introduction

The manager is checking up on the cleaning crew. 經理正在檢視清潔組同仁工作狀況。

Characters

Ned - Chef	行政主廚
Barry - Manager	經理
Gene - Janitor	清潔工
Ray - Janitor	清潔工
Michael - Janitor	清潔工

Conversation

Barry	Hey Ned, I'm going to **drop in on** the cleaning crew tonight and make sure they're actually doing something. Want to come with me?	嗨 Ned，我今晚會突襲檢查清潔組員，看看他們是否真的在好好做事。想跟我一塊來嗎？
Ned	At 3:00 in the morning? Thanks anyway; I'll sleep, instead.	在凌晨三點鐘？謝啦！我想睡覺！
	(at 2:30 am)	凌晨 2:30
Barry	I'll just open the door nice and quietly and see what the guys are doing. Hi Gene, where are the rest of the guys?	讓我輕輕地、安靜地把門打開，看看這些人在做甚麼？嗨，Gene，其他人呢？
Gene	I don't know; I haven't seen them for a while.	不知道耶。好一會兒沒看到他們了！
Barry	Don't you usually work together?	你們通常不是一起工作嗎？
Gene	Most of the time. But they helped me move all the tables, and I can **vacuum** by myself. So, I've just been working **alone** for a while. Why don't you look back in the kitchen?	大部分時間是這樣！他們剛剛幫我挪開所有的桌子，之後我就自己吸地。所以，我單獨工作好一會兒了。何不到後面廚房去看看？
	(in the prep area)	在準備區
Barry	What's this? Why are you guys **lying down**?	這在搞什麼？為什麼你們全部躺在地上？

Ray	Huh?... Oh, I guess I need to wake up. Michael, the manager's here!	嗯…啊，我想我得醒醒了！Michael，經理來了！
Michael	Oh, hi boss. I guess we got a little **tired** there for a minute.	啊，老闆！我想我們有點累，小歇一分鐘。
Barry	A little tired? It looks like we're paying you to sleep. This **doesn't look good**.	有點累？好像是我們付錢給你們來睡覺的。這狀況看來不妙！
Ray	Yeah, I realize it doesn't. I'm sorry, but we just got tired.	是的，我明白不可以這樣做。很抱歉，但我們是真的有點累。
Barry	How do I know you guys don't do this every night? I hope this isn't a habit. It's not like the rest of the people who work at this restaurant get time to sleep while they work. If you can't work at 3:00 am, just let me know. I'll find someone who can.	我怎麼知道你們這群傢伙不是每晚都這樣？我希望這不是慣性。這間餐廳的其他工作人員，可不像你們在上班時間睡覺。如果你們不能在凌晨三點工作，就告訴我，我再找其他可以的人。
Ray	Sorry, boss. I won't **let it happen** again.	抱歉，老闆。我不會讓這種事再發生了！
Michael	Me, neither. I'm sorry.	我也保證不會。對不起！
Barry	I'm going to have to write you up for this. I know you guys can do a good job. Just don't think we're going to let you work less hard just because it's the **middle of the night**.	我要把你們的狀況記點。我明白你們能把工作做好，但不要認為是半夜的班，公司就會讓你們輕鬆交差。
Ray	OK, we'll try to do better.	好的，我們會改進的。

Part I
Part II
Part III
Part IV
Part V
Part VI

Word Bank

check(ing) up on 檢視　janitor *n.[C]* 清潔工　drop in on 突襲檢查
vacuum *v.* 吸地　alone *adv.* 獨自一人地　lying down 躺下（lie）
tired *adj.* 疲累的　doesn't look good 看起來不太妙
let it happen 使……發生　middle of the night 半夜

Unit 23 管理者的職責

 Hours and Overtime 工時與加班

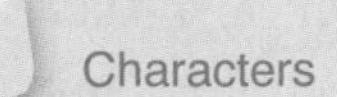 Track 91

Introduction

One of the hostesses talks to the manager about scheduling. 一位女領檯與經理談到班表安排事宜。

Characters 

Barry - Manager 經理
Missy - Hostess 女領檯

Conversation

Missy	I think I might want to go into management one day. What do you think?	我想有一天我可能會想進入管理領域，你覺得如何？
Barry	I think you might just want to stay where you are. **Seriously**, I think it's a good job. If it wasn't, I'd be doing something else.	我認為你可能想繼續做目前的工作。說真的，我覺得這工作還不錯，如果不，我早就到其他地方謀事了。
Missy	What's the hardest part of being a manager?	身為一個經理，最大的挑戰是什麼？
Barry	The part I like least is writing the schedule. Which is why I don't do it anymore.	我最不喜歡排班，所以我才不再做排班的工作。
Missy	Why don't you have to write the schedule?	你為什麼不用再排班？
Barry	Now that I'm the manager, I don't have to. But when I had **lower** management **positions**, I had to do it every week. Now the chef and the dining room manager do that **task**.	因為現在我是經理，就不用再做排班的工作。但當我只是基層主管時，我每週都必須要排班，現在是由主廚及餐區經理做排班的工作。
Missy	Why is it such a **cumbersome** job?	為什麼排班是個困難的工作呢？

Barry	The main problem is trying to get everyone the time off they want without letting someone else go into **overtime**. You really can't **justify** overtime in this business. There are always people who want lots of time off, but there are others such as yourself who will pick up extra shifts.	最大的問題是怎樣讓每個人排到他們想要休假的時間，卻不會讓別人得加班。在這個行業，你真的不能辯稱加班是合理的。總是有人想要多排假，而另外有些人又想要多排點班，像是你。
Missy	That's good for me, isn't it?	多排點班對我來說很好啊，不是嗎？
Barry	Yes, but if you get too many hours and we have to pay you overtime, it's bad for the company.	是啊，但是如果你工時太多，我們就必須付你加班費。對公司來說，這就不太好。
Missy	Because overtime costs you more.	因為加班會增加公司成本。
Barry	Yes, and with all these employees, we should be able to find enough people to cover all the shifts without anyone getting too many hours.	是的，我們要能有足夠的員工來輪所有的班，但又不能讓任何人工時太多。
Missy	Do you ever pay overtime?	公司付過加班費嗎？
Barry	Not if we can avoid it. The front of the house usually work **split shifts**, so they're easier to control. They don't work as many hours as the back of the house. Since the cooks usually work a **full shift** every day, it's easier for them to go into overtime.	能免則免。前場人員通常是分開輪班，而且不像後場人員工時那麼多，所以他們比較好管控。像廚師每天都滿班，他們就比較容易加班。

Word Bank

seriously *adv.* 認真地　lower *adj.* 較低的　position(s) *n.* 職位
task *n.[C]* 任務，工作　cumbersome *adj.* 麻煩的；困難的
overtime *n.[U]* 超時工作　justify *v.* 判斷為合理；證明是正當
split shift(s) 分開輪班　full shift 滿班

Unit 23 管理者的職責

 *Timekeeping and Payroll* 計時與薪資  Track 92

Introduction

The manager is helping a new employee understand how to get paid. 經理正在協助一位新員工了解薪資事宜。

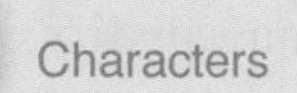

Characters

Barry - Manager 經理

Janet - Hostess Trainee 女實習領檯

Conversation

Janet	How often do we get paid?	我們多久領一次薪水？
Barry	We get paid once a month, just like most businesses. Have you learned how to **punch in** yet?	跟多數行業一樣，通常是一個月一次。你知道上班怎麼打卡嗎？
Janet	No, I really am new. I have this card, but I don't know how to use it.	不知道，我還是個新人。我有識別卡，可是不知道怎麼使用。
Barry	That's the key to everything. You use it to punch in, and if you're a waiter, you used it to ring in your orders and **print** up the checks. It's also good for your **employee discount**.	這張卡很重要，你要用它打卡上班，如果你是服務生，你也要用它來幫客人點菜以及列印帳單。你也可以透過它，享有員工折扣。
Janet	We get a discount?	員工有折扣？
Barry	Yes, if you come in to eat, your whole party gets a discount on their meals.	是啊，員工用餐所有餐點都享有折扣。
Janet	I didn't know that. That's nice. What do I do with this card now, though?	我不知道有折扣，實在太棒了！那我現在要怎麼用這張卡？

Barry	You run it through the **card reader**, just like a credit card. It will read your employee **information** and show when you punched in and when you punched out.	你把這張卡刷過讀卡機，就像使用信用卡一樣。機器會讀取你的員工資料，以及顯示你何時上班與下班。
Janet	Where does the information go?	這些資訊最後會到哪裡去？
Barry	It goes to the office assistant. We use a **payroll** company, and May in the office sends all the information to them, and they write our **paychecks**.	這些資訊會傳給公司助理。我們有一個配合的薪資公司，公司裡的 May 會把所有的資訊給他們，由他們負責計算我們的薪資。
Janet	So, if I have any problems with my pay, she's the one to talk to.	所以如果薪資有問題的話，可以跟她討論。
Barry	That's right. There are rarely any **issues** with payroll, though, as long as you remember to punch in and out. It's all done **automatically** by computer, so there isn't a lot of room for **error**. Computers only make mistakes if you do.	是的，但通常薪資表很少有爭議，只要你上下班記得打卡的話。薪資是電腦自動計算的，所以錯誤率很小。只有當你出錯，電腦才會跟著出錯。
Janet	I'll still keep track of my hours, just to be sure.	我一定會保有我的工時紀錄。
Barry	That's a good idea. Well, since it's your first day, I'll have one of the other hosts show you around and **get you settled**.	這主意不錯。嗯，既然今天是你第一天上班，我請另一位領班帶你四處看看，讓你安頓下來。

Word Bank

get paid 領到薪資　punch in 上班打卡　print *v.* 列印
employee discount 員工折扣　card reader 讀卡機
information *n.[U]* 資訊　payroll *n.[C]* 薪資表　paycheck(s) *n.[C]* 薪資
issue(s) *n.[C]* 爭議　automatically *adv.* 自動地　error *n.[C]* 錯誤
get settled 安頓

Unit 23 管理者的職責

Tips for Workplace Happiness
職場補給站
加油大使 Cheryl 來充電！

低價的服務薪資——薪資架構

服務業一直是薪資低、工時長、吃力不討好的工作，進入門檻低，經歷非用人主要考量，但仍是有人喜愛這個累人的行業。依人力銀行分析，踏入服務產業的新新人類，通常多是因為服務產業入行容易、產業模式穩定，本身不排斥與人相處，且就職的時間也不會太長久。

人力銀行曾經做過一項薪資與經歷關係的統計，服務業的薪資體制平均薪資約 2 萬 9 千元，而餐飲人員的最低薪資僅有 2 萬 4 千元，但工作時間非常地長，真的可以說餐飲服務是低價的苦命勞工。

那是不是所有餐飲人員薪資都如此的低廉？其實不然，餐飲也是有高薪資的員工。在餐飲體制下的專業廚師或是高階經理人，其薪資搭配年資也是可以非常地驚人。以下是我整理的餐飲人員薪資體制表，圖表以職務與服務年資交叉比對，現在讓我們來好好一探究竟吧！

餐飲薪資分析表（此為平均薪資，非絕對薪資）

職務	服務年資			
	1-3 年	3-6 年	4-9 年	9 年以上
餐廳服務人員	25,000	27,000	28,000	30,000
廚房助手	25,000	28,000	30,000	32,000
吧檯 / 調酒人員	28,000	31,000	32,000	37,000
餐廳低階主管（主任 / 領班）	30,000	32,000	35,000	37,000
廚房助手廚師	32,000	39,000	41,000	45,000
餐廳中階主管（副理 / 經理）	33,000	36,000	40,000	44,000
廚房主廚	-	-	-	60,000~80,000
餐廳高階主管（協理）	-	-	-	80,000~100,000
廚房行政主廚	-	-	-	100,000~150,000

看到上述的薪資，是否打擊你想加入餐飲業的熱情呢？其實，不用這樣悲觀，此為全台平均薪資的資訊，餐廳服務人員薪資，部分餐廳亦會依照特殊技能，例如語言、證照等，薪資也會有所不同，如知名的小籠包專賣店，其雙語的基本服務人員就有每月 5 萬的薪資，另知名西餐廳持有品酒執照的服務人員，其薪資每月也高達 6 萬，所以只要你有熱情，懂得增加白己的實力，相信你也可以成為餐飲界高薪資一族。

Unit 24 員工福利

1 *Flexible Hours* 彈性工時  Track 93

Introduction

A new host and a server talk about getting time off. 一個新領檯和一個服務生談到關於休假的事。

Characters 

Josie - Dining Room Manager 餐區經理

Dora - Server 服務生

Janet - Hostess Trainee 女實習領檯

Conversation

Dora	Hey Josie, my boyfriend is getting tired of me working every weekend. He wants us to **go out dancing** next Friday. Do you think I could have the night off?	嘿，Josie，我男友厭煩我每週末上班，我們下週五想出去跳舞。你覺得下週五晚上我可以休假嗎？
Josie	You know that there's a reason you work most weekends; it's when we're the most busy. Why can't you go out on Tuesday or Wednesday instead? That's when we don't really need you.	你知道這一季每週末你都得上班；這是我們最忙的時候。你何不週二或週三晚上排休？那時我們沒那麼需要你。
Dora	Because no one goes out dancing on Tuesday, that's why.	沒有人在週二晚上出去跳舞的。
Josie	Yes, I know that. I'm just kidding. **You know the drill**. Put your request in, and I'll see what we can do about it.	是啊，我知道，我只是開玩笑的。你懂意思的。你就送出請假單，我看看要怎麼處理。
Dora	OK, thanks.	好的，謝謝。

Janet	You really want to go dancing that bad, do you? It must be **tough** working every weekend. I didn't realize that I'd be doing that when I **started** working here.	你真的很想出去跳舞，是嗎？每週末都要工作很辛苦。我開始工作時，也不知道我週末都得上班。
Dora	It's not so bad. Fridays and Saturdays are always busy, so you get a lot of hours. And then you have time off when other people don't, so everything isn't crowded like it is on Saturday and Sunday.	其實沒那麼糟。因為週五和週六很忙碌，所以你會排到很多班。然後當其他人上工時，你會有一般日排休，也就不會遇到像週六和週日那種人潮擁擠情況。
Janet	I was hoping I wouldn't have to work every weekend.	我那時一直希望不用每個週末都要工作。
Dora	That's one thing that keeps people from working in **hospitality** for a long time. But it's not bad for you hosts. There are a lot of you. Not too many of you work full-time, so it's easier for you to get days off when you want. Talk to the other hosts, but I think you can get time off pretty easily, as long as you ask for it **ahead of time**.	這點就是讓人無法在接待服務業待很久的原因。但這對你們領檯來說，並不是件壞事。你們人很多，並不是很多人都全班，所以想要排休倒是容易些。只要你跟其他領班說一聲，但我想，只要事先申請，你可以很快就排到休假。
Janet	All right, I'll ask them and see what it's like.	好，我會問他們，再看狀況如何。
Dora	Keep in mind, though, that if going out on weekends is **a priority** for you, this probably isn't a great **field** to be in.	記住，如果在週末出去對你來說是第一優先要務的話，也許你不適合在這個行業。

Word Bank

time off 休假　go out dancing 出去跳舞　tough *adj.* 辛苦的；困難的
start(ed) *v.* 開始　hospitality *n.[U]* 好客；熱忱　ahead of time 提早；事先
a priority 優先事項　field *n.[C]* 領域　you know the drill 你懂規矩

Unit 24 員工福利

2 Discounted Food 餐點折扣

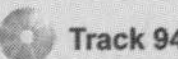

Track 94

Introduction

A new server is learning about the food discount available at the restaurant. 一個新服務生正在了解餐廳提供的折扣優惠。

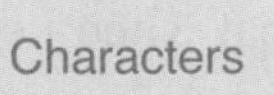

Characters

Jolene - Assistant Manager	副理
Missy - Hostess	女領檯
Sally - Server Trainee	實習生
Dora - Server	服務生

Conversation

Jolene	We're glad you decided to come and work for us. Today is your **orientation**. I'll get one of the other servers to show you around later, but first I'll explain some of the policies that we have here.	很高興你加入我們一起工作，今天會做一些環境介紹。稍後我會請另一位服務生帶你參觀一下，但首先我要說明一些這裡規定。
Sally	The one I'm most interested in is the food.	我最有興趣的部分就是食物。
Jolene	Yes, we give you a discount on food. If you come in and eat before your shift starts, you can get anything on the menu for 50% off.	是的，我們會給你用餐折扣。如果你在排班前來用餐，菜單上的任何餐點都有五折優惠。
Sally	That sounds good. I won't take advantage of that every day, but it's a nice **privilege**.	聽起來太棒了！這是個很棒的優惠，放心我不會每天利用這優惠。
Jolene	Also, if you come in to eat in the restaurant, we'll take off 25% from your entire order, **excepting** alcohol, **of course**.	再者，你在餐廳用餐，所有餐點都有七五折優惠，當然，酒類除外。
Sally	So, I can come in with my friends and we all get a discount?	那麼，如果朋友和我一起來，我們所有人都可以打折嗎？
Jolene	Yes, that's one way we say thanks for working here.	是的，那是我們感謝員工辛苦工作的方式。

Sally	I think I'll see if I can get some people together next week, **provided** I'm not working.	我想下週如果我沒有排班的話，就找些朋友一起來這裡用餐。
Jolene	We'll be happy to see you.	我們會很開心見到你。
	(the next week)	下一週
Missy	Hi Sally, it's nice to see you. And you **brought** all these people with you.	嗨，Sally，很高興見到你，你帶了這麼多朋友來。
Sally	Yes, we decided to **dine** here and take advantage of the employee discount. I've heard the food's not bad, either.	是的，我們決定在這裡用餐，同時享受員工折扣優惠。聽說這裡的食物也不賴。
Missy	It's good to see you. Here's your table. Dora will be with you in just a minute or two.	很開心見到你們，這裡是你們的桌子。Dora 會馬上過來為你們服務。
	(Dora appears)	Dora 出現
Dora	Hi Sally, it's nice to see you. You're taking advantage of the employee discount, right? All I need is your **ID card**. Just remember, the discount is only on food and **non-alcoholic** drinks.	嗨，Sally，很高興見到你。你們要使用員工折扣，是嗎？我需要你的識別卡。提醒你，折扣優惠只適用於餐點和非酒精類飲料。
Sally	Thanks Dora. I think we want to get some drinks to start with.	謝謝你，Dora。我們都先點飲料吧。

Part I
Part II
Part III
Part IV
Part V
Part VI

Word Bank

excepting *prep.* 除……以外　of course 當然　provided 假使，倘若
brought *v.* 帶來，攜帶　dine *v.* 用餐　ID card 識別卡
non-alcoholic *adj.* 非酒精的　available *adj.* 可得到的
orientation *n.* 新生訓練，環境介紹　privilege *n.* 特權，特別待遇

Unit 24 員工福利

3 *Health Insurance* 健康保險 Track 95

Introduction

A new employee learns about the health insurance program. 一位新進員工了解健康保險的內容。

Characters 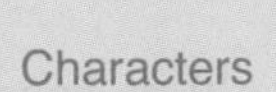 

Jolene - Assistant Manager 副理
Sally - Server Trainee 實習生

Conversation

Jolene	Let's **continue** with your orientation. Now that you're an **adult** and **actually** working, one of the big **benefits** you get is the **National Health Insurance**.	我們接著繼續環境介紹。現在既然你已經成年且確實在工作，最大的好處之一就是享有全民健保。
Sally	How does that work? I've used it at the doctor's, but I never had to worry about how to pay for it or anything.	那是怎麼運作的？我去看醫生時都會用到，但我從來不用擔心要怎麼付費。
Jolene	We take care of most of the paperwork for you. A little money comes out of your pay each month. Because we're a **private** business, we pay twice as much as you do for your insurance **premium**. The government **kicks in** some, too, so what you pay is only about 30% of your **actual** cost.	我們會為你負責多數的文件作業。因為我們是私人企業，保費從你每個月薪資支付一小部分，而公司負擔的保費則是你的兩倍。同時，政府也負擔部分，所以你的實際支出只佔保費約 30%。
Sally	That sounds really fair. Is that the same as what everyone pays?	聽起來很公平。那每個人支付的費用都一樣嗎？
Jolene	No, if you own your own business, you have to pay 100% of your premium cost. So, you're paying a lot less for insurance than the boss does.	不一樣，如果是企業主就必須自付全額保費。所以，你比老闆少付很多保費。

Sally	I never thought about that. My dad probably pays 100%, too. He owns his own business. When will I get my **IC card**?	我沒想過這些，我爸爸他自己做生意，可能也要負擔100%。那我什麼時候可以拿到健保卡？
Jolene	We have three days to submit the paperwork for you, and you'll get the card soon after that. Then, you just use it in the same way you did when you were growing up and on your parents' insurance.	提送文件大約要三天，之後很快就可以拿到健保卡。之後，你使用健保卡的方法，就跟以前健保附屬在父母那裡時一樣。
Sally	What happens if I lose my card?	如果健保卡不見了怎麼辦？
Jolene	There are National Health Insurance offices all over the island. All you have to do is go into one of them and **sign up** for a new one. I think you can also call and take care of it, if you like.	全國都有全民健康保險辦公室，你只要到其中一間，再申請一張新的就可以。我想，你也可以打電話申請。
Sally	Thanks for telling me all about this. Hopefully, I won't have to use the insurance for a while.	謝謝你告訴我全民健康保險的事，希望我不會使用到這保險。

Word Bank

program *n.[C]* 計畫；內容　continue *v.* 繼續　adult *n.[C]* 成人
actually *adv.* 事實地　benefit(s) *n.[C]* 福利
National Health Insurance 全民健康保險　private *adj.* 私人的
premium *n.[U]* 保險費　kick(s) in 負擔；捐款　actual *adj.* 實際的
IC card 晶片卡　sign up 申請；登記

Unit 24 員工福利

 Paid Vacation 有薪假  Track 96

Introduction

A new manager talks to the manager about time off. 一位新經理和經理討論休假。

Characters

Barry - Manager 經理

Alice - Management Trainee 實習經理

Conversation

Barry	As a manager, you get paid once a month, just like everybody else. And the benefits are **similar**: discount on food, health insurance, etc.	跟大家一樣，經理每個月領薪水一次，福利也差不多，有員工餐折扣、健保等。
Alice	That's pretty much what I expected. You're pretty fair to your employees.	這些跟我期待的差不多，公司對員工很公平。
Barry	Or at least we try to be, as long as they work hard. There is one thing you **receive** that a lot of other employees don't, and that's **paid vacation**.	我們盡量做到公平，只要員工們努力工作。還有一項福利是你獨有的，那就是有薪假。
Alice	So, if I go on vacation, I still **collect** my same salary?	所以，如果我放假，我還是可以領一樣的薪水？
Barry	Yes, for two weeks a year. You can sometimes take the whole two weeks **at once**, but some people like to take one week at a time. If you take it between your usual days off, then you can have nine days in a row that you don't have to work. It gives you some time to **relax**.	是的，一年有兩週有薪假。你可以一次休息兩週把它休完，但有的人喜歡一次休一週。如果你把平日休和一週的年休安排在一起，就可以連休九天不用上班，這樣就可好好放鬆。

Alice	Which I'll probably need, since managers work a lot of hours.	既然經理工時很長的話，我可能很需要放鬆一下。
Barry	Yes, that's true. In order for the restaurant to run **efficiently**, management does have to spend a lot of time here. But I think you'll find it's worth it when everything **functions** right and we have a restaurant that **runs** well.	確實是的，為了讓餐廳營運更有效率，管理階層的確需要花很多時間在工作上。但當一切運作正常，而且餐廳也營運良好時，我想你會覺得一切都很值得。
Alice	How soon can I start planning my vacation? Not that I'm in a hurry or anything.	我並非是急著想休假的意思，不過，我多快可以開始計畫我的休假呢？
Barry	Your vacation time kicks in after you've worked here a year. So don't make any plans **right now**. But you still get two days off a week; that's enough time to go to some relaxing places with your family.	年假從任職滿一年起算，所以你現在先不用計畫。但你現在每週休息兩天，足夠你和家人放鬆一下。

Word Bank

similar *adj.* 相似的　receive *v.* 收到；得到
paid vacation 有薪假　collect *v.* 收得；收集　at once 一次
relax *v.* 放鬆　efficiently *adj.* 有效率地
function(s) *v.* 產生功能；起效用　run(s) *v.* 營運，運作
right now 現在；馬上

Unit 24 員工福利

餐廳業共同福利就是吃不怕——福利架構

曾經有個好友服務於美國湖畔餐廳，他說他們餐廳員工最大的福利就是無限量的美麗湖畔景致，這是一個很有趣的觀點，我們可以解讀成，他非常喜歡這家餐廳的景致，也可解釋說餐廳福利不佳，僅有景致可以當作福利。

上一個章節我們分析了餐廳業的薪資架構，本章節再來談談餐廳福利，以下是幾家餐廳的福利介紹。

連鎖美式餐廳

- 月薪人員每日排班 7.5 小時、月休 6 天、國定假日補休、第一年即享有 7 天特休年假
- 享勞健保、團保、退休金提撥
- 同仁用餐可享優惠折扣
- 完整教育訓練、昇遷管道暢通
- 職工福利委員會每年不定期舉辦員工活動，並提供員工獎學金、文康活動及其它婚喪喜慶之補助金
- 每個人都有機會參加國際總部舉辦的各式活動，例如：各式國內外競賽活動和到國外協助其他國家開店等

知名小籠包專賣店

- 享勞健、團保及退休金提撥
- 三節獎金、績效獎金、語言獎金、禮貌獎金、久任獎金、紅利獎金
- 企業按摩師、樂活諮詢師、書籍及 DVD 借閱、年度員工體檢
- 國內旅遊、海外參訪補助（日本）
- 三節禮券、生日禮券
- 供膳、員工消費折扣、聚餐活動

連鎖麻辣鍋餐廳

- ☑ 勞工保險、健康保險、團保、勞工退休金提撥、全勤獎金、伙食津貼。
- ☑ 享有中秋，端午，春節禮金與生日禮金。
- ☑ 完整的績效考核制度及系統，定期進行個人的考核評估，作為調薪、獎金發放個人未來升遷依據。
- ☑ 新進同仁職前訓練、同仁在職訓練、專業技能訓練、進階管理職訓練、高階管理職能訓練、食品衛生訓練、環境安全訓練……等。
- ☑ 同仁免費制服燙洗、同仁休息區、置物櫃。
- ☑ 年度尾牙、同仁用餐折扣。
- ☑ 不定期同仁團康活動、團隊士氣、禮儀互動課程。

看到上述的福利，我們可以清楚了解，大致上無論是什麼餐廳皆是大同小異，當然國外的餐廳，也是依照社會文化跟國情來提供福利，但從台灣的餐廳福利來看，我們可以清楚地看到一個共通點，就是都有員工享用餐廳餐點可以享折扣。這項福利大多是餐飲業一項不成文的福利規定，至於各項的勞保、健保我想這都是台灣企業基本需要提供的，當然若您面試的是跨國連鎖餐廳，通常亦會有些海外觀摩的機會，此點也是這類餐廳招募的一項利器，在選擇是可以多方比較。

Unit 25 員工升遷

1 *Dishwasher to Prep Cook* 洗碗工到助理廚師

 Track 97

Introduction

A dishwasher is given the chance to move up to prep cook. 提供洗碗工機會晉升為助理廚師。

 Characters 

Ned - Chef 行政主廚
Duane - Dishwasher 洗碗工

Conversation

Ned	Duane, you've been here a couple months. Do you think you're going to **stick around**?	Duane，你已經在這裡工作幾個月了，想要留在這裡嗎？
Duane	Yes, I like it here. I'm not thinking of looking elsewhere any time soon.	想啊，我喜歡這裡，最近不打算再找其他工作。
Ned	Well, Eugene **left** yesterday, and we've been thinking about who we should get to replace him. Are you interested in learning how to cook?	好的，Eugene 昨天離職，我們在考慮誰可以接替他的工作。你有興趣學習廚師工作嗎？
Duane	I just might. It would probably be better than washing dishes. What made you think about moving me up?	還蠻想的，這應該會比洗碗盤好很多。為什麼你覺得要把我升遷呢？
Ned	We think you do a good job, and you seem **smart** enough to be able to learn quickly and follow the recipes. You'd just be working in the back, doing prep work. It **involves** a lot of repetitive work, doing the same thing every day, but it's not as **repetitive** as dishwashing.	我們覺得你工作做得很好，而且你看起來很聰明，可以很快學習並且掌握食譜。那你就在後面當助理廚師做預備的工作。會有很多重覆性的工作每天做同樣的事，不過不像洗碗盤那樣重覆。
Duane	I don't mind doing the same thing again and again. I'm sure it's not all like that.	我不介意一直做相同的工作。我確定不會一直都千篇一律。

Ned	No, there will be days when you have to make something different than usual. I'm not saying it's a **boring** job; I just want you to know what you're **getting yourself into**.	不會的，有時還是得做些和平常不一樣的事。我不是說這工作無聊，但我希望你知道自己投入的是什麼樣的工作。
Duane	I've seen the guys in the prep area. They seem to get along pretty well, and I think it would be fun to work back there with them.	我看過預備區的那些人員。他們似乎相處融洽，也許到後場跟他們工作會蠻好玩的。
Ned	They are a good **bunch** of guys. Like I said, we need someone to replace Eugene. It would be more hours for you as well. Prep cooks usually work a full day. I'll give you some time to **think it over**. Let me know.	他們是一群好傢伙。如我說的，我們需要有人替代 Eugene，助理廚師通常整天工作，你的工時也會增加。我給你一些時間考慮，你再跟我說。
Duane	Oh, I don't think I need any more time. I'll be glad to move up.	噢，我想我不需要再考慮，我很高興可以升遷。
Ned	All right, we'll get you a uniform and start your training tomorrow.	好的，那我們會給你一套制服，明天就開始訓練你。

Word Bank

move up 升遷　prep cook 助理廚師　stick around 逗留，穩定
left *v.* 離開　smart *adj.* 聰明的　involves *v.* 包括
repetitive *adj.* 重覆的　boring *adj.* 無趣的、無聊的
getting yourself into 專心投入　bunch *n.* 一群、一夥　think it over 考慮

Unit 25 員工升遷

 *Prep Cook to Line Cook* 助理廚師到上線廚師  Track 98

Introduction

A position has opened up in the kitchen. 廚房有個職缺。

Characters  

Ned - Chef	行政主廚
Bernie - Sous Chef	大廚
Hank - Prep Cook	助理廚師
Rose - Prep Cook	助理廚師

Conversation

Ned	Bart put in his two weeks' notice yesterday. Now we need to think about who we're going to train to replace him on the line.	Bart 昨天已經提出辭呈，兩週後離開。現在我們需要考慮訓練誰來代替他。
Bernie	I think it **comes down to** two people, and I'm sure you know who I'm talking about.	範圍可以縮小到兩個人，而且我確定你知道我想的是誰。
Ned	Yes, Rose and Hank from the prep room. But how do we choose between the two?	是助理廚師 Rose 和 Hank 吧，但我們怎麼在這兩人中間做選擇呢？
Bernie	They're both good workers, and they both have good **attendance** records. I **suppose** we'll have to ask and see if they both want it, first.	他們兩人都是好員工，而且出席率也都良好。我認為應該先問問他們意願。
Ned	That's true; maybe we won't have to **make a decision**.	也對，或許我們不需要做決定。
	(Bernie finds Hank)	Bernie 找到 Hank
Bernie	Hey Hank, have you heard about Bart?	嘿，Hank，你聽說了關於 Bart 的事嗎？
Hank	You mean that he's **leaving**? Yeah, the **grapevine** is pretty **active** around here.	你指他要離職嗎？有啊，這裡小道消息流傳很快。
Bernie	How do you feel about taking his place? Ned and I think you could do the job.	你覺得代替他的位置如何？ Ned 和我認為你可以勝任。

Hank	That would be a good **promotion**. Would it involve a raise, too?	那是很好的升遷。同時也加薪嗎？
Bernie	Yes, it would be a little more money. What do you think?	會，薪水會多一點。你的看法呢？
Hank	Sure, it'd be great to work up on the line. I know it's hectic, but it would be fun.	當然囉，能夠升任線上廚師實在太棒了！我知道會很忙，但是會很好玩。
Bernie	We still have one person to ask, but we're definitely considering you. We'll let you know.	我們還要再問另一個人，但我們絕對會考慮你，我們會讓你知道結果。
	(in the prep room)	在助理廚師區
Bernie	Rose, could I have a word for a minute?	Rose，可以跟你談一下嗎？
Rose	Sure, what did I do?	好，我做了什麼嗎？
Bernie	Oh, there's no problem. I'm just wondering whether you'd like to move up to the line to replace Bart?	沒事，我只是想知道你是否想被拔擢，取代 Bart 成為廚師？
Rose	Thanks for asking me, but I'm not really interested. I like it where I am. It's very **high-pressure** up there, and I like my **low level** of **stress** just fine. But thanks, anyway.	謝謝你問我，但我真的沒有興趣，我喜歡現在的工作。升為廚師，壓力會很大，現在壓力小我還蠻可以的。但無論如何，非常謝謝。
Bernie	You do a good job. We'll be glad to keep you right where you are.	你表現得不錯。我們很樂意讓你留在現前的工作。

Word Bank

come(s) down to 縮小範圍　attendance *n.[U]* 出席率　suppose *v.* 猜想；認為該　make a decision 做決定　leaving 離開；離職（leave）
grapevine *n.[U]* 指小道消息　active *adj.* 活躍的　high-pressure *adj.* 高壓力的
low level 低程度　stress *n.[U]* 壓力　promotion *n.[C]* 升遷

Unit 25 員工升遷

3 *Assistant Manager to Manager* 副理到經理  Track 99

Introduction

An assistant manager is being promoted to manager. 一個副理晉升至經理

 Characters 

Melody - Regional Manager 區域經理
Barry – Manager 經理
Jolene - Assistant Manager 副理

Conversation

Barry	Jolene, could you come in about 8:00 tomorrow. We have a few things we need to discuss.	Jolene，你能明天早上八點進來嗎？我們有些事情需要討論。
Jolene	Sure, I'll see you **bright and early**.	當然，明天一大清早見。
Barry	Hi Jolene, thanks for coming in.	嗨，Jolene，謝謝你這麼早來。
Melody	And hi, too.	嗨，早安。
Jolene	Oh, Melody, what are you doing here?	Melody，你怎麼在這裡？
Melody	We have an opening at our Hsinchu **store**. We were wondering if you'd like to work there.	我們新竹店有個職缺，想問你是否想到那邊工作。
Jolene	What is the position?	是什麼職位？
Melody	It's the manager; you'd be in charge of the entire restaurant, just like Barry is here.	是經理。你要負責整個餐廳，就像 Barry 在這裡一樣。
Jolene	Really? That would be great. I'm sure that's the dream of every management employee.	真的嗎？太好了，我想那是每個管理階層的夢想！
Melody	Do you think you'd mind **relocating**? Or do you really want to stay in Taipei?	你會介意搬家嗎？還是你想待在台北呢？

Jolene	I'll have to think it over. I really like where I'm living right now. But this is a great **opportunity**.	我必須考慮一下。我蠻喜歡我現在住的地方。不過，這是個好機會。
Melody	If you like, we could go down there together some day this week. You could meet the staff and see if you think you'd be comfortable there.	如果你喜歡，我們這週找一天下去一趟。你可以跟那裡的員工碰一下面，看看是不是能適應那裡。
Jolene	That's a good idea. I hate to admit it, but I've never even been in the store down there.	這真是個好主意。我必須承認，我從沒去過那裡的店。
Barry	That could give you a little better idea of whether or not you wish to **transfer** there.	這樣你會更清楚是不是想轉調過去。
Jolene	And I suppose I could **commute** there for a while, until my **lease** runs out here in Taipei. Then I could think about moving.	我想先通勤一陣子。等到台北房租到期，我才會考慮搬。
Melody	It's kind of a long way; are you sure you want to commute?	這段路程有點遠，你確定要通勤？
Jolene	I know it would take a big chunk out of my day, but I'm pretty close to **Taipei Main Station**, so I could catch the **High Speed Rail** from there. It wouldn't be too bad.	我知道通勤會花掉我大半時間，但我離台北車站很近，就搭高鐵吧，應該還可以。
Melody	That sounds OK. What day would you like to go down and **visit**?	聽起來不錯。你想要哪天下去參觀看看？

Word Bank

promot(ed) *v.* 升遷　bright and early 一大早　store *n.[C]* 商店
relocating *v.* 遷移（relocate）　opportunity *n.[C]* 機會　transfer *v.* 轉調
commute *v.* 通勤　lease *n.[C]* 租約　Taipei Main Station 台北車站
High Speed Rail 高鐵　visit *v.* 參觀

Unit 25 員工升遷

4 *Busser to Waiter* 打雜工升遷為服務生

 Track 100

Introduction

One of the server assistants is going to be moved up to server. 某位助理服務生升遷為服務生。

Characters

Barry - Manager 經理

Josie - Dining Room Manager 餐區經理

Bob - Server (Waiter) 服務生

Conversation

Josie	I think we could use another waiter. I'm **having trouble** filling in the schedule and not giving anyone too many hours. Having **another body** would be **a good move**.	我想我們還需要再多雇一名服務生。目前我有排班上的困難，不能排過多的時數給單一員工。多雇一位人手將會是個明智之舉。
Barry	Should we hire a new one, or move up one of the bussers we have now? You work with them more than I do; what do you think?	我們要再多雇一個新人，還是將其中一位打雜工升上來做服務生？你比我更常與他們一起工作，你的想法呢？
Josie	I think we have a couple of bussers who do a good job. We shouldn't need to hire a waiter. We can move one of them up. But I think we should get some **input** from one of the waiters.	我們有幾個打雜工做得不錯，所以應該不需要再雇用一個服務生。我們可以讓其中一個升上來做服務生，但應該詢問其中一位服務生的意見。
Barry	Whose opinion do you trust?	你相信誰的意見呢？
Josie	I think Bob. He's a good waiter, and he knows the bussers really well.	我想是 Bob。他是一位優秀的服務生，而且他與打雜工相當熟。
	(in the dining room)	在用餐區
Barry	Bob, could we **speak with** you for a minute or two?	Bob，我們能與你聊個一或兩分鐘嗎？

ob	Sure, what's up?	當然可以，什麼事情呢？
Josie	We want to move one of the bussers up to waiter. Which one do you think could **do a good job**?	我們想要將一位打雜工升為服務生。你認為哪一位打雜工可以勝任呢？
Bob	We have more than one good busser, but I've seen it happen **more than once** that a good busser turns into a bad waiter. For instance, Amy is one of our best bussers, but I don't think she's quite ready to **wait tables**. She's a little too quiet, and she needs more experience talking to tables.	我們優秀的打雜工不只一個，但我曾不只一次碰過優秀的打雜工變成表現糟透的服務生。舉個例子好了，Amy 是眾多優秀打雜工中的其中一位，可是對於招呼客人，我想她並不算上手。她蠻文靜的，要跟顧客互動良好，可能還需要去累積更多的經驗。
Barry	Who would you suggest, then?	既然這樣，你想要推薦誰？
Bob	I think June is the best candidate. She's really good with tables, and she's **quick on her feet**. I think she'd do well.	我覺得 June 是最好的人選耶。她與顧客互動很有一套，做起事來又敏捷。我覺得她會做的很好。
Josie	All right, I'll talk to her and see if she's interested. Thanks for your input.	那就這樣吧！我會與她談談，看她有沒有興趣。謝謝你的意見。

Word Bank

having trouble 有困難（have） another body 另一位員工
input *n.[U]* 指意見 do a good job 勝任 a good move 明智之舉
more than once 不只一次 wait tables 招呼客人；應侍客席
quick on her feet 機伶的 speak with 和……談話 what's up 什麼事

Unit 25 員工升遷

Tips for Workplace Happiness
職場補給站
加油大使 Cheryl 來充電！

我是今天值班副理——餐廳管理職

客人：「找你們主管來，你的服務太差勁了。」
副理：「您好，我是今天的值班副理。」
客人：「你是層級最高的主管？」
副理：「是的，我是今天層級最高的值班主管。」

每個公司都有其職務的階級，餐廳也是一樣，職務一樣有階級，一樣有升遷的規範與原則，惟其職務名稱跟一般公司有些不同，現在讓我們來介紹一下餐廳管理職職稱。

- 副店長 Vice Shopkeeper：協助店長管理之代理人。
- 店長（領班）Shopkeeper（Captain）：此職務一般餐廳稱為店長，飯店稱為領班。
- 副理 Asst. Manager：副理多為現場值班管理者，通常會搭配經理一同輪班。
- 經理 Manager：職務與副理類似，僅是階層不同。
- 資深經理 Senior Manager：資深經理屬後勤管理職務，較不涉及外場服務。
- 副協理 Asst. Director：部分飯店或是餐廳會設置。
- 協理 Director：主要營運管理者，控制成本與經營方向。
- 副總經理 Vice President
- 總經理 General Manager

了解職務階層後，針對餐飲管理人員又應具能力之範疇與知能呢？以下幾個管理知能提供大家了解。

- 觀念性的創造：在工作所需的認知技能中，創造不同的管理與經營。
- 領導技能：此為將腦裡的想法轉換成生產行動的能力。
- 人際管理：懂得有效與他人互動的技能。
- 行政能力：基本企業之人事及財務管理能力。
- 技術知能：對於產品製造及服務必備之知能必須清楚。
- 訓練服務：能正確且適時引導與訓練人員服務之基礎。
- 擅於組織：餐廳人員組織與工作分配得以妥善服務客人。
- 規劃流程：餐廳訂位與、點餐以及結帳流程的制訂。

- 管理進餐：進餐的流程管理與順暢度掌握。

餐飲管理近幾年一直是個熱門且辛苦的科目，許多大學的餐飲相關科系，針對餐飲管理皆有多樣化的課程提供同學選擇，通常課程內容多是以管理學為基礎，搭配餐飲概念來規劃課程，通常此為大學必須的基礎課程。

提醒各位社會新鮮人，大家在踏出校園步入職場前，餐飲管理千萬要好好學習，若你已經離開校園步入服務業，沒關係！學習時時可以進行，記得掌握以上幾個基本原則，你也可以是個出色的餐飲管理人。

Part 6
Condition
Handling
狀況處理

Unit 26 顧客受傷

1 *Slipping on Wet Floor* 在溼地板滑倒

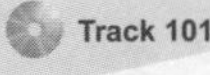
Track 101

Introduction

A guest falls on some water that is spilled on the floor. 一位顧客在有水濺出的地板上跌倒了。

Melvin - Assistant Dining Room Manager 餐區副理
Amy - Server Assistant 助理服務生
Marie - Guest 顧客

Conversation

Amy	Melvin, you have to come over here. We just had a lady slip and **fall down**.	Melvin，你必須馬上過來這裡。剛剛有位女士失足跌倒了。
Melvin	What happened? I should know as much as I can before I go over there and talk to her. Is she up and walking?	發生了什麼事？在我過去和她說話之前，我要盡量瞭解狀況。她可以站起來走路嗎？
Amy	I spilled some water out of my water pitcher and was going to find a **rag** to clean it up with. While I was gone, the woman came walking through and slipped. I think she fell kind of hard on her arm.	我拿的水壺不小心濺出水在地板上，我正要去找抹布來清理。當我離身時，這位女士走路經過就滑倒了。我想她手臂跌得不輕。
Melvin	Ok, thanks, I'll go over and make sure she's **all right**.	好，謝謝。我會過去確認她沒事。
	(at the table)	（在餐桌旁）
Melvin	Hi, I understand you fell on some water on the floor?	你好，我剛得知你因為地板上的水而跌倒了？
Marie	Yes, I was walking over there, and I didn't see the water. I fell on my arm.	是啊，我走過那邊，沒有看到地上有水，所以就跌傷手臂了。

Melvin	I'm very sorry about this. My busser said she was on the way to clean it up when it happened. Do you think you'll be OK?	對此我感到很抱歉。打雜工告訴我她其實正準備要擦乾，事情就發生了。你覺得一切都還好嗎？
Marie	I should be OK.	我應該沒事。
Melvin	I'll tell you what: If it gives you any trouble at all, go get it **checked out** by a doctor. Call me, and I'll get our **insurance** to reimburse you for it.	這樣吧，你如果覺得有問題的話，就讓醫生檢查一下。打電話給我，我們會請我們的保險公司來賠償。
Marie	I don't think that will be necessary.	我想沒有必要。
Melvin	All right, but if you have any pain, or it bothers you at all, please **get it looked at**. We have insurance especially for **situations** like this. And I do hope that it's nothing. We're sorry that this happened.	好的，但如果你有疼痛或任何不適，請去檢查一下。我們有保險處理像這樣的特殊狀況。對於發生的事我們很抱歉，希望一切沒問題。
	(later)	（稍後）
Melvin	Amy, it was good that you tried to clean this up, but next time get one of the other bussers or someone to watch the spill while you go get something to **clean it up** with.	Amy，你想做清理是對的，但下次你離開去拿東西時，先請其他打雜工或同事幫你留意一下那灘水。

Word Bank

spill(ed) *v.* 灑落　fall down 跌倒　rag *n.[C]* 抹布　all right 安然無恙的
check(ed) out 檢查　reimburse *v.* 補償；賠償
get it looked at 去檢查一下　situation(s) *n.[C]* 情況　clean it up 清理

Unit 26 顧客受傷

2 *Chipped Tooth* 牙齒斷裂

 Track 102

Introduction

A guest has injured a tooth while dining. 一位顧客在用餐時弄傷牙齒。

Characters  

John - Guest	顧客
Marlon - Guest	顧客
Jolene - Assistant Manager	副理
Sherman - Waiter	服務生

Conversation

John	**Ouch**! That **hurts**!	哎唷，好痛哦！
Marlon	What happened?	怎麼了？
John	I just **bit into** something. I think I **broke** a tooth.	我剛咬到一個硬硬的東西。我想我咬斷牙齒了。
Marlon	Oh, no! Let me call our waiter. Could you come over here, please?	噢，不！我叫我們的服務生。可以請你過來這裡一下嗎？
Sherman	Yes, is something wrong?	是的，有什麼問題嗎？
Marlon	My friend here just bit into something and broke his tooth.	我朋友剛剛咬到硬物，而且他牙齒斷裂了。
Sherman	Oh, I'm sorry. Is there anything I can do for you right now?	噢，我很抱歉。有什麼現在可以幫忙你的嗎？
John	No, I think I have what I bit into right here. Look, it's a rock. I think it was in the beans.	沒有，我想我剛剛咬到的東西在這裡。你看，是個小石頭。它應該是混在豆子裡。
Sherman	I'm sorry to hear that. I'll get my manager right away.	我很抱歉。我馬上請我們經理過來。
John	Yes, you should do that. This thing really hurts.	是的，你應該那麼做。這真的很痛。

	(the manager comes over)	（經理走過來）
Jolene	Excuse me, but I was told you bit into something?	對不起，但有人告訴我你咬到東西？
John	Yes, see this rock here? That was in my food.	對，看到這個石頭了嗎？它在我的食物裡！
Jolene	I'm sorry about that, sir. Do you think you need to see a **dentist** right now?	先生，我感到很抱歉。你現在需要先看牙醫嗎？
John	No, I think **it can wait** until tomorrow. But I'm sending you the bill.	不用了，我想可以等到明天早上，但帳單可是會寄過來的。
Jolene	Of course, and we won't expect you to pay for your meal, either. Our insurance will pay for you to get your tooth fixed at the dentist's. You only have to send us the bill, and we'll take care of it.	當然，我們也不收您餐點的費用。您在牙醫那裡把牙齒修好的花費都由我們的保險來支付。您只要把帳單寄過來，我們會處理。
John	I expect to be **compensated** for **pain** and **suffering**, too. This shouldn't happen at a nice restaurant like this.	我也覺得你們應該要彌補我的疼痛和受苦吧，這種等級的餐廳不該發生這等事！
Jolene	I agree. Sometimes, though, we get things in our food, no matter what we do. But we do try to be careful.	我同意。但有時候無論我們怎麼做，食物裡還是會有小東西。不過我們已經盡量小心了。
John	Well, you're not being careful enough. You're going to **hear from** my **lawyer**.	看來你們不夠小心。你們會收到我律師的信。
Jolene	I hope it doesn't need to come to that, sir. Just see how you feel in the morning after you've visited the dentist. We'll take care of it. And again, I'm very sorry.	先生，我們希望事情不用到那一步。明天早上您看完牙醫後再看看，我們會負責的。再次向您表達深深的歉意。

Word Bank

injured *adj.* 受傷的　ouch *int.* 哎唷　hurt(s) *v.* 疼痛　bit into 咬到（bite）
broke *v.* 弄斷（break）　dentist *n.[C]* 牙醫　it can wait 稍後再說無妨
compensate(d) *v.* 補償；彌補　pain *n.[U]* 疼痛　suffering *n.[U]* 受苦
hear from 收到……的來信　lawyer *n.[C]* 律師

Unit 26 顧客受傷

3 Broken Glass 破裂的玻璃杯

 Track 103

Introduction

A guest cuts herself on a broken glass. 一位顧客被破裂的玻璃杯割傷。

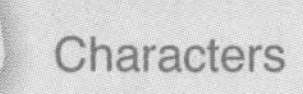

Characters

Marty - Guest	顧客
Diane - Guest	顧客
Dora - Server	服務生
Josie - Dining Room Manager	餐區經理
Barry - Manager	經理
Jamie - Bartender	酒保

Conversation

Marty	Excuse me, could you get another napkin for us, please? My wife just cut her lip on this glass.	對不起，可以請你幫我們再拿一條餐巾嗎？我太太剛剛被玻璃杯割傷嘴唇了。
Dora	Oh, no! I'll be right back.	噢，不！我很快回來。
	(Dora returns)	（Dora 回來）
Dora	Here is a towel, and I brought some ice, too. I'm really sorry this happened.	這毛巾給您，我也拿了些冰塊過來。我很抱歉發生這樣的事。
Diane	I don't really feel all that bad. I just wouldn't expect to be served in a broken glass.	我不覺得那麼糟啦，只是沒有想到會送上一個破裂玻璃杯。
Dora	No, I wouldn't, either. I'm very sorry. I'll get my manager right away.	是啊，我也沒想到，真的非常抱歉。我馬上請我的經理過來。
	(Josie arrives)	（Josie 到達）
Josie	Hello, I'm so sorry to hear you cut yourself. Your meal is **complimentary** tonight, and I'll try to find out how that happened, so it doesn't happen again. Do you need to **seek** some **medical attention**?	你好，我很抱歉聽到你割傷了。您今晚的餐點由我們免費招待，而且我們會盡力找出事發原因，以免再次發生這樣的事。您需要醫療處理嗎？

Diane	No, I think I'll be all right. It's stopped **bleeding** now.	不用了，我想我還好。現在已經止血了。
	(the next day)	（隔天）
Barry	I called this special meeting to discuss safety. We had a guest cut her lip on one of our glasses last night. We need to **make sure** that never happens again.	今天召開這個特別會議，是要討論安全議題。昨晚有個顧客被我們的一個玻璃杯割傷嘴唇。我們要確保這種情形絕對不再發生。
Josie	The glass came from the bar. I think I know how it happened. The way they stack the glasses in there, with one inside the other, seems like it would make it very easy to **chip** one, like what happened last night.	玻璃杯是從吧台拿來的。我想我知道它是怎麼發生的。他們堆疊玻璃杯的方式、是一個疊著另一個，看來似乎很容易碰裂，就像昨晚發生的一樣。
Jamie	But that's how we've always done it.	但這一向都是我們放玻璃杯的方法啊。
Barry	And I think we've been very **fortunate** that something like this hasn't happened before. It's very easy to stack those glasses too quickly when you're in a hurry. We need to come up with a better method.	我們應該覺得很幸運，這樣的事以前都還沒發生過。當趕時間時，很容易太快就把玻璃杯堆疊得太急。我們需要想個更好辦法。
Josie	One place I worked at before, they stacked them up on trays, so each **level** was separated by a tray. That way, the glasses didn't touch each other.	我以前工作的地方，他們是用托盤來放玻璃杯，每層都用托盤隔開。這樣子一來，玻璃杯就不會碰到彼此了。
Barry	I like that idea. We'll try it out and see if it's **workable**.	我喜歡這個想法。我們會試試，看看這方法行不行得通。

Word Bank

broken *adj.* 破裂的　complimentary *adj.* 免費招待的；贈送的
seek *v.* 尋求　medical attention 醫療照護　bleed(ing) *v.* 流血
make sure 確認　chip *v.* 碎裂；造成缺口　fortunate *adj.* 幸運的；僥倖的
level *n.[C]* 層；水平高度　workable *adj.* 切實可行的

Unit 26 顧客受傷

4 *Water Spilled on Guest* 水濺到顧客了 

Introduction

Two servers are talking after work. 兩個服務生下班後在聊天。

Characters

Lance - Server 服務生
Bob - Server 服務生

Conversation

Lance	What was the worst thing that ever happened to you while you were serving?	當你在服務客人時，曾發生過最糟糕的事是什麼？
Bob	One time, I had a whole tray full of desserts. I couldn't find a tray jack, so I put them up on the sidestand.	有一次，我拿了一個裝滿甜點的托盤，但我找不到托盤架，只好先堆放在旁邊的工作檯。
Lance	And the whole thing fell off on the floor, right?	然後所有東西都掉到地板上了，對不對？
Bob	Yes, and I was such a **jerk** back then that I made the busser start cleaning it up. Then I headed back to the kitchen to get the order **remade**.	對得很，當時我很惡劣地叫打雜工來清理。接著我回到廚房，請他們把該出的菜再做一次。
Lance	That's not so bad. I think mine is worse. I was serving water to a table one time, and I slipped and ended up **dumping** a whole glass of water on a guy's **lap**. He **was not pleased**.	你這還好啦，我想我的更糟。有一次我替客人送水時，不小心滑倒，結果整杯水都倒在顧客大腿上。他很不悅。
Bob	No, **I'll bet** he wasn't. What did you do?	沒錯，他當然會不高興。後來你做了什麼？

Lance	What anyone would do; I got a bunch of napkins, then went in the back and got a towel. He dried himself off as best he could, but of course he was very, very wet.	做了任何人都會做的事，我拿了一疊紙巾，然後再到後面拿了一條毛巾給他。客人急著把自己擦乾，但他還是溼透了。
Bob	What happened then?	然後怎麼了呢？
Lance	The manager **comped** the meal, of course, and gave them a voucher to come back in again. I never did see them. They probably asked to not be seated in my section.	當然經理免費招待那一餐，而且給他們優待券讓他們再來用餐，但我沒有再見過他們了。他們可能要求不要坐在我那區吧。
Bob	So that man ate the whole meal with wet pants.	所以那人整個用餐過程都穿著溼褲子囉。
Lance	Yeah, the manager told them to send us the **cleaning bill**, which shouldn't have been too bad. It was only water. And I think they were going out to a movie or something. He had to go home and change before they went out.	是啊，經理請他們把清洗費帳單寄給我們，應該不難洗，只有被水弄濕了。他們好像接下來要去看電影之類的，但他們必須先回家換衣服再出去。
Bob	I hope his car didn't have **leather** seats!	我希望他的車子座椅不是皮的！

Part I Part II Part III Part IV Part V Part VI

Word Bank

jerk *n.[C]* 笨蛋；蠢貨　remade *v.* 重新製作　dump(ing) *v.* 傾倒
lap *n.* 坐姿時大腿上方　was not pleased 不高興
I'll bet 想必　comp(ed) *v.* 免費招待　cleaning bill 洗衣費帳單
leather *adj.* 皮革的；皮製的

Unit 26 顧客受傷

客戶用餐時受傷了——公共意外責任保險

日前新聞報導一家知名的連鎖餐廳，因為免費湯品的鍋子放置位置不當，導致一名男童跌入鍋內燙傷，聽起來有些不可思議，大家會想男童能有多高，湯鍋正常應該放置於一定高度的平台上，怎麼男童會跌入呢？湯鍋總不會放在地板上吧！

其實餐廳內的燙傷案件一直是餐飲業的一個問題，舉凡員工受傷或是顧客受傷皆是，僅是很多引起原因皆非餐廳作業因素。既然難控制，是不是餐廳就任其發生呢？餐廳的作業管理機制確實不會因難控制而因噎廢食，僅是除了規範好作業外，還能有什麼保障餐廳與顧客的方式呢？

1966 年台灣制訂了公共意外責任保險制度，針對公共區域的意外責任設定一個完整的保險機制，其區分為 6 種類型，餐飲服務則規範為丙類投保場所。

什麼是公共意外責任保險制度？廣義來說，公共責任風險包括在處所內（例如餐廳內），及處所外（例如戶外區）從事營業或業務活動時，因處所設施、工作物、機械工具有瑕疵、管理不善、保養不良或因工作人員之疏忽過失，而引起意外事故致第三人傷亡或財物受損者，依法應付之賠償責任風險。台灣公共意外責任保險所承保者，僅限於被保者使用中處所範圍，故又稱為處所責任保險。

公共意外責任保險介紹

保險的理賠責任為被保險人因在保險期間內發生下列意外事故所致第三人體傷死亡或第三人財物損害依法應負責任而受賠償請求時，保險公司對被保險人負賠償責任。

1. 被保險人或其受僱人，因經營業務之疏忽或過失在保險單載明之營業處所內發生之意外事故。
2. 被保險人營業處所之建築物、通道、機器或其他工作物，因設置、保養或管理有所欠缺，所發生之意外事故。

目前公共意外責任保險投保金額是有一定的規範，依各縣市政府消費場所強制投保公共意外險規定，或消費者自治條例投保規定執行，又因各地區規定不同，投保時記得留意設籍區域之縣市政府規範進行投保，以避免觸法。

單位：新台幣萬元

法規名稱	每一人身體傷亡	每一事故身體傷亡	每一事故財產損失	保險期間總保險金額
台北市消費場所強制投保公共意外責任保險實施辦法（第 6 條）	300	1500	200	3400
高雄市供公共使用營利場所強制投保公共意外責任保險實施自治條例（第 5 條）	300	1000	200	4800
桃園縣公共營業場所強制投保公共意外責任保險實施自治條例（第 4 條）	200	1000	200	2400
新竹縣供公共使用營利場所強制投保公共意外責任保險實施自治條例（第 4 條）	200	2000	200	3600
新竹市供公共使用營利場所強制投保公共意外責任保險實施自治條例（第 4 條）	200	1000	200	2400
苗栗縣供公共使用營利場所強制投保公共意外責任保險實施自治條例（第 4 條）	200	1000	200	2400
台中市事業場所強制投保公共意外責任保險自治條例（第 4 條）	200	1000	200	2400
彰化縣營利場所強制投保公共意外責任保險實施自治條例（第 4 條）	200	1000	200	2400
台南市營利場所強制投保公共意外責任保險實施自治條例（第 5 條）	200	1000	200	2400
非上述縣市政府規定	應投保	應投保	應投保	應投保

Unit 27 失望的顧客

1 *Can't Use Credit Card* 無法使用信用卡 

Introduction

A guest's credit card has been declined. 顧戶的信用卡被拒絕交易。

Characters 

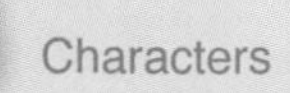

Kathy - Server	服務生
Floyd - Guest	顧客
Melvin - Assistant Dining Room Manager	餐區副理
Joanna - Credit Card Customer Service	信用卡客服人員

Conversation

Kathy	Here's your check, and you can pay me whenever you're ready.	這是您的帳單，您準備好時隨時可結帳。
Floyd	Here, I'll put it on my **American Express card**.	我要用美國運通卡付款。
Kathy	Thank you, I'll be back in just a minute.	謝謝你，我稍後回來。
	(at the credit card machine)	在刷卡機處
Kathy	Hey Melvin, the credit card machine just told me to decline this card. It said "decline – call". Do you know what I'm supposed to do with this?	嘿，Melvin，刷卡機剛剛拒絕這張卡的交易。上面顯示「拒絕交易，打電話確認」。你覺得我該怎麼做呢？
Melvin	You have to call American Express and see **what's going on**.	你必須打電話給美國運通銀行，看看是怎麼回事。
	(on the phone)	電話通話中
Joanna	Hello, American Express **customer service**, how can I help you?	你好，美國運通客戶服務部，有什麼可以幫忙的？
Kathy	I'm a server at a restaurant. One of my guests is trying to use one of your cards. The credit card machine said to call you.	我是餐廳的服務生。有位客人使用你們的卡，但刷卡機顯示要打電話給你們。

Joanna	Can you give me the **card number**, please?	可以請你告訴我信用卡號碼嗎？
Kathy	Yes, it's 3417 856382 1260.	好的，信用卡號碼是 3417 856382 1260.
Joanna	That card has been **revoked**. You are not to give it back to the customer. It needs to be sent back to American Express. We will send you a check as **compensation** for your trouble.	那張卡已經被取消了。麻煩把信用卡寄回美國運通，不要還給客人。我們會寄一張支票給你們，以做為你們的補償。
Kathy	OK, so I need to give this card to my manager and let him send it to you?	好的，所以我把這張卡交給經理，再寄給你們？
Joanna	That is right. And thank you for **denying** use of this card.	沒錯。謝謝你拒絕使用這張卡。
	(at the table)	在餐桌旁
Kathy	I'm sorry, sir, but American Express has declined your card and asked me not to give it back to you. Do you have another **form** of payment?	先生，很抱歉，美國運通銀行拒絕您的信用卡交易，而且要求我們不要把信用卡還給您。您有別的付款方式嗎？
Floyd	What do you mean you're not going to give it back? It's my card.	你不把信用卡還給我是什麼意思？那是我的信用卡！
Kathy	I don't know why, but they said I was to keep your card. You'll have to pay another way.	我不知道原因，但他們說請我們保留您的信用卡。麻煩您用別的方式付款。
Floyd	I can't believe this!	我不相信有這種事！
Kathy	Sir, you should call them and see what they have to say. In the meantime, I'll need another card for your check.	先生，您應該打電話給他們，看看他們怎麼說。同時，我需要您給我另一張卡結帳。

Word Bank

declined *v.* 拒絕　American Express card 美國運通卡
what's going on 是怎麼回事　customer service 客戶服務
card number 信用卡號碼　revoke(d) *v.* 取消；廢除；撤銷
compensation *n.[U]* 賠償；補償　deny(ing) *v.* 拒絕　form *n.* 方式；形式

Unit 27 失望的顧客

2 *Late Guests – Reservation Canceled*
客人遲到－預約被取消

Track 106

Introduction

Some guests arrive too late to make their reservation. 有些客人太晚到以致於趕不上預約時間。

Characters  

Janet - Hostess 女領檯
Oscar - Guest 顧客
Josie - Dining Room Manager 餐區經理

Conversation

Janet	Good evening and welcome. How many are in your party?	晚安，歡迎光臨，請問你們幾位？
Oscar	There are two of us, and we have a reservation for Oscar Madison.	我們有兩位，我們已經用 Oscar Madison 這名字預約了。
Janet	I'm sorry sir, but what time was your reservation for?	先生，我很抱歉，請問你預約幾點？
Oscar	It was 8:00, I think.	我想應該是八點鐘。
Janet	Yes, you did have a reservation for 8:00, but it's 8:25. We've given your table to someone else. We didn't think you were going to **show up**. But we should be able to get you in very soon.	是的，你預約八點鐘，但現在已經 8：25，我們已把你的桌位給了別人了。我們不知道你們會過來，但我們會儘快幫你們安排座位。
Oscar	Of course I was going to **show up**. What do you think I made a reservation for, anyway?	我當然會來，不然你覺得我為什麼要預約？
Janet	Yes, but it's our policy to not hold reservations **longer than** 15 minutes after they were supposed to arrive. You were 25 minutes **late**. But I'll be glad to give you the next table that becomes available.	是的，但按照規定，我們預約保留不超過十五分鐘，而你們晚了二十五分鐘。不過，我們很樂意盡快把下一張空出的桌子給你們。

Oscar	No, that's **not good enough**. I made a reservation, and I want to be seated.	不行，我不滿意。我有預約，我現在就要入座。
Janet	I'm sorry, but all our tables are full right now. That's the best I can do.	我很抱歉，但我們所有餐桌目前都滿了。我最多只能做到這樣。
Oscar	Well, that's **not good enough**. I want to speak to your manager.	嗯，我不滿意。我要和你們經理對話。
	(the manager comes up)	經理過來了
Josie	Hello, I understand that there's a problem?	你好，就我所知這裡有問題？
Oscar	Yes, this girl here says I can't **sit down**, even though I have a reservation.	是的，這個女孩說，即使我已經有預約，還是不能入座。
Josie	Sir, your reservation was for 25 minutes ago. We have people not show up all the time. That's why we only **hold** a table for 15 minutes past the time you **are due**. We'll get you in just as fast as we can. It shouldn't be more than about 5 more minutes.	先生，你的預約是二十五分鐘前。我們常常有人預約但不出現的，所以我們只保留桌子十五分鐘。我們會盡快安排你們入座，應該不會超過五分鐘。
Oscar	No, I don't like your customer service. We don't want to eat here **after all**. We'll just go **somewhere else**.	不了，你們的客戶服務我不喜歡。反正我們不想在這裡用餐了，我們去別的地方吧。
Josie	I'm sorry to hear that.	聽到你這麼說很遺憾。

Word Bank

show up 出現　longer than 比……長　late *adj.* 遲的；晚的
not good enough 不夠好　sit down 坐下　hold *v.* 保留
are due 到期（be）　after all 畢竟　somewhere else 其他別的地方

Unit 27 失望的顧客

3 *Can't Use More Than One Coupon* 不能使用超過一張以上的優待券

Track 107

Introduction

A table tries to use more than one coupon to pay for their meal. 有一桌客人用多於一張的優待券來結帳。

Characters

Josie - Dining Room Manager 餐區經理

Kathy - Server 服務生

Bob - Server 服務生

Ida - Guest 顧客

Conversation

Josie	We're **running** a new promotion. It's with a **group** called Taipei Entertainment. Their card gives you one meal free when you buy one.	我們現正舉辦一個新的促銷活動，是和一個叫做「台北享樂」的團體合作。憑他們的卡點餐享有買一送一優惠。
Kathy	How can we make any money doing that? That's 50% off.	那我們怎麼會賺錢啊？這可是打五折！
Josie	It's a promotion. The money we make from these tables isn't as important as getting people in the door and letting them know how good we are.	這是一個促銷手法。讓客人進門並且知道我們有多麼好，比起從這些桌數所賺的錢還要重要多了。
Bob	What if one person wants to order something real expensive, and the other one orders a salad?	那如果有人點了很貴的餐，另一個人只點一盤沙拉呢？
Josie	You need to take off the least expensive adult meal. We hope this will get people to order more appetizers and desserts.	那麼最不貴的那份成人餐就不用算錢。我們希望顧客會因此多點一些開胃菜和甜點。
Bob	What about if they have other coupons?	那如果他們有別的優惠券呢？
Josie	You can only use one coupon **at a time**. It says so right on all our coupons.	一次只能使用一種優惠券，我們的每一種優惠券上面都有說明。

	(later, at a table)	稍後，在某桌
Bob	Here is your check, and you can pay me whenever you're ready.	這是您的帳單，您準備好時就可以讓我幫您結帳。
Ida	We have an Entertainment card that we'd like to use.	我們想使用享樂卡結帳。
Bob	That's fine; I'll take off the **lower-priced** meal from your bill.	沒問題，我會把價格比較低的那一份餐從帳單扣掉。
Ida	We also have a coupon for 15% off.	我們還有一張八五折的優惠券。
Bob	I'm sorry, but you can only use one of those.	我很抱歉，但你們只能使用一種優惠券。
Ida	What? It says right here "15% off your total bill, alcohol **excluded**".	什麼？這上面說「全部帳單八五折優惠，酒類除外」。
Bob	Yes, but it also says "not **valid** with any other **offer**". And in your Entertainment book, you'll see that it also **states** that you can't use their card with another coupon.	是的，但上寫也有註明「與他種優惠同用時無效」。而且在享樂卡小冊子裡，也可以看到使用本卡不能和其他優惠券同時使用。
Ida	Your food is expensive. I didn't think we'd have to pay this much for dinner. We won't be back.	你們餐點很貴，我不認為晚餐要付這麼多。我們下次不會再來了。
Bob	I'm sorry. I hope you'll come back and use your other coupon **next time**.	我很抱歉，希望你們下次再度光臨，並繼續使用其他優惠券。
Ida	I don't think there'll be a next time. I'm not happy about this.	我想我不會有下一次了。我不怎麼高興。

Word Bank

meal *n.[C]* 餐點　run(ning) *v.* 運轉；舉辦　group *n.[C]* 團體；集團
at a time 一次　lower-priced *adj.* 較低單價的　exclude(d) *v.* 排除；不包括
valid *adj.* 有效的　offer *n.[C]* 特惠　state *v.* 陳述；聲明　next time 下一次

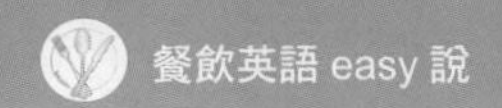

Unit 27 失望的顧客

 *Expired Coupon* 優惠券過期  Track 108

Introduction

A guest wants to use a coupon, but it is past its date. 一位客人想使用優惠券，但優惠券已經過期。

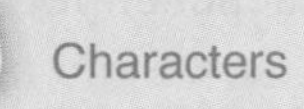

Characters

Sally - Server	服務生
Marian - Guest	顧客
Jolene - Assistant Manager	副理

Conversation

Marian	I'd like the check when we're done, please.	我們用完餐後麻煩幫我們買單。
Sally	OK, I'll make sure to give it to you.	好的，我會把帳單拿給你。
	(later)	稍後
Sally	Here you are, ma'am, and you can pay me when you are ready to go.	小姐，您的帳單給您，您準備好時就可以讓我幫您結帳。
Marian	I can pay you right now. I'll use my **Visa card**. I also have this coupon for 15% off that I'd like to use.	我現在就可以付款。我要用 VISA 卡付款，同時還要使用這張八五折優惠券。
Sally	All right, give me just a minute to run your credit card. I'm sorry, but this coupon **expired** last week. You won't be able to use it.	好的，給我一點時間刷您的卡。我很抱歉，這張優惠券上週已經過期，你無法使用它了。
Marian	Oh really? I just put it in my **purse** a while ago and didn't think about it until now. Is there no way you can take it?	真的嗎？我前陣子把它放在我的皮包裡，直到最近才想到要用。你沒有辦法收它嗎？
Sally	Let me talk to my manager and see what she says.	我跟我們經理談一下，看看她怎麼說。
	(in another part of the restaurant)	在餐廳的另一區
Sally	Jolene, could I talk to you for a minute?	Jolene，我可以跟你談一下嗎？

Jolene	Sure, what do you need?	當然，你需要什麼？
Sally	I have a guest who's trying to use one of the coupons that expired last week. Is there any way we can take it?	有個客人想使用一張上週就過期的優惠券結帳。有任何通融方式嗎？
Jolene	I'll go over and talk to them. Where are they **sitting**?	我過去跟客人講一下。他們坐在哪桌？
Sally	They're at table 21.	他們在 21 桌。
	(at table 21)	在 21 桌
Jolene	Hi, my name is Jolene. I **understand** you have a coupon you want to use?	你好，我的名字叫 Jolene。我得知你們有優惠券要使用？
Marian	Yes, I didn't realize it was expired. I was hoping you would take it, since it expired just last week.	是的，我不知道它已經過期了。我希望你們可以收它，它上週才過期的。
Jolene	It's OK; we'll **honor** it. And I hope to see you again **sometime**.	好的，我們會接受優惠券，同時也希望可以再見到你們。
Marian	I'm sure you will. Thank you.	我相信你會的，謝謝！
	(at the computer)	在電腦旁
Sally	If it expired last week, why did you take it?	優惠券上週就過期了，你為什麼還收它呢？
Jolene	This way, they'll go away happy and maybe tell their friends about us, too. If I hadn't taken it, this would have been a **negative dining** experience for them.	這樣的話，他們會高興地離開，而且或許還會告訴朋友關於我們的事。如果不收的話，他們的用餐經驗就會感覺不好。

Word Bank

past *prep.* 超過　Visa card VISA 信用卡　expire(d) *v.* 過期
purse *n.[C]* 皮包　sit(ting) *v.* 坐　understand *v.* 了解；知道
honor *v.* 接受　sometime *adv.* 在某個時候　negative *adj.* 負面的
dining *n.[C/U]* 用餐

Unit 27 失望的顧客

愉快用餐 氣憤離開——客訴處理

當年蜜月我們夫妻選擇旅遊歐洲，難得去到那麼遠的地方，當然要品嘗一下當地的特色餐廳，於是我們精挑細選了一個三星米其林景觀餐廳，價格並非我們在意的重點，畢竟機票好幾萬都花了，怎麼會在意那一點餐費呢？但很不幸的，那個用餐經驗真的是讓我不敢恭維。

法國米其林指南分為紅綠兩種，紅色指南介紹酒店及餐廳資料，綠色指南則提供旅遊資訊，在其紅色餐廳指南中，原以叉子表示等級，後續變更為星星標示。一顆星（Very Good Cooking）餐廳：「值得停車品嘗的好餐廳」；兩顆星（Excellent Cooking）餐廳：「一流廚藝，提供極佳食物和美酒搭配，值得繞道前往，但所費不貲」；三顆星（Exceptional Cuisine，Worth the Journey）餐廳：「完美而登峰造極的廚藝，值得專程前往，可以享用手藝超絕美食、精選上佳佐餐酒、零缺點服務和極雅致用餐環境，但是要花一大筆錢」。

看到以上定義，我們可以了解當時我選擇的餐廳高級的程度。其實剛進入餐廳時，我們是非常期待與愉快的，面對親切的服務生與絕美的景致，當下真的覺得飛這一趟 10 多小時是值得的，但當餐點上桌，我發現並無我想像中的美味，姑且說明是歐洲口味與我的台式飲食有落差，但當我發現食材的酸味充斥我的口腔時，我們喚來服務生說明了食材的問題，此時便是噩夢的開始。

首先是服務生先解釋我點的餐點內容，後續是管理者來了解餐點的內容，並將服務生的話重複一次，後續主廚出現了，再將餐點內容說明一次，我懂我點的內容為何，但這餐點不該有酸味，且並非我所認知的食材烹煮方式，溝通了許久我放棄了，就這樣我們草草結束用餐，進行投訴。

餐點的美味與否，其實是個很主觀的感覺，對於服務來說，客戶主觀認為不合口味，就餐廳的處理流程，可以有很多方式，如這家餐廳，推諉是客戶不懂食材的烹煮方式，或是依照客戶意願盡速更換新的餐點給於客戶，這都是餐廳管理者可以決定的。

在服務客訴處理裡，我簡單節錄以下幾個重點，是大家未來可以依循跟制訂處理規範。

掌握客戶訴求

在傾聽的過程裡，除了讓客戶發洩情緒外，別忘記把握時間，從中迅速掌握客戶訴求，客戶抱怨時，很多時候不會直接講訴他心裡真正的訴求，甚至繞圈圈迂迴謾罵，不過你要相信會抱怨一定有訴求，千萬不要相信不停抱怨不願離開的客戶說：我沒要求，只是覺得你們該改進。如果沒訴求，客戶僅會說明建議後就滿意地離開，而不會一再表達心裡的不舒服。

同理心

「我了解你的心情跟感受」這是我最常聽到處理人員跟客戶說明的一句話，重點是你真的懂嗎？處理客訴時，最重要的技巧運用就是同理心，所謂穿上客戶的鞋（walk a mile in her shoes），這不是要你真的去脫客戶的鞋並穿上它，而是提醒你，換個位置思考、體會對方的感覺，惟有同理體會，你才可以知道客戶在意的跟不舒服的是什麼，也才可以正確的提供處理方案。

提供實際的處理

要有效地處理客訴，提供實際處理方式是首要關鍵。這個動作需搭配上述的各項技巧，從傾聽中掌握客戶訴求，並運用同理心了解客訴真的感受與需求，再提供實際的處理建議。所謂的實際處理方式，指的是可以執行且迎合客戶需要，例如我那個不愉快的用餐經驗，我的訴求僅是食材並非我想要的口味，若能協助更換，服務就是我滿意的。

簡言之，客訴抱怨處理僅要抓對客戶需求、處理的方向，一切也就不難，並且可以得心應手了。

Unit 28 餐點狀況

1 *Waiter Forgets First Course* 服務生忘了上前菜

Track 109

Introduction

A server gets busy and forgets to bring the salad course to a table. 服務生太忙、忘了幫客人上沙拉。

Characters

Kathy - Server 服務生
Robin - Guest 客人
Melvin - Assistant Dining Room Manager 餐區副理

Conversation

Kathy	Here is your shrimp scampi, and the tenderloin steak for you.	現在幫你上的是白酒鮮蝦、和嫩煎腓力里肌牛排。
Robin	Wait a minute; I thought we were **supposed to** get salad first?	等一下；不是應該先上沙拉嗎？
Kathy	Oh, no! Did I really forget to bring out your first course? I can't believe I did that.	噢，不！我難道忘了幫你們上前菜嗎？真不敢相信我竟然忘記了！
Robin	It's not a big deal; we've been sitting here enjoying our wine. I just thought it was kind of **unusual** to get our entrées before the salad.	沒關係，我們還在品嘗餐前酒。只是還沒吃沙拉就上主菜有些不尋常。
Kathy	I'm so sorry. I guess I just got too busy and thought that you were already finished with your salads. I'm really **embarrassed**.	實在很抱歉。我忙得團團轉、以為你們已經用完沙拉了。真的很不好意思。
Robin	It's really OK. We don't mind eating our dinner now.	真的沒關係。我們不介意現在就吃主菜。
Kathy	Thank you for understanding. Please enjoy your meal.	謝謝你們的諒解，請享用你們的餐點。
	(in the kitchen)	（廚房裡）

Kathy	Melvin, I can't believe what I did.	Melvin，我不敢相信我會做這種事。
Melvin	What did you do?	你做了甚麼？
Kathy	I **completely** forgot to deliver the salad course to table 33.	我完全忘記 33 桌客人的沙拉沒有上。
Melvin	Oh really? What did they say?	喔！真的嗎？客人有抱怨嗎？
Kathy	They were **pretty cool** about it, but I'm still really embarrassed.	客人很淡定，但我還是覺得很不好意思。
Melvin	Don't get too upset. If that's the worst thing you ever do in this business, **consider yourself** lucky. I'll go talk to them.	不要太沮喪了。如果這是你最糟糕的狀況，你算幸運了。我會和客人談一談。
	(at the table)	（客人桌邊）
Melvin	Hi, my name is Melvin, and I'm the assistant dining room manager. How are your meals?	嗨，我是餐區副理 Melvin。你們的餐點還可以嗎？
Robin	They're good, and don't worry about your server. I know she's really busy and just forgot.	餐點很美味。對於服務生忘了上沙拉的事，不用放在心上，我知道她實在是忙到忘記了。
Melvin	We're sorry it happened, anyway. I'd like to make dessert **on the house** to make up for it.	對於服務生的疏忽，我們真的感到抱歉。我會贈送免費甜點當作補償。
Robin	That's not really **necessary**, but we'll take it anyway. Thanks.	實在不需要這麼麻煩，但我們樂意接受你們的好意。謝謝你。

Word Bank

forget *v.* 忘記　supposed to 可以；應該　unusual *adj.* 不尋常的；稀有的
embarrassed *adj.* 窘的；尷尬的 completely *adv.* 完整地；完全地
pretty *adv.* 相當；頗；很　cool *adj.* 冷靜的；沈著的　consider *v.* 把……視為
yourself *pron.* 你自己　on the house 免費　necessary *adj.* 必要的

Unit 28 餐點狀況

2 *Kitchen Backed Up* 廚房忙不過來

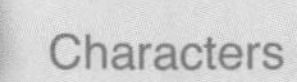
Track 110

Introduction

Two servers have to explain to their tables that their food will be delayed. 兩位服務生必須跟客人解釋餐點遲上的原因。

Characters

Doug - Server	服務生
Marcy - Server	服務生
Karl - Expeditor	傳菜領班
Paul - Guest	顧客
Andrew - Guest	顧客
Julie - Guest	顧客

Conversation

Doug	Hey, everyone, fire your orders early. The cooks are **backed up** already.	大家注意，早點和廚房下做菜單，廚房已經在塞車了。
Marcy	Really? I'd better get a couple of mine going.	真的嗎？我最好先出掉手上的一些單。
Doug	I think Raymond has a big party that they're working on now.	我想廚房正忙著準備 Raymond 那一大桌客人。
Marcy	Time to go explain it to the tables. This isn't going to be easy.	該去跟客人解釋遲遲沒上餐的原因了。要客人諒解可不容易。
	(at a table)	（在客桌旁）
Doug	Hi, folks, I just found out that we have a big party in the back that is **tying up** the kitchen right now. It may be a few minutes longer than you expect to get your meals.	嗨各位！我剛才發現廚房正忙著準備一個大團體的餐點，所以你們的餐點要比預期的再稍後一點上了。
Paul	That's OK; we're in no hurry. Do you think you could get us two more beers while we're waiting?	沒關係，我們不趕時間。那在我們等的時候可以幫我們拿兩罐啤酒喝嗎？
Doug	Sure, I'll be right back.	沒問題，我馬上回來。
	(another table)	（另外一桌客人）

Marcy	I just **found out** that the kitchen is a little **behind**. It may be a few extra minutes before everything is ready for you.	我剛剛發現廚房進度有一點落後。你們的餐點可能必須再多等一會兒才會好。
Andrew	Really? How much longer do you think it will be? We have a movie to get to.	真的？你想還要花多久？我們有個電影要看呢！
Marcy	I'll go and check on your order. Please be **patient**, and I'll be right back.	我去廚房確認一下你們的點單。請耐心等候，我馬上回來。
	(in the kitchen)	（在廚房）
Marcy	Hey, Karl, **what are the chances** of getting table 25 in the next couple minutes?	嗨！ Karl，25 桌客人的餐點有沒有可能在幾分鐘內上菜？
Karl	I don't think anything but this big party is going to be coming out for about the next ten minutes. I hate to say it, but it's true.	廚房還要十分鐘才能上完這一大團體的菜。我不想讓你失望，但實際的情況是我們做不到。
	(back at the table)	（回到桌邊）
Marcy	Sorry to **report**, but it may be 10 minutes or more before your food is ready.	很抱歉，你們的餐點必須再等至少十分鐘。
Andrew	What do you think, honey? Should we wait?	親愛的，你認為呢？我們要等嗎？
Julie	I think taking our time over dinner is more important than making it to the movie. Let's just see a later show.	我想好好享用晚餐比趕著去看電影重要的多。我們看下一場就好了。
Marcy	Thanks, we're working on getting your dinners out as fast as we can.	謝謝你們，我們會盡快把你們的餐點準備好。

Word Bank

back(ed) up 使阻塞　tying up 阻塞（tie）　found out 發現（find）
behind *adj.* 落後的　patient *adj.* 有耐心的　what are the chances 有多大機會　report *v.* 報告　delay(ed) *v.* 延遲；耽擱

Unit 28 餐點狀況

3 *Soup Is Cold* 湯冷了

Track 111

Introduction

The soup isn't hot, and the manager has to make sure everyone knows how to keep it hot. 湯的熱度不夠，餐區經理指導服務生讓湯保持熱度。

Characters

Marcy - Server	服務生
Ellen - Guest	顧客
Bernie - Sous Chef	湯品主廚
Josie - Dining Room Manager	餐區經理
Raymond - Server	服務生
Karl - Expeditor	傳菜領班

Conversation

Marcy	Here is your corn **chowder**, and the vegetarian minestrone for you.	這是您點的玉米濃湯、和義大利蔬菜通心粉。
Ellen	Excuse me, but this soup isn't really hot.	不好意思，這湯熱度不夠。
Marcy	It isn't? OK, let me get you some that's hotter.	不夠熱？我馬上幫您換上一碗較熱的湯。
Marcy	Oh, I see. The whole pot of soup isn't hot. **No wonder**; there's no water in the wells. Bernie, would it be possible to get some more soup? Someone forgot to put water in the wells, and what we have is **barely** warm.	喔！原來如此。保溫爐沒加水，難怪整鍋湯都不熱。Bernie，可以再煮一些湯嗎？有人忘了幫保溫爐加水，鍋子裡的湯都不熱了。
Bernie	Sure, go ahead and **microwave** some for your table right now. I'll get some more in **just a minute**. Could you put some water in there?	沒問題！你先用微波爐加熱一些湯給顧客，我盡快再煮一些。你可以幫忙把水加到湯爐裡嗎？

Marcy	I'm already **on it**. Hey, Josie, there isn't any water in the soup wells. Who did **setup** today? I think they don't understand how this thing works.	我已經在處理了。Josie，爐子裡都沒水，今天是誰負責保溫爐？我想他們不懂怎麼處理喔。
Josie	I'll get everyone together for a quick meeting and explain. Karl, could you buzz everyone right now?	我想召集所有人開個緊急小會做解釋。Karl，可以傳呼每個人過來嗎？
Karl	**Coming up**.	馬上就來。
Josie	I know you're all really busy right now, but whoever did setup didn't fill the water in the soup wells, again.	我知道你們現在都很忙，但是今天準備保溫爐的人又忘了加水。
Raymond	That may have been me. Sorry.	抱歉，應該是我。
Josie	Anyway, it doesn't do any good to **turn on** the heat if there's no water in there. The water against the outside of the soup pot is what keeps the soup warm. And you know there are people who love to burn their lips on the soup. So, let's keep it nice and hot, OK?	如果保溫爐裡沒有水，加熱再久湯也不會熱。湯鍋外面的水是為了要保溫。有些客人就是喜歡喝熱騰騰到會燙嘴的湯，因此鍋子要持續保溫才可以，好嗎？
Raymond	Got it. Now, can we **get going**?	了解了！我們可以去做事了嗎？
Josie	Yes, and do a good job out there.	當然可以，記得把工作做好。

Word Bank

chowder *n.[U]* 海鮮濃湯　no wonder 難怪　barely *adv.* 幾乎不；不足地
microwave *v.* 用微波爐加熱　just a minute 一下下　on it 處理這事；搞定
setup *n.[C]* 準備　coming up 馬上就來　turn on 打開電源
get going 開始進行

Unit 28 餐點狀況

4 *Dessert Takes Too Long* 甜點上太慢 Track 112

Introduction

A table's desserts are taking a long time. 甜點上桌時間太長。

Characters  

Doug - Server	服務生
Raymond - Server	服務生
Ethan - Guest	顧客
Jess - Cook	廚師

Conversation

Doug	Have you decided on dessert yet?	你們決定點什麼甜點了嗎？
Ethan	No, we're going to wait a couple more minutes. **In the meantime**, could you bring us two cognacs and two coffees.	還沒有，可能還需要些時間，這時，可以先幫我們上兩杯白蘭地、兩杯咖啡嗎？
Doug	**Certainly**, I'll be back with those in a couple minutes.	當然沒問題，馬上幫你們準備。
Ethan	I think we're ready now. My wife would like the **strawberry shortcake**, and I'll have the blackberry pie.	我們可以點了，我太太想要草莓酥餅，我要黑莓派。
Doug	Would you like that **a la mode**?	甜點上要加冰淇淋嗎？
Ethan	Yes, please. And could you **heat** the pie just a little.	好啊，就這樣。黑莓派可以稍微加熱一下嗎？
Doug	All right, I'll have those for you in just a bit.	沒問題，甜點很快就可以上了。
	(at the computer)	（電腦系統上）
Doug	How are things going on the **cold side**? My desserts seem to be taking a long time.	冷菜廚房準備甜點的進度如何？我客人的甜點一直在等。
Raymond	I had some appetizers take 15 minutes. I wouldn't be surprised if everything else was slow, too.	我客人的開胃菜已經等超過 15 分鐘，其他的菜等多久一點都不稀奇了。

	(back at the table)	（回到客桌旁）
Doug	Hi, it's still going to be a couple minutes for your desserts. Would you like a little more coffee while you wait?	嗨！甜點可能要再稍等幾分鐘，你們想再喝點咖啡嗎？
Ethan	Yes, and whatever you can do to **hurry the process** would be **appreciated**. We have somewhere we're supposed to be pretty soon.	好啊，麻煩請廚房快點將感激不盡，我們有下一個地方要去。
Doug	I'll check with the kitchen.	我去廚房問問看。
	(in the kitchen)	（廚房內）
Doug	Jess, can you give me **any word on** table 15's desserts?	Jess，可否透露一下 15 桌的甜點是否快好了？
Jess	I'm getting there as fast as I can. Things are really backed up. I'm going to try to find someone to help me in just a minute. But it'll still be a while on those desserts. Sorry.	我已經加速在處理了。今天廚房單子滿天飛，我一會兒就要找人來幫忙了。只是那些甜點喔可還要等。抱歉啦。
	(to the table)	（客桌邊）
Doug	Hi, there, the cooks say it's still going to take a bit of time to get your dessert to you.	各位，廚師說甜點還要一會兒就會好。
Ethan	I think we have to get going. Can you just bring us the check?	我想我們必須走了。可以給我帳單嗎？
Doug	That's fine. I'll have it in a minute or so, and we can take care of it very quickly. I'm sorry for the delay.	沒問題，等下就拿來，結帳是很快的。真抱歉甜點來不及上。

Word Bank

in the mean time 就在這一段時間裡；就在此時　certainly *adv.* 當然；沒問題
strawberry shortcake 草莓酥餅　a la mode 加冰淇淋　heat *v.* 加熱
cold side 冷菜廚房　hurry the process 催趕進度　appreciate(d) *v.* 感謝
any word on 有關……的事；……的消息

Part I Part II Part III Part IV Part V Part VI

Unit 28 餐點狀況

牛排吃一半囉！可以準備點心了——出餐掌控

出餐掌控是個很特別的學問，許多餐廳對於內場出餐是有些規範的，但並不會特別定義外場出餐的流程與規則。內場的出餐多由外場掌控，何時該上前菜、該上湯品、該上主餐，最後甜點何時上，幾乎都是由外場通知後，再行準備。

外場服務往往都是依照經驗與客戶狀況進行。通常客戶多時，服務人員出餐速度就會被要求快些，好讓客戶快快吃飽離開，以增加翻桌率；當客戶少時，服務人員會將出餐速度放慢，讓客戶好好品嘗餐點的美味。

雖說以上的準則是個方向，但是否出餐有其他需要注意事項與技巧呢？

出餐正確觀念

外場篇

- 學習出餐確認用量適中，避免浪費物料成本
- 餐具和抹布如有污髒，應立即更換或清洗乾淨後再使用
- 出餐區域周邊有不潔或污亂應立即擦拭乾淨後再出餐
- 食材、佐料擺放位置整齊固定，以增加產品之美觀，達到節約目的
- 尖峰時段外場人員應自我要配合內場提醒，增加出餐速度，使出餐流程順暢
- 利用空檔時間幫忙清理檯面，並經常保持乾淨整齊，且添補物料及出餐用具，確保美觀衛生及出餐流程通暢
- 出餐時，複誦內場人員所報之桌次、產品，加深個人記憶且避免因聽覺錯誤而搞亂出餐的先後次序
- 出餐至顧客面前時，應先打聲招呼提醒客人餐點已送到，離去時勿忘記說聲謝謝您或請慢用（此句用在離峰時段）
- 出餐依照餐點分類送出，例如熱食與冷食或是主餐與甜點需分開放置，不可冷熱混雜放置出餐

- 了解餐點烹煮的時間，適時通知內場準備餐點，例如前菜上後，即可通知內場準備，主餐進行至 2/3 後即可通知內場準備甜點
- 迅速回到出餐區域準備下一次出餐

內場篇

- 學習出餐餐點用量適中，避免浪費物料成本
- 鍋蓋和抹布如有污髒，應立即更換或清洗乾淨後再使用
- 出餐區域周邊有不潔或污亂應立即擦拭乾淨後再出餐
- 食材、佐料擺放位置整齊固定，以增加產品之美觀，達到節約目的
- 利用空檔時間幫忙清理檯面，並經常保持乾淨整齊，且添補物料及出餐用具，確保美觀衛生及出餐流程通暢
- 若遇出單累積過多時，適時提醒外場人員，加快出餐速度，避免客戶久等
- 出餐時，記得說明餐點桌次、產品，以便適時提醒外場

以上所述的簡易原則為出餐作業基本需知，管理者可以依照此規範來定義，服務人員於服務時則應該依照規範落實完成，惟有如此才能讓客人感覺自己受到尊重和服務周全，並高興自己選對舒適乾淨的用餐環境。

Unit 29 遇到難纏顧客

1 *Not Enough Alcohol In Drink* 飲料酒精含量太低

Track 113

Introduction

A guest is upset because he thinks there isn't enough alcohol in his drink. 顧客抱怨飲料的酒精含量不夠

Characters

Raymond - Server	服務生
Doris - Guest	顧客
Vera - Guest	顧客
Bernard - Guest	顧客
Josie - Dining Room Manager	餐區經理

Conversation

Raymond	Good evening, I'll be serving you tonight. Can I get anyone anything to drink while you're deciding?	晚安，我是你們今天的服務生 Raymond。點餐中間想問一下喝點甚麼飲料？
Doris	I'll take a Manhattan, please.	我想點一杯曼哈頓。
Vera	I'd like a glass of white wine.	我想要一杯白酒。
Bernard	And I'll take a Bombay **martini**, extra **dry**, on the rocks. And make sure to put some **booze** in it.	我想要一杯完全不甜、加冰塊的孟買馬丁尼。請記得加些酒啊。
Raymond	Yes, I'll be back with those in just a few minutes.	沒問題。等一下就幫你們上飲料。
	(a little later)	（過了一會兒）
Raymond	Here are your drinks. Have you had enough time to decide?	這是你們的飲料。請問可以點餐了嗎？
Bernard	Hey, I thought I told you to put some **liquor** in this drink?	先生，我剛剛不是告訴你、馬丁尼要加酒嗎？
Raymond	I'm sorry?	不好意思？

Bernard	This drink **hardly** has anything in it.	這杯馬丁尼幾乎沒有酒的味道。
Raymond	Sir, I'm sorry, but the bartender makes all the drinks with the same **amount** of alcohol in them. They use a **shot glass** to make sure.	先生，不好意思。酒保是用盎斯杯調酒，每一杯飲料的酒精含量應該是相同的。
Bernard	I don't care about any shot glass. I want some booze in my martini.	我才不在乎什麼盎斯杯呢，我只想喝到有酒味的馬丁尼。
Raymond	I'm sorry, sir, but there's nothing I can do. Would you like me to get you something else?	先生，很抱歉，我實在沒辦法幫你。你想要點一些別的嗎？
Bernard	I don't want anything else. I want a martini with gin in it.	我不想點別的。我只想喝加了琴酒的馬丁尼。
Raymond	I'll be back in just a minute.	抱歉，麻煩您等一下。
	(at the bar)	（在酒吧裡）
Raymond	Josie, can you help me out a minute? There's a **guy** at table 16 who **insists** we didn't put enough **gin** in his martini. Could you maybe talk to him? I don't know what to do.	Josie，你可以幫我一個忙、和 16 桌的顧客談一下嗎？他抱怨馬丁尼的琴酒沒放夠，我實在沒輒。
	(at table 16)	（在 16 桌旁）
Josie	I'm sorry, sir, but you got the same amount of gin as anyone else who orders a martini.	先生，不好意思。所有客人點的馬丁尼、琴酒含量都是相同的。
Bernard	Well, where I'm from they actually put booze in your drink when you order one. I'll go somewhere else where they don't **water down** the drinks.	這麼說吧，在我家鄉的餐廳裡、點酒類的話酒味都很夠。我就換換看去別家那種不會稀釋酒味的吧。

Word Bank

martini *n.[C]* 馬丁尼（一種雞尾酒） dry *adj.* 不甜的 booze *n.[U]* 酒
liquor *n.[U/C]* 含有酒精的飲料 hardly *adv.* 幾乎不；簡直不
amount *n.[C]* 數量 shot glass 盎斯杯 guy *n.[C]* 傢伙；小伙子；朋友
insist *v.* 堅決主張 gin *n.[U/C]* 琴酒；杜松子酒 water down 攙水淡化

Unit 29 遇到難纏顧客

2 *Guests in A Hurry* 顧客趕時間 Track 114

Introduction

A party did not allow enough time to eat and are in a hurry. 一群客人趕時間，用餐時間很匆促。

Characters 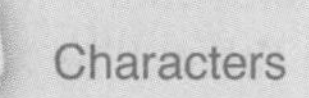 

Gus - Guest 顧客
Dora - Server 服務生
Melvin - Assistant Dining Room Manager 餐區副理

Conversation

Dora	I'll get your orders started and be back with your first course **presently**. Here is your bottle of wine. Would you like to try it, sir?	你們的點餐已經開始做，前菜回頭就幫你們上。這是你們點的酒，要不要先試看看？
Gus	Yes, that will be fine, thank you.	好啊，就這樣。謝謝你。
	(a few minutes later)	（幾分鐘後）
Dora	Here is your appetizer course. I'll give you some time to enjoy that, and then bring out your salads.	這是開胃菜，請慢慢享用，等一下就幫你們上沙拉。
Gus	Can you bring out the dinners at the same time as the salads? We're kind of in a hurry.	沙拉和主菜可以一起上嗎？我們有點在趕。
Dora	You're in a hurry? But your well-done steak is going to take a long time, and I haven't placed the order yet.	您在趕時間？全熟的牛排要好一陣子才會好，而且，我還沒有給單。
Gus	Why haven't you ordered our food? Does it look like we have all night? I have a very important meeting to get to.	你怎麼還沒給單呢？你以為我整晚時間多得是嗎？我待會還有重要的會議耶！

Dora	No, I haven't ordered your food yet. When you order a bottle of wine and appetizers, that signals to me that you aren't in a hurry and want to **take your time**.	抱歉，我還沒給單。由於你點了開胃菜和一瓶酒，暗示了你們不急、想慢慢用餐。
Gus	Well, we don't. It's not **my fault** if you think you can **read my mind**. I am in a hurry. Who's in charge here?	這樣喔，可非如此。你以為能讀心可不是我的錯。我的確在趕。你們主管呢？
	(the manager comes over)	（主管過來了）
Melvin	Sir, I'm Melvin, the assistant dining room manager. I'm sorry that you're in a hurry, but our server didn't know that. I can see if there is any way we can get your food to you **sooner**.	先生，我是餐區副理，Melvin。很抱歉，服務生不知道您在趕時間。我會想辦法，讓你可以快點享用餐點。
Gus	What is with **this place**? It took us 15 minutes just to get a place to sit!	你們餐廳是有甚麼問題？我們等了 15 分鐘才有位子坐。
Melvin	That's not **out of the ordinary** on a Saturday, sir. Let me check on your order.	這對禮拜六來說並不是非比尋常的事。先生，我去看看你的餐點好了沒有。
Gus	Never mind. I'll just make sure to never come back here again.	算了。我看是不會再來這裡用餐了。

Word Bank

allow *v.* 容許　take your time 慢慢來　my fault 我的錯
read my mind 知道我心裡的想法　sooner *adj.* 更快些
out of the ordinary 不尋常的　this place 這個地方；此指餐廳
presently *adv.* 不久；一會兒；目前

Unit 29 遇到難纏顧客

3 *Large Party With No Reservation*
人數多又沒訂位的一群顧客

Track 115

Introduction

A group of 40 people try to get a table together.

一群 40 個人想要同桌

Characters  

Missy - Hostess 女領檯
Gary - Guest 顧客
Josie - Dining Room Manager 餐區經理

Conversation

Missy	Good evening and welcome. How many are in your party?	晚安，歡迎光臨。請問有幾位？
Gary	I think there are **about** 40 of us. We'd all like to sit together.	我想約 40 位，我們想坐一起。
Missy	40? And you want to sit together? I don't really think that's going to be possible.	40 個人？要安排在同一張桌子？這恐怕很難。
Gary	What do you mean? Can't you just **slide** some tables together?	怎麼說？不能併個桌嗎？
Missy	We can for eight or ten people, but 40 is a little complicated. We don't really have **space** to put that many people all in one place.	如果是 8 到 10 位就沒問題，但 40 個人真的有難度。我們真的沒有那麼大空間可以把全部人併一起。
Gary	So, you don't ever **take** big groups? I find that **hard to believe**.	那麼，你們沒有接待過這麼多客人嗎？我真不敢相信。
Missy	We do, but they have reservations. Our manager is **right here**. I'll let her explain it to you.	我們有過，但是他們會先訂位。這是我們經理，我請她跟您解釋。

Josie	Hello, how can I help you?	有甚麼需要幫忙的嗎？
Gary	We have 40 people, and this girl says we can't all sit together.	我們有 40 個人，這位小姐說沒辦法安排我們坐一起。
Josie	And she is **correct**. It's not that we don't want you to eat here, but we have no way of putting that many tables in one place, **especially** on Friday night at dinner hour.	她說的是對的。並不是不讓你們這樣用餐，只是空間內真的沒辦法安排這麼多桌子併一起，尤其又是在禮拜五晚上用餐時段。
Gary	So, you're telling me you're going to **turn away** 40 possible customers because you won't try to put us together?	你是在告訴我，你們沒辦法安排我們坐一起，所以就讓四十個潛在客人走掉囉？
Josie	We don't really want to turn you away. We could put you at different tables in different parts of the restaurant. The only way we do really large groups is with a reservation. That way the kitchen is prepared for it.	我們不是不歡迎你們，只是餐區有空桌的地方就會幫你們安插。我們對於大型團體桌的做法，都必須先訂位的，這樣廚房才有辦法準備。
Gary	I can't believe that you're not going to let us in.	我真不敢相信，你們竟然不讓我們這群人上門。
Josie	I did say that you could come in **separately**. If you want to be all together, though, you need to let us know ahead of time.	我確實有說你們是可以分開坐的。但若你們還是要坐一起，是必須事先通知的。
Gary	**Fat chance** of that happening. Goodbye.	門都沒有。我們走吧。

Word Bank

about *adv.* 大約；接近　slide *v.* 滑動；滑行　space *n.[U]* 空間

take *v.* 接受；容納　hard to believe 難以相信　right here 就在這裡

correct *adj.* 正確的　especially *adv.* 尤其；特別　turn away 拒絕；放棄

separately *adv.* 分開地；個別地　fat chance 微乎其微的可能性（反說）

Unit 29 遇到難纏顧客

 Guest Wants A Window Table 顧客要求要靠窗位子

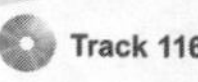
Track 116

Introduction

An unreasonable guest is upset that he can't sit by the window. 不講理的客人對於不能坐靠窗位子很生氣。

Characters

Jade - Hostess 女領檯
Tom - Guest 顧客
Josie - Dining Room Manager 餐區經理

Conversation

Jade	Good evening, how may I help you?	晚安，有甚麼需要幫忙的嗎？
Tom	We have four people, and we'd like to sit by the window.	我們有 4 個人，想坐靠窗。
Jade	I'm afraid all our **window seats** are full. We can seat you at another table right now, if you like.	恐怕靠窗的位子都滿了。如果不介意，是可以安排另一桌。
Tom	I don't understand why I can't have a table by the window. Is it that I'm not offering money? I'll give you a thousand dollars if you'll put us by a window.	不了解為什麼坐不了靠窗位子？是因為沒有多付錢嗎？如果可以安排我們坐靠窗，我可以付你 1000 元！
Jade	I'm sorry, sir, but that won't do it, **either**. It has nothing to do with money. The tables are all full, and they will be for probably another 45 minutes, **at least**.	很抱歉，先生。縱使你付再多錢我也辦不到。這不是錢的問題，位子真的都滿了。要坐靠窗位子，至少要再等 45 分鐘。
Tom	45 minutes? That's **ridiculous**! I'm not going to wait that long.	45 分鐘？這太可笑了。我可不想等這麼久。

Jade	Sir, we have tables in our second and third rows that have **just as good** a **view** as the window tables. Would you like me to put you in one of those?	先生，你們可以坐第二排和第三排的位子嗎？那裡的視野和靠窗位子一樣好，要不要讓我為你們在那兒入坐？
Tom	No. Let me talk to your manager.	不了。請你們經理出來吧。
	(Josie appears)	（Josie 出現）
Josie	Hello, I'm Josie. How can I help you?	您好，我是 Josie。有甚麼我可以幫忙的嗎？
Tom	Why can't I get a window seat? I want to sit there now.	為什麼我們不能坐靠窗位子？我現在就要坐靠窗！
Josie	Sir, we just **opened**. All of our window tables are full, and they won't be leaving for **quite a while**. There is **no way** we can give you one.	先生，我們才剛開始營業，窗邊桌位真的都滿了，客人不會這麼快離開。實在沒辦法幫您安排。
Tom	Fine, I'll take one of the other ones, but you'd better give me a good waiter.	好吧，我們就坐別桌吧。但請給我好一點的服務生。
	(to the hostess)	（Josie 走向 Jade）
Josie	Jade, seat him in Bob's section, but **warn** him he may not be in a really **good mood**.	Jade，把他們安排在 Bob 的服務區裡，但要警告他一下，這客人可不好應付。

Word Bank

unreasonable *adj.* 不講理的；過分的　window seat(s) 靠窗座位
either *adv.* 也不　at least 至少　ridiculous *adj.* 可笑的；荒謬的
just as good 一樣好　view *n.[C]* 景色　open(ed) *v.* 開門；營業
quite a while 好一陣子　no way 不可能　warn *v.* 警告
good mood 好心情

Unit 29 遇到難纏顧客

與奧客過招

在服務業闖蕩，遇到奧客是稀鬆平常的事，雖然清楚很平常，但真的遇到還是心裡一陣嘀咕，嘀咕完畢後，依舊需要好好完成服務工作，讓客戶感覺服務滿意。只是若真的遇到不合理的客戶時，只能心裡犯嘀咕嗎？不能有較積極的處理方式嗎？

客戶的訴求若合理，往往就服務立場，應盡量滿足，當然若遇到不合理的訴求，確實可以適時地說明跟致歉無法提供的原因，那要怎麼處理呢？我們用以下的案例來說明。

案例一：孩子亂亂跑，家長卻不管

狀況：客戶用餐帶了一個約 5 歲的小朋友，小孩調皮不乖乖坐著用餐到處跑，爸媽不管事倒是讓服務人員為他擔心，萬一熱湯或餐點燙傷他或是不小心撞到桌椅，那該怎麼辦呢？看來爸媽是把餐廳當做遊樂園，任小孩四處撒野。

處理：面對這樣的狀況，服務人員十足地傷透腦筋，畢竟以客為尊，即使是客戶的問題，表現上也不能太過苛責，通常處理的方式，建議先是提醒一下爸媽留意一下小朋友，避免送餐時，小孩碰撞服務人員導致受傷，若狀況依舊無法改善且小朋友可以溝通，可劃出一個小區域，請小朋友在固定區域玩耍，降低受傷的機會。

案例二：優惠過期不能享用

狀況：結帳時，客戶出示已過期的優惠券，服務人員回應優惠已過期無法使用，客戶大怒點餐時並未說明已過期，但點餐時，是否客戶有先出示優惠券呢？相信是沒有，不甘心加沒面子的心理下，客戶堅持沒優惠不願意結帳離開。

處理：確實已經過了優惠期，當然無法提供優惠，勉強讓客戶使用對於其他客戶來說是非常不公平，通常這樣的狀況，先溝通客戶了解優惠確實過期無法提供，另提供現在尚有的優惠給於客戶減免，或是使用自己的員工優惠給於客戶，讓客戶心裡舒服些。

案例三：老闆是我親戚

狀況：點餐時，客戶大聲說：老闆是我遠房親戚，他說只要報他的名字菜色可以好一點。殊不知，點餐的服務人員就是老闆。

處理：這樣的客戶不能說少，但也並非經常遇到，往往服務人員聽到客戶這樣的描述後，都是微笑回應，這是一個不錯的回應方式，當然也有些死纏爛打一定要有優惠的客戶，面對不肯接受微笑回應的客戶，服務人員是可以直接說明，公司已規定價格無員工優惠，再提供目前餐廳有的優惠活動，給客戶一個台階，也婉轉地拒絕用老闆名號要優惠的客戶。

案例四：老愛看隔壁桌的偵探

狀況：隔壁餐點送上時，客戶呼喚了服務人員，生氣的說：為什麼隔壁比我們晚點餐，卻比我們早送到？看了一下客戶的點餐 - 海鮮焗烤飯，隔壁客戶點的是蝦仁炒飯，烹調時間不同，自然無法都按照點菜的前後順序上菜。

處理：道歉是首要動作，畢竟客戶不了解餐點的製作，後續再誠實地講述餐點的烹調時間與確認他所點的餐點烹調狀況，讓客戶有個心理準備，了解餐點可能需要多耗費些時間。

世界上奧客有百百種，但他們共通的想法就是喜愛且擅於維護自己的權益，只要懂得這一點，抓住基本的處理方式，相信你也可以成為奧客殺手。

Unit 30 部落客評語

 Service Speed Is Slow 上菜速度太慢 

Track 117

Introduction

The managers are reading restaurant review and blog sites. 餐廳經理在看雜誌和部落格的餐廳評比。

Characters

Barry - Manager	經理
Jolene - Assistant Manager	副理

Conversation

Jolene	Time to give our daily look at the **blogs** and **reviews**. I hope they're all good, but they probably won't be.	該看看部落格裡對我們餐廳的評語了。我希望所有的評價都是好的，但可能不會都只有好的。
Barry	There's no **satisfying** some people, but I think we usually do pretty well on those sites.	要讓客人對我們都滿意不大可能，但這些部落客通常會給我們好的評語。
Jolene	Here's one that's not so good. "The food was excellent, but we had to wait half an hour for a table."	這裡有個不佳的評語。它說「這家餐廳食物非常棒，但必須等半個鐘頭才有位子坐。」
Barry	They had to wait because the food is excellent. That's simple. We were really busy. It's **not surprising** they had to wait that long. That's a normal Saturday.	要等是因為食物美味，這是很簡單的道理。大排長龍候位挺正常的，那可是禮拜六啊。
Jolene	Here's another one, from someone named Babe78: "The food was **delicious**, but we had to wait a long time for it. It was over 20 minutes from the time we finished our first course until the dinner arrived."	這裡有一位 Babe78 的評語：「食物美味，但候餐時間長。在吃完前菜後，還要等超過 20 分鐘，才會上主菜。」

Barry	Hmm... That's not so good, if it really was 20 or more minutes. I'll reply to her and see if I can find out more about their experience.	嗯…必須等上 20 分鐘或更久，是不大好。我會回覆留言給她，再多了解一下他們用餐經驗。
	(Barry writes a message)	（Barry 寫留言給 Babe 78）
Barry	"To Babe78: We were busy, but it still shouldn't have taken that long. We are always working to **improve**. If you will call me here at the restaurant, I'll try to figure out why your service was slow. – Barry"	給 Babe78：當天我們確實很忙，但的確也不該等上 20 分鐘這麼久。我們一向致力於改進。希望你可以打電話給我，讓我了解當天情況。— Barry」
Jolene	Hopefully she'll see it and **give you a call**. It would be nice to have more information about the **circumstances**.	希望她會看到這則留言，打電話給你。得知更多狀況是一件好事。
	(later)	（稍後）
Barry	I just got a call from the woman who said her service was slow on Saturday.	我剛接到一位女顧客的電話，她說我們裡拜六的服務速度很慢。
Jolene	What did you say to her?	那你怎麼回應？
Barry	We're going to let her come back **on us** and attempt to make her experience better. In the meantime, I'm going to talk to Ned and see about getting some extra **manpower** on the line when we're really busy.	我們應該想辦法讓她再來餐廳用餐，試著讓她用餐經驗更好。同時，我會和 Ned 談一談，看看能否在餐廳忙不過來時增加人手。

Word Bank

blog(s) *n.[C]* 部落格　review(s) *n.[C]* 評論　satisfying *adj.* 令人滿意的
not surprising 不讓人訝異的　delicious *adj.* 美味的
give you a call 打電話給你　circumstance(s) *n.[C]* 情況；情勢
on us 光臨我們餐廳　manpower *n.[U]* 人力　improve *v.* 改善；變得更好

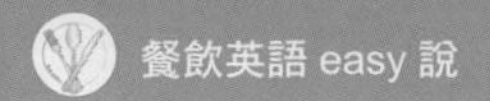

Unit 30 部落客評語

2 *Restaurant Not Really Clean* 餐廳不夠乾淨

Track 118

Introduction

A reviewer comments on the cleanliness of the restaurant. 有一位評論家對餐廳清潔度有意見。

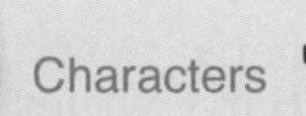

Characters

Barry - Manager 經理
Jolene - Assistant Manager 副理

Conversation

Barry	Here's another good review. "Service was prompt and pleasant, and the food was very good." I hope we see some more of those in the **future**.	這裡還有另一篇好評。「服務非常迅速，讓人舒適。食物非常好吃。」希望未來我們可以看到更多這樣的評論。
Jolene	This one's not so good, though. She says the bathroom, "had **paper towels** all over the floor. **Dust** was present on some of the pictures and posters on the wall. It gave the look of a place that needed a bit of **sprucing up**."	然而這篇就不大好。她提到化妝室，「地板上滿是紙巾。牆上的海報和圖片看得到灰塵，看來這裡需要好好打掃一下。」
Barry	That's not good. We'll have to do something about that. What would you suggest?	這實在不大好，我們必須想辦法改進。你的看法呢？
Jolene	I think we need to mention this at the **service meeting** the next couple of days. We're going to have to have the hosts check the bathrooms more often. Let's make it every twenty minutes, instead of every **half hour**.	幾天後開服務會議時，必須討論這件事。必須讓領檯更常檢查化妝室。就 20 分鐘一次吧，半小時一次不行了。

Barry	And we need to do a thorough cleaning of the front of the house. I think we've been so busy that we've **neglected** some details out there.	餐廳外場要徹底清潔。我想大家最近太忙了，都忽略了許多細節。
Jolene	Should we add it to the servers' sidework?	我們應該把這項加到服務生的雜項工作嗎？
Barry	No, I think we need to have a **professional** cleaning done. Then, we need to make sure we **stay on top of** it.	不，我認為必須請專業清潔人員來做。接下來，我們要讓餐廳的整潔度在同業當中是最好的。
Jolene	Meanwhile, I'll write a note in the blog **comments** section outlining what we're doing to fix these **problem areas**. We really do need to keep an eye on this.	同時，我會在她的部落格裡留言，約略概述餐廳已著手改善問題區塊。大家要好好留意整潔度了。
Barry	Yeah, if we don't, people might think the back of the house isn't too tidy, either.	如果我們不把化妝室打掃乾淨，客人可能認為後場廚房也不怎麼清潔。
Jolene	And that's not true. It gets cleaned every night.	這就太冤枉了，我們每個晚上都有確實打掃。

Word Bank

cleanliness *n.[U]* 潔淨　future *n.[C]* 未來；將來　paper towel(s) 紙巾
dust *n.[U]* 灰塵　sprucing up 打掃乾淨　service meeting 行政部門會議
half hour 半小時　neglect(ed) *v.* 忽視；疏忽
professional *adj.* 專業的　stay on top of 做到最好；保持最高水準
comment(s) *n.[C]* 評語　problem area(s) 有問題的區域

Unit 30 部落客評語

3 *Waiter's Attitude Is Very Good* 服務生的服務態度很好

 Track 119

Introduction

The managers find some positive comments from internet sites. 餐廳經理在網站上看到一些正面評語。

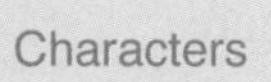

Characters 

Barry - Manager	經理
Jolene - Assistant Manager	副理
Bob - Server	服務生

Conversation

Jolene	I think I'll look up some of the review sites and see what's going on this week. I'm hoping for some **positive** reviews.	我應該上評比網看這禮拜的餐廳評比。希望可以看到一些正面評語。
Barry	We always get quite a few positive ones. We just have to avoid the negatives, which we usually do.	我們一向有好一些正面評價。我們盡量要避免負面印象，我們也一向這樣做。
Jolene	Here's a good one. "Our server, Bob, was **extraordinary**. He did everything right, plus he was a joy to see work. He obviously enjoys his work, which isn't always true in **service jobs** these days."	這裡有個好的的評語：「服務我們的服務生，Bob，是相當優秀的。他不但把事情處理得很好，也與人共事愉快。顯然他熱愛自己工作，在現在的服務產業裡、也未必所有人都如他一般了。」
Barry	Hey, that's pretty good. He keeps getting **mentioned** in the reviews. We should maybe give him something to say thanks.	嘿，這真是太棒了，很多評論都提到 Bob 喔。我們應該送他禮物表示感謝。
Jolene	Yeah, remember the one last week who said he was the best waiter they'd ever had? When we get people like that, we need to **keep them around**.	記得上禮拜有一篇評論說、他是他們遇過最棒的服務生了。餐廳裡有這樣優秀的員工，應該要好好留住他。

Barry	Yes, I wish we get a few more like him. He really does enjoy waiting tables. You can't say that about all our servers.	是的，希望餐廳裡能有更多像他一樣傑出的服務生，他是真心喜愛桌邊服務。但並不是所有服務生都和他一樣。
	(a little later)	（過了一會兒）
Barry	Hey, Bob, can you come in here a minute?	嗨！ Bob，你可以進來一下嗎？
Bob	Sure, what's happening?	沒問題，有事嗎？
Barry	We've been getting a lot of good comments about you on restaurant review sites and on our **comment cards**. We think you're a good example to our other employees, and we'd like to **show our appreciation**.	在網路評論和餐廳意見卡上，許多人對你的服務態度，都表示肯定。我們認為，你的工作態度可以作為其他員工的榜樣，謝謝你這麼努力。
Bob	Thanks guys, but I'm only doing my job.	謝謝你們的讚美！我只是把自己分內的事做好。
Jolene	And you do it **rather** well. Here's a voucher good for dinner for two in any of our restaurants. Take someone out and enjoy yourself.	而且你做得非常好。這裡倆人用晚餐抵用卷，你可以邀請朋友一起、到任何我們餐廳據點享用晚餐。
Bob	Thanks, I appreciate it. And I'll keep trying to do a good job.	謝謝你們的好意。我會繼續做好我的工作。

Word Bank

positive *adj.* 正面的　extraordinary *adj.* 非凡的　service job(s) 服務工作
mention(ed) *v.* 提及　keep them around 留住他們
show our appreciation 表示我們的感謝　rather *adv.* 相當；頗
internet *n.* 網際網路　comment card(s) 意見卡

Unit 30 部落客評語

4 *Delicious Meals* 美味的餐點

Track 120

Introduction

Good comments are coming in about the quality of the food from internet sites. 網路上對餐廳的餐點佳評如潮。

Characters

Barry - Manager	經理
Jolene - Assistant Manager	副理
Ned - Chef	行政廚師

Conversation

Jolene	We've sure been getting a lot of **compliments** on the blogs about the food lately.	最近部落格上對餐廳的食物有很多讚美。
Barry	Yes, it's really nice to see. What should we do to **reward** the cooks?	是啊！真讓人感到高興，我們該怎麼獎勵廚師們呢？
Jolene	I always thought the best reward was money. Maybe we should give them a raise.	我一直認為金錢是最實質的獎勵。也許加薪也是個選項。
Barry	I'll have to run that through the **corporate office**, but I think that's a good idea. Let me get a hold of them and see what happens.	這是個好主意，但必須經過公司總部同意。我想聽聽廚師們的想法、再看看怎麼做。
	(a couple days later)	（幾天後）
Barry	Ned, could we have a short meeting right now?	Ned，現在有空開個小會嗎？
Ned	Sure, what about?	沒問題，是什麼事？
Barry	We just wanted you to know we're real happy with the way the kitchen is running. The positive reviews have been **popping up** all over the place.	我們只是想表達說，我們對廚房最近的表現非常滿意。不斷出現許多評論、都對你們有正面評價。

Ned	That's good to hear. I think we have a good crew. I like working with them, and they put out a good product.	很高興聽到這個消息，我想我們的團隊很讚，一起工作挺愉快。他們做出的餐點很厲害的。
Barry	Here are just a few of the comments we've gotten. I'll put them up on the wall in the break room so everyone can read them. "The shrimp scampi was to die for." Our spaghetti Bolognese was **superb**." "We thought the food and service were **among** the best we've seen in the city."	這些只是所有好評中的一部分。我會將它們張貼在休息室，讓大家看一下。譬如，「白酒鮮蝦好吃得要死了。」「我們的義大利肉醬麵是一流的。」「我們認為這家餐廳的餐點和服務，是本市最出色的。」
Ned	Those are great to hear. I'm glad the other guys will get a chance to read them.	看到這些評語真讓人感到振奮。很高興其他夥伴也能一起看看這些訊息。
Barry	We have other news for you. I've talked to corporate, and all the line and prep cooks will be getting a **raise** starting next week.	還有更好的好消息呢。跟公司總部已經談過，從下禮拜開始，幫所有工作線上的廚師們及助理都加薪。
Ned	Wow! That's great. Thanks guys, I know everyone will appreciate a little extra money.	哇！這真是太棒了！謝謝大夥兒們。我知道大家都會感謝公司幫他們加薪。
Barry	You all deserve it. Thanks for all your **efforts**.	這是你們努力工作應得的。公司很感謝你們的付出。

Word Bank

quality *n.[U]* 品質　compliment(s) *n.[C]* 讚美　reward *v.* 獎勵
corporate office 總公司　pop(ping) up 蔓延　superb *adj.* 一流的
among *prep.* 在……之中；在……中間　raise *n.[C]* 加薪
effort(s) *n.[C]* 努力

Unit 30 部落客評語

我的餐廳 Blog——如何製作專屬網站

網路的世界通常是想像無限、商機無限，很多美食或是商品的崛起也是靠著虛幻的網路世界，這個章節我們要來介紹如何製作餐廳專屬的網站。

一個好的網站通常需要吸引人的元素，需要點推銷，需要增加點閱率，那怎麼達到呢？

餐廳對外網站的架構設計

網站的方便查詢與否，將影響客戶查詢後前來消費的意願，架構的完整與操作方便友善，將是網站設計的一大重點，既然是要製作餐廳網站，當然我們需要留意放置的選項，是否讓客戶方便閱覽

項目	設計重點	溝通重點	設計模式
餐廳介紹	利用一個故事來傳達經營理念	增加客戶的印象跟好的觀感	單頁顯示並利用專屬風格進行版面安排
最新消息	消息綁著優惠客戶會比較有興趣	新產品上市、節慶活動前露出預告，提供預約服務	建議使用圖文顯示、條列說明（活動時間、優惠內容、菜單介紹）
菜單	使用真實照片，並點綴餐點介紹	餐點需要分類供客戶查詢，減少客戶找尋時間	建議使用圖文顯示
會員功能	會員輸入介面需簡單且易懂	留下資訊，提供特殊優惠增加客戶的忠誠度	條列幾項可聯繫之資料輸入，避免留下過多個人資料
線上購物	區分會員與非會員購物服務，使用真實照片，並點綴餐點介紹	方便訂購與金額明確	設計以方面下單與結帳為主，並需考量安全機制
折價券下載	標示盡量清楚，圖樣要夠大，放置位置可多樣	不用怕客戶索取，優惠內容跟權利義務要載明	建議使用圖片顯示，點選進入優惠說明
分店查詢	地址、電話、MAP 要正確清楚	方便查詢、前往與聯繫	條列顯示資料，MAP 可用連結方式提供查詢

項目	設計重點	溝通重點	設計模式
網路相簿	可區分會員上傳與店家照片	增加客戶感受其他客戶至餐廳用餐的愉快經驗	利用簡單的上傳與文字描述功能進行
線上討論區	以文字方式進行討論，並可區分詢問與回覆	方便留言與查閱問題	條列顯示資料
聯絡我們	輸入介面需簡單且易懂	客戶資訊（電話或 Mail）要留下並註明可能回覆的時間	條列幾項可聯繫之資料與問題供輸入

網站特色的營造

餐廳網站的主題營造可使用的方式非常多樣。小本經營個性小餐廳大多選擇使用一般免費 blog 當餐廳網站，套用 blog 提供之版型進行設計，當然這是較省錢且快速的方式，但風險就是可能較無特色。以自行設計網站而言，特色的營造可利用以下方式來達到效果

✓設置主題音樂，增加網站氛圍
✓設計專屬 Flash 動畫，用有趣或是感性訴求的動畫增加客戶印象
✓放置專業實景照片
✓利用個性插畫增加餐廳特色
✓統整企業識別，讓網站視覺感覺一致

如何促銷網站

依照網路使用的習慣，一般瀏覽僅會專注於查詢結果的前 10 項，故目前很多搜尋網站提供搜尋排名的販售，當客戶利用關鍵字查詢時，搜尋網站可依照你希望的顯示排名提供資料，以增加你的網站的曝光度，而以下是幾個促銷的方式

✓成立 FB 粉絲團（免費）
✓加入團購網或是美食網（免費）
✓Yahoo 排序前 10 名（需計費）
✓Google 排序前 10 名（需計費）
✓E-dm 廣告宣傳（需計費）
✓部落格廣告宣傳（需計費）
✓廣告輪播網（需計費）

專業的網站經營者可花點時間閱讀其他專業網站的精心設計，相信你會發現不同於你原本管理與經營的思維，甚至於從文章點閱與轉分享數量中，你也可以收集到客戶對於餐點或餐廳氣氛的喜愛喔！

餐飲英語 easy 說
Learn Smart! 011

發行人	周瑞德
作者	Mark Venekamp & Claire Chang
企劃編輯	Elaine Liu 劉雅麗
特約作者	Cheryl Lin 林瑜娟
特約編輯	Claire Chang 張蘋
封面設計	King Chen
內頁構成	華漢電腦排版有限公司
印製	世和印製企業有限公司
初版	2013 年 3 月
定價	新台幣 369 元
出版	倍斯特出版事業有限公司 電話／(02) 2351-2007　傳真／(02) 2351-0887 地址／ 100 台北市中正區福州街 1 號 10 樓之 2 Email ／ best.books.service@gmail.com
總經銷	商流文化事業有限公司 地址／ 235 新北市中和區中正路 752 號 8 樓 電話／(02) 2228-8841　傳真／(02) 2228-6939

國家圖書館出版品預行編目（CIP）資料
餐飲英語 easy 說／ Mark Venekamp & Claire Chang 作 .
-- 初版 . -- 臺北市：倍斯特 , 2013.03
面；　公分 . -- (Learn smart ; 11)
ISBN：978-986-88732-0-9 （平裝附光碟片）
1. 英語學習　2. 餐飲行業　3. 會話
805.188　　102002114